FROM
THE BROKEN
TREE

ALSO BY LEE LANGLEY

NOVELS:
The Only Person
Sunday Girl

STAGE PLAY:
Baggage

Lee Langley

FROM
THE BROKEN
TREE

Thomas Congdon Books E. P. DUTTON *New York*

For information contact: E.P. Dutton, 2 Park Avenue, New York, N.Y. 10016

Library of Congress Cataloging in Publication Data

Langley, Lee
From the broken tree.

I. Title.

PZ4.L28 Fr	*1978*	*[PR6062.A535]*	*823'.9'14*	*78-7813*

ISBN: 0-525-10988-9

Published simultaneously in Canada by
Clarke, Irwin & Company
Limited, Toronto and Vancouver

Production Manager: Stuart Horowitz

Designed by The Etheredges

10 9 8 7 6 5 4 3 2 1

First Edition

For Simon

Truly, though our element is time,
We are not suited to the long perspectives
Open at each instant of our lives.
They link us to our losses; worse,
They show us what we have as it once was,
Blindingly undiminished, just as though
By acting differently, we could have kept it so.
—PHILIP LARKIN

                                No world
Wears as well as it should, but mortal or not,
A world has still to be built.
—W. H. AUDEN

PART ONE

She had always kept a few souvenirs in her jewel box, tucked out of sight. Now she pushed aside some pearls and scrabbled at the bottom of the mahogany case, picking up fragments of her life. A photograph, badly creased and bent at the corners: a group of girls, clustered together, captured at some moment of celebration. One of them, with knees slightly bent, drooped in a self-conscious attempt at grace; the next girl was trying not to laugh. Another, with a hand up to push back the curls at her neck, was frozen in that pose. She herself wore a white dress, her hair in braids. They stood outside a flat-fronted house in a foreign street in the pale light of a spring sun, faded over the years into a yellow fog. Within that arbitrary frame, the smiles, jokes, secrets were merely suspended, waiting to be released. Outside, wars occurred, and family quarrels. The casual blows of history, anguish of one sort and another, death, took their toll. In the photograph everyone lived on, unmarked by change or decay. Only she changed. She put it down irritably. She had never really liked those girls anyway.

There were other things: a menu from a wedding dinner, a theater program. Brittle, age-spotted documents in Russian and Polish. A page torn from an old newspaper, folded to show a picture of some shabby men—"Strikers Win Battle." In the center of the group a sturdy, blunt-featured man, fist raised in triumph. Leah felt suddenly tired: why had she agreed to this foolish idea, this digging up of the past? The past was full of pain, and betrayals small and large. Better left alone. She removed the remaining papers without looking at them and dropped them quickly into an already half-full cardboard box on the dressing table. And so she failed to notice the yellowing photograph of a baby, smiling widely, held in the arms of a thin, dark-haired girl. Covered by a dog-eared wedding picture, it lay unseen among the other papers.

From the jewel box she took her rings and slipped them, one by one, on fingers misshapen with arthritis. She ought to be feeling excited: this was her son's big day.

On the morning of his investiture, Emmanuel Raeburn received a slightly worrying letter. Only slightly worrying, nothing serious: the failure of a small project in an unimportant overseas territory. Still, irritation persisted, troubling him like a piece of grit in his shoe. A small project, but it should have gone smoothly. Raeburn Enterprises usually went smoothly.

He put on his top hat, straightened his silver tie, and left with his wife and son for Buckingham Palace. As the Rolls threaded its way across London, he realized that already he had left a lasting mark on the city: With satisfaction he noted how, on every side, his high-rise buildings caught the eye, dwarfing the surrounding, older structures. He never could understand why some people disliked modern developments. He saw them as monuments, not only to his own prosperity, but to the capitalist world. When Harold Macmillan said that most of the people had never had it so good, he certainly spoke for Emmanuel Raeburn. First the financial rewards; now the accolade. A property developer with a title! Sir Manny, that's what his friends would call him. And it was still only the summer of 'sixty-six. With a bit of luck, by the end of the decade he might make the House of Lords. He didn't anticipate much trouble, personally, from the Labour government.

He was aware that the sky was blue outside, but through the tinted glass of the Rolls it had a thunderous gray tinge. Over Trafalgar

Square hovered a cloud. A little cloud like a man's hand. Was that a sign of something? He wished the question had not occurred to him. He wished the small disappointment had not come to mar a day of crowning satisfaction.

He was a stockily built man, too short to carry off successfully the formal elegance of a morning suit. He was not handsome, but when he smiled—which was often—his solidly fleshed face broke up into little mounds of humor, the dark eyes narrowed into amused slits, and he gave, against all the odds, an attractive impression.

In the front seat, next to the chauffeur, his son sat, silent as usual. One of those *nebechy* romantics, Manny sighed to himself, the sort who turn up their noses at a perfectly good modern building but signed petitions to save every old ruin ready for demolition. Twenty years old and he still had a neck as thin as a schoolboy's. Emmanuel experienced a rush of tenderness toward him. He heaved himself forward and grasped Joe's neck with affection. His son flinched and twisted his head around questioningly.

"What's the matter?"

Emmanuel felt foolish, awkward. Off-key somehow. "Your hair needs cutting." And then, to soften the statement, he asked, "When are you seeing Simeon?"

"Tomorrow. You should know. You fixed the date with him, I didn't."

Why are even the briefest encounters with one's children so unsatisfactory? Emmanuel wondered.

There was a clucking of irritation from beside him. "Manny! Do move over." His wife was spread across two-thirds of the seat, sitting stiffly, like a doll, trying to remain uncreased. She floated, crimson with excitement, in a bubble of anticipation. Buckingham Palace came into view and she gave a gusty sigh of pleasure: the palace, the title, the pinnacle of their achievements. "It's the pinnacle of our achievements," she said aloud.

"Yes," Emmanuel agreed.

It should have been the most thrilling day of his life. Why, then, did he feel this sudden, unaccustomed twinge of unease?

Simeon Abrahams bobbed across the entrance hall of the Garrick Club like a clumsy craft navigating a choppy stretch of water, his shambling figure enveloped in a flapping, tentlike suit.

"Joe, my dear boy. Good of you to come." They shook hands.

Joe had met Simeon many times over the years, but they had never exchanged more than a few words. He looked curiously at the pouched face, the small, brilliant eyes gleaming from beneath thatches of dark eyebrow.

The Garrick, with its massive staircase, lofty ceilings, walls crowded with paintings in carved, gilded frames, could make some men look puny in comparison. Simeon's bulky figure, too big for the cramped proportions of modern rooms, here assumed the proper relationship with its setting. A Johnsonian girth was a sign of stability: like the place, he was solidly made.

"I thought we'd go straight in to lunch," he suggested, "if that suits you."

Between the entrance hall and the dining room, their progress was constantly halted by one acquaintance or another: an old associate, a fellow-member of some committee, all pausing to greet Simeon. He was, as Joe knew, a busy man. He ran his publishing house with a very personal hand on the reins, yet his vast bulk and benevolent presence were to be found at the top table for every fund-raising dinner, in a well-placed box at every charity gala, and on the speakers' platform at meetings for anything from flood relief to prison reform. To the causes he espoused he gave not only time and money but the benefit of a complex network of social contacts. He knew everyone and he used everyone: when he came on the scene the right people found themselves approached in the right way at the right time, and into Simeon's hairy paw dropped the jackpot, to be passed on to the deserving cause concerned.

A waiter led them to their table and fussed around them like a good nanny. Simeon glanced at the menu. "The salmon, I think. For me. Joe? Perhaps you'd care for something else?"

"No, no. The salmon."

While Simeon chose the wine, Joe was free to enjoy the shadowy room, with its canvases by Zoffany covering almost an entire wall. The tables were placed well apart: indiscretions would spread no further than intended.

Simeon, studying the wine list, lips pursed thoughtfully, at the same time studied Joe. The boy had changed a good deal since they last met: the vestiges of schoolboy gawkiness had gone, and he was slender now rather than skinny. In honor of the Garrick he had exchanged his normal student attire for a dark Italian suit and a white, high-collared shirt. He was taller than his father by several inches, but he had Manny's dark, narrow eyes, set in a high-cheekboned, slightly sardonic face. With his pale skin and brown hair he lacked the vividness of his parents' coloring. His looks and his reserve had been bred into him by England. Environment, Simeon thought to himself, had certainly modified the family physique.

Wine selected, Simeon turned to Joe. "So you're to spend a year working in London, I hear."

"It's part of the normal architecture course: to give me some practical experience in an architects' office before I go back to Cambridge for the next stage."

Simeon said amiably, "Tell me, Joe; what are your ambitions in the long run? Are you one of those highly motivated young fellows?"

Joe laughed. "I'm about as unmotivated as you can get. Becalmed, actually. Floating on a wide Sargasso Sea."

"That sounds uncomfortable."

"No. Yes—perhaps I enjoy the discomfort. The only suffering I'm likely to experience. Perhaps I'm afraid I'll be proved incapable of action if the opportunity does arise. Fatally flawed." His tone was mocking.

"The times don't favor Aristotelian heroes." Simeon murmured. "Our excesses lie in other directions."

The waiter poured an inch of wine and stood waiting. Simeon sipped and nodded his approval. He turned back to Joe. "It must be very hard for young people in our sort of circle today, surrounded by a generation that fought its way to the top of the tree and who therefore *must* see the top of the tree as the best place to be in order to justify the struggle. The younger generation, nesting there from birth, might not see its charms so clearly."

Joe waited, refusing to be drawn. Was the real purpose of this lunch after all to be no more than a plea for greater understanding of his parents? A salmon-flavored sermon? Surely not. Simeon was too shrewd to waste his time on inconsequential chat. This meeting was simply the latest variation on a theme of parental manipulation. Joe saw no reason why he should assist in the operation. He certainly would not be the one to steer the conversation into personal channels.

"How's business? Anything interesting in the autumn list?"

"There's a rather rude, six-hundred-page novel by a new American fellow. . . ."

They continued to talk publishing. Joe asked all the right questions and listened attentively. He was being scrupulously polite, and Simeon knew from experience the value of politeness to a private person; effulgent courtesy was a good weapon for deflecting awkward questions. He knew exactly what Joe was doing: he was stonewalling.

The salmon arrived, small, neat portions flanked by rows of thinly sliced cucumber. The waiter fussed again, seeing they had everything they needed. The world's disorders had no place here: a cozy, second-childhood serenity reigned. Simeon said casually, "I believe Manny has told you about this rather quixotic idea of mine for a book?"

"He . . . touched on it."

Joe was rather pleased with the phrase. Suitably noncommittal. His father had indeed touched on it, in the course of an abrasive encounter. Striding up and down the room on his short legs, furiously jingling the small change in his pocket, he had first muttered, and then shouted a good deal. "What's the matter with you, Jo-Jo?" he had asked. "A fine education, meeting the right people, short of nothing. You've had the best of everything!"

"That," Joe had explained, "is the trouble. You've raised a lotus-eater."

For the next ten minutes he had held on to his pose of studied politeness while his father expressed his feelings. Finally Manny had run out of breath and expletives simultaneously. He sat down.

"Right. While you're thinking great thoughts about how you propose to fill your time for the next forty years or so, there's something you can do. Oh, nothing to do with *business*," he had added sarcastically. "Very much your kind of thing. Nothing to do with *trade*. You can go and talk to Simeon, it's his idea. Some book about Peszno. I don't know what it's all about really, but he seems to think you might be interested. Perhaps you'll spare him an hour, give him the benefit of your vast intellect. Shouldn't be too tiring for you. Would you do that

⊻ 8

for me? I'd be much obliged. Well, I'd better get some work done. You'll be wanting to get on with your—what is it?—lotus-eating."

Now Joe nodded at Simeon. "Yes, he touched on it."

Simeon registered the lack of enthusiasm in Joe's voice. "Does it irritate you, that old people go in for nostalgia so much? It's a mark of progress. It's how we measure our achievements. Looking back, we can see how far we have come. That can be comforting."

"I suppose it might."

"Oh, yes. Take my own example. If my parents had stayed in Poland, my dear Joe, I would certainly not be talking to you now. One pogrom or another . . . one war or another; the Russians or the Germans or the Poles. . . . To hear my parents talk about that place you would have thought it paradise lost. It always annoyed me. They starved in Peszno, they suffered there, they had the good sense to get out —and then they never stopped talking about it. The Diaspora syndrome. You've heard it from your grandmother—"

"But you can't feel any of that," Joe protested, "Any more than I do. You were born here, like Manny, not in Peszno. *This* is your country."

"Of course," Simeon agreed. "When I got to school they said, 'You're English-born' as though I had won a prize. . . . You cannot imagine how intoxicating it was, teachers telling me about English his- tory—'my' history and 'our' empire. At home they were still talking Yiddish and here I was, learning about my heritage as a British citizen. It was irresistible. I'm afraid I was rather impatient with my parents. I feel guilty about that, now."

"I know the feeling well."

The linking of parents and guilt had been a mistake, Simeon realized. Perhaps the whole meeting had been a mistake. Perhaps his instinct about Joe had been wrong.

"I read something of yours once . . . a school essay on some metaphysical poets—"

Joe looked astonished. "How on earth?"

"Oh, I was doing some fund-raising nonsense, and a tour of the school was on the itinerary. Anyway, I remember it. The metaphysics of nostalgia, too, could be interesting. And the question of identity. Dan- gerous stuff, easy to lead memory astray, digging into the dead land."

"Why do you want to do this book, Simeon? You're not that in- terested in Peszno."

"I'm interested in people."

9

"That hardly covers it."

"No. Well, then let's say it's a question of links. We happen to have links with a small Polish town, a *shtetl*, that some of us knew and some have only heard about. There are still links with that town and the old traditions, the old ways. There are still a few left who remember how it was. But sooner or later the last link will go. And it will be as though the place never existed—vanished like Atlantis. Oh, the *town* is still there, geographically speaking. But that world only lives through the people who knew it, and it will die with them. I would rather like to preserve something of that lost world Joe, so that it isn't forgotten."

"But who on earth would be interested? Who would read it? A small Polish town, a group of aging Jews—it's hardly your Book of the Month Club choice, is it?"

"Well, Joe: I suppose *I'd* be interested. And I happen to be in a position to be able to do something about it. I know this is going to sound hideously sentimental, but I suppose I just don't want that world to die unrecorded."

"I can see it'll make a lovely coffee-table book, packed with nostalgic, sepia-tinted illustrations. I can even see why you want to do it, in a way," Joe said, "but I still don't see where *I* come in. I mean, why me? I'm not a historian. I'm not even a writer. Why don't you get an established writer, a big name? You know all the big names."

"Big names come expensive. I thought I could exploit you."

For a moment Joe was exposed to the extraordinary radiance of the Abrahams smile. He realized that Simeon was not a pretty man: in terms of weight and measurement he exceeded the acceptable. His features were neither refined nor regular. But his face had the ambiguity of a Rembrandt portrait: the ungainliness was transformed by humanity.

"Can you name me an established writer with grandparents who came from Peszno? You have that advantage. We're great survivors, but there is always a question mark, isn't there? The last couple of thousand years have had their bad times, but a time like the present is just as bad in its own way. Indifference is another enemy. Handing on to the next generation is always an act of faith. There's something in the Bible somewhere: 'A shoot shall spring from the broken tree, a branch shall grow from its roots. . . . ' Isaiah, I think. Remembering is part of survival." He shrugged again. "The old ones remember, all too well and all too often, I'm afraid. Young men forget."

He saw Joe's skeptical expression. "Don't dismiss it too quickly. With your fondness for history you might find it more than moderately entertaining. . . . You might even find it illuminating. Your grand-mother is going through her papers for photographs, letters, and so forth. Why not take a look at them when term's finished? No hurry, it's the sort of thing you could do in your spare time—I don't imagine Manny's architects will be exactly running you off your feet. Anyway, think about it."

On Sunday morning Joe lay indolently in a deck chair. He was glad he had accepted Nicky's invitation to stay for the weekend. Next to him she was sunbathing, her blond creaminess stretched out on the grass. Her father was systematically destroying the newspapers, spreading pages around him like crazy paving. Behind them the yellow Cotswold stone of the Matthews' Georgian house reflected a golden light.

The garden was a sheltered hollow, a cupped hand of sunshine and warm shade full of flowers and trees, birds and an occasional bee. Joe was on the verge of falling asleep.

Nicky's father slapped *The Sunday Times* irritably. "This prop-erty-development business is getting out of hand! Something ought to be done about it."

Joe said lazily, "Oh, people are becoming aware of the dangers. . . . The press is doing quite a good job—"

His host grunted impatiently. "Rubbish! The press is bought. They know which side their advertising's buttered. *And* the architects —charlatans, most of them. I don't expect *you* to agree with me of course dear boy, but the fact remains that it's a ramp. Vast fortunes are being made by these shysters, growing fat at other people's expense. . . . The usual element, like Mr. Greenberg here." He banged the paper.

The usual element. Joe felt the familiar exhaustion settling over him like a fine, clogging mist. Once again the declaration, embarrassing to others, irrelevant to himself, that had to be made. "Had you forgot-ten," he asked lightly, "that I'm one of the tribe?"

11

Either Nicky's father was genuinely unembarrassed or he covered it well. He shrugged crossly. "Oh, I'm not talking about people like you, you fool. You know the type of person I mean."

He did indeed. He could hardly have avoided it, over the years. A Semitic cast of countenance might have been a social asset: at least people would have known where they stood. As it was, with his public-school patina, he blended into the background, and people spoke freely, the semantics of prejudice coloring innocuous conversation, making him aware of the gulf between ordinary him and ordinary them: "A sharp little Jewish lawyer . . ." or, "One of the brethren, of course . . ." or, "A financier, frightful man, you know the type: talking in pounds and thinking in Yiddish."

Traditional Christianity had its part to answer for. At prep school once he had heard the vicar explaining that Jesus was a Christian, surrounded by Jews who resented him. "But Jesus was a Jew," Joe said. "Not in the *accepted* sense," replied the clergyman.

Ah, the *accepted* sense! Just as the Nazis measured noses and held medical examinations to trace Semitic characteristics, the nicest people went through their own process of categorizing: Property developer? Yes, he'll be one. Loud-mouthed entrepreneur? Almost certainly. Crooked company director? Definitely. Rich vulgarians and chaps in big cars smoking fat cigars? Oh, all of *them*. When it came to artists, the focus tended to blur a bit: the refugee violinist was just a musician with a foreign name. Scientist? Well, he could be a runaway Russian. On the whole, *poor* Jews lacked credibility. Prejudice, he saw, was never dispelled, merely contained. And it found a thousand tiny vents through which to emerge.

He glanced at Nicky. She was looking at him anxiously, apologetically. Nice girl. He would miss her, this year away from Cambridge. He smiled at her reassuringly and closed his eyes. But the sun was too hot, the garden shrill with the squawking of birds, killers all, in their way. There wasn't a snail or a worm that was safe from their stabbing and their rending. The bees carried built-in menace. Even the deck chair was at the wrong angle. Nicky's father, with the land, and a Gainsborough on the drawing-room wall, and the old money on which the dust of respectability had long since settled, would have described himself as "well-to-do." He would call Joe's father stinking rich, if asked for an opinion.

Joe got to his feet abruptly. "Rather sticky out here. Think I'll cool down inside for a bit." He strode away rapidly across the lawn.

12

"Oh, *Daddy!*" Nicky said reproachfully. "You're so bloody tact-less."

Her father shrugged. "That's the trouble with these people—they're so oversensitive."

Leah opened the door and stared at Joe appraisingly.
"Hullo, Gran."

Her severe expression did not alter or soften. "Hullo, Joseph. You never come to see me anymore."

"I've come now, haven't I? How are you?"

"What do you care how I am? No one cares about an old woman. Why should they? Nobody even troubles to ask me how I am anymore."

He kept his voice even: "*I* just asked how you were."

She closed the door of the flat and shooed him before her into the sitting room. It was as brightly lit as a stage set, every highly varnished surface aglitter, the carpet like a crimson river swirling around their feet. "How *should* I be, with my bad back and the trouble with my hands? I'm wonderful."

She was nearly eighty years old. And she had spent close to sixty of those years in England, but, Joe noticed, she still said "vunderful."

"Ah," he said, switching off. To attempt to go along with Leah's complex routine, to attempt to deal rationally with her as she unloaded her fundamentally unanswerable questions and her complaints, could put him flat on his back with a two-day migraine and high-pitched bells in the ears. Hers was the rhetoric of self-pity that merely required an audience. Joe was an old campaigner. He moved around the over-furnished room, picking up and examining the little silver bowls, knickknacks, and onxy ashtrays, putting them down, nodding and rais-ing his eyebrows expressively, and hearing not a word.

When she had exhausted her complaints and herself, Leah said briskly, "You'll have some tea." Joe registered the change of voice, and tuned in.

"No, I don't think so." He knew that to accept right away would diminish her sense of power.

"You'll have some tea."

He sat down, conscious of having played his part in that particular exchange, word-perfect. He watched her through the open kitchen door: her round body bulged comfortably in her cashmere dress. Her hair, drawn into a bun, was like silver floss. Rich old men and women, Joe had noticed, seemed to go silver in one jump, missing out on the dreary, streaked gray; the pepper-and-salt of the less well-endowed. As he had grown, she had shrunk, hunching down into herself. The fierce, dark eyes were hooded by heavy, wrinkled lids, and, with her neat, curved beak of a nose, gave her the look of a watchful old turtle.

She called out, "I hear you're mixed up in this book idea of Simeon's." The cups and saucers clattered angrily. "I thought he would have more sense. Worrying old people who do not want to talk of private things."

Joe suspected that every old trout for miles around was aching for the chance to talk, but he kept his peace. Leah carried in the tray and offered him a plate piled high with little round cakes. He began to shake his head but she ignored him and pushed some of the cakes onto his plate, her black eyes flashing like coals reflecting a light.

"I made them myself, they won't poison you."

"Delicious," he said, truthfully.

"No, really? Not too sweet? A bit heavy perhaps?"

He reassured her.

"You weren't here for Pesach," she said accusingly. "I don't suppose you even knew when it was."

Meaning to humor her, Joe ended—as so often—by being driven to hurt her, through irritation with her arrogance and her iron rigidity on matters of ritual. "I always know when it's Passover because of the chocolate Easter eggs Scott and Jeanette are stuffing themselves with." The indiscretion was not a serious one, but Leah's eyes widened in theatrical horror. "Easter eggs! You will tell me next they have Christmas stockings."

"They do. And a tree with colored lights."

She said, sepulchrally, "I have lived too long." Bernhardt could have done no better with a line from Racine.

14

Joe said, more sharply than he intended, "What does it matter now, anyway?"

Her brimming tears vanished like a child's. "Don't talk like that! People died for those beliefs."

"They believed. That was their right. I do not. Can't I have the same right? Can't we leave it like that?"

She shook her head violently. "You think you can just shake it off? My boy, you know nothing. One day you will have to answer for your ancestors. You cannot escape the covenant."

The overheated air of the apartment was suddenly stifling. The whole thing was eerie, this obsession with the past. He had nothing to do with these people; they were people of the shadows, they breathed air dank from ruins and soured by the poison of the gas chambers. Whenever he tried just to be himself he got slapped in the face from one side or another. ("The usual element," Nicky's father had said, casually pigeonholing him with the undesirables.) You did not choose. You were chosen.

He looked at his watch, and she noticed. "Always in a hurry. . . ."

"Thanks for the tea."

"Must you go? So soon? You just got here."

He touched her cheek briefly with his lips, but she seized his head and pulled him down for a smacking kiss. He felt mauled.

"I have collected some bits and pieces for Simeon's precious book, going through my trunks, as if I haven't enough to do. You can take them now."

After he had gone she carried the tray into the kitchen, wondering why she behaved as she did with him. So much that mattered left unsaid. So much said that was meaningless. Partly, it was the language: as she grew older, her thoughts ran ahead of her tongue. In Yiddish or Polish she could still have kept pace with them, but English had become tiring, and so she kept to the easy paths of familiar conversation. On those routes they could never open their minds to each other. She blamed herself for getting sidetracked, discussing stupid details, and arguing pointlessly. She was genuinely worried about Joe: the boy seemed increasingly unreachable.

Sifting through Leah's cardboard box, Joe had glimpses of her life across the years—steppingstones to the present. Scraps of paper, old cuttings, letters, recipes, yellowing photographs. Faces that, old and young alike, gazed out of the pictures with an innocence that no longer seemed possible. Young men in suits that seemed too small for them, and peaked caps that seemed too large. Venerable gentlemen with broad-brimmed hats and black coats and beards; some young girls, slight and shyly grouped together, one in the center wearing a white dress with many buttons, her hair tightly braided. A girlish figure, heartbreakingly slender, a mouth that curled with humor. With a shock, Joe identified Leah, Leah as she had once been. But this was a stranger; her form bore no resemblance to the grandmother he knew. Except for the eyes—the long almond eyes she could still use so eloquently.

There was a postcard of Southend; a wedding photograph of his parents: his father—with sleek black hair—smiling fatuously at his mother, slimmer and flirtatious-eyed. How they had changed! These were the familiar faces. Others were less easily identified. He paused at a photograph of a baby, sitting on the knee of a girl with dark hair.

He began dropping the whole faded collection back into the box. As he picked up the cheaply mounted picture of the young boy and girl, some newspaper clippings tucked into the backing fell onto his desk. He spread them out, puzzled. All from English newspapers, they appeared to have no relation to family or Peszno: "John Middleway, promising young barrister who had distinguished himself at the Nuremberg Trials" . . . "John Middleway Knighted in the New Year's Honours" . . . a blurred photograph of Sir John and Lady Middleway and some titled friends at Ascot . . . one, dated a little later, was a news report: "High Court Judge Injured in Car Accident."

Intrigued, he began to dial Leah's number: she would have the answer. Then he remembered that Manny and Rebecca had carried her off on a Mediterranean cruise for what he could only feel was a family penance. He threw the cuttings back into the box.

After a moment he took them out, flicked through them again: Nuremberg, the Royal Enclosure, Covent Garden Gala. . . . He reached for the telephone directory.

The house overlooked Hyde Park. Joe rang the bell and waited. The girl who opened the door wore faded jeans and a loose T-shirt. She had a thin, childish body and dark hair cut very short around her hollow-cheeked face. She waited silently, peering short-sightedly at Joe through enormous, slightly tinted glasses. A daughter home from school, he guessed.

"I have an appointment with Sir John . . . Joe Raeburn."

She stepped back and motioned him into the large hall. "His train's been delayed. He shouldn't be long. I'm Samantha."

The hall was very formal and slightly austere. An intricately carved mirror hung on the dark green wall; below it was a narrow marble chiffonnier. The girl hesitated in the doorway of the drawing room and moved on. "Let's go into the library."

She waved him to a chair and collapsed on the leather sofa, curling her legs under her and pushing aside a book lying open, face down beside her. Joe's eye was caught by an illustration of a Star of David on the cover—not something he would have expected to find in a Gentile stronghold like this. He craned his neck slightly to try to read the title, and she at once passed it over to him. It was, he saw, yet another account of life on a kibbutz in Israel.

"Are you enjoying it?" The question was mechanical, her response warmly gushing.

"Tremendously! I'd love to go and live on a kibbutz, it must be *fantastic!*"

Joe winced inwardly. He was about to declare himself but she

≱ 17

went bubbling on: "No possessions to worry about, no formalities. A beautiful way to live."

"I rather like having my own things round me," Joe remarked.

"Oh!" She waved away the comment. "If you tried the communal life—"

"I did, once." He was reluctant to hurt her feelings; he, too, had been through a phase of breathless idealism when he was younger, but all this warmth was a bit overwhelming.

"I spent a summer with a bunch of people who were running a commune—the whole bit, milking the goat, sheets drying on bushes, all that."

"And?"

"And after a while I realized it was just daft: sitting around with flowers in our hair eating wholemeal bread and denouncing the evils of capitalism, and when we needed something badly enough, one of us just tapped our evil, capitalist parents. Pointless. So I chucked it."

"But a kibbutz. That isn't artificial. It's a genuine community."

"But your presence there, as a sort of sunshine patriot, that would be self-conscious, wouldn't it?"

"Not if my work were honest. They need people. Well, I'll have to make up my mind about it soon. I've been putting off making a decision quite long enough."

"I find one can get by indefinitely without making a decision," Joe said. He was bored with the discussion. These starry-eyed upper-class girls were all the same; he had known them as sisters of classmates. First you got the monologues about service and equality, and then in due time they had their debutante season and married suitably into their own circle in the old family church, started breeding, and left the crusading to the next generation.

She sensed his withdrawal. "I'm sorry, I'm boring you. One person's obsession can be another person's blind spot. My mother can talk for hours about the value of wheat germ to the nervous system." She smiled, suddenly uncertain. The huge glasses dominating her face gave her a slightly comic vulnerability.

Joe felt a pang of remorse. "Look, don't let anyone put you off your idea. Few enough people want to help others, and soon it'll be too late. You'll be doing sensible, dreary grown-up things." Even as he spoke he knew the words were pompous and condescending, but it was too late.

She frowned. "What do you mean?"

"I mean if you want to do it, do it. Have you asked your parents?"

She looked at him kindly. "How old do you think I am?"

She looked about fourteen, but he realized she might be older. He decided to play it safe. "Eighteen?"

"Oh, *God!*" Her reaction was part amusement, part indignation, "I'm twenty-one, and I've been working for two years."

There was no way to retrieve the situation. Obviously she wasn't a child. How could he have failed to recognize that? The hair with its smooth, geometric precision was modishly cut—probably Vidal Sassoon. The body was slight but as she sat back on the sofa he saw that beneath the shapeless T-shirt were small, high breasts, narrow hips. He began to mumble apologies.

"Oh, don't worry. I do understand. I'm used to it actually. I'm quite a social failure. I talk like a Saint Trinian's sixth former—yes I do, I know it. And even though I buy the latest gear from Biba and Mary Quant and stay up half the night to try and get madly experienced-looking bags under my eyes, nothing helps."

"At Cambridge I once told one of the dons his mother was looking for him and it turned out to be his wife," Joe said. "I just have no eye for these things."

She granted him a small smile.

"What do you do?" he asked.

"I'm a cook."

"A cook?"

"That's right." She stared at him. "You're wondering why, aren't you? Not the trendiest thing you can think of, is it?"

"On the contrary, it could be—"

"I'm not very successful with the swinging crowd. I tried being a receptionist and they simply didn't take me seriously. I tried the BBC and *they* didn't take me seriously. I was a bit of a joke. Jolly hockey sticks. Anyway, I'm a good cook. I'm Cordon Bleu trained. As a cook I'm taken seriously."

The front door banged, and she jumped to her feet. "There he **is.** You're *very* late!" she called.

A tall man, rumpled and a little out of breath, was walking down the hall. He had a slight limp. "Blame British Rail. Held up for two hours, and *then* they blithely tell us we've missed the connection."

Through the middle-aged blurring of jawline and throat and the crosshatching of wrinkles, Joe could discern a classically handsome bone structure. Middleway would be an impressive figure in his judge's robes and wig.

He turned to Joe, eyes twinkling. "Now, let me see: my secretary said you wanted to ask me about some personal, family matter? Is that right?"

Joe nodded, thinking to himself that the man's air of absent-minded vagueness could have been an asset when he was a barrister.

Samantha took her father's coat. "I'll leave you. I've got to get ready for work."

Joe brought out the newspaper clippings from his pocket and handed them to Middleway. "I'm going through material for a book about a Jewish community in a small Polish town called Peszno. I'm trying to trace people who might have had something to do with the place. When I found these cuttings among the material, I thought. . . ."

The telephone rang, and Middleway reached across the desk to answer it. He glanced at Joe, "Forgive me for just a moment. . . ." Tactfully, Joe wandered over to the bookshelves and stared up at the titles. He heard Middleway ask, solicitously, "How is it going, when d'you think you'll be back?" And then, after a pause, "I miss you." He put down the telephone and began to glance through the cuttings. He shook his head regretfully. "Poland, you say? I've never been to Poland."

He shuffled through the papers again. "Perhaps it was simply Nuremberg. A lot of people were fascinated by the trials, you know. It could have been just that. Whoever cut out the early bits went on keeping pieces about me for a while. It happens."

Samantha pushed open the door. "I'm off." She had changed into a thigh-length shift and long sleek boots. Even Joe could see that she in no way resembled a schoolgirl.

"Look in when you get home, I'll be up," Middleway mumbled, still looking at the cuttings. Samantha waved a picnic basket at Joe and disappeared down the hall.

"Whose are these?" Middleway asked.

"My grandmother's."

"Have you asked her about them?"

"She's away. I'm afraid my curiosity got the better of me—I thought you might be able to clear it up right away."

"Wish I could. Polish . . . lose family in the camps, did she?"

"Yes."

"There you are, then. It'll have been Nuremberg. Nothing whatever to do with your book." He handed the clippings back to Joe. "You know, I wouldn't bother your grandmother with it. Chuck 'em away. Old people can be easily upset, she might not want to be reminded about Nuremberg, might churn her up."

He nodded briskly at Joe. "Well. Sorry I couldn't help." The interview was clearly at an end.

At the front door Middleway shook hands cordially.

"Goodbye, Sir John. Thank you for giving up your time."

"Not at all. Good luck."

Walking toward the car, Joe glanced back and saw Middleway still standing by the door, watching him.

The following Saturday, Joe went to a party in Chelsea. The crowded, noisy room depressed him, and, glancing about, he was suddenly aware how brash and overconfident the girls seemed. Some wore skin-tight leather, others were strutting around in over-the-knee boots and dresses that barely covered their buttocks. The whole thing was like a parody of itself—a self-consciously swinging scene.

"Isn't this bloody marvelous?" a girl shouted through the smoke, writhing vigorously to the Rolling Stones, her flesh intermittently visible through the linked plastic discs of her brief dress.

"No."

"No? What's wrong with it?"

"What's right?" he asked, pleasantly.

"Oh, you get on my tits, darling. You're so bloody po-faced." She stopped dancing, chucked him under the chin, and headed in the direction of the bar. "My advice to you is to get pissed," she shouted. "Then you might loosen up and have a bit of fun."

Loosen up. Easier said than done. The music, the company, and the mood seemed suddenly stale and indigestible. He left early.

He let himself into the apartment and wandered through the

21

empty rooms, putting on all the lights. There was something chilling about the place despite the mildness of the evening. He could sense the warm air flowing through the rooms, rippling over the clinically tidy bed, neatly placed chairs and tables. The rooms were cones of silence, deafening him. He coughed and felt he had disturbed the stillness. He stared malevolently at the large sofa and the circular white table. He liked the stuff in a way, but he had not chosen it. The Notting Hill apartment, like his life, came professionally designed, ready furnished, prepaid. Everything supplied, nothing left to chance. Or choice.

Given such conditions there seemed no way of defining himself, or indeed his life. He planned nothing: things were drifted into—holidays, casual relationships, a career. Living in the present was hard: no imperative emerged, no one thing presented itself as worth the effort. His was the stasis of indecision.

It seemed to him at times that he suffered from a condition he could only describe as weightlessness: the very ease of his life provided a fatal antidote to struggle. Joe was conscious of this weightlessness while remaining helpless to do anything about it. Mere action was useless—a charade, a do-it-yourself puppet show in which he was both Punch and puppet master. He could wear homespun and share a commune for a summer vacation, or go on a Landrover pilgrimage to India which broke down in Athens. None of it mattered, really. The car was always parked somewhere, ready to be picked up; the jet could get him home in time for tea. Nothing mattered, neither the doing nor the failing. Security made everything possible and simultaneously rendered it sterile. He would never need to cry for help.

He still hoped, in his moderate way, that there might be an answer somewhere if he could only think of the right question. That he might find something in his life that would inspire, possess him, for which he could—what? . . . sacrifice himself? Suffer? Something that would free him from his ridiculous self-despair.

A long time ago he had played with the idea—seductive, thrilling —of thwarting his father's compulsive generosity: of refusing to go on taking, because, unknown to the donor, the price was too high. But it was already too late: the mantle of acquiescence had grown to fit him too well; he could no longer shake it off, though it stifled him.

One must make a decision sooner or later, the Middleway girl had said to him the other day. But why bother? Primroses, it seemed, grew beside all paths, even the weariest river wound somewhere safe to sea. One field was like another, one city like the next. Girls varied only in their availability. The Middleway girl was certainly different—a bit of a joke, as she said. But an original, with her schoolgirl vocabulary and her myopic eyes shielded by smoky glass. A joke, but she stuck in the mind.

He dialed her number. "It's Joe Raeburn. I wondered what you were doing." Now *there* was a sparkling opening, he thought glumly. A great start.

"I'm reading an improving book."

"Do you want to go on reading it, or do you feel it's improved enough?"

She refused to let him pick her up at home: "I'm used to finding my way about, I'm very independent." Twenty minutes later her car pulled up outside. He was waiting for her in the downstairs lobby.

Inside the apartment she glanced around the big room, noted the reference books stacked on shelves to the ceiling; the drawing board surrounded by sheafs of papers, the big desk. "Bit grand for a mere youth."

"Not if the youth's father owns the building."

"How tidy you are."

"It's a manifestation of a deep insecurity," Joe said lightly. "Only a man at ease with his universe can treat it carelessly. I tried scattering newspapers and socks about the other day, to try to humanize the place, but it didn't help: I realized I was cheating. And even my untidiness was orderly."

She picked up an illustration from the drawing board. "What's this?"

"The Tower of Babel. A ziggurat. I'm rather fascinated by the idea of the ziggurat."

"Joe, dear: I went to a very posh boarding school where they taught us to sit with our knees together and to stand with our tummies and bums tucked in. I'm a demon lacrosse player, and I can do you a lovely floral arrangement. But I don't *know* anything. You better explain what a ziggurat is before we go any further."

He explained, and she listened, studying the drawing closely. "So it was a kind of high-rise of its time in a way then?"

"And at the top there was a temple, a sort of guest house for the passing god, in case he felt like dropping in."

"That's a hospitable idea."

"Very hospitable. It came furnished with bed and compliant virgin."

"Well, as a virgin I have to admit I'd be a bit of a failure," she said, "but I could try being compliant." She tilted her head back, looking up at him, mouth curved in amusement, eyes invisible behind the dark glasses.

"I thought everyone treated you as a kid," Joe said.

"Perhaps that's why I had to show them they were wrong." She put down the drawing. "I'm actually quite good at it," she added reassuringly, "and I'm on the pill of course, so there's no need to worry."

Joe, who tended to invest occasions of this sort with a degree of romanticism, was slightly disconcerted. "Do you do this a lot?"

"Not that often, actually, but only because I don't meet many people I like enough to want to go to bed with. If I really like someone, I just can't think of a good reason not to. It seems so awfully silly."

The contrast between the cool practicality of the statement and the childish phrasing was too much for Joe. His seriousness crumbled.

"Oh, I do think a laugh's a terribly good start," Samantha said approvingly.

She unzipped her dress and stepped out of it. Her tanned flesh was patterned with a white bikini mark, like a phantom swimsuit. Her body was supple, its angularity unexpectedly graceful. She curled up on his bed, waiting, watching him.

"I can't see your face," Joe said, touching her glasses.

"I don't quite feel safe without them," she explained. But she removed the tinted shields.

They came together with the minimum of fumbling or awkwardness, physically in harmony. Joe saw that she was right: even this poor mockery of a ziggurat could have its moment of ritual splendor. A fine consummation.

Lying next to each other afterward, they talked; Samantha less jokey, Joe less guarded than usual. Toward midnight she said, "I better go. Daddy will wait up for me. He always does, and he's on his own. Mummy's not back from the health farm till tomorrow."

"I'll see you home," he said. "And no arguments."

"All right. How would you like a scrambled egg? I'm starving."

The streets were empty and the two cars kept pace, side by side. At red lights they continued to talk, calling through the windows to each other. Laughing at nothing, elated, Joe relished the inconsequentiality—the fun of it all. Preoccupied with Samantha, he lost, for a little while, his pervading sense of futility. He forgot himself in delighted contemplation of her uncloying sweetness. Without even being aware of it, he allowed himself to feel safe with her.

They parked and walked up to the house. It was dark except for a light in an upstairs window, and Joe waited while Samantha unlocked the door and pushed it open.

"Samantha? Is that you?" A high, clear voice called from above.

Samantha looked startled. "Mummy's home." She switched on the hall light. Lady Middleway, slender as a mannequin and as neat-boned as her daughter, came down the stairs wearing a camel-hair dressing gown. "Where on earth have you been?"

"Mother, this is Joe."

Lady Middleway's narrow, brilliant smile flashed in Joe's general direction as she held out her hand. "How do you do, Mr. . . . ."

"Raeburn."

"Mr. Raeburn." She paused. "Any connection with. . . ."

"Emmanuel Raeburn? He's my father." It was a question, Joe found, that came up in certain circles. Samantha glanced up at him, so close that he could see the huge black pupils almost obscuring the dark brown of her eyes.

"We're just going to have a snack in the kitchen, we won't disturb you."

Lady Middleway's face had sharpened and seemed paler than before. Joe had thought her beautiful at first sight. Now he noticed lines of strain tugging at her muscles.

"I rather think, Samantha, that we should say good night to Mr. Raeburn now."

The tone was peremptory, and Samantha frowned. "We're just having something quick—"

"Oh, I think not. It's a little late. We mustn't keep Mr. Raeburn."

Joe said cheerfully, "Perhaps it is a little late." He was not surprised by the snub. But it angered him. Also it was unexpectedly graceless. He looked up and saw Samantha's father, shadowy at the top of the stairs, waiting.

"Good night, Sir John."

Joe drove away, taken aback by the strength of his own anger. Surely he should have learned by now. No one was fooled. He was not Joe Raeburn, a speck like any other speck . . . lost in the universe. He was Joseph, son of Emmanuel, who had been Rubinstein before he was

Rubin before he was Raeburn. Never quite belonging. Somewhere within the blood, like a virus, a strangeness lurked, to confound him, to defeat him. He could never count on being one of the crowd. Never melt into the blanketing darkness. Even when he himself was unaware of it, otherness clung to him like phosphorus.

At last he slackened pace, turned, and drove slowly home.

He was still asleep next morning when the doorbell rang.

"May I come in?" Samantha was very formal. She walked in, unsmiling, and moved around the room restlessly.

"I wanted to apologize for last night. And if you want me to leave, I'll understand. But I *am* dreadfully sorry it happened. You certainly saw Mummy at her best."

"She's not unique, you know," Joe said.

"No, but she's too intelligent for that sort of rubbish—or should be. I think she's sick, it's a sort of sickness. She's always been the same, even at school. . . . She's never actually said she doesn't like Jews. But one gets the message after a while. The really hilarious thing is that I hadn't even realized you were Jewish until she went into her panic act last night."

"Under the circumstances, she can't be too happy about your idea of going off to work on a kibbutz—you might as well suggest joining a leper colony."

"Oh, I haven't told her. She doesn't know about that. Nor does Daddy. I started years ago, not telling them things that might upset them. It's easier. They worry about me frightfully. About something happening to me. It's a terrible responsibility, trying to keep them unworried.

"Did you know I was adopted? People say adopted children have an easier time of it, that adopting parents are more relaxed. Don't you believe it. They seem to worry all the time. Mummy'd spent years trying to have kids, and finally they told her to forget it unless she wanted to kill herself. And I suspect she tried that too, at some point. I know she had a bad turn, went a bit wild—not that anything's ever been *said*, of course. Nothing is ever *said*, too embarrassing. But one gleans the odd hint, and Daddy's always fussing about her."

Apologetically, she added, "All this makes her sound like a neurotic monster, but actually, she and Daddy gave me a wonderful childhood. Not a shadow anywhere. I haven't one memory that isn't golden where they're concerned. I remember her saying once that if you have a marvelous childhood, whatever happens later, you'll always have that, they can't take it away, you'll always have a sort of glow that you remember. I suppose I should be grateful for that. I *am* grateful for that."

She shrugged nervily. "I'm sorry to go on like this. I'm talking far too much, and what do you care about my mixed-up family anyway?" She had hunched herself up into a ball at one end of the sofa. Her face looked even smaller than usual, her mouth turned down at the corners.

He took her hand and pulled her to her feet. "I'm glad you came."

"Honestly?"

"Honestly. Actually, I was about to pulverize the entire Middleway family with a set of hideous Yiddish curses—really settle their hash unto the third and fourth generation. But on consideration I'll spare you. On one condition: with your qualifications I assume you can make a decent cup of coffee, and I haven't had breakfast yet."

"Let me put that right—it's the least I can do—"

"And please stop apologizing for your family. Wait till you hear about mine."

She halted in the kitchen doorway: "You're amazing. Even the *kitchen's* tidy."

"I know. It's the Jewish mother in me."

Joe was checking specification charts at the architects' offices when a secretary looked in from the next room. "Joe: your father just rang. He wants to see you at Raeburn House right away."

"What, now? I'm in the middle of something."

"It sounded pretty urgent. He said right away."

The traffic was heavy, and it took Joe more than half an hour to reach Mayfair.

Manny was at his desk, cigar clamped into position. "What kept you?"

27

"Traffic. How was the cruise?"

"I don't talk about holidays in office hours. Of course you wouldn't know the difference, but to me, it's unprofessional."

Clearly a bad morning. Joe assumed his most wooden expression and waited for Manny to continue. His father sat shifting papers about testily, finally glancing up to check that Joe was paying attention.

"I've been thinking. This book of Simeon's, it's occupying a lot of your time. I know you only took it on as a favor. Well, I think we should tell Simeon to find someone else."

"As a matter of fact it's proving more interesting than I thought. I really don't mind—"

"Oh, you don't *mind*? Well, that's terrific. You're *supposed* to be having a year of practical work. This is when you're *supposed* to spend a bit of time, amazingly enough, on architecture."

"I was doing that, this morning, until you got me over here. Look: don't worry Dad, I'll handle the book in my spare time. It won't get in the way—"

"Of course you would prefer the arty-crafty side of things. Better than work, isn't it? Scribbling! When I was your age I was—"

"At my age you were running two businesses, three if you count the one that didn't appear on the books. Yes, I know, Dad. You just have to face it: your talents and mine don't lie in the same direction."

Manny began to go red in the face. "Talent! Don't flatter yourself, *boychik*! What you have a talent for wouldn't buy you a smile from your fine friends if it weren't for my money. Think of yourself as something special, don't you? An artist, maybe. A cut above the sort of 'roughyak' your old man is. Artist? You couldn't create a bagel to keep the wolf from the door. You couldn't create a pair of shoes to keep your feet dry."

Bad scenes with his father were nothing new, but Joe could not as yet work out what had sparked this one off. "What, actually, is the matter?" he asked. "What have I done?"

"When have you ever done anything? You're spineless. It's my fault. I've been too easy with you." He stood up, pushing back the heavy swivel chair. "I'm switching you to another outfit, they'll teach you a lot, it's a big opportunity, they're doing it for me. You can stay until you have to go back to Cambridge."

"It's awfully good of you to be so concerned about my welfare," Joe said sarcastically. "Pity I've just mastered the internal telephone system and got to know the secretaries' names. Who are these people?"

"Franks and Sayer. They're based in Sydney—"

"Sydney, *Australia*?"

The suggestion was so absurd, so eccentric that Joe hardly knew how to deal with it. "Look: sorry and all that, Dad, but I don't actually want to go to Australia at the moment."

"Your views have nothing to do with it. You're going. It's as simple as that."

"If it weren't for your face I'd think this was some kind of joke. Dad, people just can't be shipped off to Australia anymore. Forget it."

"Just this once," Manny shouted, "you'll do something you don't want to do! Because I say so! Because *I* want you to!"

Joe kept his tone mild. "Dad, I have not done anything I really wanted to do since I was about five years old. Everything I have done has been because you wanted me to. The schools I went to, the clothes I wore, the holidays I took, what I'm doing at Cambridge. *You* chose, all along the line. I agreed. You're right, I *am* spineless. I've gone along with it all. But I'm not going to Australia. Because it's bloody ridiculous."

Manny began the agitated walk up and down the office, an invariable sign that his temper was about to get out of control. "I'm not discussing it any further. I'm a busy man. A few months in Australia will do you good. They're putting up a lot of interesting stuff there, you'll learn something. Better than wasting your time going through a lot of old papers, and getting mixed up with upper-class *shiksas*!"

Something about the way Manny slurred over the last few words suddenly gave Joe the clue to the whole bizarre episode. "I'm surprised at you, Dad. You've been nobbled by the Middleways. I'd have expected better of you. Lady Middleway is having kittens at the thought of her nice daughter being defiled by a Jew-boy—well, that's in character. But what are *you* getting so upset about? It's a bit early to worry about me getting seriously involved, I've only just met the girl. Anyway, *screwing out* is okay, isn't it? It's *marrying out* that's the ultimate crime."

Manny's face was a dark, congested crimson. "I'll make it very plain. I pay your rent. I pay your bills. I pay for everything. This is just a little on account. Don't see the girl again."

"You're asking too much."

"I'm not bloody asking. I'm telling! And that's an order."

Joe forced himself to move normally, to open the door and leave the office, closing the door carefully behind him. Dimly he could hear Manny shouting, but the clamor inside his own head was too loud for him to distinguish the words. He walked quickly to his own office.

Leah's cardboard box was still on his desk. He picked it up and walked out of the building.

Manny's secretary hovered by the door. "You haven't forgotten the meeting? They're waiting for you in the boardroom." She handed Manny a bulging folder as he stormed past her, cursing.

He was short with everyone at the meeting, and at the working lunch which followed it he swallowed his food half-chewed and suffered violent cramping pains in the stomach. The ingratitude of children was almost beyond belief. You did everything for them, asked nothing in return. Gave them love, gave them everything. But it was a one-way transaction: there was no deposit account to draw on, you didn't build up any credit. Ask them for something, a favor, for the best of reasons, and you got a kick in the teeth. Well, this was not going to be the end of this particular business. There was more he could do yet.

He shouted as he returned to his office, "Molly! Get me the Middleway number," and a moment later his secretary buzzed him.

"Lady Middleway on the line, Sir Manny."

The clear, high voice sounded anxious, a little breathless. "Manny? What's happened? What have you done?"

"What d'you mean?"

"She's gone. Samantha's gone."

Leah was sitting watching television when the telephone rang. She turned down the sound with a sigh: such a good play too. She always enjoyed the afternoon programs.

It was Joe. "Gran, I'm sorry to bother you, but I want you to listen carefully. I want you to let mother know I'm all right. She's at one of her charity meetings and I can't reach her."

"Why should you not be all right?"

"No reason at all. I just want her to know I've gone away for a while."

She knew at once that something was wrong. "What has happened?"

"Nothing. Don't worry."

"You've had an upset with your father."

"Gran, tell me something. What do you know about John Middleway?"

"What are you talking about?"

"In that box of yours, the papers you gave me, there were some press clippings about him—"

"In that box? Impossible! Where are they? I don't know what you're talking about."

"Look, don't worry. It doesn't matter anyway. I must go, I have a plane to catch."

She cried out, "Joseph! Please write! For God's sake don't be a stranger, don't disappear. We have lost too many in this family."

"I must go."

"At least tell me where you're going," Leah said quickly.

"Israel. I'll be—" The electronic tones sounded in her ear and they were cut off.

She tried to reach Manny but he had gone out. She put down the telephone, tempted for a moment to start weeping. It would have comforted her. But the moment passed and she sat dry-eyed in her brightly lit room, with the girl on the television screen, silently mouthing words. She was filled with foreboding and a sense of loss that she had known before, long ago. She had forgotten, thought it gone. But it had only been blanketed, overlaid with the weight of the passing years. She felt very tired, and closed her eyes, hoping to sleep for a little. But sleep eluded her.

PART TWO

Peszno was not a large town, and the river looped tightly around one end of it so that the lower part of the town was almost an island. There were two squares: one with a bandstand where the Russian military band played on Sundays and holidays; another, smaller one down in the Jewish district. There were three churches, an officially recognized synagogue, and some twenty small rooms here and there regularly used for prayer meetings by devout Jews whose piety was second only to their irascible temperament—each man his own rabbi might have been the ideal solution.

A cemetery for each community lay outside the town, and a town hall that tried to cater for both stood on the west side of the main square. Neatly laid out in rectangles and oblongs, the residential area consisted of a grid of ten streets intersected by six larger avenues. Perhaps the casual visitor would not at once have discerned that there were two Pesznos: the upper part, with the town hall as the focal point, and the lower end, with its market and its maze of little shops and stalls. Here, every alleyway, corner, and street sprouted its merchandise. Even doorways and window ledges were brought into use—heaped with goods and cheap materials. The whole area swarmed and pulsed with humanity about the business of buying and selling.

This lower market was filled with the brilliant colors of vegetables and fruit, bales of cotton and wool, rows of leather boots, and baskets of live poultry. Tubs of herrings were lined up beside open shopfronts, and rows of tallow candles hung from hooks. The smells were pungent and bewilderingly varied: the sharp tang of the pickled cucumbers; the warm, yeasty aroma of fresh-baked bread; plump olives, black and green, that exuded an odor like wet, porous stone; and alongside the tallow candles, rough lumps of local soap that tickled the nostrils and made children sneeze.

Against the mounds of jewel brightness, the glistening, fresh-picked color, the women in their black dresses and headscarves were somber figures. Heads tightly bound in the traditional kerchief, they stood, some mute, some hectoring passers-by with loud, challenging voices, each offering something special—a bargain on no account to be missed. Perhaps a pyramid of green peppers like fat silken pincushions, or a basket of pearly eggs from the hens kept in the back yard. Or a few fresh cucumbers piled onto a cloth on the pavement, their speckled skins encrusted and warty like the backs of toads.

The peasants, faces raw and flayed by the wind in winter, burned brown in summer, shouldered their way through the market in thick jackets and bulky shirts, their trousers tucked into the tops of their vast, muddy boots. The Jews with their black hats, beards, and gabardine coats flapping around their ankles looked very urban in contrast.

The Jews always seemed to be hurrying from one place to another —between home and synagogue; between one business deal and the next. The dreamy expression on the thin, bearded faces might be religious fervor, or the elation following a satisfyingly profitable turnover.

Once, when Leah was a very small girl, she had asked her mother why nearly all the stall holders were women. "Where are the men?" And her mother, almost surprised to hear the question, said, "Studying Torah, of course."

Perhaps there was an element of wishful thinking in the reply, but the point was that in an ideal world all the men *would* be at religious studies. There were in fact men who were shopkeepers, innkeepers too, but they were somewhat looked down on if these activities kept them from loftier things. Leah's own father had a little shop at the side of the house, but it seemed to her that the pots and pans he sold, and the bookkeeping that kept track of it all, occupied a small proportion of his day. Luckily he supplied the local barracks with tin plates and mugs for the men, so he could devote himself to the luxury of study without worrying about where next week's Sabbath chicken was coming from.

The week had a relentless rhythm at the lower end of town: Sunday was for washing clothes. Even as a baby Leah could remember watching her mother and big sister almost hidden in clouds of steam, banging at the linen with large wooden bats as the clothes boiled and bubbled and the house filled with the smell of soap. On Monday the great stiff bundles were humped to the pressing woman, to be folded and flattened between huge rollers.

Tuesday was market day. Leah held the baskets for her mother as Rachel examined flapping poultry, sniffed cheese, and bought rounds of butter wrapped in wet cabbage leaves, harangued by the stall holders, bargaining, conceding, clinching an acceptable deal.

By Wednesday the pace was already quickening toward the Sabbath preparations. On Thursday, market day again, Rachel bought the fish for Friday, opening their gills and pinching the glittery, scaled bodies to check for freshness. Then the children were bathed, their underwear changed, hair washed. On Friday, with the Sabbath only a sunset away, Rachel was racing against time to have everything ready. The chicken must be sent to the ritual slaughterer; the meal prepared, the house cleaned. Around midday, Leah's father, like most other men, stopped work or study to go to the bathhouse, and by sunset, with a final burst of speed, the Sabbath was welcomed in.

For twenty-four hours calm reigned within the house, troubles and worries officially banished. Leah had heard her wicked cousin Mordecai whisper once that the real, practical value of the faith was that the Sabbath did indeed, as the Talmud said, provide even the poorest with a moment of consolation: the nearest they could hope to come to a glimpse of heaven on earth.

In the unfashionable part of town near the synagogue, the streets were less symmetrically drawn, and one of them curved, following the contours of a small hill. Walking home, Leah could gauge the curve as every step brought into view a little more of the approaching houses with their long, shuttered windows and iron balconies. The street was not only curved, but steep. That, Leah knew as her steps grew slower in summer, the heat becoming more intense, bouncing off the cobbles and striking her body like a blast. In winter when the wind blew more bitterly into her face she seemed to be climbing her way home.

Along the street, every twenty yards or so there was a tree. They were slender, delicate trees with trunks slim as wrists, and they bowed even to the lightest wind. In summer their graceful heads were forever nodding and rustling and their feathery leaves shimmered in the breeze. In winter they were buffeted, bending before the gales, their bare branches thrashing like a light bundle of twigs. Winter and summer the trees were always moving, moving in the wind.

The town was not large, but to Leah it seemed enormous. There were entire neighborhoods she had never seen. As she grew older more of its mysteries were revealed, but at eight she had thought it limitless, and with reason: the far end of town was itself a foreign territory, somewhat feared. People told stories of their forays to the other end as though recounting travelers' tales. Now at twelve she knew better. She was on the point of becoming a much-traveled person. She was going on a train, to visit her uncle Simeon.

It may have been Simeon and his wife Malka, a sharp-eyed woman of boundless kindness, who unwittingly infected Leah with the bug of curiosity about the outside world. She had always been an alert, inquiring child, not even the Torah safe from her questions.

Her mother hushed her reprovingly when she began yet again: "But why? . . . " Her father moved her baby brother from his lap where the child had been dozing, and put Leah in his place, cradling her in his arms in the absent-minded way he had. At once Leah felt more peaceful, the contentiousness draining away. He stroked her black braids while he talked about the difficulties, the imperatives of ancient times, and the way the Law should be understood. Leah, unconvinced by his argument, was soothed by the gentle voice.

"She has a boy's head on her shoulders," Simeon said once, on a visit. "She wants to know about everything." Leah's mother looked worried. A girl who wanted to know about everything did not, to her mind, sound like an ideal daughter *or* a good marriage prospect. She could see the marriage broker's expression if he heard the girl had a boy's head on her shoulders. . . . They would probably have to increase the size of her dowry if all these questions went on. They had already had problems, when little Daniel was about to be born, four years ago.

"Where does the baby come from?" Leah had asked.

"The midwife brings it in her black bag," her mother said, shifting about in the narrow iron bed.

Later, when the midwife arrived and hurried up the stairs to the bedroom, Leah had gazed at the black bag, longing to peer inside it and see whether she was to have a brother or a sister. If the midwife brought the baby in the bag, she thought, why was her mother screaming?

But now she was to visit Uncle Simeon. Very early in the morning when only the market people were about, her father walked her through the slumbering streets, through the familiar crisscross of buildings to the upper section of town where everything was strange. Then out, past the Catholic cemetery and over the fields, to the place where the railway track was flanked by a small, rutted platform and a wooden shelter large enough to hold two people in wet weather. There they waited while the mist lifted off the fields and the sun began to glitter on mile upon mile of steel track. They waited, watching the track until at last it came: a tiny puff of smoke on the horizon, and then the train was in view across the fields, slowing, grinding to a halt.

Jacob lifted Leah onto the train, handing up her little carpetbag and putting her in the charge of the guard, who knew her uncle Simeon, a man of some consequence at the frontier post.

The huge iron monster tearing across the countryside with such speed, so effortlessly, was for Leah like some vision of the future out of one of her cousin Mordecai's books—which her mother would have forbidden her to read had she known of their existence.

Simeon's home was only a mile or so from the German border, and on the second day of her visit he took Leah with him to the frontier post. While he performed the mysterious tasks that concerned him, she was free to examine the station and the trains. The trains particularly fascinated her, seething with steam and splashed with thick, claylike mud along their sides. The noise, the uniforms, the crowds, the strange languages . . . it all seemed bigger and brighter and freer than any life she had acquaintance with. That freedom was not equally available to everyone, she learned soon enough, but it was not until she was much older that she realized that her uncle's sphere of activity was one officially known as bribery and corruption. It was, of course, on the most high-minded level. Nevertheless, when Simeon arranged for a Jewish prisoner to be provided with such extreme luxuries as a bed in his cell, a blanket, and some food, it was through the unofficial transfer of coins from one palm to another.

She was watching the wheel tapper, working his way laboriously up the train, when Simeon came over to her. "Run to the house and tell your aunt to prepare. I'm bringing a family home." She watched him hurry back to the customs man, plunging again into his argument, waving his arms, smacking one fist into the other, shrugging in exaggerated despair, beard waggling. He was an energetic man in discussion. Through the tiny window of the customs house Leah could just make out a group of emigrants; ragged, exhausted, and clearly terrified. The Abrahams family—the father in long Hasidic coat, fur hat, and shabby boots; the mother crouching like an animal, her clothes ballooning over her huge stomach, at her knees two small children. Their possessions were scattered around them, wrapped untidily in bundles. Their hair was matted and dusty from two days of traveling already, from some distant village near the Russian border.

When they limped into the house with Simeon carrying most of the bundles, Malka went to work with brisk authority: she took the woman and children into the kitchen and gave them all baths. Then she washed their hair, combed it, tied bright ribbons on the children's braids, and picked over their belongings for some better-looking clothes. Simeon attended to the father. Then the bundles were retied, neatly. After that, food and rest.

Leah was fascinated by the contrast between her aunt and uncle and the emigrants: Simeon and Malka were full of vitality, they knew what had to be done and how to do it. The travelers had a terrible passivity—waiting to be spoken to, moved from here to there, advised, even it seemed, to be preyed on.

Already, with the journey hardly begun, they had been robbed. An old trick, and a common one: the friendly stranger offering to save them from the humiliation of the enforced bath at the German border.

"I keep telling the authorities," Simeon groaned, "if they are concerned about the infection and infestation, why pick on the Jews? Why strip *them* of their clothes and subject them to the disinfectant bath? The Sabbath bathing, the hand-washing, the dietary laws . . . we *must* be more hygienic than the peasants!"

Leah looked at the Abrahams family and reflected that, though they looked clean enough now, she would not have risked one of her precious kopeks as a guarantee of their freedom from lice before Malka's ministrations.

"You should not have handed over the money," Simeon said severely. "Two rubles for each of you—ridiculous!"

"He seemed such a good man," muttered Abrahams, shaking his

head sadly, "and a Jew too. He promised we would get on the train with no bath needed."

Grateful to be spared the barbaric and unpleasant public bath, the family had waited, trustingly, only to discover that their philanthropic friend had deserted them. The German authorities, unimpressed by stories of rubles and promises and friendly strangers, were firm: no bath, no train. It was at this point that Simeon had come upon the scene.

When it was time for the train he led the family back to the station: neat, well-dressed, cheerful, and obviously clean. "Abrahams family," Simeon announced crisply.

The customs man, reassured by the appearance of the travelers, and with certain practical arrangements concluded privately with Simeon, waved them onto the train. Just before it pulled out of the station the woman leaned from the window and clutched Simeon's hand. She placed the other hand on her stomach.

"The little one, if it is a boy, will be Simeon, for you. May God bless you for your kindness." She was crying.

Leah did not respond to the touching scene. She found the family dull, stupid, and lifeless. But she was greatly impressed with the energy and practicality of her uncle and aunt. This was the way to help people, not with pious lines from the Scriptures, but with deeds. Help in this world, not promises of help from some distant God.

When she said as much to Simeon he was not pleased, hearing, behind her words of admiration, disapproval of her parents' way of life.

"Deeds alone are not enough. They are like flowers without roots. They will have no lasting value. The Torah provides the roots for good deeds to flourish and bear fruit in their turn."

Leah twitched one of her braids, tossing it behind her shoulder, a gesture she unconsciously used when she was not fully convinced by something but realized that further argument would be unwise.

The train had left the station. They were bound for England, they said. What would life be like there? Were there places in the world that were so different from Peszno that she could not even imagine them? The train gathered speed, growing smaller, until only a distant cloud of smoke showed the direction it had taken.

It was barely light when Leah heard her mother get up. She made almost no noise, yet Leah knew from the lightest footfall and the smallest movement exactly what she was doing. A splashing: the hand-washing and quick morning prayer. Now the clothes. Footsteps down the stairs, a scrape and clatter: the range was ignited. Soon it would be time for her to get up. Sunk deep in the soft feather bed, eyes closed tight, she listened to the clink of china, the sound of her mother getting bread from the cellar, pouring coffee from the large metal container to be heated with milk for breakfast.

A few feet away, Daniel was still asleep. His thumb rested close to his mouth on the pillow; probably he had been sucking it during the night. Just the two of them slept in the room now. Hirschl was sixteen, a man, and slept in the passage next to the kitchen when he was not traveling between towns for his father. Leah could remember the time all three of them had shared this little room, when Daniel became old enough to sleep in a bed. There had been a time, earlier, when their big sister Ruda, too, slept in the room—before she got married and moved out to live with Shmuel's parents. Leah knew they were lucky to be just the two of them now, when some families slept five to a room, children and parents together. She realized they were privileged—not rich of course, but privileged. They had nice china to eat off, and sheets on their beds. Sometimes she had a dress from Germany to wear for the festivals, finely stitched by machine instead of the everyday, handsewn ones.

Far away down the street, at the bottom of the hill, Leah heard the sound of wheels and hooves, and a muffled cry as the coachman urged the horses faster. Then, clear in the morning air, the sound of the trumpet. It was the post coach from Warsaw. Always the coachman played the same air on his trumpet at the same point, just near the bottom of the hill, as though to encourage the horses to hurl themselves up the slope, their hooves crashing and slipping on the cobblestones. Now the coach was gone, on toward the main square.

One of the drivers was married to a relative of theirs, and he had once allowed Leah to try her skill with the trumpet, but though she blew until her cheeks ached, no sound could be drawn from it. Another example of exciting things that apparently women and girls could not do.

Next door, more movement. Her father was getting up. Leah flew out of bed, flung off her nightgown, and was into her skirt and petticoat, blouse, knickers with the elastic that bit into the skin, cotton stockings rolled above the knee, and down the stairs by the time her father had completed his prayers and appeared in the bedroom door.

"Good morning, Father."

Tall, thin, his dark eyes looking almost black against the pallor of his skin, Jacob had a slightly startled look when addressed directly by any member of the family, as though roused from deep thought—as was indeed often the case. His dark beard and curly hair were the same texture as Leah's long braids: glossy and wiry, growing thick.

"You're up early, child," he said approvingly, imagining she had been helping her mother in the kitchen. Leah, looking demure, did not enlighten him. Thin like her father, she was small for a twelve-year-old, with a narrow, high-cheeked face, bright, slanting eyes, and a broad brow. She watched him go off to his morning prayers in the synagogue and slowly went back upstairs to call Daniel. He lay, awake now, placidly sucking his thumb, waiting for her to tickle him out of bed. Nearly four years old. Soon he would be going to school—some boys had already started, at three, but father said four was soon enough. Would he be allowed to suck his thumb at the *cheder*, or would the teacher stop him, tell him that was for babies? Filled with sudden tenderness, Leah hugged him, breathing in the sweet, milky breath. He laughed as she began to help him dress, tickling him.

Leah's father called from the front door, "Someone to share our breakfast, Rachel." Leah and Daniel, still at the big kitchen table, looked up to see who it was this time. Hardly a morning went by without her father bringing home some beggar or pauper from the synagogue, to share their food. This morning's was typical: emaciated, dragging his heavy boots on their clean floor, his thin face almost invisible behind the bushy beard and curly side-locks. A long coat, stiff and green with age, and his hands grimed with dirt. Leah's stomach contracted with revulsion, and she moved her plate nearer to Daniel's. Perhaps the beggar *prayed* regularly but she doubted if his bathing was as regular.

"Leah, I hear the postman."

She opened the front door before the man could knock, the letter grasped in his large, grubby fist, picked out from the loaded satchel. He was in no hurry to hand it over, looking frankly at the name on the back, and the stamp, to see who had written to the Levis and from where.

"Germany, eh," he said encouragingly.

"Yes." Leah closed the door on his disappointed face.

Jacob had escorted his guest to the corridor where, as well as Hirschl's bed, a washbasin, jug, soap, and towel were placed in readiness. Hirschl himself was in Warsaw delivering an order of enamel pans. Leah watched, craning from her chair. As she had expected, the "guest" merely poured water over his hands in the token ritual handwashing. Her father, himself using a plentiful supply of soap, tactfully passed it over to the beggar, who, to his surprise, found himself actually washing his hands without altogether knowing how it had happened.

The two men came into the room, and the stranger sat down next to Leah. She gazed furtively at him, curling her feet under her chair in case she accidentally touched the filthy creature, and watched him begin to eat. When she had her own home, she vowed, she would have a separate room for beggars to eat in. It simply was not fair to inflict them on your own family.

Her mother's lips were drawn tightly together, and she offered coffee to the guest in somewhat clipped tones. He accepted it and gobbled some toasted bread spread with plum preserve. When the plums were ripe, Leah's mother brought them home in barrels, boiled the fruit with sugar in the tiny yard, and then packed the preserve in big earthenware containers that were kept in the cellar with the apples, which they spread out on straw to keep all winter. But it was spring now, and not many earthenware jars remained. Leah watched resentfully as the stranger spooned more preserve on his bread.

Breakfast was over. The "guest"—after a second cup of coffee and another piece of bread—departed, thanking Rachel for her hospitality. But there was a certain condescension in his manner which let her know he was aware that by giving her the opportunity to perform a good deed that day in the eyes of God, he had done *her* a favor.

They began to clear the table. It was a small house: the kitchen and corridor occupied the whole ground floor, with the two bedrooms above. Up another cramped stairway was the loft. Next to the kitchen, through a door off the corridor, was the shop, just one room with its own little door to the street. Jacob went through the connecting door. Around him, arranged on shelves, were dozens of different types of kitchen utensils and enamel plates and dishes. The shop was dark and smelled of metal and lamp oil.

He opened the street door and prepared for the day. Leah heard the squeak of hinges and bang of wood, the green door rattle, and pictured Jacob settling himself at the narrow, unpolished table he used as a desk.

If business proved slow he would open a book and study quietly for a while. He was constantly reclaiming small pieces of the working day for calm and silence; his face relaxed, his eyes dreaming. He was not a man of action like his brother Simeon, but Leah knew they shared the same curious confidence in the world's goodness.

Rachel was busy in the kitchen. Leah knew that all morning, while she was at school, her mother would continue to be busy, and would go on being busy all afternoon and evening too. Leah found it astonishing that her mother did not share her resentment that their way of life—obedience to the Commandments and the Law—made it necessary for Rachel to be continually occupied with practical, repetitive tasks. With a sense of escaping it all, she picked up her books and left for school.

Daniel looked like a little convict, his head shorn of the thick, dark curls and only the earlocks remaining as evidence of his babyish prettiness. In his knickerbockers, dark jacket, and a peaked cap a little too large for him, he was ready for his first day's schooling.

Everyone kissed him, and Rachel gave him a little package of black bread, cheese, and pickled cucumber, neatly wrapped in thick, greased paper and then a strip of linen, for his midday meal. Then Jacob lifted him and carried him effortlessly down the street. The *cheder* was not far away but Jacob was gone for some time, staying to see the child settled before the books and chatting to the *melamed*, whose normally ferocious expression was smoothed into a temporary serenity as he talked to the quiet man with the dark, heavy-lidded eyes.

Daniel was not frightened because he was accustomed to the atmosphere of learning. At home, he often sat on his father's lap while

45

Jacob went on with his reading. Since his father seemed to get so much pleasure from reading, Daniel assumed that he, too, would find it enjoyable. He waited for the lessons to start.

True, as he gazed down at the tiny, black print filling the pages of the thick book he wondered how he would ever be able to read and understand it. But everyone else did, so he knew he would too, in time.

He moved his finger along the Hebrew letters, trying to locate a familiar shape, when suddenly, onto the page fell a shower of small sweets, a coin or two, and some nuts. Daniel looked up, delighted, to try to see where this magical shower had come from. His father, behind him, also gazed upward in apparent astonishment. Daniel grabbed the sweets and stuffed them into his pocket as his father patted him encouragingly on the head and left the *melamed* to get on with his work.

It was a tiny room. The fifteen or twenty boys between three and five years old were crowded onto benches around a battered table which was covered with a worn oilcloth. The same room, outside school hours, was also used for cooking, eating, and sleeping. The range was against one wall, two narrow beds against the other, and on rough shelves were the cooking utensils and chipped plates. Not much light penetrated the dusty window, and the air was thick and stale.

"Well, well, enough of the time wasting. There's work to be done!"

The *melamed*, knowing that a man who is forced to the extreme indignity of being paid to pass on his learning is a sorry creature indeed, took out his despair on the small pupils in his power. As Jacob's footsteps died away, the *melamed*'s thin, deeply lined face once again bunched into his normal expression of impatience and disappointment.

His wife had nagged at him half the night; he knew already that his earnings this week were insufficient, and here were these boys, all better fed than he, supplied with bulging bags of bread and cheese or sausage, while he and his wife had barely enough to keep them from actual hunger at the end of the day.

"Begin!"

He rapped out the command to one of the boys and the child began at once to chant, parrot-fashion, the letters he knew. He made a small mistake and the *melamed*'s cane came down across his shoulders. The child began to cry.

"Next!"

The next boy in the row began to chant and managed better.

The *melamed* grunted and moved on. He nodded impatiently at the following boy, who happened to be Daniel. Eyes wide, Daniel gazed up at him, waiting for some guidance, so that he could do whatever was expected of him. Unconsciously his small fist moved up to his mouth and he began to suck his thumb. The *melamed* gave a roar of rage and his cane whistled down on Daniel's fingers, knocking the thumb from his mouth and leaving a raw, scarlet weal on the skin. He was an obedient child and had never been beaten at home. This unfair and unexpected punishment dazed him. He sat, too shocked to cry, covering the caned hand with his fingers.

"So: whose turn is it now?"

The *melamed*, at last recognizing that he had called on a new boy to read, passed on briskly. Boys must be taught respect and obedience, and an occasional injustice would simply give them a taste of the outside world, where injustice was all too plentiful. The chanting went on and Daniel listened, uncomprehending, the pain of his bewilderment greater than the pain of his hand. He was about to raise his thumb again, when he froze, remembering. He licked his lips nervously and rubbed at his eyes with the back of his hand. There was no ventilation, and as the hours passed and the room grew hotter, the tang of body odor soured the air.

The window was so grimed that no one saw Leah, on her way home from school, peering through the glass to see how her little brother was getting on. She saw him rub his eyes quickly, and saw, standing out red against his skin, the weal from the cane. Watching him sit there, knowing how many more times the cane would sting him, knowing the weariness and boredom he was to experience, she felt angry tears filling her own eyes. She blinked them away. Boys had to study for long, dreary hours, even little boys, because that was the way to know the Law. She turned and went on to the market. Her mother had given her a list, there was food to be bought. Girls had to know about marketing, that was one of their duties.

Faintly, from within, she heard the *melamed*'s voice: "Next!"

Suddenly Leah was aware of spring all around her, a million unseen movements: leaves, buds, seeds, all reaching for the light, stretching, bursting, blooming, so that there was a thrilling restlessness —the very soil and air seemed to be tugging at her with tiny fingers.

Passover was the watershed of the year: summer seemed nearer, the worst of winter over. Color returned to the town after the blacks and grays of the last few months. Pale sunlight picked out almost forgotten touches of yellow and brown and red on the crumbling walls of houses; lit up the pale green shoots of the first leaves on the trees in the street, even struck jewel-glitters from the cobblestones.

Rachel needed help, scrubbing the house from attic to cellar; Leah put away the ordinary dishes and plates and brought out the special ones kept for Passover, and burned her fingers boiling the metal objects used for cooking, to purify them.

The evening before Passover began, Jacob led the children around the house, candle held high, armed with a feather to find any crumbs of flour that might have been overlooked. It was a ritual search and all knew it, though when some crumbs carefully left in position by Rachel were pounced on by Daniel, Leah noticed his dark eyes blinking with genuine excitement and, for a moment, she was almost reconciled to what she regarded as the absurdity of it all, though she prudently kept her views to herself.

She had a new dress for Passover, white and high-necked with a long, tight bodice and a flat bow that tied low down at the back. She felt the bow pressing into her as she sat at the table, *Haggadah* open before her. As a young child she had always surreptitiously turned a few pages ahead of time, to enjoy the appalling drawings of the ten plagues, and now she noticed Daniel doing the same.

His hands still bore bruises and marks from the early weeks of *cheder*, but he was quick and alert and soon had the measure of the *melamed*'s powers. When the wretched man's larder needed replenishing, and, in the absence of the necessary coins, he fell on a few of the boys—usually the smaller ones—confiscating the food their mothers had supplied them with, Daniel was prepared: he had already divided his packet into two. He could not always avoid the beatings, having his ears viciously twisted, his head cuffed. But at least he had some food to keep him going through the interminable, airless afternoon hours.

Now, at the table covered with a fine white cloth, they were waiting for him to begin. He was the youngest and must ask the questions that set the Seder ceremony in motion: "Why is this night different from all other nights?"

And with Jacob's response, they were off, into the familiar rhythm: "Once we were slaves unto Pharaoh in Egypt . . ."

The children always enjoyed the Seder. The *Haggadah* was full of good, lurid stories—the plagues, the parting of the Red Sea. . . . And the suspense of wondering whether, this time, the prophet Elijah just might drop in and occupy the place set for him, for which reason the front door was left open. Then there was the singing, and the search for the *afikomen*, the hidden piece of matzo.

Passover had its excitements, its "special" feeling. But it also meant something else: it meant Easter. And above all, Good Friday.

Good Friday was the worst day, always. The tension mounted slowly through Lent, beginning with Ash Wednesday and building toward that black, bitter climax, when the very church seemed to grow larger, its stone front towering over Leah as she approached it, waiting to crush her in punishment, the cross throwing a shadow that marked her: Christ killer. As the congregation filed out of the arched doorway after the Good Friday service, every Jew in town who had any sense was off the streets.

She had been inside the church once, though her mother never knew, smuggled in as a toddler by a Gentile peasant girl who came in to clean the house while Rachel was recovering from a fever. The girl had wanted to attend the wedding of her best friend, and she took Leah along. The child stared at the richly encrusted altar, the plaster saints, the figure of the Virgin all blue and gold and ivory, the paintings and the flowers, the flags, the incense burning in the filigree containers. The candles glimmering by the dozen. All of it astonishingly different from the unadorned plainness of the synagogue. In church, men and women stood together, families were not divided. Though even here, she noted, God could not be addressed in the language of every day. Just as

Hebrew replaced Yiddish in the synagogue, here the Polish congregation mechanically repeated the litany of Latin phrases. *"Boruch Ato Adonoy . . ."* they muttered in the synagogue. *"Benedictus qui venit in nomine Domini . . ."* chanted the Catholic congregation.

But on Good Friday, she knew it was very different, the church stripped of its ornaments, the altar bare. Christ was dead and they mourned. "Vengeance is mine, I will repay," saith the Lord. Leah felt a chill at the phrase. She disliked thinking of God in terms of vengeance, though there were times when it was unavoidable. And Good Friday was one of those times.

For Friday was Sabbath eve too, and sooner or later the men and boys would be forced out of their safety for the Sabbath service, to be taunted, jostled. As women wept helplessly some bewildered man or terrified child was seized to have his face bruised by the cobbled street, his earlocks shamingly sheared. Infidels. Unbelievers. Anti-Christ. The Jews deserved to be punished. It was a Christian duty. Kill a Jew for Jesus.

Not that many of these peasants would have actually killed anyone. Most of the time they got along well together, the townsfolk and the "Old Testament People" as some called them. But it was a time for settling scores—some of them secret, some trivial, some unworthy. These were complex transactions.

A few weeks before, Leah had noticed a laborer passing by, probably still hungry after his scrappy Lenten meal of pickled cabbage and herring, pausing to sniff the rich, comforting smell of Rachel's Sabbath chicken. A feast in preparation for the Jews, misers, he thought to himself, if nothing worse. Getting rich at his expense.

This same peasant had once asked Jacob to write a letter for him—"Levi, I need to send word to my nephew in Warsaw . . ." and Jacob had written the note, and in turn made use of the peasant by asking him to light their lamp—"The Sabbath is in already and I must not kindle a light, will you do me the kindness? . . ."

And while Jacob had glanced with unconscious distaste at the peasant's red and grubby hands, the laborer, in lighting their lamp, could not help noticing the shiny spoons and forks on the table, the white cloth, heavy silver candlesticks. . . .

All morning Rachel in her apron and thick cotton dress dashed from stove to table, a patch of moisture dark under each armpit, rubbing her hands fussily on her apron, humming tunelessly to herself, sighing in irritation when her mother-in-law got in her way to lift the lid of a pot and sniff critically at it.

The *shnorrers* were already making their rounds: confident, almost arrogant, each collecting the small pile of coins established by tradition as his due.

Good Friday was always bad.

"Take care," Rachel said mechanically, as Jacob, Daniel, and Hirschl set off for the bathhouse with their bundles of clean underwear under their arms.

As they turned the corner, trouble confronted them: a gang of youths in their path, strung out across the street, a barrier of human flesh, each swinging an improvised truncheon or knout. Big peasant boys, full grown, with strong arms and heavy shoulders.

"Why are you not in church?" from the leader.

Jacob remained silent but he and Hirschl closed up, keeping Daniel between them.

"We must show these poor sinners the way to church, boys. Make sure they get there." They ringed the little group, pushing, nudging. Jacob began to speak, but one of the young Poles struck him glancingly on the mouth with his fist and Jacob's head snapped back, blood oozing from his lip.

Daniel, a tiny shadow-creature in his dark jacket and trousers, pressed close to his father, almost invisible against the long black coat. He clenched his teeth so that he would not whimper or make any sound, but his eyes moved, flickering around the deserted streets, searching for some way they might escape.

So it was Daniel who first saw the group of boys who came into the street from one of the intersections and stood silently, waiting for the peasants to notice them.

They looked different from the usual Jewish boys of the town. Daniel recognized one among them, his cousin Mordecai Shoobotel, and he called out before he could stop himself. The peasants swung around, and paused, clearly surprised by the businesslike appearance of the newcomers. Without the traditional gabardines and hats they looked very capable of defending themselves. But they were, after all, only Jews, so would probably put up no fight.

"Clear off, this is no concern of yours," one of the young Poles snapped.

Daniel's already wide eyes stretched wider as he saw the boys begin to advance on the peasants. Their movements and the way they held their arms looked odd, almost like a dance without music. Then a number of things happened very fast: the peasants were contemptuously waving their truncheons at the approaching boys, when the truncheons were seized, and certain swift, bewildering, and unexpected actions were carried out, accompanied by hoarse cries and shouts in some foreign language. It was all over very quickly, and a moment later the peasants were picking themselves up off the cobblestones, limping away down the street, shouting abuse and threats, but with no wish to prolong the encounter. That, they thought, was the trouble with Jews: you couldn't trust them—not even not to fight.

"Shall we continue to the bathhouse?" Jacob suggested shakily.

The bathhouse was a square, one-story building near the synagogue. Its high windows streamed with condensation and the air had a steamy, soapy quality. Inside the front door, a few steps down, lay the central bathing area, a large rectangular pool that doubled as the men's communal bath on Fridays, and for the rest of the week served as the ritual bath, the *mikva*, in which the women immersed themselves to be purified after menstruation. Along the walls were the small cubicles for private baths. The stone walls, gray and porous-looking, were always running with moisture and the floor was slippery underfoot.

The male attendants were busy replenishing water and supplying soap. Jacob, immersed to his neck, the steam wreathing itself around his head and beard, recounted the story of the boys who had arrived to save them from an unpleasant situation on their way to the baths.

"As well for us they came along, God be praised."

"They wouldn't thank you for saying so," commented Meir, the attendant, pouring a bucketful of boiling water into the steamy pool. "They are modern fellows, freethinkers, they go around talking about workers' rights and the need for self-defense."

"Well, they certainly defended us."

"Naturally! People who look for trouble will find it."

"Why should they be looking for trouble?"

"They want to try out their ideas, things like this new Japanese nonsense, this craziness they found out about in some Warsaw magazine. Jujitsu combat it's called—"

"You seem to know a great deal about it all," one of the bathers remarked.

Meir shrugged impatiently. "My younger boy talks about these things. Of course I never let him get mixed up with them, but you can't help hearing about it. This jujitsu is the latest thing: the weak overcome the strong, by using skill."

"With God's help, that sounds like a good Jewish idea."

"Well, they have been heard to say that self-defense works, with or without God's intervention."

Jacob frowned. Of course they were young, mere boys, but Shoobotel was a cousin, and he did not like to hear blasphemy from a member of the family, even a distant member. "More hot!" he called sharply, and decided to change the subject.

Leah stood by the window, watching the street through the lace curtain. Behind her, she could hear the little noises of female movement: her grandmother groaning slightly as she shifted her stiff muscles; her sister Ruda singing to the baby on her lap; her aunt Malka muttering over a prayer book; her mother sighing deeply in that patient, long-suffering way of hers, the prayer book open before her. Outwardly the room was at peace, but there was a tremor of anxiety . . . the candle flame wavered.

The incident on the way to the bathhouse had unsettled them all, and Leah had wanted to keep Daniel back from the synagogue, fearful of the tiny figure venturing out again into the streets. But Jacob had been firm, and Rachel silenced Leah, so the menfolk had gone to the evening service as usual, leaving the women to prepare for the Sabbath meal, light the candles, and pray uneasily at home.

"Well? Can't you see them yet? Aren't they in sight?"

Leah shook her head, glancing for a moment over her shoulder at the room. The table was ready, its damask cloth almost hidden by the large dishes, the candles in the silver candlesticks burning with a high, bright flame in the warm room.

Her nostrils catalogued the spicy smells drifting through the air: the sharpness of the gefilte fish, the sweet cinnamon tang of the apple cake. There were times when she resented the constant dietary obsessions: a pots-and-pans religion. And the Friday-night ritual entwined food and piety in the very soul of children and adults alike. Maybe this was why so many mothers urged their sons to "Eat, eat,": with a full stomach, you were somehow nearer to God. . . .

A figure was in sight at the far end of the street. Now Leah could see her father, then Daniel toddling manfully, Hirschl lagging behind as usual. Her brother-in-law Shmuel, Uncle Simeon, and then, half hidden by her father, two more figures, strangers.

She mentioned them to Rachel, who sighed and got up to look. Leah hoped today's unexpected guests would not be tramps. She knew her mother shared her reservations, but Jacob's hospitality was blind and possessed no nostrils: he really did not seem to notice when the guests smelled or scratched or picked their noses. She squinted again at the strangers.

The man, next to her father, nodding in answer to some remark, she could hardly see: his coat hung down to his ankles, the broad-brimmed hat rested on his ears, and a dark beard concealed almost all of his face. He was small and thin, but she could be sure of little else.

Behind Daniel she saw the second stranger, a boy about her own age. Frail, his bones visible even at this distance, his eyes dark holes in a thin, pointed face. Some *yeshiva* student by the look of him, half-starved, picking up a dinner where he could, existing on "eating days" contributed by families who could afford hospitality.

She felt the usual impatience rising within her: life should be more than old books, however holy, more than devout thoughts in skinny bodies. She promised herself she would make Daniel run and jump and climb trees in the summer when they were out of sight of their parents. From swaddling clothes into prayer shawls. No freedom for the limbs—nor for the mind, which must not wander from studying God's Law. Had Leah expressed these dreadful thoughts aloud, her mother might have suspected the influence of a *dybbuk*—"A devil has entered the girl!"; it must be the evil eye to give her such thoughts. Then there would be threads drawn from her skirts and flung onto the fire with snippings from her hair; and lumps of coal placed in her pockets to protect her from harm. It had happened, when she was younger, but now she had learned discretion and Rachel was unaware of the heterodoxy blooming on her very hearth.

Leah smoothed her long-bodiced dress and twitched her braids back over her shoulders. On one arm her mother had tied a narrow scarlet ribbon to ward off the evil eye after the photographer had remarked on her beautiful hair yesterday. Leah hoped she would be allowed to keep the photograph when it came: Rachel had been reluctant about it in the first place, until Uncle Simeon reassured her.

Leah could never altogether make up her mind about the evil eye: in bright daylight it all seemed very improbable. But at night, in her little room, with the lamp blown out and only the chinks in the shutters filtering moonlight into the darkness, it was another matter—the devil seemed very real.

Leah found it hard to picture the devil. She realized that, strictly speaking, the devil was a non-Jewish problem. The God of Abraham did not insist that they were all miserable sinners. Improvement was possible, by your deeds shall ye be judged. But still, there he was, the devil, a figure of horrifying fascination, built up of all the most dreadful images her mind could encompass.

Life was full of sinister, unmentionable figures who lurked, thrust out of sight, in the back of Leah's mind: like the enema woman her grandmother talked of sometimes, from her village. The gross, red-handed enema woman with her goose quill and her sheep's bladder, who came to deal with those whose overcharged systems needed cleansing.

Leah's flesh crawled at the idea of the enema woman and her activities. Her own mother used herbs to settle the family's disorders. But not all horrors were faraway figures. There was the man who came, mysteriously, in the night, every month or so, to empty their earth closet, the little shed screened by bushes, which stood in the corner of the tiny yard by the side of the house.

No one ever talked about him, the nightsoil man with his horse and creaking cart. He came when they were all supposed to be asleep, and it was proper to behave as though he did not exist. But sometimes, waking, Leah heard weird sounds—scrapings, and thuds and once a muffled curse—and she longed, sick with fright, to know more. To *see* him. Hirschl told her once that the man also skinned dead animals: horses and dogs, and she wondered, horrified, whether he came to their yard with his hands dripping the blood of dead dogs; were his clothes made of mangy skins sewn together with the guts of disemboweled cats?

Outside the house the plane trees shivered and swayed and a few drops of rain gathered into the wind's palm were flung into the faces of the group walking up the street. They quickened their pace. The wind whipped their clothes close to their bodies and to Leah they looked like a cluster of dark saplings, blurred and mysterious in the dimming light.

As the men hurried toward them, up the last steep stretch of cobbled street, Leah was conscious again of the Sabbath calm in the house; the time for the women to draw breath. To pray. But not to think. Deep thoughts were for menfolk. Would thinking get the chicken cooked? The bread baked? It was attention to these details that kept the day spinning along with due respect to the Law. And so her mother darted about the house, eyes everywhere, hands busy, mind blank, until at the setting of the Friday sun she was ready: buttoned into her rustling silk dress, her stiff wig respectably in position over her cropped hair.

"Here they come," said Leah. The men were home, her father urging everyone forward, gently pushing them toward the door held open in welcome, introducing the strangers, first Solomon, and then his son, the thin, anxious-looking boy.

"And this is Chaim."

The blessing for wine, for the washing of hands, for the first fruits of the season. So many blessings. Chaim relished them all. "Blessed art Thou, O Lord God, King of the Universe. . . ." Living with these little rituals Chaim felt his life at moments had a chance of matching a pattern of divinity. There was a benign, healing quality to a life lived God's way. A chain that encircled the day, the year. A chain as insubstantial as a promise and as strong as steel. Familiar and reassuring in a world where so much, suddenly, seemed to be frightening.

"My father has been talking of moving . . ." he muttered to Leah, in answer to a question about his future.

"Move where?"

"Perhaps across the border to Germany." The presence of the border tempted thoughts of a fresh start in a new country, but Chaim was oddly reluctant about Germany. He knew that Poland had little enough to offer. And alone in the world as they were, he and his father, a move seemed a practical idea. Peszno had been his mother's town.

"Have you no family here?" Leah prompted, as the boy seemed to have come to a stop.

"My mother's parents died in the epidemic, the same week as

she did. My father's parents . . ." The almost inaudible voice died out completely. Leah leaned forward, waiting. He shrugged and shook his head. "They used to live in Vilna."

They ought to move, Chaim thought. Even he could see that business in his father's little shop was not flourishing. It was a good shop, respectable. But holy books, candlesticks, and prayer shawls did not have the turnover of, say, vegetables or groceries.

They were frugal, and, since his mother's death that terrible summer, people had been kind—often they had been carried off for a Sabbath meal in some family home. Like tonight. But there was, too, the question of military service. He was thirteen. If they stayed on here, he risked conscription to the Russian army. Years of loneliness and hardship, drudgery in some outpost of the Czar's empire, forbidden to worship his god and forced to speak Russian. Officially Poland did not exist, it was "the Vistula region," and if Poles were second-class Russian citizens, the Polish Jews were barely considered human. Consequently, for them, military service was increased to twenty-five years.

His religious studies might prevent his conscription, but one could never be sure. The authorities could decide otherwise, and there was no arguing with them. Bribery had been known to work, but his father did not even possess the means to safeguard him that way.

There was a burst of animation from his father. "Spinoza!" Solomon said vehemently. "Don't talk to me about Spinoza! A disgrace to his own people! A traitor!"

"It is his philosophy I am talking about, not his personal behavior," Jacob put in mildly. "What I am saying is—"

But already the conversation had left philosophy behind in impassioned discussion of notable Jews. The women tended to remain silent, confining themselves to nods of agreement or sounds of disapproval.

"Now a man like Hafkine, there is what I call a good Jew, even if he does come from Odessa," commented Hirschl. "To combat the cholera, to save lives . . ."

Simeon was talking of Marx, another unpopular name. "A typical Jewish anti-Semite," he commented regretfully. "He will do much harm to his own kind. That sort of self-hatred is always dangerous."

Jacob coughed gently. "As I was saying—"

Chaim withdrew into contemplation of the military service that probably lay ahead for him. There were twelve hundred Russian soldiers quartered in the town. The men lived in huts, pitilessly cold in winter, stifling in summer. Chaim had talked to some of them, had seen how they lived, miserable, cut off from their families, no comfort in their lives. The officers, on the other hand, occupied houses at the upper end of town, and they had stylish wives, dressed always in the latest German fashions.

The socially ambitious among the townsfolk competed for the honor of having them as dinner guests. From the doorway of the little shop, Chaim had watched the officers' wives out on a shopping expedition, lighting up the narrow gray streets with their bright clothes—too bright, too opulent for his liking, walking, as Isaiah described it, "with stretched forth necks and wanton eyes." They chilled him.

For Chaim, the only justification for the soldiers in town was the military band. It played on Sundays and holidays in the main town square. He tried to arrive early, to watch them get ready, and he would wait near the bandstand, poised like one of the musicians, ready for the opening bars. They always began with "God Protect the Czar" before going into the first familiar tune. As the notes rose like silvery threads in the air, Chaim seemed to rise with them, floating, losing himself in the music.

The band would be playing on Sunday—Easter Sunday was a particularly festive day for the townsfolk, with the priest going from house to house, sprinkling the food-laden tables with holy water, blessing the homes. But this Sunday Chaim would not be in the square. Easter was not a good time to go out.

His stomach full from the Sabbath meal, he felt very comfortable in the Levi home. The family lived well, almost elegantly—that was clear. The room was warm, the big blue enamel stove that had come from Germany shone in the lamplight, giving out a marvelous heat.

Germany was the source of delicacies of every sort. A relative, back from a trip across the border, had come on a visit not long ago and brought some German chocolate for Chaim. His father, breaking the chocolate in two, had told Chaim to take half to the two Polish children down the road. The children, like so many peasants, did not go to school, and every day when Chaim went past on his way to class, the boy would chant anti-Jewish songs and throw stones after him. Now he had to take chocolate to them. Reluctantly he held out the dark, shiny slab and the children snatched at it, like wild puppies.

They stood, chewing, gazing at him mistrustfully, wriggling their bare toes in the dust, the chocolate sticky in their grubby hands.

Chaim should feel sorry for them, his father had explained, untaught, ragged animals. But Chaim had also watched them climbing trees in summer, through the closed window of the schoolroom, seen them munching sweet, stolen apples in the sunlight while he tried to concentrate on the Talmudic ruling on the maturity of fruit trees. Indeed once, lost in a dream, he had failed to answer to his name, and the teacher's strap crashing down on his shoulders had been his reward.

From the day he started at the *cheder* at the age of three he could not remember a time allocated to play. It simply did not occur to his father that such a thing was required. No wonder the peasants laughed at them, joked about their white, indoor faces. But the peasants would never know the fascination, the exaltation of that slow progress through the labyrinth of learning. "If two men grasp a garment . . ." Simple beginnings, first steps. At times bafflement. Until the sudden illumination, and the old words gained fresh meaning, filling his mind with light.

In the room, talk had turned to the worrying increase of Russian interference in Jewish districts, the intensifying of incitement to violence, encouraging of pogroms—apparently spontaneous, in fact carefully organized. One of the men who traveled a good deal was talking about a pogrom in a town near the Russian border. Of course it would not happen here, they all agreed, relations with the townsfolk were too good, but still it shattered the ease of the room.

Chaim was a shy boy; the easy geniality of some adults only accentuated his stiffness in company. But Jacob had a quiet confidence that he found comforting. He looked up at the tall, sharp-featured man with the small child on his lap. Both father and son had those curious, long eyes. Daniel was pale with exhaustion, but neither he nor anyone else thought of his going to bed before them.

Chaim thought: *Should one not protect children from the world a little? When I have a son, I shall try to make his childhood joyous. So that he does not learn too soon what the world is.*

It had been an unusual evening. In most of the houses he was invited into, even those where money was not short, meals were haphazard affairs, cutlery flung into a heap in the middle of the table, people helping themselves. Here, the table had been laid so that each person had not only his own spoon and fork but even a knife, sharp, with a smooth wooden handle. The brass oil lamps brightened the simple room.

More talk of pogroms. "Please God, it won't happen here," Rachel murmured. But how could you be sure? Now his father was talking, telling of their trip to Vilna, to visit Chaim's grandparents, Solomon's mother and father. Must they relive the experience over and over, Chaim said to himself, as a sort of payment for their supper? He tried to shut out his father's voice, but it was too late. In the glowing fire within the stove, a little flame shot upward, and in his mind the flames licked and curled as they had in Vilna, in the narrow street of houses with their iron shutters and iron doors. But even iron shutters could not protect everyone.

". . . All around us were people, running; mothers dragging children, babies, old people falling, crying out for help . . ."

The Cossacks howled as they rode in, so that the air was filled with unearthly shrieks and cries like souls in torment. Solomon's parents might have been safe, but they had delayed securing the iron door, hoping Solomon and Chaim would reach the house. They did, but the Cossacks had gotten there first, by a few seconds. Hidden by a water barrel a few yards away the two of them witnessed the whole scene. Solomon's father had been dragged out and felled with one saber blow, his mother, giving a terrible gutteral cry of mingled terror and grief had rushed out of the house to try to protect the old man—to be knocked flying like a weightless scarecrow as the Cossack urged his horse on. Her skull was crushed by the horse's hoof . . . horses, with neither anger nor malice in their heads, were innocently quenching life all around.

Chaim's father, with an extraordinary calm, clutched hard at Chaim's shoulder and drew him quickly into the shadows, as they crept down a side street. The house was already burning fiercely. Solomon kept saying that God would protect them. Chaim, seeing in his mind's eye that slashing saber, that hammer hoof, wondered why God was not protecting the people being butchered in the next street. But there was no time to think further, for a Cossack at full gallop came tearing toward them, ahead of the main party, whirling a saber glittering in the light from a street lamp.

Solomon remained standing, Chaim pressed close to his body, face hidden in his father's coat. The boy did not know that Solomon was uttering the final prayer, preparing to meet a certain death. There was a thud and he pitched forward, and lay prone in the street with

Chaim crushed under his light frame. Warm liquid poured onto Chaim's face, into his mouth and nostrils, choking him. He opened his mouth to scream and the liquid filled his mouth. His father's blood, tasting like rusty iron. Vomit rose in a jet from his stomach and he twisted his head, retching violently.

Through eyes obscured by blood he saw horses' hooves clattering a few yards away, the main Cossack party rattling past, shouting, yelling, riding by the prone body of a Jew cut down by the roadside.

As the sound of the horses and men died away, Chaim squirmed out from under his father's body and tried to lift him. Blood was trickling from the side of his head and around them lay the shattered fragments of an earthenware pot. Slowly his father stirred and groaned. He sat up and clasped Chaim to him.

"God has protected us."

Chaim was prepared to believe it. He knew that an earthenware pot aimed at an approaching Cossack from an upstairs window had struck Solomon an instant before the sword swishing toward his head. The pot had knocked him to the ground, and his apparently lifeless body, concealing the child, had therefore been ignored by the following Cossacks. All this was fact. The hand of the Almighty was to an extent conjecture, but Chaim joined his father in a prayer of thanks. God had indeed protected them.

The world was changing, no doubt of that. And the outside world was imposing more and more rules, intruding on their traditional way of life, limiting, forbidding, punishing. Every day there was talk of leaving. Many had gone already, some to America, some to England. And there was Germany, so close. But despite everything, life was good here, familiar. . . . Chaim drifted sleepily in the warmth of the great, blue-tiled stove.

"Chaim!" his father's voice broke into the boy's reverie. "Here is a little problem for you. We are just discussing . . ."

This was always happening: in the midst of some complex discussion on the finer points of the Law, his father would draw him into the conversation in order to give him a chance to shine in company. Finding himself the center of attention, the eyes of the room on him, had the effect of making Chaim lose his wits. *If ever I have a son,* he promised himself, *I shall not embarrass him publicly, nor require this outward show of learning. We will be close, we will share our knowledge and our love, easily, privately.* Meanwhile he had not heard the question. His father repeated it. Not a difficult one, just the reasons for the ritual concerning the eating of hindquarters of lamb or cattle. Hardly a fine theological point, but his mind went blank.

Leah, nearby, smoothing her skirt with her fingers and rather bored, looked up casually at the thin boy and saw what no one else did: his private fear. Moving unobtrusively and apparently to warm her hands, she had her back to the rest of the room and she caught Chaim's eye. Her foot clattered against a pot and under cover of the noise she whispered, "Jacob and the angel."

His face cleared. Of course! At once he began to recount the Biblical episode: the night-long struggle between Jacob and the angel, the enigmatic description of the injury sustained by Jacob—"in the hollow of his thigh" . . . the men nodded as he went on; the women listened placidly to the familiar story. ". . . So before the hindquarters of lamb or cattle may be pronounced kosher, the hip muscle must be removed."

Even today, Leah knew, they had to learn, and live by, rules concerning hip muscles and sunsets, cloven hooves and sea creatures, the mixing of wool and cotton, milk and meat. Surely all this would be swept away soon—by the twentieth century and the revolution her cousin Mordecai was always talking about.

Chaim looked at Leah as he finished, at her mischievous eyes and wide brow, and smiled for the first time that evening. The stove shimmered with heat and Chaim's eyes smarted from the fumes. He loved to sit very close to a fire. Around him the whole room seemed to be constantly in motion: one woman rocking a baby, another jigging the small boy on her lap, singing an old song; the men rocking as they argued together, the words rippling through the room, forefingers jabbing the air, arms flapping impatiently, shoulders shrugging, heads nodding, bodies swaying . . . movement was life.

Lulled into drowsiness, Chaim was unaware at first that the animation was dying away, that attention was focused elsewhere, until as the last voices faltered into silence, he, too, heard what the others were hearing: the noise of heavy boots and staccato, official voices. Of orders and loud responses.

They sat silent, waiting. The baby cried, was quickly hushed. When it came, the sound they were waiting for still startled them. The hammering on the door was so heavy that the wood shuddered and bounced under the blows.

Leah's father rose and crossed the room, not hurrying. He unfastened the door and held it open. The policeman outside knew him and paused for a moment, embarrassed by what he had to say. "Levi, we have to search your house."

Rachel gave a cry of protest, but Jacob, like the policeman, knew the form must be observed. He stood aside.

"May I ask what you are looking for?"

"We have been informed . . ." He avoided Jacob's eyes and waved his men in.

They shouldered their way through the door, their brawny uniformed figures bulking hugely in the kitchen. In their presence the room grew cramped, seemed suddenly to press in on the occupants like a prison cell.

"There has been a large consignment of saccharin smuggled across the border. . . ."

The noise of the men was everywhere, their boots loud on the floors, their voices loud, rasping from the attic, echoing from the cellar. Jacob said calmly, "I am not a smuggler."

The sergeant, his men out of the way for a moment, was able to shrug helplessly. "*I* know that, Levi, but what can I do? An informer has given the word. I have my orders. . . . Do you want me to get into trouble? Put yourself in my position."

The men were methodical: they flung open doors and shutters so that the cold night air rushed into the house with the sound of the rain; they turned over mats, emptied drawers and wardrobes, rattled ornaments. Rachel kept various little hoards of coins in vases around the room, each for its own special purpose, charitable gifts, journeys, clothes for the children. The soldiers shook out the money suspiciously, keenly, as though discovering something incriminating.

They went into the shop and the enamel crashed from the shelves. Rachel sprang to her feet but Jacob shook his head quickly and she sat down again without a word.

They were thorough. They poked at bags of barley and sugar and flour, plunging their dirty hands into the contents, occasionally licking their fingers. They examined the cooking utensils and searched the kitchen shelves, mixing up the separate dishes for milk and meat. They stripped the beds and probed the mattresses and someone slit the fat pillows on several of the beds so that suddenly the silent group in the kitchen was engulfed in a cloud of small white feathers, floating and whirling down the stairs, settling on heads and shoulders, frosting the men's black beards with white. When enough time had been spent on the pointless but officially ordained search, the sergeant recalled his men.

One of them, striding through the room, almost tripped over Chaim's foot. He stopped and gazed down at the boy with an intensity of hatred in his eyes so fierce that it shone from him like a flame. Chaim felt himself falling into those eyes like someone falling into a pit of fire: the flesh was burned from his bones, his very bones were consumed by that hate, a hate that had nourished itself over centuries, passing like the worm itself from generation to generation, self-perpetuating.

What harm have I done you? Chaim longed to cry out. *What crime have I committed?* The question would have been irrelevant. He harmed the man by being what he was. His existence was his crime.

The policeman spat on the floor, kicked aside Chaim's foot, and strode to the door. The sergeant, unseen by his men, shrugged again at Jacob. "There *has* been smuggling going on in town," he said apologetically.

He followed his men out, leaving the door open. The shutters swung and banged, and, in the darkness outside, the white feathers swirled and danced like huge snowflakes. Chaim looked around the room: smashed china, flour and grain trodden underfoot, milk trickling from a shelf and forming a muddy pool on the floor, Rachel weeping silently.

Outside, the feathers danced like living things. But in the room, Chaim realized, no one moved. For the space of a long breath there was absolute stillness. A curious noise broke the silence: a bubbling, snuffling sound. The baby had fallen asleep and was snoring.

The little group progressed down the street like a ship under full sail: in the center, the *melamed*, carrying the youngest member of the class. Around him, clinging to his greasy black satin coat the four-year-olds, stumbling, tiny legs unable to keep pace with the teacher's long strides.

Then in an outer ring, the oldest boys, veterans of five, already accustomed to the journey, who had established a sort of trotting movement which they could keep up for the whole journey. Daniel was an experienced member of the *cheder* now: he joined the group as it passed the door, grabbed a spare handful of coattail, and fell into the jog trot.

The leaves on the trees shimmered pale green, almost silvery in the spring sunlight. As they reached the bottom of the hill, Daniel glanced wistfully at the words painted on a black board above a wide gateway: A. CHOMSKY WOOD MERCHANT. Before he had become a big boy Leah used to take him with her on mornings like this, to play hide-and-seek in Chomsky's timber yard. But there were no holidays for *cheder* boys.

It was the girls, mostly, who played in the timber yard, on holidays or after school, usually with a small brother or sister slung on one hip or dragged along by a fat wrist, and they spent hours there, eluding Chomsky's watchful eye, running for cover if he spotted them, exploring corners of the yard. There were long stacks of roof beaming piled up like old hulks at the back of the yard, nettles growing up between them and chickens idly pecking here and there.

In an open-sided barn lay the seasoned, more expensive wood, and everywhere, underfoot, were chippings and shavings and sawdust lying like a sandy beach, yellow in the sun. This was the place the children came for their secret games, to play Egyptians and Israelites or soldiers on horseback, astride narrow planks of wood. In the timber yard with its mysterious, resin-fragrant alleys, its mazes of wood, hide-

and-seek gained an added thrill from the fear that Chomsky himself might at any moment stumble on them.

He was a short but immensely powerful-looking man with bulging, overdeveloped muscles, and he used to stand, thick legs straddled slightly apart, shouting lurid curses and threats at the children, his small eyes red with rage.

He could have shut and locked his gates, but they were wrought iron and heavy, so he left them permanently open, and in time the gates had sunk into the earth and could not be moved anyway.

The timber yard was for the spring. But as summer approached, the wood seemed to generate heat and the alleyways trapped air heavy with resin, making breathing difficult. The sound of the saw hummed in the air like the buzzing of distant bees, accompanied by the *whirr-clunk, clunk* of its steam engine.

So in the summer Chomsky was at peace, and the young ones gathered in the small square with its faded blue wooden seats, with the drinking-water fountain, and on each side the small, busy shops: Cohen the spice merchant and Stein who mended shoes and Slumkow who kept the little café where the men sipped their tea and read the newspapers, passing them from one to another.

The older boys and girls wandered off to the river—boys with boys, girls with girls, as befitted young adults of marriageable age—and leaned over the bridge, gazing into the clear green water as they chatted. The younger ones hung around the square, listening to adult squabbles, playing five stones, kicking pebbles, and generally spinning away the summer days in an amiably wasteful fashion.

Leah's friends waited for her, sitting on one of the benches, kicking their feet, stirring up dust, and giggling at nothing in particular. When she arrived, they wandered off arm in arm, gossiping. The square was like a big communal backyard: outsiders never came through, it led to nowhere in particular and contained nothing of interest except to locals. There was a casualness about its encounters: women shouted messages across the square. Old men paused and murmured together, nodding beards, or sat motionless by the hour on rickety metal chairs, gazing at a chessboard set out on an upturned wooden box from the fruit stall. The games of chess could last all day, the players unaware of the boisterous activity around them.

Occasionally Chaim, released from the shop or his studies at the *Beth Hamidrash*, was allowed a game, pitting his wits against old hands like Golomstok, a tiny, twiglike figure with sleepy eyes, who once said consolingly after the game, "The mistakes have all been made, before we start. We just discover them."

In the summer, Leah's cousin Mordecai spent most of the day in the square. The Shoobotel home consisted of two rooms and a little balcony for the four of them. His father had once, briefly, enjoyed prosperity on the strength of his wife's dowry, and he had opened a bookshop in the square.

There he stood, smiling, rubbing his hands, encouraging passers-by to enter, examine the stacks of old books he had assembled from second-hand shops in Warsaw. But the pious needed nothing outside their holy books, and no one had money to spare for reading matter. So he shut up shop and went back to peddling carpets in the market. In the two cramped rooms the Shoobotel boys had grown up surrounded by hundreds of battered books, stacked against the walls, balanced on top of wardrobes, pushed under beds, behind cupboards. Books fading, gathering dust, their pages growing brittle and brown.

Mordecai began to look at the volumes first because some had pictures. Later he learned to read them, and found he enjoyed them. He was already doing well at his studies. Even so, on the family's finances he would have got no further than elementary school had it not been for an ingenious plan thought up by his friend and crony Jochanon. Jochanon's father was a wealthy merchant—his house one of the biggest in the neighborhood—and one day he sent for Mordecai.

"I hear you're a clever boy, Shoobotel."

"That is true."

"Not modest though."

"Not if modesty is incompatible with truth."

"Quite. Well the truth is my son is not clever. He must be educated, and his studies are hard for him. He tells me you can be of help. I have a proposition." It was a simple proposal: Mordecai would go to the Polytechnic with Jochanon, discreetly doing most of Jochanon's lessons for him. As a boarder he had the added incentive of getting away from the dingy family home during the school year. In the summer the square became his forum.

Leah had known Mordecai since they fought over the same wooden clothes peg as two-year-olds, and every summer they renewed their friendship. For Leah, Mordecai had something of Uncle Simeon's "outside world" about him: he had read so many books, had so many fascinating ideas. Not that he was gentle, like Uncle Simeon. His ideas were expressed violently, his views were often shocking, or hard to understand, like this notion of self-defense through Japanese jujitsu.

It was felt by some that young Shoobotel was introducing provocative and un-Jewish activities into the neighborhood and influencing boys who should know better, so that they neglected their studies. Luckily Jochanan's excellent school marks reassured his father, and the "arrangement" continued.

For much of the day Mordecai was the center of a group of boys, listening to his ideas, sharing his plans. But early in the morning, before his followers joined him, Leah managed to get him on his own.

Today when she arrived he was already deep in some printed leaflets. She dropped onto the seat beside him, the wooden slats vibrating. He looked up, nodded, unsmiling. "The most remarkable thing, astonishing. Leah, this is something we should all study. You should look at this—"

"Are girls also to throw people over their shoulders?"

He shook his head impatiently, resetting his *yarmulkah* on his wiry hair. "This is something new! An amazing invention. I read about it in a newspaper and I sent for these." He waved the leaflets. "A Dr. Zamenhof—an oculist in Warsaw—has invented a new language, an international language. He calls it Esperanto."

Leah looked bored and stirred the dust with her shoe. "Haven't we enough languages to learn?"

"But that's just the point!" He leaped up and began circling the wooden seat vigorously. "Think how wonderful this could be! You and I can talk Polish; our parents communicate in Yiddish, we pray in Hebrew, the Russians insist on teaching us Russian, and talk French in refined circles! And in France or Italy they have similar problems. England, Germany, the same. But with Esperanto people could talk to each other no matter what their own language might be. Think what that means! International understanding! We could talk to complete strangers from across the world, like brothers."

"It must be very difficult," Leah said doubtfully.

He flung himself down again, thrusting leaflets at her, pointing at words already ringed in ink, turning pages, his energy engulfing her. Mordecai, she thought, was a very un-Jewish boy. Or rather no: his Jewishness was inspired, overflowing the narrow world of the ghetto. Ideas, theory, debate—that was his world too. But he refused to be confined by it, and that was where he clashed with others who felt his very energy to be a dangerous sickness.

"See: there are words that already exist in several languages, like *park, theater, nature, character.* Then Zamenhof takes root words, common to languages of Romance and German origin, see . . . nouns end in *o*, adjectives end in *a*, there's only one conjunction to the verb —why, it's *easy.* Look: here he gives the Lord's Prayer in Esperanto— '*Patro nia, kiu—*' "

"Mordecai, that is a prayer for gentiles."

"*If* there is a God at all, there can only be one, so a prayer to him is reaching its destination whether a gentile is muttering the Lord's Prayer or you are chanting the *Shema.* 'The Lord our God is One,' isn't that so?"

The square, pugnacious face was almost peasantlike in its outlines, so different from the other slender, pale boys she knew. He was often outrageous, yet his grasp of the Law was as good as any *yeshiva* student's. And when she was with him, Leah felt her own frustrations slip away. She had no need to conceal her curiosity in the outside world, to apologize for being a girl yet being so boyish in her mentality. Indeed, with Mordecai, perversely, she sometimes felt it necessary to play the traditional female role of practical doubter, in order to make him expound even more vehemently his theories and wild plans of action.

Suddenly he shuffled the papers together, picked up a dark cloth bundle from the bench, and sprang up. "I have to go." He began walking rapidly away.

"Wait for me!" Leah ran to catch up with him.

"I have an errand to do." She glanced at the bundle under his arm and said nothing. "I am on my way to Avrum's father."

The pawnshop. Leah kept her face expressionless but she knew how he must be feeling. The pawnshop hovered darkly on the edge of everyone's lives: into it went precious items, a brooch, some pearls, a superior piece of clothing, and then came the desperate scratching around to earn the money to redeem them—not always achieved. Mordecai shook the bundle. "My father's Sabbath coat. I hope we can get it out by Friday."

"I'll come with you."

As they approached the corner shop with its cluttered window, Mordecai's steps slowed. On impulse Leah asked, "Shall I take it in for you?"

He looked astonished. "Why should you?"

She had never been inside the pawnshop. Rachel would have starved before suffering such humiliation. Now, her curiosity overcame her reluctance.

"It really doesn't bother you?" He looked relieved. She took the bundle, and quickly, before her resolution could weaken, marched inside. There were a couple of women in the shop, trying to look invisible, waiting to see how much their little treasures were worth. Across the counter, Avrum's father peered at a necklace, his mouth turned down disapprovingly. It was clearly a thing of little value and would be worth even less after his eyes had examined it.

Leah disliked him; he had a keen, questioning look, he seemed to sniff like a hound for customers. She hated the way he ran the rubles through his fingers, as though reluctant to let them go, before handing them over. The women scuttled out and she went forward. He looked surprised to see her, and slightly pleased. She put down the coat silently and he shook it out and held it up, looking closely at the cloth.

"But this is not your father's!" he exclaimed. "This belongs to a shorter man altogether."

"So?"

"So where did you get it?"

She stared at him feeling herself growing red in the face. "What is that to do with you?"

Surely he did not imagine she had stolen it? Her shame was exceeded only by her rage. She was about to snatch back the coat and march out, but she remembered that Mordecai was waiting, and his mother needed the money to buy food for the family. There must be women in here every day who felt like this, sick at heart, watching the old man's grimy fingers touching their personal possessions uncaringly, putting a price on everything. To have to depend on someone like this, to put up with his sneering smile, accept his decision! Women should not have to suffer it.

He shrugged and ran his hands over the coat: "This is Sabbath wear . . ." He held it closer, "But not new, quite worn. Remember, if you want it out for Sabbath, I close early." He shoved the coat behind him and took a small pile of coins from a stack standing by the cash desk. He ran them through his fingers like beads, several times, and Leah watched his hands, listening to the rippling clink of the coins. When he handed them over she counted them quickly. "Is that all?"

70

"More than it's worth," he snapped, giving her a receipt token.

As she fumbled for the door, almost dizzy with the need to get out of his presence, she again heard him pick up some coins and run them through his fingers.

The Esperanto classes began the next day. There were eight of them in the group, Leah the only girl. There was Yossel the baker's son, who arrived with flour on his sleeves from helping his father load the oven; Josef, whose widowed mother ran a stall in the market; Dovid and Shmuel, whose father was an attendant at the bathhouse and who always smelled faintly of soap; Jochanan Minsky, the merchant's son, who often brought along nuts or sweets for the group to share; and Avrum from the pawnshop.

Pushed and urged by Mordecai, the group stumbled through the grammar, learned some vocabulary, and even exchanged formal little conversations together, sitting crowded on the bench in the square, some perched on the backrest while Mordecai, too restless to sit still, danced around them like a boxer, waving the grammar book, encouraging and applauding as they made progress. Now and then he stopped to grab a sweet or nut before circling on again. Leah, knowing how little he got to eat at home, was amazed at how solid and healthy he looked.

Old men at the tables outside Slumkow's café sat watching them, sipping tea, straining the liquid through pieces of sugar held in their teeth, shaking their heads. The lessons went on all through the summer.

"This is the last year of the century," Mordecai reminded them. "We must greet the twentieth century with the language of the future!"

In the autumn things changed. School began for Mordecai and Jochanan in Warsaw, others had work and study. The days grew chilly, and only the little ones—racing from tree to tree, playing pointless games of catch and tag—found it warm enough to be comfortable outside for long.

Crossing the square one day Leah had to shelter from a sudden, flurrying rainstorm, the sky blackening, rain sweeping across the street, slanting in the wind. The yellow leaves, heavy with rain, dropped from the trees, spreading in a golden tide on the ground.

A few drops of rain splattered Leah's cheeks as she stood waiting, and she felt inexplicable tears, hot and stinging, rise to her eyes. She blinked rapidly and shook back her braids with an impatient gesture.

Why was she crying? She was not crying, she answered herself, she must be getting a chill.

The storm passed, the sun wavered through the shredding clouds, picking out the few ocher leaves still left on the trees. The chess players had moved indoors to the café and the old men sat looking through the steamy windows.

Leah hurried home to knead and roll the dough for the *lokshen,* an Esperanto grammar book propped on the kitchen table. Rolling out the dough paper thin, folding and slicing it with the sharp kitchen knife, she punctuated her movements with her growing vocabulary of nouns and verbs. Jacob, appearing from the shop for a moment, surprised her in midsentence. "What's this, what's this?"

"Esperanto."

"Ah. The Warsaw lunatic who thinks he can make us all understand one another."

"So we will. Nineteen hundred will be the year of international understanding!"

"It will take more than a new language to make that happen, my child. But who knows? This may be a beginning." He patted her head and went out. She spread a clean sheet over Hirschl's bed, draped the slivers of *lokshen* over it to dry, and began to scrub down the table, leaning sideways so that she could go on reading the book.

As usual, extra places were laid at the table, but tonight she knew whom they were for: Chaim and Solomon, frequent visitors, were coming.

"My big girl here is studying this new Esperanto," Jacob told Solomon after they had eaten. Chaim's father shook his head. "Why do you allow your children to waste their time with passing fashion?"

Leah felt irritated. The usual, narrow-minded ghetto bigotry. No interest in anything outside Torah and tradition. "Not all new ideas are just a fashion. Perhaps the children of Israel should have told Moses to take his Law somewhere else: it was a new idea after all!"

Solomon laughed, nettled. "Well, occupy yourself with Jewish new ideas then."

"Dr. Zamenhof, the inventor of Esperanto, *is* Jewish!" Leah cried triumphantly.

Chaim watched her: so full of life! The almond eyes gleamed, the black braids twitched as she tossed her head. Jacob watched her too and wondered whether these outside influences were good for a girl. But he hesitated to confine her, and secretly he enjoyed her liveliness: Rachel was a good wife but preoccupied with her work. Hirschl was a good boy, who tended to arrive home tired out from so much traveling. Danielsche was still almost a baby. Leah's head was full of nonsense, but she made him smile; through her he remembered dimly what it was like to be young.

It was in the bathhouse that Leah noticed the specks of blood on her underclothing. She thought at first that she must have cut herself, and she searched for a graze. Then, as she dried herself, she noticed the smear on her rough white towel, and slowly, with mounting terror, discovered she was bleeding. Her mother was in the next cubicle, but it was impossible to call her without attracting the attention of the inquisitive attendant who prided herself on knowing everyone else's business before they knew it themselves.

Leah hastily washed the drops of blood from her underwear, and the long, red streak from the towel. She touched herself again, fearfully, between her legs, and her stomach lurched as she saw the red moistness of her finger tips. She dressed, pressing her legs together and praying blindly to be saved. *Whatever it is, please God, look after me. God will protect.*

She unlocked the door and waited. After a while Rachel called, "Leah? Are you ready?"

"Mama, I'm not feeling well."

Rachel rushed in, all anxiety, as Leah knew she would. She stopped at the sight of Leah, fully dressed and apparently quite well, standing pressed against a wooden partition. Over her shoulder Leah could see the attendant already sniffing drama. "Shut the door, Mama."

Rachel closed the door, frowning impatiently. "Now. What is hurting?"

Leah said tremulously, "I am bleeding."

73

For a moment Rachel failed to understand. Leah and Danielsche were linked in her mind as the babies, and Leah was small for her age. She thought the child might have stepped on something, cut her foot. Then she looked at Leah's pale, tear-stained face and suddenly realized what she meant. Her hand flashed out and slapped Leah hard on each cheek.

Leah burst into tears again: did her mother think she was making it up? "It's *true!*" she exclaimed.

Unexpectedly, Rachel smiled, reassuringly. "I know. The slap is to give you a good color, so that you will always look well and rosy. Bring the blood to your cheeks. My mother did the same for me. There is nothing to worry about. This is something that happens to all women."

Women? It was the first time Leah had been called a woman. She was a girl, surely. She did not want to be a woman. Women worked and hurried and never had a moment to think. Women got married to people chosen by their parents and cried when they were widowed or when an epidemic took their children from them. And then women grew old and sat by the fire like her grandmother Hannah, and sighed and groaned and got in everyone's way and talked about the past. She did not want to be a woman.

"What is it?" she whispered.

Rachel was busy, ripping a strip of calico off her petticoat, improvising a sort of diaper which she tucked around Leah, while she thought what to say. Leah was a quick child and clever but she was innocent, as Rachel herself had been, in personal matters. Rachel had discovered her own menstrual blood in the bed one morning, and had been convinced that a vampire had been feeding off her during the night, or that Baba Yaga, the ogress who rode through the night on her cauldron looking for children to eat, had been enjoying a passing gulp of her blood.

She tried now to explain, but she simply did not know where to begin, how to put the words together. These matters were not spoken of: women learned what they needed to know when the right time came, and then the subject was closed again. Her own wedding night had made many things clear to Rachel that had puzzled her before, but she could not bring herself to speak of them to Leah. Not even with Jacob had she discussed them. There were certain things a woman did or had done to her that were not talked about. Much of it was unpleasant, and occasionally there were unsettling, fleeting moments of pleasure which, as a decent woman, she did her best to conceal. Leah would learn all this for herself when the time came. But now, this, today, must be explained.

"Leah: you know the law for married women to go to the *mikva* every month, to be cleansed, to be purified. It is after . . . this, when it stops, that women come every month to the *mikva* for the ritual bath. So that their husbands will not be defiled by touching them."

"You mean I will bleed like this every month? *Forever?*" Leah moaned.

Rachel said sharply, "You are a woman now. You must behave like a woman. No more tears." She was embarrassed by it all, she wanted to get out of this tiny cubicle. All around them, from other cubicles she could hear the splashing of water, the calls for the attendant, and then her mother-in-law, summoning her to do up her boots. Thankfully she unlocked the door. "Bubeh is calling."

Leah asked, "Why does this happen? Is it an illness?"

"Illness? No! It means you are a woman. You are able to bear children."

Bear children. But her mother had told her the midwife brought the babies in her black bag. Now it seemed she was telling her something else. Leah realized her mother was not to be trusted. Nor could she ask her father. He would become abstracted, murmur something about it being written in the Talmud in such and such a place, and vanish from the room. Well, she would have to find out for herself.

Chaim and Solomon were invited for a Chanukah meal, as was the Shoobotel family, although Rachel did not really feel at ease with them. Jacob's cousin Shoobotel was a feeble creature and his wife a misery, and the boys were odd. The younger one was sickly and no wonder, with the nourishment he got. And Mordecai. . . . Mordecai was a mixture of a peasant and a madman. True he was a brilliant student, but such ideas! And his appearance! He refused to wear the long black coat and hat, and went about in a jacket and a cap, looking like a postman. Her own relatives were more refined altogether, but now that her parents were both gone, there were fewer opportunities to reunite the family and in fact she had never really liked her sister. Still she wished sometimes that Jacob was not quite so benevolently disposed toward his highly unsatisfactory relations.

The nine-branched candelabra bore its first candle and the pilot candle. Leah had a new dress, lavender with the ruffled sleeves the officers' wives had already introduced. There were gifts for the children, hair ribbons for Leah, and a new drinking mug for Daniel with a painting of a boy on it. And Benjamin got some slippers. For Chaim and Mordecai (though they were now men, being thirteen and having had their Bar Mitzvahs) there were also presents: an embroidered *yarmulkah* for Chaim and a long, warm scarf for Mordecai.

In the course of the evening Leah drew Mordecai to one side. "I want to ask you something."

He waited, eyebrows raised.

"I want to know about babies."

"What about babies?"

"All about babies. How they are made."

"How—" He stared at her in amazement. "You really don't know? Not at all? It doesn't seem possible!" He recognized that Rachel was a rigid woman, and, as a man, Jacob could hardly. . . . He wondered how to explain. It should have been easy. But with Leah sitting so close that he could see himself in her wide eyes he was suddenly aware of her, physically, for the first time, and the straightforward explanations were strangled in his throat.

"Ah. Well, it's very simple really. But I shall have to explain another time. I shall draw you a diagram. It's very scientific."

He had struck the right note. She nodded, satisfied. "Tomorrow then. Don't forget."

But the next day there was a snowstorm, and it was later in the week that she put on her boots and walked to the square and saw Mordecai standing in Slumkow's café doorway. She waved, and he put down his glass of tea and came toward her.

The square looked larger in the snow, the trees standing like skeletal sentinels. Here and there, where the snow had slipped off the benches, their blue gleamed like reflections of the bright sky. Mordecai was still wearing his old jacket, with the new scarf wound around his neck.

"Well?" Leah began at once. "Babies?"

He took a notebook out of his pocket, and then with a quick movement swept the snow off the nearest bench. People hurrying across the square, women in headscarves and stout boots, carrying bread, or milk in metal containers, looked curiously at the two young people sitting talking on a bench as though it were summer.

Mordecai was scribbling squares and circles in his notebook. "Have you never seen animals, climbing on each other?" he asked abruptly.

"Yes. People throw stones and they run away. So?"

He sighed. Then he said rapidly, "All right, this is the way it is," and gave her the facts.

". . . And *this* goes *here*, and then the egg. . . ."

She stared at the paper. "It's really like that? Always? That's the only way?"

"Haven't your friends talked about all this?"

"We talk, but no one knows. The older ones only talk to each other." She sat, lips compressed, gazing at the café doorway and its clouded glass. "Why don't they tell us from the beginning? They should tell us," she said at last, flatly.

"It's hard for parents. They were brought up to believe these things are shameful, secret. It is up to us to change that."

She nodded. "Thank you, Mordecai."

Again he felt the new, disturbing awareness of her presence. He said, tentatively, "When the time comes for you to marry, did you ever think you might . . . choose someone for yourself?"

"Choose? But that's impossible. Father will decide." She felt walls closing in on her; her life was being decided, possibly even now, by other people, and she would have no voice in the matter. It had never occurred to her before that she should. But now, for the first time, she thought that perhaps she might like to shape her own fate.

"I never heard of anyone . . . choosing."

"Oh," Mordecai said casually. "In the outside world it happens all the time."

"Couldn't I marry you?" she asked. "We get on so well."

He began to laugh. "First of all, your father would be horrified. Your mother would faint. And in any case . . ." He faltered, and then went on more firmly, "And in any case I don't believe in marriage."

"How can you not *believe* in marriage?"

"The world is changing. There must be more freedom for men and women to choose partners, but to live like comrades."

"Without marriage."

He nodded. "After the revolution—"

"Oh! The revolution! There will never be a revolution, the Russians will not allow it."

"There must be a revolution. For equality, for the workers, for justice, for . . ."

She stopped listening. He was in full flood about the proletariat and unconditional historical necessity, and she had heard it all before.

77

What occupied her thoughts now was this extraordinary new idea about partnership. He would like to live with a woman in freedom, and without marriage. As comrades. It seemed very exciting. If she were to embark on such a partnership she would live in a big city and, she supposed, find work and go to revolutionary meetings with him and share his thrilling experiences, instead of being left at home like other women with the saucepans and the children.

Children. Suppose there were children. What then? What about the freedom and the partnership? She felt suddenly chilled and got up from the bench.

"I'm cold. I must go home."

He stopped in midsentence and realized she had not been listening. "I brought you a book. It will explain why there *must* be a revolution."

She took the book and he said, with a confidence he did not fully feel, "Well, here's to freedom and partnership." He held out his hand and she took it, slowly. She was not wearing gloves and she felt his rough skin, surprisingly warm, against her smooth fingers.

"Yes," she said.

But when he came home for Passover it was all settled. His mother gave him the news: Leah was betrothed to marry Chaim Rubinstein. Mordecai went straight to her house without even dropping his bag. Leah put down the knife she was scrubbing and opened the door. He asked, wonderingly, "What happened to freedom? To choosing for yourself?"

She said woodenly, "You could not understand."

"Oh, I understand. I understand, but I cannot forgive! I thought you had more spirit. I thought you would fight."

She did not argue, simply stared at him, her eyes flat with resentment.

"And the usual obscene arrangement! Marrying off children! Medieval. This is nineteen hundred, and girls of thirteen are being married off!"

She said quickly, "I'm fourteen now. And besides the wedding will not be for another twelve months. Not until I'm fifteen, father said."

"So old!" he mocked her. Then as the corners of her mouth drooped, he relented. "I apologize. It's not for me to criticize your family arrangements, and Chaim is a good boy. I expect you will be happy enough. But I had hoped you would . . ." he shrugged, "do more with your life."

"But I shall!"

He shook his head. "A betrothed girl is already halfway to a married woman and you must play your traditional part. Well. Good luck."

He took her hand and shook it. At the door he paused as he picked up his bag and asked her a question in Esperanto. She looked guilty and stammered a brief reply. "I haven't had much time, lately . . . to study . . ."

"Of course." He nodded, smiling, and went out.

Leah went back to scrubbing knives. The Passover bakehouse, specially purified, had been turning out matzos for weeks; the house was upside down and everyone was busy cleaning, scraping, rubbing. Leah was drying the knives when she suddenly stopped, dropped them on the table, and hurried up the stairs, past the little bedrooms, up into the loft with the dark wooden roof supports arching over her like exposed ribs.

As usual, the household linen was hanging over lines strung across the loft, drying in the warmth that rose from the rooms below. Leah had always come up to the loft when she wanted to think. She loved the smell of soap and clean linen, and the way the sheets dried stiff as boards, so that she moved between hard white linen walls which flapped and swung stiffly, giving off a hollow sound when she tapped them with her knuckles. In the dim, shadowy light everything looked mysterious. She used to play hide-and-seek up here with Daniel when they were both younger, when he was still a baby. The pillow cases hanging on the lines looked like small shrouds, shrouds for the children who died every year, for the babies who succumbed to the fever or the lack of nourishment, or the cold. . . . She thought of Daniel, how he used to lie in bed sucking his thumb and waiting to be dressed. She supposed she would have children—was that after all, not the reason for her decision? Because the choice had been hers. Mordecai would never understand, so there was no reason to tell him—but nothing had been forced on her. The decision to marry Chaim had been her own.

When the little rat-faced man had come to see her father she did not recognize him as the marriage broker, the *shadchen*, but he had, it seemed, for some time been noting details of her in his little book. He followed Jacob into the shop, shutting the door officiously.

"Leah," Jacob said, when he had gone, "it is time to discuss your future. You are no longer a child. . . . Of course we are not talking of anything immediate, but it is time to be thinking about marriage."

"You want to be happily married like your sister Ruda, surely?" her mother broke in.

Since Leah found her brother-in-law a bore she might have answered sharply, but her father was talking again.

". . . You have known each other some time now, he is a very fine young man . . . a good scholar. . . ." He went on at some length. ". . . In short, Leah, we would be very happy to welcome Chaim into our family, but of course you must have the final word. We are not old-fashioned. In my day parents did not discuss, but the world changes and I want you to be happy. It shall be your choice."

"Why make such a conversation about it?" Rachel cried nervously, "the *shadchen* has made the necessary inquiries, the terms are suitable, she must be happy with such a good choice of bridegroom."

Leah's mind flickered over her future. She could refuse. She could say, "I do not wish to marry and settle down to pots and pans. I wish to live in freedom, to choose . . . a partner, a comrade."

And then? She saw Chaim's face, pale like Danielsche's, childlike, though he was older than she by two years. And she saw Mordecai, striding down the street, exploring some new horizon, filled with some new idea. And always he was striding ahead and she was trying to keep up. And one day she would have children, clinging to her skirts, a baby heavy against her breast. Trying to keep up, stumbling. Being, perhaps, left behind?

She said, "I am happy with your choice, father."

Rachel gave a cry of relief and kissed her on both cheeks and Jacob smiled and kissed her forehead, and after a little while Leah went upstairs into the loft and wept silently and for a long time against the unyielding sheets, the stiff, rough linen softening gradually beneath her tears.

Now, standing again in the loft as the sheets dripped steadily like trees after rain, Leah stopped thinking. She forced herself into a deep blankness that comforted her, that allowed her a healing, restful oblivion. She did not know how long she stood there, her clothes growing damp and sticky from the sheets around her, but at last she stirred and sighed and walked back to the low doorway and the stairs. She had to finish the knives.

Mordecai came home for the summer holidays with a new idea: they were to have a library. Of course it would have to be done secretly, the authorities would never permit it—indeed it might have to be kept secret from some of the more religious parents, who would surely disapprove.

"But we have no money," Chaim pointed out. "How will you organize a library?"

Mordecai began circling the bench, arms flailing. "Simple! In my home we have enough books for two libraries! I shall choose the best books, catalogue them, and then . . ." He was off. No one else spoke much, though they nodded from time to time.

At last he paused for breath and Leah asked, "What about a room?"

"A room. Yes, we shall need a room, some shelves—wooden shelves for the books, and a table, a chair, a bench—"

"Why not a carpet and a chandelier?" Leah asked.

Chaim said quietly, "We have a cellar that is not used now. My mother . . . kept the preserves there, but we do nothing with it. I could ask my father—"

"Oh, he'll refuse!" Avrum exclaimed, knowing how his own father would respond.

Leah said, "He will refuse if you tell him the full story. But if you simply tell him some young people wish to have a room for study because their own homes are not big enough, he may agree. He need not know more."

Mordecai looked at her with admiration. "Leah, you have the mind of a politician. What a pity—" he stopped. "Chaim will ask his father then, and we shall hear the results."

With Leah's prompting, Chaim managed for the first time in his life to tell less than the whole truth to his father and as a result obtained permission for the cellar to be used. They visited it during shop hours so that they could speak freely without being overheard by Solomon.

"It needs cleaning . . . smells damp."

"So we'll clean it. Shmuel can bring soap from the bathhouse," Mordecai said.

Yossel added, "My father has some whitewash. . . . If we painted the walls white—"

"Excellent!"

Minsky, who could afford to be indulgent, gave Jochanan a stack of wood for shelves, and Leah brought a chair from Jacob's shop. Plans went ahead, walls were washed, painted, floors scrubbed, shelves inexpertly hammered together and books selected, catalogued.

For most of the young people, even a few kopeks a month was a consideration, but they were excited by the prospect of joining a library, of having unlimited reading material. Most people in the town had to rely on the miserable stock of the traveling book peddler with his horse and cart, who appeared on market day every few weeks with a tattered selection of sacred Hebrew works for the men and a few Yiddish tales aimed at the inferior minds of women. The subscriptions mounted.

The group took turns to supervise the library, between work or studies. Leah enjoyed it, she found time to read, and in a curious way it renewed her relationship with Mordecai. Chaim had been drawn into the group, assimilated and, because of his amiable disposition, accepted as a friend.

The sting was drawn from Leah's bitter encounter with Mordecai, and an easy, three-way relationship established itself. She had never been happier: she was combining her two worlds, participating in Mordecai's outside interests, but from a position of safety.

As the library became more popular, its existence could no longer be kept a secret. Parents found out about the books—in some cases sampled them. In other houses there were explosive scenes.

"I will not have such works in my home!" Slumkow roared, banging the table. He flung himself back in his chair so violently that his *yarmulkah* almost fell off his head. His wife made soothing noises and glanced anxiously at Solly, sulking on the other side of the table.

"Are there not enough good books, that you need this—dirt?" He pushed the Polish novel, a highly moral tale, away from him with the handle of a knife.

Jacob looked into the library that afternoon and found Leah busily replacing returned volumes to the shelves. He took down one volume and began to read it, smiling reminiscently. "You shouldn't spend too much time in a damp cellar," he remarked in his absentminded way. "Your mother imagines you are gossiping in the square with your friends."

Leah looked alarmed. "You won't tell her?"

"I shall tell you first, if I decide it is necessary."

Leah and Chaim were to be married in the autumn, on a Tuesday, that being a particularly auspicious day for a wedding.

"Why a Tuesday?" Mordecai asked irritably, realizing he would have to miss classes to come home for the so-called celebration.

"You know!" Leah exclaimed, straight-faced. "After creating the first Tuesday, the Almighty, blessed be He, looked on His creation and repeated *twice,* 'It is good.' Which makes it a lucky day for weddings."

"Idiocy! Unbelievable idiocy!" Mordecai banged his head. "We live by magic and superstition and insist that we are fulfilling the true Law. Lucky Tuesday! Sheer superstition."

"Goethe said that superstition is the poetry of life," Leah said demurely.

"He wasn't Jewish."

"Oh, I'm sorry. I didn't know you had to be Jewish to pronounce on poetry."

"You don't. But to pronounce on superstition . . . !"

He was busy fastening a Warsaw newspaper between wooden clamps so that library members could read it, as they did in the proper library near the gymnasium. It was in the library newspaper that Leah first became aware of Zionism. Mordecai knew all about it, had read Herzl's *Judenstaat* in some illegal publication, and told her a little about Herzl's idea of a Jewish state. He was impatient with her ignorance.

"You're like ants scrabbling in the dust, here. There's so much going on. Revolutionary groups are meeting, there is talk of strikes—"

"But who *are* all these people?" Leah wanted to know. "Who does the organizing, who does the work?"

"The Bund. Three years ago in Vilna a few people got together and formed the Bund. I know one of the men who was there . . ."

Word of the Bund spread fast. It was a secret society of the best sort: not only revolutionary but Jewish! Meeting in synagogues, even in cemeteries, holding mock funerals to escape the eye of the authorities. But it was not only authority they had to beware of: almost everyone —for various reasons—was against the Bund. The Orthodox were outraged by the Godlessness; the better-off disliked the socialist principles involved, and the ghetto dweller feared the upheavals that must follow such a program. Surely life was not so bad, they thought. Why could they not be left in peace to live quietly and make the best of things? Small wonder that there was treachery on the part of comrades, information passed to the police so that meetings could be prevented or broken up.

"Are you involved in all this?" Leah asked Mordecai.

"Not yet, not much. But I shall be. A boy from the Polytechnic told me about an idea for talks between the Bund and the P.P.S. Wouldn't that be magnificent? No more gentiles and Jews but workers, Polish Socialists, united against oppression."

"But not all Jews are workers. And not all Poles are workers. What about the people who do not feel oppressed. What will you do about them, the people who are content?"

"If they have more than their needs that is unjust, and they will have to lose some of it."

Leah thought: *They will not be happy about that.* And she thought of the power and authority that lay in the hands of those people who would not wish to be helpful. "Mordecai, you will be careful?"

"Careful? Why? Will being careful achieve anything? Anyway, what can happen?"

The next time she saw him he had a broken arm and two cracked ribs.

"They broke up one of our meetings. . . . Someone informed. There was no chance of getting away."

He had brought home some more books and Leah was helping him put them in order in the library, dusting them with a clean rag. He was perched on a stool, using his good arm to leaf through books and hand them to her.

She watched him concentrating on a paragraph, nose wrinkled, lips thrust forward in a soundless whistle. *He must be brilliant,* she reflected. When he took the entrance examination to the Polytechnic with more than three hundred candidates trying for the seventeen places available to Jews under the quota system, not only had he been accepted, but he had managed to complete Jochanan's paper too. "What will you do, Mordecai, when you finish your studies?" she asked.

"Who knows? Maybe I shall work for the Bund."

"Go away, you mean? I shall miss you."

She was crouched on the floor next to him, surrounded by books, her dark blue skirt billowing around her like a collapsed flower.

"You could have come with me," he said. He put down the book he was holding and took one of her black braids in his hand, tugging gently, so that her head tipped comically, like a doll's. "I wonder if you know your own mind after all." He leaned forward and quickly, clumsily, almost falling off the stool, he kissed her mouth. Leah's pale face flooded with dark color, then drained so that her eyes looked even darker against the pallor. Her veins were on fire; she was, for a moment, unable even to breathe as she gazed, horrified, at Mordecai.

Her body was trembling and she was aware of sensations never before dreamed of: her breasts felt as though they were leaping inside her blouse; her heartbeat banged almost audibly, and within her body a vibration shook her so that her thighs and belly quivered inexplicably. Invisible hands seemed to be touching her all over, the hammering of her heart was like the thump of a drumbeat between her legs.

Mordecai was astonished by her reaction. It was the first time he had kissed a girl, but she, surely, as a betrothed woman, must have been kissed before? He, too, felt the heat gathering within him, stirring blood, nerves, muscle.

They remained frozen, he on the stool, she crouched before him, facing each other, breathing unevenly, until Leah, shaking free of the trancelike state, got to her feet and was out of the room and running up the stairs before Mordecai could stop her. He raced after her, banging his arm painfully against the wall, and just caught sight of her dark blue skirt before she turned the corner. He ran after her, not even noticing the stares of the passers-by.

Leah dared not head for home. Her flushed cheeks, her excitement, might arouse Rachel's curiosity. Where then? Undecided, she paused, and heard Mordecai call out "Leah!" as he hurried after her. Without turning her head, she started off again, running, beginning to gasp for breath. At last she turned in at the open gateway of Chomsky's timber yard.

Alleys lined with crisscross stacks of wood led away in all directions; the yard seemed deserted, but the saw rasped and clanked in the distance. She made for the far corner, away from the sawing shed, her feet scuffing up the wood shavings and the white dust on the path. She stumbled into the old hiding place she and Daniel had used in so many children's games. Half-kneeling, her hands covering her ears, eyes closed tight, Leah waited, heart thudding. Perspiration, trickling from her brow and temple, mingled with the dust on her face.

She had not heard him approach but she felt his presence as he stooped to enter the wooden cave. She kept her eyes closed, licking her lips, terrified. Then she heard him laughing. *Laughing?* Furious, Leah snapped open her eyes and glared at him, forgetting her panic.

He was sitting a few inches away, grinning at her. "You're like a little mouse, all dusty and bedraggled," Mordecai explained, still looking amused. "And what do you think I'm going to do? Eat you?"

She felt foolish. Tears welled up, tears of mortification that he should find her ridiculous. Mordecai wiped them away, gently, almost dreamily. He began to stroke her face, her throat, her breasts. She made no attempt to push him away. Her arms hung helplessly by her sides. Each touch of his hand ignited her flesh until she blazed and quivered under the exploration. The fragrance of the resin was overwhelming in the hot, still air. Mordecai's face wavered and seemed to grow larger as he leaned over her.

The square lay bleached and dusty in the sun. Under the trees, sunlight and shadow rippling over them, children played hoops or ball games. Two little ones were trooping around and around one of the trees. A thirsty child gulped at the drinking fountain and a small black dog barked cheerfully.

Chaim was alone in the shop when the policeman came in.

"Not many customers today," the officer remarked.

"Money is short and food comes first."

"Before God? Food comes before God?"

"Not before God. Him you can speak to in your heart. But before the purchase of objects, yes."

Without altering his tone, the policeman asked, "You're mixed up in this library foolishness of young Shoobotel's, aren't you?"

"What library?"

The sergeant sighed. "All right. There is no illegal library run by no silly young people and therefore no informer can have told me where it is to be found. So when I send some men to search a certain cellar which does not exist, they will of course find no books there and no one will be prosecuted. Good."

Chaim, matching the sergeant for woodenness of expression,

risked a question: "When would your men search the cellar, if there were such a place?"

"At six o'clock this evening the new guard comes on duty. That is often a good time for such visits."

"Thank you," Chaim said.

The policeman shrugged amiably. "When you get a few more customers, you can thank me in a more practical way. No hurry, but bear it in mind." He went out, saluting a passing townswoman.

Chaim stared through the dusty window, waiting for his father. When he appeared Chaim said quickly, "I promised Leah I would call on her," and was halfway down the street, his coat flapping, before his father had finished nodding.

Mordecai was not at the library. His parents were not at home. Leah was not in and her father thought she was visiting a friend. Which friend? Chaim stood, indecisive, debating what to do next. It was almost three o'clock, when he would normally go back to his studies. He could do so, and let events take their course. The library was not his concern, he did not even wholly approve of it, he found some of the literature dangerously freethinking, not to say Godless.

For a count of ten he stood, deep in thought, considering possibilities. Then he set off at a trot, around the town. He found Yossel at the bakehouse and beckoned him out; a minute later they split up and Yosell dragged David and Shmuel away from a game of cards outside the bathhouse while Chaim found Jochanon stretched out in his garden reading. The five of them hurried back to the library, pausing for a moment at Yossel's father's shop to borrow three huge breadbaskets, while Chaim stopped at the milkman's yard to ask for the loan of a handcart for an hour or two.

By a quarter to six they had done all they could. Chaim flew up the stairs into the house and grabbed every object he could carry that might pass for religious in tone: candlesticks, an embroidered cloth, a brass plate, a silver cup. The boys sat down on the bench, and Chaim opened a holy book. Two library members who had wandered in were pushed onto the bench, the books they carried hastily stuffed into jacket pockets. Chaim was nervous, but he was calmed by one thought: Sergeant Krapoc was a kindly man, and even better, would hardly want to endanger his forthcoming bribe. The visit would be no more than a formality.

The clock nearby struck six, and Chaim gave the signal: the boys began to chant, the sound drowning out all other noise, so that the hammering on the door of the cellar came as a real surprise—they had not heard the policemen's boots clumping down the steps. The door was flung open and Chaim looked up, not at Sergeant Krapoc as he expected, but another policeman. For a moment he was at a loss to know why the face seemed familiar, until he remembered: that night at the Levis', when the police had searched the house. This was the man who had kicked his foot aside. The man with the fires of hate burning in his eyes. He had been promoted; he was a sergeant now. The boys stopped their chanting and swaying, and waited.

The police were clearly surprised and disappointed, glancing at the sergeant for guidance. There were—as yet—no regulations against praying in cellars.

The sergeant, who had remained by the door, walked very slowly around the bare cellar, looking carefully at the shelves, then at Chaim. "What have you done with them?"

Chaim regarded him inquiringly, instinctively stepping back a pace as he met the man's eyes. The sergeant was looking at him as one might examine a poisonous fungus found growing in a dark corner—with an impersonal, curious disgust. It reduced Chaim to an object. The object might be ignored or it might be destroyed, but either way it did not exist as a person.

"What have you done with the books?"

Chaim's mouth was so dry that he was unable to speak. He shook his head.

The sergeant swept the sacred ornaments from the shelf, sending them crashing to the floor. "You Jews think you're clever. But the time will come when your cleverness will not help you." He glanced at the boys. "Military service should take care of some of you, and there are . . . other arrangements possible."

He walked toward the door. In the entrance, Leah and Mordecai stood, gazing in astonishment at the room. Chaim tried to catch Leah's eye, to reassure her and prevent her from speaking, but she was looking around the room in an almost demented manner. Had Chaim been calmer he might have wondered whether there was some other cause for her agitation.

"Where are the—" she began.

"—The others are late. We started the service without them," Chaim broke in hastily. The sergeant's eyes blazed at Mordecai, who drew Leah aside to make room for the policeman to leave.

No one spoke or moved until the sound of their boots had died away down the street. Then Mordecai demanded, "What has happened? Where are the books?"

Chaim told him, with Jochanan and the others joining in, describing their frantic journeys wth the handcart, loading and unloading, the race against time, hiding the books in Jochanan's summer house, staggering up and down the steps with the breadbaskets. Even Chaim sparkled with an animation he normally reserved for the synagogue.

Mordecai said formally, "It was very good of you, Chaim. I'm grateful."

Chaim shrugged. "They would have burned the books. And I know how much the library means to you." But he was looking at Leah as he spoke.

She was examining him intently, like someone memorizing details of a place soon to be left: the tentative smile, the anxious eyes, the gentle face that was still so thin despite the meals Rachel set before him. She looked away, frowning, blinking.

The chatter broke out again . . . they would have to be more careful . . . it would mean moving the library . . . they must beware of informers . . . make new plans. . . .

Under cover of the noise, Leah said quietly to Mordecai, "I cannot do it. I cannot tell him."

He said roughly, "Then I will."

"No." She shook her head. "Everything will go on as arranged."

He looked incredulous. "But that is impossible! You said—"

"I cannot hurt him. It will never be spoken of again."

Leah was very calm. Unnaturally calm, perhaps, but they all agreed that of course she and Chaim knew each other well; one could almost call it a love match, not like some in which the bride might not have seen the groom more than half a dozen times before the wedding day and then never without relations listening and interfering on every side. The preparations for the wedding were lengthy and exhausting. For weeks Rachel and Ruda and Leah were busy.

Earlier, on Yom Kippur, Leah had prayed as always for forgiveness of her sins. But never had she been so sincere. She remembered her past, childish Days of Atonement, when she had prayed mechanically, "Forgive me for sins I may have committed unwittingly," when the worst offense she could summon up was a moment of disobedience to her mother.

Now she prayed fervently for her sins and for herself. Forgive me for . . . for what? For discovering that her body had desires, could respond to someone else in a way she had not dreamed possible . . . in a way that frightened her. . . . Forgive her for loving Chaim and thinking of Mordecai when she woke and when she fell asleep.

Mordecai that summer afternoon, the timber yard deserted, warm and fragrant in the sun, the resin almost intoxicating in the air, and Mordecai finding her (as perhaps she intended?), holding her, touching her. . . .

"Forgive me, Lord . . ."

Rachel was busy with food and drink, the cellar already full of preserves and jars of borscht and wine, and each day adding to the pile. For Leah it was almost unrelieved wretchedness: Hannah had regained her health as if by some miracle cure and, as resident grandmother, was determined that everything should be done properly. She braided Leah's hair into tiny plaits with a small lump of sugar at the base of each, "So you should enjoy a sweet life." Leah had to try on new clothes, be fitted for the wedding dress, and all the time she grew thinner. Rachel was in despair. "Every time we make the dress fit, you grow skinnier! It will hang on you like a sack!" Rachel's movements became increasingly frenzied. So much to be done, so little time. . . .

On the day of her wedding, Leah woke early and looked across to see if Daniel was awake. But the narrow bed was empty. She remembered with a shock that tonight Chaim would have that bed. Daniel would sleep downstairs in a corner of the kitchen from now on.

No breakfast. She must fast until the celebration tonight. But already Rachel was hurrying her, "So much to be done . . ."

They cut her hair. The lumps of sugar in her braids had melted with the warmth of her body and stuck to her scalp, so that every snipping movement was painful. Rachel said sympathetically, "Cry, cry yourself out, it's lucky." But she remained dry-eyed.

They tried the *sheitel* on her, and everyone exclaimed how nice the wig looked, the hair just like her own, and so fashionably dressed. But no more braids bouncing on her shoulders, no more running her fingers through her heavy hair when she washed it. From now on, with her hair cropped short, she would cover her head with a kerchief during the day and with her pious wig at other times. She snatched the wig off and looked in the metal mirror hanging in the kitchen: her face was gaunt, and above it the scarecrow tufts of black hair looked like a scrubbing brush chewed by rats, some still sticking flat to her head with the melted sugar, some standing up on end wildly. Weeping at last, she went to the bathhouse for her immersion in the *mikva*. She bathed first, to wash herself, in the usual little cubicle, then sat like a statue while the attendant cut her fingernails and toenails and gathered up the cuttings to be ceremonially burned. Afterward she went down the steps and into the *mikva* three times, the water green around her and over her head, the attendant calling out in a harsh, birdlike voice, "Here is a true daughter of Israel!"

"Here is a sacrifice on the old altar!" Leah wanted to cry. But then she thought: *Who is making the sacrifice? Nobody forced me. The decision was mine.*

Minsky had offered the use of his house for the wedding feast, and all day a stream of women carried provisions between Leah's home and the merchant's spacious house.

Leah's dress, a warm ivory which Rachel felt was kinder to her pallor than a stark white would have been, was—as predicted—not a good fit.

"I knew it! It hangs on you like a sack!" wailed Rachel when she saw Leah standing in the bedroom, shoulders slumped, arms hanging by her sides in a graceless posture. But the wig and much pinching of her cheeks improved matters, and Rachel thought the veil would help to cover up some of the shortcomings.

Already weak with hunger, Leah was seated on the little bed in the kitchen, waited on by relations she hardly knew she possessed. Not only Ruda and Hannah and Aunt Malka and her mother's two sisters and Mordecai's mother, but half a dozen others as well, all fussed around her, pinching her cheeks, adjusting her wig, and remarking with determination on how lovely she looked. After a while, Chaim was led in by the male relatives. He, too, looked even paler and thinner than usual and kept his eyes on the ground. Leah thought his new silk caftan made him look almost elegant, and with a sudden lifting of the heart she remembered that he was not a stranger, that she loved him like a brother, and that life with him would not be a penance. She smiled as they put the veil on her, and the women exclaimed at her sudden radiance and dissolved into a shower of sentimental weeping.

It was growing dark. Each guest lit a candle, and the procession slowly began to wend its way to the synagogue. The candles guttered for a moment as a breeze swept the long street. Leah's white shoes were thin, and she could feel the curving cobblestones pressing into her through the soles. As a toddler she had fallen over, tripping on the uneven surface, once scraping her nose. In winter, ice made the cobbles treacherous; in summer, dust lay like gray fur between them.

Ahead of her and behind, the long line of candles glimmered and wavered in the darkness. From windows along the street more candles gleamed. And in the synagogue courtyard there was a crowd waiting, men on one side, women on the other, with the richly embroidered canopy, the wedding *chuppa,* held aloft on slender poles, waiting for her.

Chaim was there already. The rabbi lifted the veil from Leah's face and let it fall before beginning the ceremony: prayers, benedictions, the sipping of the wine, then Rachel leading her seven times around the bridegroom. More prayers and the veil lifted for the last time and thrown back. Then Chaim placing the ring on Leah's finger, his voice wobbling, "Behold thou art consecrated unto me, according to the Law of Moses and Israel."

Finally the goblet from which they had sipped, wrapped in a white cloth and stamped underfoot by Chaim, the glass breaking with a loud crack. A cacophony of good wishes erupting from the guests— *Mazel tov!* Good luck!"

Jochanan's father had set lamps blazing in every window, and the house looked like a palace in a picture book. Leah and Chaim, almost fainting from hunger, exhaustion, and nervousness, were conducted to the place of honor. Guests crowded the room, gifts piled up on the long table by the window, and, from those who gave money, small envelopes were tucked into Chaim's pockets.

The moment Chaim had been dreading most was at hand. He had to stand before these people and deliver an impressive speech, but he was not an impressive speechmaker. His tongue seemed to be filling his whole mouth, and his knees were shaking. He stood up, and the chattering around him was replaced by a cheer and then silence. For a moment the silence pressed in on him; he swallowed.

"My dear father, my parents-in-law, Rabbi, friends, and relations, this is a very important day. Today I am a bridegroom. Now what is a bridegroom? A bridegroom is a lucky man, because he has fulfilled the instructions of the Torah: he has found a wife, a prize beyond rubies. But more: a bridegroom is a happy man. Why is he happy? Because he is no longer alone in the world. Because he has found someone to share his joys and sorrows. He has found . . . a partner."

Leah looked up, startled. Why had he chosen that word?

"As I say, he has found someone to share the good times and the bad times, to comfort and be comforted by, to love and be loved by." He paused.

"Leah is known to you all . . ." murmurs and cheers, "so I do not need to tell you of her many skills and good qualities, of her intelligence and her kindness. But there is another quality that she possesses which I would like to speak of.

"These are strange times we live in. Uncertain times, and it may be that black days are again looming upon us. In our history the women of Israel have always played a queenly role, however humble their lives. They have not allowed the enemy—whoever he was—to break their spirit. I know that, whatever happens, Leah has the quality that will help us to fight on and survive. The quality of courage."

There was a moment's puzzled silence before the master of ceremonies led the applause. A strange speech, not the usual thing at all.

Chaim sat down, and Leah, filled with an emotion she could not name, squeezed his hand and flung herself into Jacob's arms, burying her face against his chest. He stroked her head, carefully now, for fear of dislodging the wig. No more affectionate tugs on her thick black hair. "He is a good boy, your Chaim. You will make a good couple."

Across the room Leah saw Mordecai, staring at her. He turned away and began to tease an old man sitting next to him.

The musicians were installed in an alcove at the end of the room; Fishbein, a small monkeylike man who did bookkeeping for the Army, played the fiddle, while his younger brother accompanied him on the flute. Yossel's father had found a cousin, Saul, who played the accordion—in fact, had spent some time in Paris and as a consequence was regarded as a professional. The noise, a mixture of sweeping, lilting music, laughter, shouting, arguing, clapping, stamping, and calling of greetings, roared in Chaim's head like thunder. The dancers moved across his line of vision like ghosts floating past, their outlines blurred.

Men and women did not dance together, except for a few daring young married couples, and they danced linked by a handkerchief, so that the older folk would not be upset by seeing them actually touching. The old men danced, in groups, holding hands, arms raised, heads bobbing, feet nimble. At one point Hannah took to the floor, rheumatism once more forgotten, to circle the room with a vast *challah* loaf in her arms.

Chaim's head ached, but he regarded the crowded room with affection; the traditional ways had the charm of familiarity and around him he felt nothing but goodwill.

At last, when they had been kissed by everyone, congratulated by everyone, given valuable and conflicting advice by everyone, the happy couple, limp from the strain of the day, were escorted back to Jacob's house and into the bridal chamber. Door closed, family departed back to the celebration, the two were at last alone.

Chaim sat down on his bed and Leah on hers. She wondered whether she should begin to undress herself or whether that was the bridegroom's traditional task. For a minute or two they sat in silence, Chaim avoiding her eye. Leah thought: *Probably he is saying the prayer for before approaching your wife.* She would wait.

Presently it would begin, the touching and coming together. They would really be man and wife then, united by their flesh and the fire in their veins. She felt a small fluttering of excitement inside her, and, deciding that even a devout man had prayed long enough, she began to take off her jewelry. Chaim gave her a startled glance and continued to sit on his bed. Leah removed her shoes and then, rather quickly, her white and now rather crumpled dress.

Around the tops of her legs she felt warm and a little shaky, and she turned toward Chaim, wearing only her petticoat and white silk stockings rolled above the knee. He had not moved and was still wearing his silk caftan, and, she saw with amazement, his *hat.* Surely that could not be right? Did really religious men keep their hats on, even at such moments as these?

She began to slip the petticoat off her shoulder and Chaim gave a twitch of anxiety. He cleared his throat noisily. "Leah!" His voice came out too loud, and he hastily brought down the volume. "Leah; this is a little difficult . . ."

"You must not be concerned about me," she said eagerly, "I will do whatever you want, whatever you wish."

He looked increasingly gloomy. "The point is that for years I have learned the duties of a husband; I know the laws and interdictions, I know the legal points and rules of connubial conduct—"

"Good!"

"Yes. But in practical matters . . . details are not always clear . . . the rabbi does not discourse on them. Which is to say, of course in general terms, naturally, we all . . . but there are particular questions . . . in specific areas—"

"You don't know what to do," Leah said.

He flinched. "You must not distress yourself. We cannot be the first to approach this matter in mutual discovery—"

Leah crossed the room, opened her clothes chest, and lifted out a small, battered tin. She reached beneath the bed for a key concealed in a cracked floorboard, unlocked the tin, and took out a scrap of paper. It had been folded and unfolded so often that it was almost falling apart, but the drawings and words were still visible. It was Mordecai's diagram of how a baby is made.

She handed it to Chaim. He took it, puzzled, and gazed at it for a moment. Suddenly the meaning became clear and he put the drawing down, obviously embarrassed.

"How do you come to have this?"

"It is the truth, Chaim. Should we be ashamed of the truth?"

He picked it up again, reluctantly, and looked at it quickly, then looked away. "Yes," he said, "I see." Another pause. "But should we be . . . standing up or lying down?"

Leah had not considered this somewhat technical point. "Perhaps if we try first one way, and then the other . . . ?"

Chaim began to undress, and Leah waited with lively interest to see what he looked like. Danielsche she had seen of course, but a child, she assumed, was not the same. Yet when Chaim had taken off his caftan and shirt he bent over the lamp to blow it out.

"Oh, why?" Leah protested. He looked shocked.

"We cannot approach each other except in the dark, you must know that." At least he was familiar with the Law. Chaim blew out the lamp, finished undressing, and moved toward Leah in the dark. His bare foot stubbed against the bedpost and he let out a yell of pain. He stretched out a hand and encountered her bare flesh. Leah had dropped her petticoat.

Chaim quickly and silently spoke the appropriate blessing, and pressed himself against her hopefully, trying to keep the diagram in mind. Something was definitely wrong, no progress seemed possible. "I think the bed," he said finally. "The Talmud does after all speak of men and women lying together."

"Yes." Leah stepped back. "Chaim, I must open the shutters, it is airless." She flung open the shutters and turned back to him, knowing the moon would be up. The ghostly light flooded into the little room, glimmering silver on his boyish body. Chaim was standing uncertainly by her bed, naked except for his skullcap and his *tallis koton* around his thin shoulders. She had not expected this and found the sight somehow ludicrous.

Perhaps after all the Law knew best: if a man risked looking ridiculous, darkness was preferable. She moved closer to Chaim, closed her eyes, and drew him toward her. She lay back on the bed. And her wig fell off.

She had forgotten about the wig. Did women remove them before "lying with" their husbands? If he kept on his *yarmulkah*, should she not keep on her wig? Considering what a freak she looked without it now, it certainly was as well that the lamp was out.

Stretched out in her narrow bed Leah suddenly began to laugh. They were so ridiculous with their ignorance and their attempts to follow a childish drawing. For a moment she hated Chaim for not knowing what to do, for not being masterful, for not being cruel and full of authority and experience. She opened her eyes again. He was perched on the edge of the bed, and she thought of his chicken-wing shoulders and bony knees, and she started laughing again. It was partly exhaustion, and Chaim realized this.

"I think we should sleep now," he said. "We have plenty of time for learning. We have all our lives." He kissed her quickly on the forehead and she went on laughing until tears ran down her face, and then without being aware of the change she stopped laughing, and she found she was weeping in despair.

Let him kiss me with the kisses of his mouth, for thy love is better than wine . . . the Song of Solomon ran in her head with a new meaning. *His left hand is under my head and his right hand doth embrace me* . . .

But the whole preparation for marriage was an attempt to make the woman as undesirable as possible—an extension of women's exclusion, their separateness. Like the rule that barred women from the synagogue floor and kept them segregated at social gatherings, it was all part of the process of reducing female power and dangerous charm. Cut off the gleaming tresses, blow out the lamp, the woman's body must not be seen even in the moments of love. Even King Solomon, who had loved many strange women, would have found it difficult to compose his passionate song faced with the shorn-headed, rough-handed workhorse a betrothed girl became upon marriage.

She had herself never understood the Song of Solomon properly until she found herself being embraced by Mordecai, the way his hands had moved over her, exploring her. She thrust her face into the softness of the pillow and did not hear Chaim whisper, "Good night." All she could think about was the hot, pine-scented air of the timber yard that afternoon, and her body fluttering like a bird, and the touching. And she knew that even with a lifetime of learning, this would be different. That Chaim might approach her with love, but there would be no fire in the veins.

On April 19, 1903, Easter Sunday coincided with the last day of Passover.

All week an uneasy feeling hung over the town, a sense of waiting. The rumors from the big towns were not reassuring: the activities of the Bund were proving an irritant to the authorities, and the activists found hostility even among their own families.

"Why must they stir up trouble? If we stay quiet and keep the peace nothing need happen," Rachel said fretfully. "This is not Warsaw. We have no trouble with the townsfolk, hardly any, not often at all."

Chaim was at the *Beth Hamidrash*, where he spent an increasing amount of time, lost in the byways of Talmudic exploration, poring over the old books, the chanting. It was Friday and he would soon be home to collect his bundle of clean underclothes and set out for the bathhouse with Jacob and Daniel.

Rachel, busy as usual, hurried into the kitchen wearing her "so much to do, so little time!" expression and began setting out dishes. She kept glancing irritably at Leah as though expecting some response. At last Rachel said vehemently, "This is the twentieth century. People are civilized. We are not living in the Middle Ages."

Leah did not contradict her mother. She touched her wig, its stiff strands set in a suitably modest style. Beneath it her own hair had grown again. She looked around the room, saw her grandmother crouch nearer the fire, sighing heavily, her face lined and crumpled like a screwed-up brown paper bag, her sagging body twisted with rheumatism. Only Hannah's *sheitel* remained unchanged: neither age nor anxiety whitened the black wig, which sat with shining, incongruous youthfulness on the old face.

The town was very quiet, the churches full, the streets empty. Only the Jewish quarter still pulsed with life, the last few hours of marketing, dealing, cutting and sawing and stitching, lending and borrowing, before the Sabbath put an end to it.

In Warsaw, the Bund members were busy with great plans: every town was divided between allegiance to one party or another, one ideal or another—Socialists or Zionists or something else again: "Gather five Jews together and you have five opposition parties," Chaim said wearily. The Russians, Leah reflected, need do nothing: if divide and rule was the aim, it was being done for them by the Jews themselves.

Every café, every shop, every stall in the marketplace had its knot of men discussing possibilities. So much discussion. So little achieved. Talk. Theory. Debate. Abstract problems. Analysis. "Why must there be a revolution? I'll tell you why there must be a revolution. For three reasons . . ." "Why is Zionism contrary to God's law? For the following reasons . . ." Examine the argument, question it, demolish it. But action? Action was not natural to them, traditionally, and they were, above all, people of tradition.

The year before, a friend of Mordecai's, a shoemaker called Leckert, had tried to assassinate the governor of Vilna, shooting wildly at the man as he came out of the circus. The boy had failed, of course, but he was executed all the same. And the reprisals followed. So what had that piece of recklessness achieved? Families bereaved, yet another ukase issued; measures introduced against the "revolutionaries"—in other words, the Jews.

And so the town waited, nervously.

The men began arriving about midday on Sunday, cartloads of them, strangers, carrying no baggage, and without, it seemed, anything in particular to occupy their attention.

One, brawny and heavy-shouldered with a face like a malformed turnip, brought a horse to be shod at Mendel's forge. Generally a customer exchanged gossip while the work was done, Mendel mumbling his words around the nails he held in his mouth, but this stranger, stolid and expressionless, stood silent after a brief greeting in Russian, his gaze idly moving over the maze of streets that led into the market. Mendel felt a tightening of muscles in his stomach. Perhaps he was hungry, that must be it. Surely he could not be frightened of this lumpish man? It was absurd, nothing out of the ordinary was happening.

"What brings you to town?" he asked, also in Russian, as he wrenched off the worn iron shoe and threw it aside.

The stranger did not reply at once. Then he said, carelessly, "I was called in to control some vermin, the town is having trouble with rats. . . ."

Mendel found his lungs suddenly needed more air. He took a quick breath, like a gulp, and nodded slowly. "Over by the warehouse I suppose. I never know what is going on at the other end of town."

There was no response. Mendel hammered in a nail and looked up fleetingly, to find the man staring down at him. Perhaps it was because the blacksmith—stooped over the horse's hoof—seemed much smaller than the stranger, that Mendel felt for a moment like some tiny animal gazing up at a hunter. He felt suddenly trapped, cornered, the man's heavy boots looming, mud-caked and scarred. He felt the boot would move in a second, smashing into his body, crushing it, and he heard himself give a pathetic, ridiculous squeak as life was extinguished.

Mendel straightened, speaking firmly, despite the fluttering breathlessness he felt. "You work over Easter then?"

The man smiled. His eyes were again moving across the network of streets visible from the wide door of the forge. "Rats are rats any day of the week."

* * *

Jacob said soothingly to Rachel, his glance resting on Daniel, "Nothing is going to happen."

"Isn't that what I have been saying?" Rachel's voice was a little shrill. Chaim and Leah exchanged a quick glance and went on eating. The old lady, munching noisily, seemed unaware of the tension.

In the time since her marriage Leah had come to accept that, for Chaim, the greatest excitement, the fiercest thrill was to be found in the airless little *Beth Hamidrash*, losing himself in the past. But she had no such escape. She had to remain in the unsatisfactory present.

The little bedroom had witnessed warmer scenes than the wedding night failure, but it was warmth rather than passion that the two shared. She wondered how Mordecai was. They had received letters from him, full of the work the students were doing, promising great things. *What great things?* Leah wondered sourly. *More strikes? More botched assassinations? More reprisals?*

Daniel said, "Someone is at the door."

Rachel rose to her feet, but Jacob shook his head slightly. "Who is it?"

Muffled through the door: "Mendel."

Jacob drew back the bolts and Mendel almost fell into the room. He was breathing unevenly and had obviously been running. He stood blinking at them. "It is beginning," he said.

They had all been declaring confidently how normal everything was, yet now nobody found it necessary to ask him what he meant.

Rachel gave one despairing moan, then closed her lips tightly and said no more. They waited, listening, trying to hear from where it would come, whether it was near. Usually trouble began with a gang of drunken peasants or a group of fevered churchgoers inflamed by a Christ-killer sermon, rushing out into the street and breaking down a few doors. But this was different.

"There are men with carts at the entrance to all the streets leading into our part of the town," Mendel told them. "They are moving slowly, but they are covering every street."

"Have they sabers? Horses?" Hannah asked, with memories of the Cossacks galloping through the streets of her youth. He shook his head.

"They have fire."

Fire? They were all shocked into silence.

"What are they doing?" Leah finally demanded. If no one else would ask, she preferred to know.

"They have kerosene in the carts and rags and sticks. And they have axes. They smash a window, throw in a blazing torch, and wait. If the family runs out they shout, 'Vermin escaping' and club them down. If they don't appear, the men nail planks across the door to trap them inside while the house burns."

Now they could smell it, the smoke. And hear faint noises, growing louder.

Rachel asked, without panic, "What shall we do?"

"Perhaps we can still reach the river, get across."

Mendel broke in, "They are stationed at the riverbank already. And the bridge is guarded."

Chaim suddenly sprang to his feet, almost knocking over the chair. "Father is alone! I must go to him."

Mendel said, "He is not there. I knocked at the house, on my way. I thought to bring him with me, but the house was empty."

Chaim looked distraught. Jacob said, "He will be with friends, perhaps they can get him out of town."

"We are encircled," Mendel said, shaking his head.

Jacob stood, silent for a moment, biting almost absently on his thumbnail. "So we are . . ." *Trapped,* he was going to say, *like the rats we are described as. We are in a corner and we will scream and burn or be driven out to have our skulls smashed in.*

"So we are . . . obviously better off here," he ended briskly. "Mendel, will you stay with us?"

"I have others to warn. At least they can be prepared. *Shalom.*" He hurried away as Jacob locked the door behind him. They heard him knocking at the Steins', next door.

It was Hannah, surprisingly, who took charge. The frail, bent figure gave orders, her voice harsh and cracking with the strain. As a girl Hannah had lived through the bad times, the massive pogroms, and she had not forgotten. The experience had taught her what was needed now.

She hurried them along as they followed instructions: They pulled all the wooden furniture across the room to stand against the street walls. A large cupboard was placed near the window, and Rachel flung down tablecloths and rags next to the door and the windows. Then she began filling every container in sight with water from the two large barrels that she kept in the cellar—it was no longer safe to go out to the pump in the street. Leah, Chaim, and Daniel carried the water up to the bedrooms while Rachel soaked bedcovers and sheets and dragged them up the stairs, packing them around the door to the upper part of the house. Hannah hurled water into the big stove and poured more water over the wooden stairs, drenching the walls, expertly soaking everything in the center of the house and leaving only the street wall dry. The door from the street to the shop was barred and shuttered but they dragged tables and chairs over to stack against it, and against the door to the yard. So often Jacob had talked of putting in a big window to the shop, to make it light, but now they gave thanks. One room less to defend.

By now the noise from outside was very loud indeed, no more than a street away, and they worked feverishly, pouring more and more water on the stairs until Hannah told them to stop: they must keep some water in reserve. She gave them final orders, muttering the words quickly, a wild witch figure, her face streaked with dirt and perspiration, her wig awry. "We must not move when the torch is thrown in. It must appear to have set fire to the room, and be seen to blaze. If we put it out they will see and throw in more."

This was the worst time: the preparations made, they blew out the lamps and waited in the darkness, huddled out of sight on the stone steps leading to the cellar.

The street was full of the sound of splintering wood and glass tinkling to the ground; the smoke already seeped in under the front door, swirling in like a spy, seeking them out in their inadequate hiding place. Among the crashing noises and the boots clumping on the cobbles came the human voices, some shouting in pursuit or giving orders, others crying out, calling, children screaming for mothers who could no longer protect them.

Leah crouched, holding her hands over her ears, trying to blot out the sounds, trying not to see in her mind the terrified creatures younger than Danielsche, some clutched in mothers' arms (though that proved no defense), fleeing from flaming homes or trapped inside, as the houses blazed like huge beacons.

Then it came, so loud that they jumped: the crash on the shutters—axes splintering the wood. The window gave way, and the room was suddenly brilliant with the light of the fires outside. Leah caught a glimpse of a man's head at the window and almost shrieked aloud, positive that he had seen her huddled against the wall. Then the torch thudded in, scattering sparks and flames, and the rags around the window caught at once, blazing up fiercely.

Then the rags at the bottom of the front door began to burn, the smoke pouring under the door into the street. Hannah had thought it out well. The effect was of a house burning briskly.

On both sides of the door, people waited. Inside, choking in the thickening smoke, holding wet cloths to their faces, the family waited, watching the flames spread, watching the wood begin to catch. How long dare they let the fire burn unchecked?

Outside, patiently, the men waited, axes and clubs ready. After a few minutes, orders were shouted and the hammering began again. Planks were nailed across the door and window to prevent the vermin scuttling out.

Then the thuds and crashes again, from next door this time. But now the screams came quickly, for Stein had decided to try to reason with the men. He opened his door—and the vermin were dealt with, swiftly, before they could argue their case.

Chaim and Jacob crept forward, soaking cloths wrapped around their mouths, to throw more water onto the floor. Chaim had a long-handled broom, and he edged nearer the window to stir up the flaming rags and make the conflagration more convincing. As he leaned forward, cautiously prodding the blaze, one of the rat hunters, disappointed by the swiftness of the Steins' extermination, lobbed another torch over the crisscross of nailed-up planks and into the kitchen. It struck Chaim full on the side of the head, felling him and igniting his clothes in a sheet of flame.

Like a cat, Leah streaked across the room, flung the rug over Chaim, and hauled him by the heels away from the worst of the blaze. The room was filled with smoke, choking her, burning her lungs. Her face, like Rachel's, was contorted with panic, but they made no noise. The hunters' ears were tuned to the sound of any squeak their quarry might make.

Her stomach turned at the sickly smell of burning flesh: the side of Chaim's head was raw and blackened, the hair scorched away. His body, too, had been burned when his clothing caught fire. One hand hung from his sleeve like a lump of half-cooked meat.

Rachel, Daniel, and Hannah half-carried, half-dragged him down the cellar steps, and Rachel began to attend to his burns while Leah took his place in the kitchen. Jacob, eyes streaming, started to order her back to the cellar, but then he nodded. She pushed at the burning rags, pressing them to the street wall. They blazed bright through the broken window, licking at the planks. The front of the cupboard was on fire, though Jacob continued to pour water over its back and sides.

103

The shadows leaped and shrank as the flames rose and fell: the room was an oven, and for all the water they had slopped on the floor, tongues of fire took hold—one licking a forgotten curtain, another a wooden mantelshelf—and the blaze began to spread. Now, creeping closer to the window, Jacob peered through the smoke and saw that the rat hunters had moved on. He jerked his head and Leah joined him, flinging more water on the shelf that was now burning steadily, and stamping the tattered curtain underfoot.

Coughing and retching painfully, they began to damp down the blaze, leaving the window until last. The fire must be visible, without becoming a funeral pyre. . . .

Hours passed. Hannah had sent Jacob and Daniel to the bedroom windows to watch for the return of the men. By each window they had ready a cooking pot filled with oil-soaked rags. It was difficult to see what the street looked like. Across the road the house was almost gutted, and thick smoke from their own downstairs window obscured the view. Suddenly Jacob pulled back from the window and gave a signal. A moment later, the cooking pots were flaming in the windows. From the street it seemed as if the house was burning strongly, upstairs as well as down.

The men went by without pausing. When footsteps and wheels could no longer be heard, the family put out the flames. The kitchen was ruined—the walls charred and filthy; the mantelshelf destroyed, the beautiful blue-tiled stove blackened and cracked.

They gathered in the middle of the room, moving very slowly, fatigue and pain making every movement an effort. Chaim's hand and head were bound up with cabbage leaves, herbs, and strips of clean rag, but to some extent all were burned, their hands raw, clothes singed. They gazed at each other, dazed, scorched, their eyes shining in the darkness.

Leah suddenly became aware that she had lost her wig. It smouldered among the rags by the window, looking like a small dead animal. They all listened, hearing only the occasional crash of a falling beam in a blazing house, and a cry that might have been a shout or a scream. At last, silence.

Still they waited, unmoving, in the kitchen, huddled together as the hours passed. When the first dawn light filtered through the broken shutters, Rachel stirred, moved stiffly to the stove, and then, bringing her sore, burnt hands up, she clamped them over her mouth and at last began to weep. She turned to Jacob. "I was about to make some tea. And there is no fire to boil the water!"

Seeing her stricken face, Leah and Daniel began to laugh unsteadily, and the others too, even Rachel, while her tears were still tracing a sooty path down her cheeks.

Jacob said, cautiously, "God has protected us." He turned to Hannah for confirmation. His mother sat, crouched in her customary pose, on the basement steps. But as he touched her shoulder she toppled and fell into his arms, light as a bundle of twigs. The old lady had summoned up a last burst of strength for the campaign. But there would be no more battles.

Even grief and mourning must wait their turn. Rachel, who had quarreled daily with Hannah, cried noisily for a few moments while Jacob laid his mother's body gently on Daniel's bed and covered her.

It was time to go outside. Leah tied back her hair and bound a kerchief over her head. At that moment she knew that she would never wear a wig again. Jacob drew back the bolt, but the door was nailed shut with planks. Daniel got an ax from the cellar and smashed open a shutter. Then, carefully, Jacob and Leah climbed out. She pressed her lips together, biting them, unable to hold back a moan of horror as she looked around. The street was littered with debris, still smoking. And with bodies. Some had been clubbed down as they ran; others, trapped in their flaming homes, had jumped from upper windows to be smashed on the cobblestones. Some were hideously unrecognizable; others, appallingly, looked unmarked, seemingly asleep, until she approached nearer and saw a neighbor, his child, the crushed skull, the broken neck. The Steins, all four, lay sprawled at their door as though felled by the same stroke. The blood had dyed the pavement a thick, rusty red.

Jacob wrenched the plank from their door, and the others limped out, Rachel supporting Chaim. At other windows, Leah saw furtive movements, proof of life. They ran from house to house, whispering names, trying to discover who survived. Two doors away the Adlers were at their window, feebly attempting to free themselves. They passed the baby out to Leah while they struggled with the planks. The Adlers had, years before, made a second, lower cellar with a tunnel for ventilation. Last night it had saved them.

Jacob said, "I shall stay here to help people out of their houses. Go with Danielsche to the *shul* and see if anyone is there—if the building is still standing."

Chaim, too weak to go with them, whispered with hope, "Father will be there."

Rachel began to drag out the ruined furniture, while Leah and Daniel, eyes flicking away from bodies as they passed, hurried down the wrecked street toward the synagogue. As they crept around the corner they stopped, staring in amazement.

Behind its railings, the synagogue building was unmarked. Not one of its tall windows was broken, not a beam charred. Its huge doors were intact. And emerging from it was a crowd—men, women, and children, blinking in the light, pale with fear and exhaustion, but unharmed. At one side Leah saw Chaim's father. She hurried over to him. "What happened here?"

He shook his head and shrugged, "Every minute we expected them to break in, murder us all, but they just passed by."

It was Golomstok who supplied a possible explanation: "Who were these men they sent to our town? Strangers. Russians. In the night they see this building with its domes and tall windows, surrounded by a courtyard and railings. They have been told to attack our homes, our dwellings. The orders are plain. They do not recognize our synagogue —perhaps they think it is some town building—maybe a church!"

But were they safe yet? Had the strangers gone, or would there be more rat catching today? Cautiously, boys crept through the streets to the main town square, to the police station, to the town hall. No carts remained. No men. The town slept. For this occasion, at least, it was over.

Broad daylight now, and the town awoke, self-consciously attempting to maintain normality. The night's events were not of local making. This time, peasants could murmur sympathetically—and in some cases sincerely—over a Jewish acquaintance's misfortune. The Czar was a friend to no one, though such opinions were best kept to oneself. Certainly it would not do to become involved; informers were everywhere. The townsfolk kept to their own end of the town while the ghetto buried its dead.

The task was an appalling one. The Talmud said "the whole body" must be buried, and so the very blood-soaked earth beneath the battered head or torn limb must be scraped and scooped up; even the cobblestones pried out of their places, "so that the poor souls may rest in peace."

The burying took a long time. Normally the wails and cries of mourners would be loud in the air. But now, with disaster on such a scale—the angel of death calling not to pluck one selected victim from a family but sweeping half the ghetto under his black wing—there was only a muted sound of weeping, not in the open-mouthed, open-hearted style of the funeral ceremony, but in the deep, racking, inward way that marks an incommunicable woe.

Mourning was a luxury none could afford. There was a desperate, almost superstitious need to erase as far as possible the signs of the pogrom. Ruined furniture and possessions were taken by the cartload to the dump outside the town; the blackened walls left standing were scraped down, the littered streets cleared inch by inch. The women worked quickly and silently. Officially, nothing was said. It seemed almost as though the incident had not occurred at all. Only the gaping, gutted houses, the people missing from the congregation, gave the lie to the charade of normality.

Later, when the news came in from other towns, they realized they had been lucky. "At Kishinev," Hirschl told them, "the pogrom lasted three days. The whole Easter holiday was celebrated with killing."

"Zionists are being watched, arrests are being made," Jacob commented, reading the paper from Warsaw. "The Czar is getting interesting advice from this man Von Plehve. He says, 'The revolution will be stifled in Jewish blood.' What good will that do? How many Jews are there in Russia? Will killing them prevent anything?"

Leah took the paper from him and read on. She felt starved of life, and she seized on occasional letters from Mordecai like crumbs from the banqueting halls where decisions were being made.

"Theodore Herzl has been to St. Petersburg," he wrote, "to ask

Von Plehve to stop persecuting the Zionist societies. The wily old vulture said that if the Zionists were committed to establishing a homeland for the Jews *elsewhere*, he certainly would not stand in their way. . . . In other words, he'd be pleased if we would all trot off to Palestine. Which is just what we cannot do if we want to be part of the future of this country."

Jacob had lost almost his entire stock in the pogrom: the contents of the shop was ruined, cracked and split or furred with a thick bloom of sooty black. Replacing it would be a slow and expensive business. Leah felt the pawnshop moving nearer.

Spring came and summer; the year passed in a sort of numbness. They always prayed for fine weather on Succoth, the Feast of Tabernacles—particularly Rachel, who hated getting her wig wet. And Jacob was firm about building a properly flimsy structure, as instructed in the Talmud, ". . . through which the stars may be seen." ("And the wind may blow" commented Rachel tartly.)

In previous years Leah had enjoyed the special feeling of eating outdoors surrounded by the fragrant, leafy trellis of the *succah*, on cold nights wrapped in her father's coat. But this year she felt different about it: perhaps it was the sight of the abandoned houses on all sides, their beams exposed like blackened bones, that reminded her of the last Passover night; or Chaim's head, the pink, lumpy scar where the flaming torch had struck him and on which the hair would never grow again. Or his hand with the tight, bright pink scarring. Perhaps the very flimsiness of the *succah* in which they sat reminded her how insubstantial their safety was.

Whatever the causes, the uneasiness she felt about her birthplace grew stronger. Sometimes she imagined herself taking flight, swooping into one street after another, a great bird the color of night, peering in through different windows, hovering over other rooftops to eavesdrop on other families, to see their private faces and catch their hidden thoughts. Did anyone know what anyone else was thinking? Gossip and talk were endless, but who spoke out about his secret fears? What were they thinking, the shopkeepers, as they bargained, as they fought over a kopek? Did their days fill their minds? Or was there an inner compartment where lamentations, cries for help, despair, were all shut away and silenced in the cause of survival and the struggle for a livelihood?

That autumn Leah wrote to Mordecai in Warsaw that she was

prepared to do more to help the Bund; she hardly knew what form her help could take, but she was willing. The answer came sooner than she expected. The following week, when she returned from market, Mordecai was waiting for her, full of news.

For months the Polytechnic had been seething with revolutionary activity. Classes had become little more than an excuse for debating sessions. "Even the professors have become involved—the discussions go on through the term, speakers are smuggled in: P.P.S., the Social Democrats—even the Bund!"

There had to be some kind of climax to it all, and finally the explosion had occurred: a meeting, a call for action, resolution, professors making anti-Czarist speeches, enthusiasm getting out of hand: "Someone snatched the portrait of the Czar off the wall of the hall, and a moment later it was burning—right there in the middle of the floor."

The next day the Polytechnic was closed, other colleges shut down, with the students—and in several cases the professors—busy demonstrating, holding meetings, spreading the word. Then some arrests and deportations to Siberia were swiftly carried out and another little uprising was nipped in the bud.

"How were you not arrested?" Leah asked, amazed.

Mordecai sprang up, arms waving, dramatizing the story: "They came in the night to the lodgings, to check our papers. I heard the wheels of the post carriage—you remember one of the drivers married my cousin Rivkah? I jumped straight out of the window onto the coach, praying it would be the right driver. I was lucky. We were out of town before they had been through the house."

Officially Mordecai was studying and helping out in his father's almost nonexistent business. Unofficially, he was working for the Bund. He called in Leah and the old group. Packages arrived, delivered by the helpful post-coach driver, and Leah and the others distributed the Socialist proclamations, reading them first so that at least they could answer any questions that might be thrown their way. After a while the packages grew too dangerous: too conspicuous to be risked.

"We can provide our own copies," Mordecai announced cheerfully. "I know a man who can get me a hectograph copier."

The following week the great Peszno revolutionary duplicating enterprise began: Leah and Jochanan learned how to operate the hectograph, laboriously making the master copy with the special ink, and then carefully pressing it into the gelatin bed. Then, vainly trying to keep paper and fingers clean, they attempted the next stage. Copies were certainly made, but whether they were readable was another question. The group left them everywhere, all over town, slipped under doors, behind counters, through open windows.

There was much talk of capitalism and workers' solidarity and encouragement to strike for better conditions, but for most of them, finding time to help the underground between working in the bakery or bathhouse or marketplace, was all part of an exciting game. But Mordecai fretted, feeling under-used. He was not fooled by the letters of congratulation that headquarters managed to get through to him— he knew they were merely playing at revolution, while in the deeper waters real risks were being taken.

Then things changed. When Chaim came home from the *Beth Hamidrash* one afternoon, Leah said, "We're going to visit Uncle Simeon."

"Why now?"

"Because Mordecai has heard from headquarters and needs Simeon's help."

Chaim's spirits dropped. Mordecai's needs tended to intrude increasingly into their lives. "More revolution? God's will is what matters. What will you achieve with all this striving and plotting if you do not ask God's help in the enterprise?"

"*You* ask God's help," Leah said sharply. "You are on closer terms with Him. Meanwhile we'll talk to Uncle Simeon. Surely God won't mind having an assistant?"

They waited for the train outside town and climbed aboard. As always, in addition to the men traveling for business and the inevitable handful of soldiers, there were a couple of families laden with bundles and babies, on the move to a new country, hoping for a new life. Leah watched them, feeling not so much pity as irritation: *Why must they always run away?* Mordecai had said once that they were all trained in submission, their very elders practiced it, encouraged it, enforced it. Suppose they were to fight back? Then she looked at the gaunt, shortsighted men, the thin women dragged down by their babies. Of course, fight back. Easy, against sabers and clubs and heavy boots. She felt a stab of shame for her earlier irritation.

Simeon welcomed the couple warmly. He looked in astonishment at Leah, so energetic and so modern, with no wig, her own dark hair tied neatly in a bun. She was a young woman now, and filled with ideas in the manner of the young. But she had always been bursting with ideas, even as a child. He remembered her legs and arms like sticks, thin little face, and narrow eyes taking in everything. How she asked questions! But now she seemed to have answers of her own. It was all talk of the Party and workers and Socialist internationals.

Then came the reason for the visit: "There is to be a Party congress in Germany and some delegates must be smuggled across the frontier to attend. Some will need our help. They will have false papers and temporary passes issued by a magistrate, but even so they will need help to get through."

To Leah's surprise Simeon was not keen to get involved. "I look after people, individuals in need," he said. "It seems to me that your Party doesn't really require my help."

But in the end he agreed. He would be at the railway station to smooth the path of the delegates. He and Chaim discussed ways of making the passage easier. And then the subject was dropped and they devoted themselves to Malka's vast dinner.

When the delegates arrived in town, even Mordecai was daunted by the task of getting them unnoticed past the customs barriers. A dozen strapping young men with hard, quick eyes and a way of standing that was at once relaxed and aggressive. How on earth were they to be explained away?

Chaim and Simeon found an answer: long, Hasidic gabardines, outsize black hats, and lumpy, untidy-looking bundles. Dressed so collars turned up to their ears and laden with parcels, they might get through. There were two danger points on the journey: the embarkation, and the customs check before they were allowed into Germany. Simeon could help them past the first, but for the second they needed a man whose beard and earlocks would stand scrutiny. Mordecai said thoughtfully, "What we need is one genuine, studious, innocent Jew."

"Yes, I suppose so," Chaim said absently. He stopped and blinked rapidly at Mordecai. "No! I am not a member of your group; I do not even support all that you stand for!"

"I don't ask you to support us, just help get us through. You will even have false papers, no one can trace you, there will be no risk afterward. It's for Poland, surely you care about that? Would you support the Czar instead? All who are not for us are against us."

Chaim sighed. Mordecai and Leah both had a certain relentlessness of manner when their wishes were opposed. He agreed to go. Dressed in his own clothes, he took charge of the passes and agreed to step forward if questions needed answering.

111

At the checkpoint, leaving the delegates in the background, he handed in the passes and waited with the others to have them returned. As each name was called out, the owner would step forward to retrieve his papers. Waiting nervously in line, Chaim suddenly felt dizzy; the blood drained away from his head. Too late it occurred to him that he had not examined his own false papers. He did not know the name he was traveling under.

For a moment he contemplated flight, but they would catch him. He could not even get back on the train because without papers he would not be allowed to reenter Poland. He stood, frozen, his mind blank. This was his punishment for meddling in politics. At least with false papers he would not implicate the family, but he was trapped. He could see Mordecai, up ahead, but could not reach him. Worn out by tension, he felt unable to stand, to move another step. He sank to the ground, supporting himself on the bundle of books and clothes. He was so tired that his head drooped. Slumped there, he listened, eyes closed, to the slow roll call of names and responses. He prayed fiercely for God's forgiveness for the duplicity he had taken part in, hoping only that the cause was good, that this socialism he was helping would indeed allow the Polish people a freer life and the Jews the tranquility of worship. As he finished praying, an idea tentatively presented itself. Not a great idea, but it might work. He remained slumped, his limbs slack, eyes closed. Feigning sleep, he actually drifted into it.

He was awakened by a thump in the ribs from a boot and a roar of derisive laughter. He struggled to his feet, blinking at the customs man.

"You Jews. You'll never amount to anything, feeble lot you are. Less praying and more work would do you a lot of good. Build up your muscles, give you some stamina. Here."

The customs man thrust the papers forward, and Chaim took them, still blinking. Everyone else had been waved through. He quickly joined the others on the train.

When the delegates had returned and gone their various ways, life in town seemed unbearably dull. It was boredom as much as anything that led Mordecai to set up the Peszno fund for arming the Bund.

"Asking for contributions is no good," he said impatiently. "With money so scarce, we could hardly finance a bow and arrow through contributions. We must be inventive."

112

At the end of several months of inventive and tiring activity Mordecai called the group together and made a stirring announcement: they had raised enough money to make a significant contribution to the arming of the Bund! In practical terms—one revolver. Everyone cheered and Yossel asked about ammunition. "That will come later," Mordecai said hurriedly.

The revolver was purchased in some secrecy and the good news passed on to headquarters. The gun, carefully wrapped in layers of clean white linen, was looked after by each of them in turn while they waited for a reply, for further instructions. But headquarters had other things to worry about at the time—the Russo-Japanese War was keeping the government busy and the Bund took advantage of the lull in arrests to stage demonstrations and cause disruption wherever possible. So no one actually found time to tell Mordecai what to do with the revolver. They continued to pass it from one to another, taking great pains to keep it clean and to ensure that parents remained in ignorance of its existence.

In January came the news of the Bloody Sunday in St. Petersburg, where a workers' demonstration had been fired on by troops. Perhaps this was the start of something. Mordecai, who had the revolver at the time, cleaned it yet again. He wished they had managed to raise money for ammunition but things had been bad that winter: even Jochanan's father had been hit by lack of business; Jacob's small savings had gone to try to rebuild his ruined stock. The Shoobotel family, penniless at the best of times, could barely scrape enough to stay alive. Benjamin was not healthy, but he helped the new man at the forge, and Mordecai earned a few coins writing letters to relatives abroad on behalf of unlettered neighbors.

"Things are getting very bad," Leah said somberly.

Mordecai flung out his arms in excitement. "All the better! You don't get a revolution when people are comfortable. There is a delicate balance between need and earnings . . . if you can maintain that, people will put up with a great deal. But if that balance is upset things begin to happen. Already the peasants are muttering about the injustices of the landlords; even in the armed forces there are ripples . . ."

He is beginning, Leah thought, *to talk like a public meeting.* Sometimes, she felt that politics was very bad for conversation.

But what he said was true, she found. Chaim, who still went to listen to the military band when they played in the square, heard from some of the soldiers that they were growing restive about the conditions they lived in. They knew something of what was going on. "Fifty thousand men were lost in two weeks, fighting the Japanese last September. It could be our turn next." They lived and died like cattle and they were becoming aware of it. It was a bad winter.

Perhaps in an attempt to break out of the depression that hung over the town, the Purim festivities erupted with greater spirit than usual that spring: the streets were filled with children in fancy dress— miniature versions of Queen Esther, the hero Mordecai, King Ahasuerus, and Haman—the evil counselor with his ambitions of genocide, foiled by a neat palace counterplot. "The first Jewish conspiracy . . ." Mordecai commented dryly.

"Now it came to pass in the days of Ahasuerus . . ." The children sat spellbound in the synagogue, fingering their finery, listening to descriptions of a long-dead Persian kingdom that once a year sprang to life and color in the mouths and minds of worshipers. "Fine linen and purple, silver rings . . . drink in vessels of gold and royal wine in abundance."

And at every mention of the hero, Mordecai, the children cheered loudly, and each time they heard the name of Haman, whistles, hisses, stamping, and the clatter of wooden rattles filled the synagogue, deafening the indulgent congregation.

The splendor of the palace they could only imagine; the characters were names in the Book of Esther. But the situation was one they were all familiar with, even the youngest: the recurring need for someone in authority to decide it was time to root out the stranger in their midst, the foreigner with his foreign ways of worship, whose Sabbath fell on a different day, the man who would not bow: the threat, the outsider casting a shadow of otherness, the enigma, the Jew.

Later, hurrying home, Rachel set out the "Haman's ears" made of golden pastry with a dark, glistening poppyseed filling, and the neighborhood was fragrant with honey and rosewater, vanilla and chocolate, as plates wrapped in white cloths were carried from house to house. The sun shone, spirits rose. Drinking was never a ghetto pastime, but on Purim it was ordained that the wine should flow.

The mood changed from that day. Spring came early and the crops were good. The indications from Moscow and St. Petersburg were encouraging for once. The Czar, it appeared, was considering . . . the Czar was discussing . . . the Czar felt the time was approaching . . . and finally, unbelievably, in August came the news: The Czar had granted the Imperial Duma. There would be a lower house of representatives, an elective legislative council.

"True, they will be responsible to the government," Leah told Jacob, "but still, it means representation, more than most people would have dared to hope for."

The town buzzed, the differences between Jew and Gentile, between innkeeper and policeman, debtor and creditor forgotten. It was time to celebrate. The newspaper from Warsaw carried the words that few had seriously believed they would ever live to see: "Freedom! Long live the constitution!"

Elders of the various synagogues were approached to organize their people in a grand parade of loyal thanks to the government the following day.

Leah studied the newspaper, but facts were hard to grasp, since so much of the space was filled with jubilant proclamations and formal statements of gratitude. Mordecai was due back from Warsaw and she watched for him by the window. When he came in sight she flung open the door, keen to hear all he had to say, and to give him the local news. "There is to be a grand procession in the morning—" She saw his expression and stopped.

"They throw you a crust and you leap for it like a mongrel! I'm joining no grateful procession. If I march it will be with the workers, to restate our demands."

More demands? She was crestfallen. But the more they discussed it the more she saw that Mordecai was right, as usual; that they should stand firm for justice and that this "freedom" was a sop. But how should they make their views known? He intended to canvass the town at once, making contact with any militant worker groups. There would be support from the workers. "Anyone who cares about justice should be prepared to march for his beliefs."

Over supper, Leah broke the news that she intended to join the workers' march. Rachel was at first disbelieving, then scornful, then angry, and finally she burst into tears. She turned on Jacob and Chaim. "This is your fault, both of you! Always she has been indulged, spoiled. As a child by her father and now by her husband. For shame! A good Jewish girl marching like some peasant woman with no education and no morals!"

Leah began to laugh. Rachel's wig was crooked and her face flushed with fury. She began to clatter the pots and pans noisily.

Leah appealed to Jacob: "You do understand? This so-called

freedom does nothing to guarantee the workers a better way of life. The Czar is as powerful as ever. The exploitation of the masses continues. That is why we march against it. We want more."

Jacob thought: *She sounds as if she is addressing a public meeting.* He shrugged. "Let us hope it is not too much."

She nodded at her brother. "Hirschl? You must have *some* opinion."

"Oh, I have an opinion, but you won't like it. I mistrust revolutionaries, because they say they want freedom, but what they really want is power."

She turned to Chaim. "Are you against me too?"

He threw up his hands helplessly, "When were workers not exploited? And if your workers gain control, shall they not exploit those in their power, as Hirschl says?"

"No, no. It will be brotherhood, a Socialist brotherhood!" She knew she had got her way.

When her parents went to bed, she and Chaim stayed down in the kitchen. She had put Daniel to bed in their room for the night, and Hirschl had tactfully gone to bed, shutting the door into the corridor. After a while there was a tapping at the front door. Mordecai, Jochanan, and a man from town, unknown to Leah, came in quickly.

"Have you got it?" they asked.

Leah nodded, and produced her old red winter skirt, with the seam already ripped open. She cut out a rectangle, spread the cloth on the table, and began to stitch lengths of white tape to the flannel, the tape forming words: LONG LIVE THE REVOLUTION, DOWN WITH THE CZAR, DOWN WITH TYRANNY, LONG LIVE POLAND.

One sentence was in Yiddish, the next Polish. The work was slow and they took it in turn, when fingers began to ache. Then the banner had to be attached securely to two slim poles. It was long past midnight and she could see Chaim's eyelids drooping wearily. Jochanan had gone home, and the stranger, Stefan, was dozing by the range. She and Mordecai worked on, sore fingers pushing the thick needles through the red cloth. She felt a serene glow of pleasure that things had worked out like this. Chaim was good and kind, and she felt safe with him, as she now felt safe in her friendship with Mordecai. There was in the smile she directed at the two of them a trace of complacency.

At last the flag was finished and rolled up, ready for the next day. They said good night to Mordecai and crept upstairs to bed, whispering in order not to disturb Daniel, curled in a corner. They went to their separate beds without embracing: Leah's menstrual period had finished the day before but she was not yet ritually pure without a visit to the *mikva*. She might have rejected the pious wig, but Chaim stood firm on the Law as it affected their life together.

By seven-thirty the next morning Peszno was already in a state of excitement: the processions were timed to reach the main square at ten, so at nine the people began gathering, Poles in their section of the town, and Jews outside the synagogue. Slowly, with flags and banners raised high, the two processions moved off from opposite ends of the town. In the broad boulevard leading to the square they joined up, the two streams swelling into one colorful river, the banners mingling, Polish saints fluttering in the breeze along with gleaming Stars of David.

The workers' procession, joining neither, formed a separate stream, with Leah's red banner at the head, along with others bearing similar slogans. It, too, made its way to the main square, now jammed with waving, cheering people. At a balcony, officials waved and smiled, and the sun glinted on embroidered silver and shiny silk as the flags bobbed over the heads of the crowd.

The workers' procession edged up to the front of the square, to catch some of the words booming from the balcony through a megaphone. Mordecai listened for a moment or two, then turned disgustedly to Stefan and Leah. "Pickled cucumbers and celebration wine! Meaningless! Let's go!"

Chanting slogans of freedom and equality, the proletariat, small in number but large in spirit, swept out of the square and headed back to the Jewish quarter. The little square there was quiet, abandoned by all but old women and small children, playing peacefully in the sunshine while the oldest of the old men brooded over their chess, as though no processions were taking place at all. Suddenly the empty square was filled with people, banners, flags, shouting, noise.

Mordecai, bounding onto the wooden seat where the Esperanto lessons had taken place, began to address the crowd. Arms whirling, hands jabbing the air like a boxer, he radiated energy. Light seemed to spring from his fingertips and hover like a nimbus around his head. Leah blinked, dazzled for a moment, and caught her breath, seized— treacherously—with a sudden excitement that had nothing to do with the revolution and everything to do with Mordecai's eyes flashing with enthusiasm and a memory of the touch of his rough fingers on her flesh. Never with Chaim had her body leaped, awakened as she knew it could be. As—thumping with excitement and filled with tremors—it now was. Cheering with the others as Mordecai jumped down from the bench, she found to her dismay that tears were running down her cheeks.

"Is that a tribute to my oratory?" he shouted above the noise. She felt his hand on her arm, and she smiled and nodded vigorously, safe in the lie.

They marched back to the town hall and again the officials appeared, thinking to repeat the earlier performance, until one of them noticed the slogans on the banners and heard someone shouting, "Death to the Mock Parliament and the Czar!" Smiles and officials vanished. The workers stood their ground, shouting slogans and clapping in unison. Leah, glancing about her, noticed the policemen first, two of them, casually circling the edge of the small crowd, making notes.

"I think we should go now," Leah said, tugging at Mordecai's sleeve. He looked around and he, too, noticed the uniformed figures. He nodded. "Perhaps it's time."

The next day the town returned to normal, and few seemed to notice that freedom had lasted no longer than Freedom Day, as Mordecai kept pointing out.

The euphoria of August drained away into an anxious autumn: trouble in Odessa; the general strike, a mutiny on the battleship *Potemkin.* Finally there was news of an organization calling itself the True Russians, formed to deal with insurrection and terrorism. Unfortunately, it seemed that terrorism was best fought with terrorism, and that the main target for the attacks was to be the Jews.

"Why the Jews?" Leah asked.

"Why not?" Chaim replied. She thought of Haman and Pharaoh, of the Romans and the Polish princes, the Crusaders, of Von Plehve, and thought: *Why not indeed?*

Jacob was out with Hirschl, delivering a consignment of plates to the barracks. He hurried home, out of breath, looking worried. "Arrests are being made . . . I heard some talk—I told Hirschl to stay and see what he could find out. Apparently the leaders of the workers' procession have been named."

Rachel, predictably, began to cry. "I knew evil would come of it . . ."

"How much time is there?" Chaim asked.

"It has been slow so far . . . collecting names, arranging papers, it takes time. Then, suddenly, they can be swift. Delay would be—unwise."

They talked the matter over, quietly. Mordecai was away again, on one of his mysterious, flitting trips to Warsaw, but he would be warned by one of the others. Stefan had already left. Leah, quite clearly, must leave too. She protested vigorously. "They won't arrest me. They will never believe a woman could be worth arresting."

Jacob said, "Your friend Stefan . . . Well, his sister was arrested yesterday at a meeting." He turned to Chaim. "I think you should go. For Leah's safety."

"Yes, of course. What remains to be settled is where it shall be."

Rachel, swallowing her sobs, wanted Germany. "Hirschl is often there."

Jacob suggested America: there was a large Jewish community in New York; Americans did not persecute. In America it was possible to find true freedom.

Unexpectedly it was Chaim who made the choice. "England has allowed Disraeli, a Jew, to rise to the highest position in the land. There must be justice in England."

So the decision was made: it would be England.

They huddled together in the little shelter beside the railway line, watching the steel tracks vanish into the mist. A fine rain seeped from the gray sky. Rachel talked incessantly, full of last-minute instructions: "Avoid speaking to foreigners; look for the nearest synagogue, rely on the rabbi's advice, eat nothing on the journey except what you have with you." It was a wicked, nonkosher world they were entering.

A figure came toward them across the fields. Certainly not a policeman, Chaim thought—not one, alone. They waited, watching. For a moment of surging hope Leah thought it was Mordecai, returned in time to say goodbye. But it was only young Slumkow, come to wish them a safe journey.

Daniel, like Jacob, said nothing, but stood very close to Leah, and whenever their glances met, smiled widely, determined to be grown-up about the separation. Hirschl had stayed behind at the house, in case there were awkward visitors who might arrive to ask questions. They would not be safe until Simeon had seen them across the border.

Chaim's face was puckered in concentration as he tried to gather their baggage closer together, constantly shifting a box or a tin trunk, rearranging a bundle. Most of the boxes contained religious objects, the basis of the shop he would be setting up in England. Clothes had been kept to a minimum. Regretfully Leah thought of her mother's store of tablecloths, the elegant china, and the cooking pots. Still: in this way Chaim would be in business at once and they could buy more china and linen very soon. Solomon helped his son with the bundles, making sure the knots were securely tied, loose ends tucked in.

"Shouldn't the train be here by now?" Rachel asked fretfully. Presently she would sob, when Leah got on the train. For the moment she felt only frightened and helpless. Why did Leah have to go so far? Perhaps the police would not have come. She sighed heavily.

Leah saw the trail of smoke first. How many lifetimes ago had she stood here in the early morning sunshine, hair braided painfully tight, waiting for the train to take her on her first visit to Uncle Simeon?

"The train!" The others had seen the smoke now, and began to make vague, pointless movements in preparation for the farewell. Daniel's fists were clenched tightly and thrust deep into his pockets. He had been sure he would not cry, but the slow, panting approach of the train seemed to be forcing the air out of his lungs, and he knew that the moment he drew another breath, the tears would start. He began to blink quickly.

Leah noticed. She had kissed Jacob and Rachel and Solomon. Now she turned and flung her arms around the boy. "Danielsche . . . little brother . . . baby . . ."

She wanted to say something but her throat was blocked by tears, aching as she tried to swallow. As she kissed him, quick little pecks under the ear, on the temple, on the cheeks, the way she used to when he was a baby, he saw that the tears were welling up in her eyes, dripping onto the collar of her dark coat, already bedraggled by the rain.

They said nothing in the end. Just rubbed cheeks and held each other close, and then she got on the train, Jacob lifting her as he had so long ago. The baggage was quickly taken aboard, and the steel monster began to strain and move. And was gone.

Daniel had been holding his breath again. He let it out now in a great gasp, and, resting his head against the shelter wall, at last gave in to his tears.

Simeon took charge at the frontier. He settled Leah on a trunk and took Chaim off to the customs office. She sat, crouched among the bundles, muscles slack from exhaustion. The journey had hardly begun and she felt drained. She realized with a twinge of dismay that already she had taken on the hopeless, passive look of the emigrant. Waiting for the train. Waiting for the customs. Waiting for the boat. Waiting to be told where to go next. Where was her usual sprightliness? Her spirit, her confidence, her impatience? Of no use now. Impatience here would only arouse hostility. She slumped on her trunk like the poor Abrahams woman Simeon had helped all those years ago, unmindful of how long she waited. Deep in thought, she did not notice the approach of the stranger until he spoke to her. In Yiddish he asked her solicitously if she needed help.

His manner was so pious, his coat so long, his beard so luxuriant that at first Leah took him for a rabbi. Then she saw his eyes. Small and dark, they shone with a zeal which, had it been religious would have amounted to ecstasy, but this zeal was of a different nature; the eyes were little pools of greed, sparkling with rapacious alertness; the muscles of his face were ordered by guile, so that features in themselves quite ordinary assumed a repellent aspect.

Leah had not seen the man who robbed and tricked the Abrahams family, but it must have been just such a man. Maybe this very man. Her weariness left her and rage flooded into her body on behalf of Simeon, working against an army of serpents like this man, and on behalf of the poor wretches already swindled and those still to be robbed.

She smiled up at him tremulously, and the man was startled by the sudden radiance that lit up the pale face above the drab overcoat. "On your own? And a long way to go, I dare say. The world is very big and frightening when you are alone . . . ."

A hundred yards away, Leah could see Chaim and Simeon waiting in line. She smiled. "Yes. Very frightening."

He squatted down beside her and became very confidential, paternal almost. "I can help you. I have a friend in Germany who has

121

helped several girls like you to make a good life. He can find you work with a good kosher family, you will be treated like a daughter of the house— They have a fine home, nice furniture, and the pay is generous. What do you say?"

"You're very kind . . ." She looked doubtful, and her reluctance spurred him on.

"No, no, it's nothing. What does a little kindness cost? I like to help in any way I can. Now, I can put you on the train—"

Leah broke in, her voice almost quavery. "But I have not changed my money."

"I can do that for you—you'll get a better rate if I do it for you. How much do you have to change?"

Leah mentioned a modest sum, and patted her bodice. Anxious to move his quarry on to a less prominent place, the man began to count out German currency from his wallet, while Leah fumbled inside her bodice for a thick envelope. Still some way off, but walking toward them, she saw a policeman, young and pleasant-faced. She decided to put her faith in human nature. She held out the envelope and with her other hand took the money, which she slipped at once inside her dress.

"Tell me sir . . ." She had not yet relinquished her envelope. ". . . The kosher family who will treat me like a daughter . . ."

He moistened his lips, smiling reassuringly, "Yes, my child?"

"When will they go away to visit friends? Soon, I suppose. And as they are so kind, they will take me with them. All the way to Buenos Aires, like the other girls who are looked after by people like you and your friend."

The sharp eyes widened in amazement, and then as Leah gave a small shriek and began to cry loudly, the man whispered hurriedly, "Hush! Do you want to make trouble? Do you want to attract the police? You know what happens? You will be thrown into jail and *never* get across the border!"

He looked nervously over his shoulder—to see the young policeman gazing inquiringly at him. But when he tried to move unobtrusively away he found Leah clutching the hem of his long coat with a surprisingly strong grip.

The policeman said curtly, "What is all this about?"

Leah turned a pathetic face toward him. "Sir, this man is trying to rob me. He has taken an envelope that belongs to me."

The man waved the envelope in the air, agitated. "I have stolen nothing! This envelope is mine! The poor child is deranged—weary from traveling."

122

The policeman plucked the envelope from his hand and glanced inside. He raised his eyebrows and held out the packet to the man. "Letters. This one begins, 'My silly little goose'—Are you *sure* this belongs to you?"

The trickster stared in disbelief at the sheaf of letters: "But she has my money, my marks. Give me back my marks!"

Leah lowered her head and wiped her eyes pathetically. The policeman handed her back the envelope. How lucky, Leah thought, that Mordecai wrote to her in Polish.

The policeman turned to the man. "Any further trouble and you will find yourself answering to the captain."

Rage, dismay, incredulity that this could actually be happening to him—the changing expressions flitted across the man's face. As the realization hit him that he had lost even a small sum of money, a wail of pain came from his lips and he turned away, hunched, rocking in misery.

"Thank you, sergeant," Leah said gratefully. He smiled condescendingly. "You see how even your own kind are ready to rob you. You should take better care of your possessions." He walked on, stretching his back muscles lazily.

At the other end of the platform Chaim and Simeon had completed their transactions. Leah saw them hurrying toward her. She tucked Mordecai's letters back inside her blouse. *Well,* she thought, *if this is the outside world, perhaps it will not be so bad.*

Another train, another country. Noise. Dirt. Strangers. At one frontier Leah lost Rachel's tin of goose fat. Somewhere else Chaim ripped his coat on a nail. Small disasters, but depressing. The boat was crowded. And of course, filthy. They were seasick.

When had she last slept in a bed? Washed? How far away, now, was England?

Leah felt as though she was to spend the rest of her life sitting on a trunk, encircled by bundles. She closed her eyes to shut out the vast, iron-beamed cavern that surrounded her. But this only seemed to intensify the noise: so many voices, echoing in her head, calling, so many incomprehensible words in this ugly foreign language. She would never be able to learn English, and she wished she were back in Peszno at the big kitchen table, warmed by the old blue stove instead of being lost here, in Victoria Station.

She had clenched her muscles to try to stop shivering from cold, and now she was frozen stiff, so cold that all sensation seemed to have left her limbs. How long would Chaim take to find the man who was supposed to meet the immigrants? Perhaps there had been some problem with his papers, perhaps he had been arrested, was even now on his way to jail or in a train speeding away from here, and she would remain here until she froze to death or some figure of authority forced her out on the street. And then where should she go? *This must be how a newborn baby feels*, she thought dimly: *thrust violently into a world full of noise, where nothing makes sense and you can understand no one.* She wished that, like a baby, she could curl up tight and suck her thumb. Danielsche used to suck his thumb, and when he fell asleep the thumb would slip gently from his lips and rest, moist, next to his mouth. . . .

She felt a sense of dizziness, of falling. A soft voice at her shoulder speaking the vile English roused her, and she looked up to see a middle-aged woman gazing down at her anxiously. "Are—you—lost?" inquired the woman. Leah stared at her blankly. The woman tried again. "Do—you—need—help?" she asked more loudly, and then, louder still, "I am from the Young Women's Christian Association. We can help you."

Leah wondered miserably if she was doing something wrong by sitting here, since the woman was shouting at her. Exhaustion from days of traveling, lack of sleep, hunger, and the strange dizziness that kept sweeping over her as the noise grew louder in her ears, all combined to rob her of the ability to think or act. She tried to speak, but the effort caused an almost physical pain. She glanced suspiciously at the woman: Was this another slave trader trying to trap her into a life of shame? The woman's eyes looked kind, but Leah knew she could trust no one.

A sudden weakness overcame her, and she would have fallen from the trunk but for the woman, who grabbed her shoulders and held her steady while she rummaged in her handbag. She knelt down next to Leah and placed a tiny bottle under her nose. Leah breathed and then gasped as the searing sharpness rose in her nostrils. She sat up and pushed the woman violently away from her. Chaim, hurrying up with a small, fussy-looking man in a black hat and long coat, was horrified to see Leah apparently struggling with a strange woman. He called out, and Leah cried in relief at the sight of him.

The small man spoke to the woman in English, rapidly and curtly. Her smile faded. "I just thought she needed help," she murmured.

As she turned away, Leah saw that the woman's expression was in fact gentle, and that her actions had been well-meant. "Perhaps we should thank her. She was good to me."

The black-coated man said sharply, "These Christians! They start by helping and end by trying to force conversion on you. Have nothing to do with them. We do not want their help."

Outside the station the streets were bewildering, so many people hurrying about, so much traffic. Their fussy helper piled them and their luggage into a horse-drawn cab and began talking rapidly while they drove through the London streets. Chaim was not to imagine that money was easily gained here, he warned; life was hard. People should stay where they belonged. London was getting too crowded, and all these foreigners coming in were arousing hostility; even Parliament was talking about it. He clearly thought of himself as English and shared the resentment he spoke of.

Gradually the houses grew meaner and more dilapidated, the people shabbier, the streets less well swept. At last the cab stopped, and they climbed down at the entrance to a large, bleak building. Over the entrance were some words in Yiddish that Leah read aloud: "Jewish Temporary Shelter." Slowly they made their way inside, into yet another cavernous room—smaller than Victoria Station, but just as crowded. All around the room were pathetic family groups with bundles of clothes, sticks of furniture, children crying. The only difference was that the noise was a familiar one: even the crying had a Yiddish tone to it.

They sat and waited. A meal would be provided. But they must wait. Someone would come and talk to them soon. But they must wait.

Waiting, Leah thought again about the woman at the station. Was it right that a friendly gesture should be repulsed? Had they as a people been rejected so long, so often, that rejection had itself entered their character?

PART THREE

Sometimes it seemed to Chaim that with their coming to London, all logic, all reason went out of life. The ordered pattern of existence was ruptured, and in its place a sort of madness reigned. He turned increasingly to God for encouragement; never had he felt so in need of help.

January in London was cruel. The black fog crawled down Chaim's throat as he trudged in search of premises for his shop. The fog hurt his eyes and clogged his nostrils. An attack of bronchitis that had kept him in his bed for weeks had left him weakened so that the London streets seemed to stretch as he walked them; he lost his sense of direction and perspective in his fatigue.

In the spring Miriam was born. A difficult birth, the midwife (who had herself come over some years earlier from a town not far from Peszno) told Chaim, "Your wife is too much of a thinker," she said disapprovingly. "She keeps analyzing childbirth instead of getting on with it. This can only make it more difficult."

The baby was rounded and healthy looking, a touching contrast to the thin London children with their scrawny bodies and unsmiling, angular faces in which the eyes loomed huge and shadowy.

Chaim watched from the grimy window a child from the decaying house next door carrying home broken boxes to make firewood and a few pieces of rotting fruit from the market barrows. He was a boy of eight or nine, not a pretty child: dark, with a shambling, ungainly walk, but he had a good-natured cheerfulness that Chaim found astonishing in the circumstances. Childhood here, Chaim realized, had nothing to do with fairy tales and magic or even the chafing security of granny's apron strings and *cheder* as it had in the old country.

He and Leah had rented two rooms in Whitechapel, and shared the lavatory in the yard with the rest of the tenants in the house. When they had seen the familiar squares of Yiddish newspaper threaded on strings, hanging on the wall of the lavatory, both for an instant felt more at home, reassured. But this was a flush toilet, something new to them. Water from a pipe, always available at the pull of a chain! Otherwise, water had to be fetched from a tap on the next corner and sometimes there was a line of women waiting to fill their buckets. In the cold weather the wind came stinging around the streetcorner, the women flinched, and the icy water slopped over their shabby shoes and hems.

Their lodgings, furnished with two rusty iron beds, an unsteady table, and two chairs from the junk man, looked wretched despite all Leah's efforts. When they had first walked into the place she stood for a moment staring at the stained, flaking walls, the rotting floorboards. Chaim stood next to her, feeling guilty and helpless. "I must find the synagogue," he said, and left her to unpack.

The rooms looked better now: she had made cupboards and a dressing table of a sort from orange boxes carried back from the market and covered with cheap material, and she put up curtains of the same bright, cheap cotton. But she could do nothing about the splitting floorboards and cracked windows.

It was an odd life, in which simply surviving this day, this week, this month, was an achievement. The noisy, Yiddish-speaking neighbors, sharp but kindly; the shop fronts with their Hebrew letters over the entrance; the smells and sounds and weekly routine reminded her of home. The bathhouse was nearby with its *mikva*; the cut and thrust of market day reproduced the sounds of the Peszno market; ritual circumscribed their days as it always had.

"It isn't a new life we're making," she said once to Chaim. "It's just the old life in a new place." She sensed that outside their little bit of London, exciting things were happening, a different world was blooming, and she wished they could have been part of it. But when she did venture outside the ghetto, fear set in: she lost her way; the incomprehensible, ugly English bemused her. She retreated, reluctantly, into the known. But she did begin to learn English.

Chaim had found premises. The small shop looked attractive, yet it soon became clear to him that it was not succeeding. He kept the fact to himself and began calling on the pawnshop with precious items wrapped in newspaper. But he was unaccustomed to subterfuge and soon enough Leah found out.

There was no one they could turn to for help. As it was, Chaim's father had written saying he, too, was thinking of going to England. Leah knew that the new government act had virtually cut off such possibilities, but he might get through. On the other hand, if Solomon came, he would be a responsibility rather than a help. Leah began to find even cheaper ways for them to eat. The late shopper at the market, willing to accept leftovers—bruised vegetables, overripe fruit—could save a good deal over the week.

She did not tell Chaim she was pregnant again, but before long it was obvious that there would be another mouth to feed. To his dismay Chaim found himself thinking about it even in the synagogue. The world intruded. He looked at the small group of men, each apparently rapt in his loud and energetic communion with God. Was he the only one who was failing to make contact?

There was a large synagogue a few minutes' walk from their lodgings, but newcomers tended to find it too orderly, too English, and Chaim, like the others, had found his way to one of the little rooms that flourished in every street, each fresh group of immigrants forming the nucleus of yet another tiny, independent congregation.

This particular *shul* was in Simcha Solomon's front room. During most of the week the room was in full use as a buttonhole workshop: the entire family and two work hands, crowded there for twelve hours every day—and often for longer if work was urgently needed. Stacked around them were hundreds of half-finished jackets and waistcoats, all waiting for buttonholes. The clothes were piled high on the worktable;

they overflowed from large boxes on the floor and cascaded from cords strung across the room from wall to wall.

But on Friday afternoon, Simcha banged on the worktable with his heavy metal scissors and work stopped. The clothes were carried in armfuls up the narrow wooden stairs and carefully laid out on clean sheets spread over the floor. Needles were anchored in large, steel-hooped pincushions, thread gathered up, and within a few minutes all signs of clothing and sewing had vanished. Rebecca Solomon swept the room, and Simcha opened the battered mahogany sideboard that housed the prayer books. The room was ready for its Sabbath role.

The "congregation" arrived, about fifteen men filling the room, taking their prayer books from the sideboard and hitching their prayer shawls around them briskly. A large wardrobe was used as the Ark, housing the sacred scroll.

Rebecca, her daughter, and a few of the wives climbed up the stairs and crowded together in the gloom of the upstairs landing, from where they could hear the service—or some of it at least. The *shammes,* a fussy, cross-eyed man with a reedy, high-pitched voice, stationed himself at the door to relay key points of the service to the "upper gallery" from time to time, bawling up the stairs.

After the service Chaim waited as the others drifted away with handshakes and murmured Sabbath good wishes. "Simcha . . ."

Busy putting away the prayer books, Simcha grunted without looking up. Chaim did not feel encouraged. He sifted through suitable phrases. Simcha threw him an impatient glance: "*Nu?*"

"I need some money—"

"You're not asking to borrow, I hope?"

"No, no!" Chaim looked shocked. "I must find work. I am giving up the shop—or rather it has given me up."

Simcha rocked back on his heels and looked hard at Chaim's earnest face, the gentle eyes blinking anxiously at him. He reached out and took Chaim's left hand, studying it in amusement. "A student's hand we've got, so fine and smooth. Such soft skin, the nails long, and so clean and white! Do you know what these hands will look like in a few weeks, with my kind of work? The needles that press into you, that prick again and again? The tough thread that cuts like the edge of a knife? The skin will be scarred and calloused, the fingertips will be raw until they harden slowly into lumps, the nails will be cut short. The nice white fingers will be gray from grease that nothing will wash out. They will be painful. And ugly."

Chaim held out his right hand, palm down. The skin on the back of his hand was hideously scarred, pinched and pulled by the old burn, the flesh a harsh pink. "Have you got work for me?" he asked.

Simcha pursed his lips doubtfully. "You are unskilled. With buttonholes you can't afford a mistake—a snip in the wrong place can mean a whole jacket ruined. I have class trade here, my jackets go to Ascot, they go to West End balls, I can't take the risk. But I know a man who could use you. He's in linings. Linings, you can learn in a day. Later, after more practice, we'll talk again."

On the way home Chaim walked jauntily. He felt more optimistic. He would work hard, they would eat properly, life would continue. Soon he would be doing buttonholes, spring meant better weather and everything would look brighter.

It was still bitterly cold and Chaim huddled inside his inadequate overcoat. It was long but the material was thin stuff and the wind sliced through it, sharp as . . . *a knife* he had been thinking but he changed it: *Sharp as button thread.* He smiled radiantly and an old woman passing muttered, "Idiot!"

On the corner, his neighbor Mrs. Abrahams was trying to crawl home with a full bucket, dragging it, crippled with arthritis. Chaim picked up the bucket and carried it for her, helping her along. Against her dirty black sleeve his left hand stood out very pale. He had never been conscious before of how very white his skin was. And clean. For a moment he felt a pang of regret for the secluded life: the occasional customer looking for a prayer book; a pair of candlesticks. There was no harshness in such transactions; he had been spared the true marketplace. His had been more an exchange of views and news, to which the exchange of goods and money had been incidental.

The wind was heavy with rain now and he shivered, walking slowly because of the bucket of water. He put it down, shrugged off the Abrahams woman's thanks, and paused in the mean street for a moment. He longed for summer, and in his mind he saw the square in Peszno, the main square with the scarlet flowers in their neatly tended beds, and the military band, instruments dazzling in the sunshine, the sound of trumpet and drum, the music rising in the clear, warm air. . . .

Leah was apologetic about Ruth. Two girls. A man expected a son.

Miriam and her baby sister slept in the drawers of an old chest, pulled out and placed on the floor. Leah spread blankets over the drawers to protect baby fists, and sang to them when she felt strong enough, but she was very low in spirits.

After the letter came she wrapped herself in despair and became unreachable. They were utterly alone now. The enormity of the loss still seemed impossible.

"We have terrible news for you," Simeon had written to Chaim. "You must prepare Leah gently."

But Chaim, confined to bed with a return attack of bronchitis, had to lie and listen, helpless, while Leah herself read out the letter in a hard, flat voice. "Daniel was taken for military service. They just came and took him away, and young Shoobotel, Benjamin, who is already in poor health, God help him. Mordecai will be taken if he returns.

"Jacob and Rachel went to Warsaw to try to find out where Daniel had been sent. We heard rumors about trouble in Russia and on the day they arrived, there had been an armed uprising in Moscow. Nerves were very bad in Warsaw. Jacob and Rachel were in the street when a demonstration organized by the Bund came round the corner. The affair got out of control and the troops fired on the crowd. Rachel and Jacob were in the middle, unable to get out. They were in the direct line of fire. It is a dreadful thing. Try to comfort Leah . . ."

She put down the letter, her face gray. "God," Chaim began.

She got up and stood over him, the long eyes blazing. "Do not," she said very slowly and clearly, "do not speak to me about God." And she left the room.

Chaim went off early every morning to Simcha Solomon's workshop. He was in buttonholes now, and, in addition to his twelve-hour day in the workroom, he brought home garments to stitch by lamplight until late at night. He was so thin that his face seemed to be made of bone, the forehead, temple, and nose gleaming white, fleshless, and the dark eyes sunken and lacking luster.

He still attended the *shul* in Simcha's front room, but perhaps because the weekday smell of cloth and sweat and stale tea hung over it even on the Sabbath, Chaim no longer found the peace and exaltation in prayer that he had in the past. It was like holding a precious and familiar book and not daring to open it because of a terrible suspicion that, unperceived, a thief had stolen away the beautiful words, leaving emptiness behind.

All around him the old ways were being abandoned. Pavements thronged with young people on Friday nights; the newspapers were full of people changing their names— "I, Maurice Irwin Homes, heretofore known by the name of Moses Israel Hominowitz, do hereby give notice that by a deed poll dated . . ."

Leah, for different reasons, found the neighborhood unsatisfactory. The realization that the ragged, crippled creature down the street was the Abrahams woman, who had been helped across the border by her uncle ten years before, was at first deeply depressing to her. It pressed home her own drop in the social scale. Once she would have regarded the Abrahamses and people like them with pity touched with a certain contempt. Now she shared their condition and found that it was not necessarily due to stupidity or laziness. The boy, Simeon, named after her uncle, was a lumpen child with none of Danielsche's grace and slenderness, but his remarkable, glowing smile had stopped her as she was turning away from him in the street. "Come and see me one day after school," she had suggested, to her own surprise.

Since then, he had been giving her English lessons every day. They sat side by side at the scratched table, the babies at their feet occasionally clambering up to be rocked absently as the lesson proceeded. They made a faintly absurd picture: the slim, brisk young woman with the imperious tilt to her head, carefully following the words of the brown-skinned, shaggy child, his features looking all the heavier next to her sharp bones.

She paid him in food, which saved his family from giving him a midday meal. He had other ways of supplementing an inadequate diet. "Sometimes I help the boys with their mathematics, and they give me monkey nuts after school—there's a stall in Frying Pan Alley where they sell them hot, fresh roasted." She gave him a whole penny to buy some for himself the next day.

135

"Why do you leave the house so early?" she asked one day, seeing him pass by.

"I do shopping errands for Mrs. Horwitz and Mrs. Katz before school," he explained. "Three farthings a time." After school he had Hebrew classes and then helped his father with the slipper making. Only Leah knew that even later at night, when the family was asleep, he did schoolwork, sitting in the lavatory so that he could have light.

Simeon had a corduroy suit provided by the Jewish Free School. He also appeared one day in new boots, clumping about in them proudly. "The school people are getting very clever. The last pair they gave us, mother pawned and then didn't have the money to get them out again. So when I went to school I had to wear her old shoes and of course they noticed, and found out what had happened. So this time the school lady came around and said to mother that if I lost my boots again I would be sent to prison because they are really the school's property. And mother believed her!"

"Well," Leah asked after the lesson, "am I making progress?"

"Very good. You'll be an English lady."

"*Nya!* Ugly language. But I don't want to be a foreigner like those poor women who can only go into Yiddisher shops. I want to go one day to the real London, to see Buckingham Palace and Hyde Park and Harrods!"

A charity visitor from the Board of Guardians had told her about Harrods, the magical store with a moving staircase so thrilling that women fainted and had to be revived with free glasses of brandy at the top. Of course Leah realized that people like herself would not even be allowed into such a treasure house. But one day perhaps. . . . "Let us go over the lesson again," she said to Simeon.

"I'll read you a poem," he said. "Listen: 'He clasps the crag with crooked hands . . .' "

At the end Leah commented, "Hands? Who ever heard of a bird with *hands*! Claws, or maybe talons, but hands! That's English for you. The *goyim* just can't write poetry!" But she read the poem aloud, as he instructed.

Miriam began to mouth the words after Leah with the accurate mimicry of children. "Cockneys we'll have in the family!" Leah remarked, amused. Both girls looked like Chaim, with thin faces, pointed chins, and huge eyes. Leah did her best to keep them clean, and mended their clothes so that they were patched rather than ragged.

Chaim had only a few minutes each day for lunch. He washed

and they sat down to eat. There was a cloth on the table and even a few wild flowers in a cup, gathered by Leah from the crumbling wall outside where they sprouted defiantly. What the table offered to eat was less attractive: some thinly sliced bread, a pickled herring fillet, and an end of cucumber chopped into some sour milk. They ate silently, weariness emptying their minds of conversation. Chaim chewed on his bread quickly, anxious to return to the buttonholes. His work was neat and well executed but he was still slow. The sore fingers hindered his speed with the needle, and he had to be careful if the thread bit through the cracked skin, not to get blood on the garment.

Perhaps he should try the machining: the smell of machine oil was unpleasant, but the work was quick. He glanced up to mention the thought to Leah and saw her head drooping, her eyes dull. She had always been so animated, so full of life. He longed to be able to make her smile, to see the flash and snap return to her eyes, the curl of humor to the corner of her lips.

Leah sensed him looking at her and tried to conceal her bleak mood. "Simeon is teaching me English. He actually likes the language."

"He is a clever boy—the only one in that family with a head on his shoulders. I wish he came to synagogue more often." He meant simply that he would enjoy seeing the child, but Leah took it as a criticism.

"Perhaps he feels that study at school will help him eat while study in *shul* will only allow him to starve virtuously."

She had never spoken so sharply before and Chaim was shocked. "God's commandments—"

"—Oh that!" she said in a tired, dismissive tone. "I read somewhere that to be religious means to recognize our duties as being commands from God when actually they're just the voice of our conscience. If you have a strong conscience you do your duty. So where does God help?"

He did not like arguing with Leah, but he could not allow this. He began to talk, patiently, reminding her of the demands and rewards of their faith, of the divine mission. At one point she tossed her head slightly, and her hand rose to her neat hair. She flicked at it restively, and his voice faltered. For a second he saw her as a girl, tossing her head at Rachel, throwing back a braid of black hair. He knew she was not listening to him.

"I must go." As he left, Leah was beginning to sweep the room, keeping up the constant battle against dust, crumbling plaster, and the grime that overlay everything in this gray corner of a gray city.

Chaim walked quickly but cautiously back to work. The streets were greasy and hazed with a fine sleet. In the gutters, blackened, filthy scraps of paper swirled in the gusts of wind. On the flaking brick walls were notices in Yiddish—police announcements, a sign explaining what to do in case of fire, and others that still amazed and offended Chaim— posters put up by synagogue authorities. Passover was approaching and the notices offered "Seats, seats, seats! In airy comfortable halls. With good cantors." What was it, an opera performance, that they flaunted the skill of their singers, the luxurious premises?

And the seats of course were not free. The crowded synagogue on High Holy Days financed the less well-attended regular services. Not all Jews were devout synagogue-goers. So on the few days in the year when everyone wanted to put in a word with God, they paid for the privilege. It shocked Chaim, but he knew that if they were to attend, he must purchase their tickets. On the other hand the rent had to be paid, food bought. The gas meter consumed their pennies with increasing speed. He would have to master the sewing machine.

Kolinsky's sweatshop made Simcha Solomon's buttonhole workroom look like a palace: it was partly below ground, ill-ventilated, and crowded with six machine hands and two finishers. Clothes, completed or partly finished, hung from cords and railings all over the room, forming a crisscross "ceiling" of clothing which ended a few inches above the heads of the machinists. The machines clattered noisily, the high tables were piled with cut-out fabric waiting to be stitched, and every inch of the room contained boxes of scraps for collection by the piece sorters, or bales of fabric waiting to be cut.

Kolinsky himself did not operate a machine, but moved from one to another, encouraging, exhorting, and complaining without pause. He was there first in the morning, and he was still there when the last worker rose wearily from his seat to go home. Kolinsky was a small, round man with a round head like a balloon and tiny ears which grew red when his voice rose in anger. He shouted a good deal but the machinists ignored this, partly because they knew they could go no faster, and he knew this too, and also because he was not really unkind, not vicious as some work bosses were, imposing fines on their employees if they slowed down or were ill. He paid low wages, wickedly low, but at least he paid them. He demanded a full twelve-hour day, but he could call upstairs to his wife to make Russian tea for everyone if the day was so cold that the machinists' fingers turned blue and clumsy. On one occasion he had even brought in a bag of bagels for them, bought cheap because they were yesterday's, to mark his son's Bar Mitzvah.

Chaim occupied the corner farthest from the window—if he craned his neck he could just see the shoes and lower parts of people's legs going by on the pavement. The shoes were always cracked and dusty, the skirts and trousers frayed. The electric light bulb, hanging from a dust-furred flex, was several feet away. As he bent low over his small black hand machine, it occurred to Chaim that almost all of his life he had been stooped over some table, straining his eyes in bad light. From his first day in *cheder*, to these trousers in worsted and Prince of Wales check, he was always bending, stooping, straining to see, becoming accustomed to the cramped, airless existence. It seemed as though one had been an apprenticeship for the other.

Hard to remember now, the pleasure he had found in those hours of study, although at *cheder*, too, he had glanced up occasionally to look through the window at the apple trees, white with blossom and then soft green, lit with the brilliant globes of scarlet apples. But he had never climbed them, never picked a forbidden fruit or sunk his teeth in the crisp, juicy flesh.

At least they could eat on Kolinsky's wages, and Leah had whitewashed the walls of their two rooms so that, for a few days, the London soot was banished and they sat in sparkling whiteness, bright curtains shutting out the street.

When he looked in at the uncurtained windows he passed on his way to work, Chaim was appalled: the Londoners seemed to have given up the struggle against their surroundings. There was one house, a tenement on the sunless side of a drainlike street, where he often paused for a moment. In the ground floor front room a man, his wife, and two children lived and slept. The ragged, barefoot children sat on the floor among the litter and scraps of food, aimless. One of them, not totally dulled by this existence, had taken to catching Chaim's eye as he passed, and occasionally they exchanged a quick wave of the hand.

In a corner a heap of crumpled bedclothes had been pushed aside to make room for the husband's mildewed armchair, rescued from some rubbish dump. The chair was turned away from the window and all Chaim saw of the man was a tangle of dirty yellow hair and a flushed cheek slumped against the rotting fabric.

The smell from the room reached Chaim's nostrils through the broken windowpanes. But what horrified him almost more was that he saw with a shudder of recognition that there was something about the haggard woman that was not unknown to him: that downward-looking, listless despair he saw in Leah sometimes and knew he himself must share.

"Rubinstein! Admire the scenery, enjoy yourself, dream, but in *your* time, not mine!" Kolinsky was at his shoulder. Chaim turned back to his machine and his boss moved on, ears reddening, balloon head bobbing across the room. "Dreamers! Idlers! We're all here to work! There is no time for dreamers!"

It was late when Chaim left the workroom, carrying some half-completed garments for finishing at home. As he approached the tenement with its broken windows, he wondered if he would see the child, exchange a wave. Perhaps he could make a doll from a piece of wood and dress it with scraps. . . .

The crowd around the door did not at once strike him as unusual. But as he came closer he saw policemen and noticed the light blazing in the ground-floor window. He slowed down and tried to understand what the crowd was talking about. At last he noticed young Fishbein, a fellow-machinist, who had followed them over from Peszno. Fishbein had picked up English very quickly, and Chaim plucked at his sleeve. "What has happened?"

Fishbein shrugged. "Some drunken fool has killed his wife."

"In that room?" Chaim asked. Fishbein nodded.

How was it possible? The woman had been listless, despairing. But she had been alive. Just a few hours ago he had looked in, caught that tableau of motionless figures, that familiar drooping head. *Killed his wife.* How had he killed her? What instrument could a husband use against a woman he must have loved once?

Fishbein had been listening to the crowd. He turned back. "It seems he came home drunk, expecting the children to have picked up a bit of food from the market barrows. There was no food and he decided to thrash the children for their failure. When the woman tried to make him stop, he turned on her. Beat her to death. Some of these people saw it happening and sent for the police, but it was too late. He had kicked her too much in the head and body and she was dead."

Chaim pushed through the crowd to the window. The room seemed to be full of policemen, surrounded by bits of smashed and splintered furniture. Where were the children? No sign of them in the room. What would become of the children, the one who waved? He stumbled clear of the people and began to walk home. What kind of a world was it, where a man attacked his own children, killed his own wife? The Poles, too, beat their wives, brutally, savage like animals. It seemed the whole world was an arena for barbarians.

He started to walk more quickly, his mind spinning with thoughts, flooded with light: to be physically exhausted but in hopeful spirits was a familiar condition and one that he had accepted, even at times enjoyed. But weariness of the spirit was something else—a vast, coiling snake of despair that slowly stifled all will, all joy, all hope, until the walking shadows that were once people lost the desire even for the effort of existing, and gave up the ghost.

Chaim had not fully acknowledged the creeping evil in their lives until he recognized it in the unknown woman's face. And now it filled him with a shock of fear that woke him from a long trance. It must not creep over them, he resolved; they must rise above it. They must improve themselves. He would take home more garments, work later hours. At home men studied far into the night—in Vilna he had met a devout man who slept for only three hours and spent the rest of the time studying. He would do the same. But in the cause of the family's survival his work would take the place of his studying.

That night he said a *Kaddish* for the dead woman. Ashes to ashes. One garment less for Kolinsky, he could bear that loss. But a woman slumped with downcast eyes should be remembered by someone, prayed for by someone as she lay in the morgue with her head and breasts kicked to destruction. Moses said, "I have put before you this day life and death; choose therefore life." But you did not *choose* life, Chaim realized. You fought for it. Well, he would fight.

Summer was upon them like a wolf that year, before they could prepare themselves. The icy streets of winter were now tunnels of hot, gritty air. Milk soured before it reached the table; butter turned rancid. Ruth and Miriam cried fretfully, their faces damp and flushed, and Leah sponged them down with water from the rain barrel, hot as bath-

141

water when the sun was at its height. The smell from the shared lavatory, intensified by the heat, was as sharp as ammonia and filled the house.

No one could sleep, and, when the sun set, people carried their kitchen chairs outside and sat by their doors, fanning themselves and talking quietly. Every few yards, grouped around the open front doors, spilling out of the tenements, they gathered in a caricature of continental sociability, the heat and discomfort of their homes driving them outdoors and giving the street a deceptive look of summer ease.

Above the rooftops the sky looked black and thunderous, with no moon visible. Leah sewed by the light slanting from the open window behind her. *At home,* she thought, gazing up for a moment, *the sky would be a deep midnight blue, studded with stars.* There was a Polish song she knew as a child about the night sky and the prince of the moon riding his silver steed through the silent darkness, vaulting the sky from horizon to horizon. She was aware of the vastness of space there, the great empty arc, the immensity. Here, the sky was reduced to a sulphurous-looking strip visible between mean buildings.

At home a slow, healing night silence stole in over the fields, then a bird called sleepily from a nearby tree. A dog barked in some distant farm and from far away came the faint sound of the train whistle, floating across the empty miles. And then the silence fell again, a silence composed of space and stillness through which she felt the slow rhythm of the earth breathing.

Here she was surrounded by the sounds of humanity. They buffeted her: children cried and were hushed, someone was selling nutmegs and horseradish in the next street, calling and ringing a hand bell. From every doorway came murmured Yiddish, an occasional muted laugh. It was too hot for arguing and only the strongest could raise their voices. Ruby Golski, seventy-two and crippled, managed it. "Anarchists!" she rasped. "They should go back to Russia where they came from! Them and their revolution and their nonsense. We don't want them here— These foreigners are nothing but troublemakers!"

At last, with a slight cooling of the air, Leah put down her sewing and took the sleepy children inside to the bed they shared. Then she made a glass of tea for Chaim, who was still working at the kitchen table, the tiny sewing machine whirring, clattering. They sat for a while at the table, Chaim blinking slowly, his eyes sore from the strain. Suddenly Miriam gave a cry and sat up in bed, scratching furiously, rubbing at huge red weals on her legs and arm.

"Chaim, get the disinfectant," Leah said. She pulled the bed away from the wall. On the flaking plaster was a dark red, glistening patch, spreading like a huge splotch of blood as she watched. Bugs. A small army of the blood-hungry creatures brought out by the hot weather, erupting from invisible cracks in the wall and hidden resting places in the floorboards, looking for nourishment.

"I thought I had finished with them last time." Leah sighed and cursed silently. At the thought of the annual battle with the bugs her strength almost failed her. She wanted to pick up the girls, one on each hip, and just carry them away out of the door to somewhere clean and cool. . . .

Chaim found the disinfectant and hurried over with it, but already the bugs, sated with blood, were in temporary retreat. Even as Leah began pumping the handle of the tin spray, the heaving red blanket scattered and the gorged bugs vanished into the wall. From outside Ruby Golski heard the squeaking of the spray. She stuck her head through the open window. "What are you doing? You kill one and thousands come to the funeral!" She cackled and moved off, gripping a homemade paper fan in her crooked fingers.

The next day Leah began the usual campaign against the bugs, burning sulphur candles, filling the rooms with choking fumes while she took the children with her to market. That night she poured soft soap into the upturned lids of empty tins that she placed under each bed leg. The following morning the green, oozy substance was thick with the bugs trapped in it. The chamber pot she had left under the bed for the children had also trapped its quota of bugs, drowned in a sea of urine.

She sealed the rooms, fumigated again, plastered up cracks in the wall, repainted them. Then, as the heat reached its climax the next afternoon, from their hidden nests, from cracks unnoticed and holes invisible to the eye, the bugs emerged, advancing in search of food. Like everyone else, Leah gave up the battle.

Leah left Ruth and Miriam with Mrs. Golski, and she and Simeon took the bus to Hyde Park. As the streets grew cleaner, the houses more spacious, her spirits rose: at last she was to see Speakers' Corner! The sun shone, there were window boxes spilling over with flowers, and ladies in dresses almost as colorful. She had on her best dress, but suddenly she saw how shabby and dull she looked, her hair scraped back, her hands coarsened with work. She could not think when she had last bought something new for herself, but it must have been in Peszno. In London she hardly looked in a mirror. The days of rustling silk dresses brought back from Germany by Hirschl and bright ribbons in her hair seemed almost beyond the reach of memory.

Simeon, despite the heat, wore his Free School corduroy suit, partly because he was so proud of it, and also because it happened to be the only one he possessed. He was glancing about, memorizing the sights of fashionable London, and for a moment Leah felt a stab of regret that it should be this ugly child and not Danielsche enjoying the day with her. To have had that delicate figure beside her—the little brother—would have enriched the day. She realized that in her thoughts he was as he had been at their last meeting. If alive, he would have grown up. He would be a young man now, in army uniform, his body perhaps scarred by wounds, or maimed.

Simeon, sensing a drop into melancholy, turned and gave her a wide, encouraging smile. She smiled back, ashamed of her earlier thoughts. It was Simeon who had to find the way, leading her along the wide, busy street past the vast new store in Oxford Street. "Why not spend a day at Selfridge's?" Leah read out loud from the sign in the windows. "In these clothes," she added, "they would not even let me in!"

They soon saw the crowds listening to the speakers and pushed their way into the thick of them. One man, nicely dressed and prosperous looking, was talking in a well-modulated, clear voice that Leah found she could follow quite easily. He was referring, it seemed, to certain undesirable people who did no work and lived on charity. ". . . They come pouring in, these incapables. They speak no English, learn no skilled trade, they know nothing of the qualities that enrich civilized communities. . . . The Aliens' Immigration Act *must* be maintained!"

Leah felt a shock of dismay: was this how the English saw the immigrants? "What does it mean, incapables?" she asked Simeon.

"Not able to do anything. Useless."

The man was still speaking. She heard the words "dirt" and "ignorance" which needed no translation and pulled Simeon away. "Let us listen to another speaker."

A few yards farther on, a worker in a cloth cap and grimy suit was haranguing the crowd: ". . . Means must be taken to prevent them from taking the bread out o' the mouths of starving English artisans. They belong to no trade unions, they work all hours of the day and night for a few coppers, these . . . immigrants. The alien trade puts away the shekels under their floorboards and gets rich while British workers starve! I ask you, is it right?" The crowd cheered.

In the bus going home Leah was very quiet. Could they ever feel at home in this country where they were so much resented? The man in the next seat was reading a newspaper and Leah noticed him nudging his neighbor and pointing out some cartoons. He read the wording aloud: " 'Yes, guv'nor, I'm the last English bloke in this street.' And look at this one— 'A well known chair-maker tells how the fair and reasonable price of nine and six a chair has been brought down by the Alien Trade. They beat machines, they can produce a chair for three and six . . .' Look at that, Joe. There it is in black and white. The Alien Trade. I tell you, they're after our jobs—"

"Excuse me, mister! You mistaken!" Filled with rage, Leah tapped the man's arm. "You wrong! Vee not alien trade, vee . . . incaperles . . . living on der charity!" She felt a vast sense of frustration that her grasp of English was so limited. There was so much she wanted to explain to the man, but she hoped her sarcastic rebuke would reach its target.

He stared in amazement at this excited young woman who seemed to be so angry with him. Her accent was so thick that he could not make out even a word she was saying. "Look, lady," he said soothingly, "I don't follow you, I'm sorry."

She stared at him. He had called her a lady! He had apologized!

145

The English were totally illogical; she would never understand them.

Simeon hurried home to do some slipper finishing, and Leah waited for Chaim outside the Jewish Reading Room: the workroom was on short time for a few days. While she waited, she watched the bustle across the road: opposite the reading room was the Pavilion Theatre, glittering with lights and jammed with people arriving to see the latest Yiddish drama.

Leah suddenly longed to be part of that crowd, to be going out, to be going into a theater to watch a play! These people, chattering, at their ease, seemed to belong to the city. They had chipped away at London and made themselves a niche.

As Chaim came out he saw her looking across the road, her eyes alight, her whole body radiating a sort of yearning. He did not altogether approve of the theater, and they could afford nothing but the barest essentials just then. He came up to Leah as she gazed ardently at the theatergoers. "Let's see the play," he said.

Their seats were right at the back, high up under the roof of the theater. Although they were very far from the stage, Leah was entranced by everything. The first short play was a comedy, and the audience roared happily at the familiar jokes.

In the interval, the theatergoers plunged their hands into the baskets they all had brought with them, to grab pieces of cold fried fish, salt beef, bagels with smoked salmon, even legs of chicken. The whole audience seethed and heaved, a sea of humanity from whose undulations occasional arms would reach up like shipwrecked sailors, grabbing not for a spar but for a sandwich.

The noise was deafening. Yiddish, Russian, Polish, English, and Dutch, all filtered through the mouthfuls of food being munched with ferocious enthusiasm. Chaim noticed Kolinsky and his scrawny wife sitting below them in the better seats. Kolinsky's bald balloon head was a shiny pink, his ears bright red, and he waved a sandwich energetically in the air to make a point, a piece of salt beef falling out, unnoticed, onto his lap.

The next play began. The setting was Vilna, though it looked like no Vilna Chaim had ever seen. Leah suddenly sat up in her seat, frowning in puzzlement. She clutched Chaim's arm. "But this is Leckert's story—you remember Mordecai's friend, the shoemaker?"

Watching the mummers on the brilliantly lit stage, with the voices drifting up to them through the darkness, Chaim for a moment was back in Peszno, listening to Mordecai's stories of the Bund—the intrigue, the mistakes, the hopes of unity and freedom that all seemed to have withered away.

But it sounded different here—the Bund members were giants of daring and courage, their every act a magnificent achievement. The play reached its climax: the brave shoemaker shot at the governor and was condemned to death—a noble martyr. Around them the audience wept freely, munching the last of their food, sweating, applauding, enjoying the melodrama.

What, Chaim wondered, had become of Leckert, the real Leckert, and the botched assassination that had achieved only reprisals for others and a pointless death for the shoemaker? What had become of reality? He saw that all their pasts ran the same risk: of becoming a comforting fantasy. Already he was no longer sure that he remembered it the way it had really been.

The move took place just before Christmas. Chaim never referred to Christmas of course, nor Easter, but the fact of Christmas could not be overlooked, with shops brightly decorated, and stockings of silver-wrapped tangerines and walnuts hanging outside greengrocers, flanked by miniature Christmas trees.

The move itself brought Christmas forcibly to Leah's attention when she was packing their few bits of china and found a page of an old *Jewish Chronicle* lining a drawer. She was more at ease now with English, and she crouched on the floor, reading a report of a sermon on the Wandering Jew. "If Jesus could return," she read, "the spirit which was in Jesus would spring up again and dominate the Christian Church and the wanderings would be at end, and an end to their persecutions and their disabilities. . . . Jesus was a Jew not only in his birth and state but in his opinions, his convictions, his religion. He did not teach new doctrines. There was no reason why his followers should not remain Jews in their religious belief. As for the doctrines called Christian teaching, he knew nothing about these . . . the Jews whom Christians have so hated and so persecuted for rejecting Jesus have been much nearer to his thought and life than their persecutors."

Mischievously she showed it to Chaim, who merely commented, "And if Antiochus had wiped out Judaism as he wanted to, there would have been neither Christmas Day nor Chanukah to celebrate."

Another pregnancy had almost run its course. Leah hated her own awkwardness, the slowness with which she did everything. Miriam at four was already skilled at looking after her little sister, and Chaim was being helped by the Slumkow boy as he filled boxes and trundled a loaded handcart through the streets to their new home.

Leah was still confused about the whole idea of the move: "If we do not have money enough for two rooms, how is it that we can rent a whole house?" she inquired anxiously.

Chaim said, more confidently than he felt, "It is a question of progress. You have to take a leap, move forward." These brave words covered several days of doubt and self-examination that had begun when he passed the Butler Street Jewish Soup Kitchen and recognized another face from Peszno, Golomstok's son Israel, a tailor who had been a regular at Slumkow's café in the square.

Things had not gone happily for Israel in London. "I ask myself sometimes, Chaim, if I did right to come. On the one hand there are no Russians, there is no pogrom in the night. On the other hand, there is no work to speak of, I lost my wife in the influenza epidemic, and I am left with the child."

Chaim was shocked at the way the death of Golomstok's wife was catalogued, but he realized that not all marriages were as close as his and Leah's. An arranged marriage to a girl chosen by your parents need not result in a meeting of soul mates, whatever the Talmud said.

Israel talked on about his troubles, his voice taking on almost musical cadences. Half-listening, Chaim had a revelation that left him almost giddy. "I can rent you a room, cheap, and get you steady work," he said.

Israel's face lit up, the hollow cheeks creasing hopefully.

And so it came about that as the last days of the year spun out, Chaim, Leah, and the girls moved into the seedy spaciousness of the house in Sidney Street with six rooms and a lavatory all to themselves.

Leah chose two rooms for them to sleep in, on the first floor, and the kitchen downstairs. Israel Golomstok had an attic room for himself and his six-year-old son Abbie, for which he agreed to pay five shillings and six pence a week which Chaim would take out of his earnings. The other attic was rented to a friend of the Abrahamses who also needed work. The front downstairs room became the workshop, for this was the grand, the daring plan. By renting out the two rooms to employees, Chaim ensured both a regular payment toward his own rent, and a steady flow of work from his two lodgers.

Leah commented wonderingly, "You have become a work boss."

"I am simply safeguarding our livelihood," he said sharply. But both statements were true.

Golomstok had no furniture, so he and the child slept on a pile of bedding in one corner of their attic. They ate mostly bread and soup which Abbie fetched from the soup kitchen. The Abrahamses' friend, a sad, solitary man named Segal, cooked himself vile-smelling herring meals on a little range he picked up in the market, filling his room with smoke and fumes that curled down the staircase, finding their way all over the house.

"Look here, Segal," Chaim said irritably. "Your herrings are everywhere. The garments smell of herring, the machine oil is beginning to smell of herring. It must stop."

Leah felt too heavy and fatigued now to do more than sit in the kitchen and try to keep herself warm. Londoners were celebrating New Year's Eve. She recalled another December's end, twelve years before, when she and Mordecai and the others had welcomed in the twentieth century. Esperanto and international understanding and free thought would change all their lives. Where had it gone? She was twenty-five, and she felt a million years old.

Simeon, who had brought over his schoolbooks the day before, had made her read out some lines, one of which, to her surprise, she found she remembered: "She is older than the rocks among which she sits."

She felt a weariness of the eyelids and the soul. Sitting in the kitchen she saw nothing of what went on in the street, and Chaim was busy moving in the rented sewing machines, the big tailoring tables, and the rails for the completed garments. So no one paid any attention to number 100, the house across the street, and in any case they would hardly have been struck by the appearance of any dark, foreign-looking, furtive men coming and going. Almost everyone looked dark and foreign and furtive in Stepney on a cold January morning.

Two days later, as her contractions began, Leah abandoned

149

her warm kitchen and moved upstairs. The midwife came and went, promising to be back later, and Mrs. Golski sent her daughter over to help. Leah waited apprehensively as each wave of pain receded, dreading the next, wondering how long it would be. Through the night she slept fitfully, waking suddenly to cry out as another spasm gripped her body. The midwife had pronounced that nothing would happen before the next day, and had gone home to sleep.

A little before dawn Leah woke, startled, tensing herself against expected pain, but no contraction followed. Something else had wakened her, some noise. She sat up and found Chaim peering down at the dark street. "What is it?"

"Police. The street is full of police." The window was blurred with frost and grime and he rubbed at the glass to try to improve the view. From outside came the muffled sound of voices, and men moving quietly. Then silence. Suddenly Leah's body heaved convulsively. She cried out, "Chaim! It's beginning!"

He began to dress hurriedly. Why had the midwife gone home? These women were too confident. How could you be so certain of the time of a birth? With the two girls he had been out of the way when it happened. Now he was involved. And he did not know what to do.

"What should I do?" he asked. But she was too busy trying to control her breathing to answer him.

The sky was lighter now, and Chaim could see clearly what was going on outside. The police had surrounded a house across the road, and, as he watched, two officers walked up to the front door and one of them knocked loudly. From above his head, from a second-floor window, there came a burst of gunfire and Chaim saw one of the policemen drop to the pavement with a faint, astonished cry.

Leah heard the shots and sat up again. "What are they doing?"

"Shooting at the police."

She gasped, and gulped water thirstily from a cup next to the bed.

"Someone is knocking at the door, perhaps it is the midwife." Chaim clattered down the stairs and Leah heard voices, then the sound of people climbing the staircase, going up past her door. Someone wanting Golomstok perhaps. More knocks, more murmurs, more people climbing. From time to time Chaim looked in, saw that things were much the same, and disappeared again. From the street, more shots, but Leah had lost interest. What did she care about some madman firing on the police? The contractions were almost continuous now, and she began to feel a powerful urge to push the center of pain out of her body.

Chaim, looking dazed, put his head in the door. "Are you all right?"

Before she could answer, another knock from below sent him flying down the stairs, but this time he reappeared followed by the midwife, looking unperturbed. She put down her bag, took off her shapeless coat, rolled up her sleeves, and crossed unhurriedly to Leah, writhing on the bed. "Now," she said briskly, "let me have a look at you."

Dimly, through her absorption with her own body, Leah heard the increasingly loud noises from all around. Shots and shouts and the boots of running men. From overhead too, there came noises—there were, it seemed, people on the roof.

Around noon the child was born, and Leah, exhausted, noted with satisfaction that it was a boy and that he had a lusty cry. She knew already what he should be called: Emmanuel, which meant "God with us." "Butter and honey shall he eat," said Isaiah, "that he may know to refuse the evil and choose the good."

Chaim held the child and wept, and he touched Leah's soaking head. Then he was gone again to answer the door. More clattering up the stairs, then some shuffling.

Chaim came in diffidently. "Leah, would it trouble you if some neighbors stood by the window to watch?"

Leah stared as a bunch of strangers invaded her bedroom and crowded around the window. The midwife was washing the baby, and one or two of the women looked away from the street to glance at the child and exclaim approvingly. But mostly they confined themselves to the scene outside.

"Hundreds of police! With guns! Are those soldiers?" "Morrie says that's the uniform of the Royal Engineers, he makes their jackets. . . ." "Did you see the smart fellow in the top hat and well-cut overcoat? The Home Secretary, that's right, Winston Churchill, very nice overcoat, lovely quality. . . . He took a cup of tea from—Look, there's the fire brigade now."

"What is happening?" Leah asked.

The midwife looked bored. "Anarchists. Always making trouble."

From the group at the window a sudden gasp of pleasurable horror: "The house is on fire!"

Leah slowly got out of bed, wrapped herself in a blanket, and moved over to the window. She could glimpse number 100 over the shoulders of the others, billowing smoke, and seeping through the gaps in the window came its acrid smell.

Weakness and panic overcame her. The sound of fire, the shouts, the smell of smoke; in her mind it spelled pogrom. She sank back on the bed, pressing the floppy pillow to her face and ears to shut out the smell and sounds, weeping.

From the doorway Chaim saw her prone body and his head cleared. The sense of unreality that had descended on him when the first group at the front door pressed money into his hand for the privilege of a view from his rooftop had grown into a fever, a wild dream of riches fluttering his way, endless ten-shilling notes. But now it left him. He strode into the room and said sharply, "It is over. Everyone must leave. My wife must be quiet."

Reluctantly they jostled out of the room and down the stairs. Then slowly, the people from the roof went. At last the house was empty. Leah went to the window. The house opposite was still smoking, but Chaim told her the charred bodies of the besieged men had been removed. There were rumors that others had escaped.

The soldiers had withdrawn, the crowds had gone home to eat and gossip. In the street, unnoticed, lay the two dead bodies of unwitting participants in the battle: a cat and a dog.

The workshop should have been a success.

"There is plenty for everyone," Kolinsky had told Chaim. "For the first time the British workingman can buy new clothes for everyday instead of secondhand castoffs from lords and ladies that they pick up from the old-clo' men. These people from Leeds—Marks and Spencer— are opening a branch in London. Maybe you should see if they have something for you?"

Chaim got customers, but something was wrong. Delivery was slow, the customers grew irritated. Chaim had never been a work boss, merely a supervisor. He sat at a machine himself, and soon he was sitting longer, his treadle rocking faster, his fingers hardened like seasoned leather. For the truth was that Israel Golomstok and Segal were not good workers. They appeared, yawning, when Chaim had already opened up. They spread out their work reluctantly, they disappeared upstairs at lunchtime for an hour or more, and their working day grew shorter as the months passed.

"Throw them out," Leah advised.

"I will talk to them again. Perhaps they will change."

She looked skeptical. "You know what it says in the Torah: 'Can the Ethiopian change his skin or the leopard his spots?' Throw them out."

It was amazing, Chaim thought, how often Leah quoted from the Torah. The freethinking daughter of a pious man could be a hard companion at times. But he still hoped that if he made the position clear, the men would understand. He made the position clear: "I cannot pay you for work you have not done."

They nodded mournfully. They understood. But they did not change. They ate at the soup kitchen whenever they could; their rooms were almost rent-free since Chaim could hardly extract money from the now-penniless lodgers. And he was too soft to get rid of them.

A few days later Simeon called in after school. Leah hugged him affectionately and handed him the baby while she made him a glass of tea. "I heard about the siege . . . about the anarchists. I thought you might have been involved."

"Oh!" Leah shrugged sadly. "My revolutionary days are over. Now I'm just a spectator—I know nothing of all this."

He walked up and down as he sipped his tea, pausing to tweak the baby's head absent-mindedly. Leah saw he had something on his mind. "How are the lessons?" she asked. "No more poetry for me? How are you doing at school?"

"I'll be leaving soon. I'm nearly thirteen."

"You could stay on, get a scholarship, a clever boy like you."

"Dad wants me to help in the business."

The business. A grand name for slippers, Leah thought. She watched him pacing.

"There is to be an inspection at school tomorrow. A visit from one of the school governors . . ."

"So?"

He pointed at his feet, and she saw that the boots, flapping and split at the sides, were a woman's castoffs. "Mum's pawned my boots again."

"But I thought the school authorities told her—"

He shrugged, but she saw his distress. "I think I'll just stay away tomorrow. They probably won't notice."

"No. It's not right."

She thought for a moment. "Have you the token?"

"It's on the mantelshelf at home."

Leah went to the square tin where she kept a small stock of coins, saving them up with painful slowness toward a treat she had long dreamed of: a day at the seaside. She emptied the tin onto the table. How few coins it held after so many weeks! "Is there enough here? Take what you need."

"I can't—"

"Don't talk, hurry! You can redeem the boots before the shop closes. Don't let your mother catch you. And here—" She thrust Chaim's freshly ironed white shirt at him. "Borrow this, you'll look like a prince."

The next morning, Sir Samuel Morgenstern arrived in Leman Street in his automobile and was helped out by an official of the school. The inspection began—boys standing stiff and nervously ill at ease, Sir Samuel placidly bored.

At last he reached the oldest boys. He paused theatrically. "Well, boys. This is the important moment. My annual visit is more than a routine look at your fingernails. I like to see a well-polished pair of boots, but I'm interested in what's inside your heads too. The boy I choose will come and live in my home, have the finest education in the country. It will give him a chance to reach the very top. Now," he said, turning to the school official, "which boys have the best marks?"

"Simeon Abrahams has the best marks, Sir Samuel."

Morgenstern's face fell slightly at the sight of the clumsy youth. "In what subjects?" he asked hopefully.

"All subjects."

Next to Simeon stood a graceful, languid boy with lustrous eyes and a slender face. Morgenstern thought how handsome he would look in decent clothes; already he stood well. Perhaps he should think over the choice, issue his decision later, privately. . . .

Simeon, reading his mind, understood his problem, and, catching Morgenstern's eye, he gave him a reassuring smile. Morgenstern caught the full strength of that enveloping warmth. He found himself smiling back at the boy. "Abrahams, eh? And what do you want to be, Abrahams?"

Confident in his polished boots and clean white shirt, Simeon said, "A lawyer, sir."

"Lawyer? What made you settle on that?"

"Shakespeare, sir. I thought: With a good lawyer Shylock would never have got himself into that situation."

Morgenstern's smile broadened. "A lawyer then. Right. I shall be seeing you."

After school Simeon leaped up the stairs, searching for Leah. "I'm to go to Charterhouse!"

She stared at him uncomprehendingly.

"Morgenstern! The inspection! A miracle, but he chose me, and I'm to go to his old school, it's a great public school. I'll spend the holidays at their home, travel—"

Leah hugged him, thrilled. "It is God's will," she said, quite sincerely.

Leah was pregnant again. She thought sometimes that the price of the infrequent and none-too-wonderful physical relationship she enjoyed with her husband was astonishingly high. The months of discomfort, the growing clumsiness, the pain, the extra work, the expense.

It was the arrival of Sarah that brought matters to a head. Sarah was the smallest, the thinnest of the children, with a long pale face and tiny bird bones. Manny had been small, but sturdy. This one was frail. But her energy showed at once, as though she knew instinctively that, in her situation, lying still would get her nowhere. As Chaim bent over her and murmured a blessing, she tossed her head sideways, the minute fingers reaching up to her ear. He gave a rare chuckle of amusement.

"As is the mother, so is the daughter," he quoted. Leah, unaware of her own gesture of impatience and equally unaware that Chaim had long ago recognized and analyzed it, thought he was simply being sentimental.

Something had to be done. The last of the "siege money," all those ten-shilling notes that had fallen so painlessly into Chaim's hands the year before, had been used. Even though he worked harder than ever, Chaim realized that the rent of the house was beyond them. They would have to move again.

He reread the last letter from his father: "There are rumors everywhere. The barracks are empty, the soldiers are being moved secretly, and no one knows what will happen. The talk is worrying. Thank you for the money you sent last time, you have been a good son. . . ."

In the street he heard the news vendors crying out with relish the headline of the day: "Suffragette throws herself in front of King's horse! Derby tragedy!" What sort of woman killed herself for the sake of a piece of paper? Chaim wondered. Why were they so violent? What did they want from life so badly that they were prepared to sacrifice life itself?

He went to the synagogue to give thanks for his new child—"even though it is a girl" as the service phrased it—and there, while Chaim was praying, Moses Mendel entered his life.

"You look like a man with problems," Mendel said. "Problems, like blessings, should be shared." Mendel had the head of a fish, which stuck out grotesquely from his long, greasy coat. Beneath the black hat, his jutting nose, large glassy eyes, and nonexistent chin sloping away to his collar gave him the look of an earnest herring. The puny body was stooped, curving, the fish head poking forward so that with his small, shuffling footsteps he slithered along the pavement as though balancing on his tail. When he spoke he had a way of lifting his arms slightly away from his body and then letting them fall again against his coat. It looked as though he was breathing through gills. Winter and summer he wore the same clothes, hat and overcoat, though in the coldest weather he added a mottled green muffler, like a trail of seaweed around his throat.

Chaim told him about the workshop lying idle, about the lodgers, equally idle, and his increasingly large family. Mendel listened intently, eyes glistening sympathetically, arms moving almost imperceptibly as he breathed. At the end he nodded, blew his nose thoughtfully on an ancient handkerchief, and said, "I can help you. This is what we must do."

The following day Golomstok and Segal were roused at dawn by a loud hammering on their doors. "Where's Golomstok? Where's Segal?" shouted Mendel. "Why are they not at work!"

The miserable wretches struggled down to the workroom, barely awake, and began nervously to sort out garments, giving the newcomer puzzled glances. Chaim sewed quietly. Mendel stormed about the room, kicking aside cardboard boxes, shrugging irritably, rheumy eyes dribbling, gills opening and closing rapidly. As the work speeded up he flashed a rare smile, revealing a glimpse of sharp teeth that filled his mouth in yellow profusion. Suddenly he was no longer a mild herring, but a different kind of fish altogether—the sort that was capable of opening its jaws and snapping up sprats like Segal and Golomstok with one flip of its fins.

The machines rattled, the work was sent out, and the rent was paid. But Mendel saw the customers and did the books. Chaim was busy at the machine. When Leah realized what was happening, she, too, stormed at Chaim. "He has become your work boss, he keeps the money, you get a wage like those two upstairs. What has he contributed? Why should he be the master here?"

She marched down to confront the usurper. Mendel was eating a herring sandwich, feeding it rapidly into his wet slit of a mouth. He looked up questioningly, his eyes swimming. Leah said firmly, "Mr. Mendel, I cannot allow you to take over my husband's workshop in this way. You have been very kind, giving him your time, and you should have some return for that, but these are *his* premises and he must have control."

He put down the sandwich and stood up, looming over her. "Must? *Must?* There is no must, Mrs. Rubinstein. Your husband was about to become a pauper when I took over his business—"

"Took over? What did you do, exactly?"

"I brought it to life! Have you been out in the streets, woman, have you seen the laborers waiting for a few hours' work? This is a slack time, men are being told there is no work for them. You want the soup kitchen again, Mrs. Rubinstein? The handout of a piece of bread? Are your children eating? Do they have shoes on their feet? Do you have a fowl, maybe, on a Friday night, coal in your grate? Do you remember the coal tickets, Mrs. Rubinstein, and the empty grate when the week's coal is finished and the children are crying, hungry? Don't come talking to me about who has control. Your husband is a good man, Mrs. Rubinstein, but he has a scholar's head on his shoulders. A *maggid* he could be. That is bad for business. Lucky for him I can look after the business and leave him free to work and pray with his mind at peace. Just feed your family, Mrs. Rubinstein, and give thanks, give thanks for Moses Mendel."

"But you take everything. He has a wage like any other worker. And you do nothing. Can that be right?"

"Because I am here, you are eating," he said. "If I was not here in this workroom your good husband would be busy praying for help from God and you would be pawning your coat to feed your children." He picked up his sandwich. "Now don't bother me."

She went into the kitchen. Emmanuel woke and began to cry, which set off Sarah in her basket. Leah picked him up and rocked him against her shoulder, absently, soothing Sarah with her other hand. She knew, with a terrible certainty, that Mendel was right. Unjust, wicked as it was, his presence made the difference between existing and starving. From the bedroom came the sound of Chaim coughing nervously, and then he started down the stairs. Mendel did not give the workers long for their meal break.

She listened to him coughing and gasping for air, and she was overcome with a sudden reckless fury: Mendel was not God. He could be defied. She counted the coins in her little tin and stood waiting for Chaim. "Tomorrow we shall have a holiday. We shall spend the day by the sea!"

It was August Bank Holiday Monday. There was an uneasiness in the air, a sense of waiting for no one knew quite what. They sat on the train, tense with anticipation, gazing out the windows, the children hardly able to believe in the miles of green, curving countryside. At Southend they walked very slowly from the station to the beach. The children stared silently at the great, flat expanse of water: endless, unreal. It was their first sight of the sea. Chaim carried Sarah against his shoulder and Manny held on tightly to his big sisters' fingers.

There were other children on the beach, in light summer clothing, sailor suits and straw hats, with spades and buckets, laughing and running around like puppies. The Rubinsteins were not dressed for such activities. In their dark clothes and heavy boots they stood like a clump of shadow on the sunny promenade, ill at ease, out of their element. Finally the children took off their shoes and stockings and gingerly walked across the grayish sand to stand with their toes in the shallow, lapping surf. Ruth and Miriam grew more daring and looped up their petticoats to paddle energetically, beckoning Emmanuel to join them, but he shook his head gravely, walked back to Leah and Chaim on the promenade, and carefully dusted the sand off his bare feet.

Later they ate some bread and cheese and apples, trying not to notice the melting glories of vanilla and strawberry ice cream being consumed by others not bound by the dietary laws. Such food could not be kosher. Ruth did venture to say that she found it unlikely that pork fat would be found in ice cream, but it made no difference. Then the girls paddled again until it was time to catch the train home. As they walked away from the beach, Leah looked back for a moment, and it seemed as though the bright, glittering scene was already far away, the tiny figures leaping happily, dwindling while she watched, seen through the wrong end of a telescope. When she turned back to walk on, her eyes dazzled from the sun, the street suddenly seemed darker, as though a cloud had passed over it.

The summer heat had brought out the bugs as usual, but Leah was too tired to fight back. The day after their trip to Southend, while the dark red predators swarmed the walls in constantly changing patterns, the women and children retreated to the pavement outside the front door, sitting listlessly in the shade cast by the buildings. From inside came the endless whirring of the machines. Leah, her head full of shifting patterns of blue sea and sky, sat slackly, breathing through her mouth so that she could avoid smelling the foul air.

Moses Mendel came rushing down the street toward them, his face shining with a mixture of exultation and perspiration. "Good news! We must get more machines, we shall be extra busy. We will be making uniforms, they will need a lot of uniforms."

"Why?" asked Leah, dull from the heat. Spiritless from fighting bugs and dust, she had not read a newspaper for weeks.

"Why?" The fish face gaped at her. "For the war, of course."

And so, as naturally as one season of the year moved into another, peace gave place to war, and everyone's life was changed.

David was a big, fair-skinned child unlike any of the others —"My English boy!" Leah said, laughing at him. She had no trouble with David: an easy birth, an easy baby. A smiler. He had a slow, almost astonished grin that invited complicity in his pleasure.

Emmanuel, from the very beginning, took a special interest in the new arrival. Later he taught him how to grip his rattle, moulding the fat baby fingers around the handle. "We shall be partners," he said to the infant, who grinned happily back at him.

"Already he is talking like a businessman!" Chaim marveled, with a tinge of dismay. "Where does he hear such talk?"

"Not in this house, *nebech*!" snapped Mendel, who kept his piety strictly for the synagogue and would have welcomed a more business-like atmosphere in the establishment. He and Golomstok collected bales of khaki cloth regularly. They had made new patterns—civilian suit patterns were no use, a uniform was something else.

"Cut economical!" Mendel exhorted. "Narrow seams! And watch your hems, keep them small—what d'you think, they're going to grow out of them? A uniform has a short life."

And the men? Chaim wondered. *Will they, too, have a short life?* The material was thick and coarse, hard to stitch. Chaim rubbed the back of his hand gently across the cloth: the men who would wear these uniforms, some of them would be seasoned soldiers with hard bodies. Others would be young boys, off to fight unknown enemies, the cloth chafing and scratching their flesh. As he repeated the endless, unvarying movements—sending the cloth forward, turning, turning again, stitching—a moment's lack of concentration sent the needle plunging into his finger.

The blood welled up, a scarlet drop splotching onto the material and vanishing like rain soaking into sand. Chaim stared, hypnotized, at the blood trembling on his finger. Would some boy fall, bleeding, in this uniform now taking shape beneath his needle, the blood soaking the thick cloth until it was dark and stiff, the flesh stiff within it. . . .

"Faster!" screamed Mendel, slithering up and down between the tables. "We have to deliver tomorrow, not next week!"

Gradually there were changes that became impossible to ignore.

"You sure you're not German?" The burly cockney in the vegetable stall stared at Leah and Chaim. "You got a funny accent."

"My accent I can't help but German I am not and never was." To Chaim she added in Yiddish, "He seems to think we're Germans."

"What's that yer talkin' then?" the man demanded. "Sounded like German to me." He turned to his mate. "It all sounds the same to me, bleedin' foreigners, they're all German, wherever they come from. Oughta be locked up."

Every day Chaim took David on his lap as he repeated the morning and evening prayers. The child listened, his eyes fixed on his father's lips. Leah recognized Chaim's growing fear that the English, gentile influences which he himself kept at bay might erode the old traditions. She sympathized, but she made sure the children spoke English together. It was no good always to be a stranger in a strange land. The children must belong here. Now, especially, a foreign accent, a foreign name, was an embarrassment. She approved of the fluent cockney that flowed from the children's lips. They had made a good beginning. Perhaps the family should change its name. The Finkelsteins had just changed their name to Firman. A foreigner, once merely a source of amusement, was becoming an object of suspicion. It could be dangerous.

A German brass band used to play on Sunday mornings and Chaim loved the sound of it. He raised his head from the machine and nodded in time to the *oompa! oompa!* of the march as the men went swinging down the street. But the band had quietly been disbanded. Mendel had changed his name to Menderby, although nobody used the English version, least of all his English customers.

Mendel was very happy with the way the war was going. The threat of a short war—"We'll have the boys home before Christmas"— had not pleased him; that would hardly have done more than help them over the slack summer season. As it was, the demand for men grew and so did the demand for uniforms.

Young Jacob Fishbein had enlisted and vanished into the Army, to his mother's despair. "This is not our war," she said bitterly to Leah. "But you see: our blood will be spilled." Simeon wrote to say he had volunteered and would be going into the Flying Corps.

On a lamppost in the street Leah found a crude painted sign: BUY BRITISH, STAMP OUT THE ALIEN TRADE.

"We shall need more hands," Mendel said briskly one day, "a couple more at least." He arranged everything. The house was filled with cloth, and now he reorganized the sleeping arrangements. "Golomstok and Segal, you must move in together. We need the room for machines." He put two worktables in one of the attics and moved an old iron bedstead for himself into a corner of the downstairs workroom.

Chaim breathed in the tiny furry particles dislodged from the cloth, and his cough grew worse. "Why do we allow it?" Leah asked Chaim one night. They were sitting at the kitchen range, Chaim huddled close to the source of warmth as always. "You work night and day, you look like a ghost, and you earn laborer's wages. Everyone thinks we are getting rich with the uniforms!"

Chaim's cough saved him from the humiliation of answering. He had a bad attack. Ruth, bringing in a container of milk still warm from the cow in the stables down the road, gave him some to soothe his throat.

Fortunately, Mendel's frenzied searching for more and more work resulted in an order for parachutes for the balloon observers. The zeppelin raid on the Guildhall had made everyone very conscious of the possibilities of war in the skies. The parachutes were difficult to handle, billowing, slippery, spreading everywhere. But the silk was fine and smooth, and, given a respite from the fuzzy fibers of the uniforms, Chaim's lungs eased a little.

While Ruth and Miriam went to the Free School with Abbie Golomstok, Leah took Emmanuel and Sarah down to the local infants' school. Every day David begged to be allowed to go too. He was not yet four but big for his age, and so keen to share the adventure of school that in the end he got his way. When he was initiated into the mysteries of English nursery rhymes he at once passed them on to Chaim:

> . . . There I met an old man who wouldn't say his prayers,
> I took him by the left leg and threw him down the stairs!

Chaim shook his head, convinced anew that beneath the apparent civilization of this country lay a barbarity of a particularly ferocious kind. He thought for a moment of that unknown dead woman, trying to protect her children from their vicious father, and murdered for her pains. . . . What was it about the English? They seemed to reserve their worst brutality for the helpless: for children, for wives. Toward strangers they tended to behave with restraint, though their nursery rhymes bore evidence of an underlying violence. An old man who wouldn't say his prayers. . . . Perhaps the old man was of a different faith? Other prayers, other ways, throw him down the stairs. It was not hard to see in the mind's eye a pogrom.

He realized that he could be accused of worrying unnecessarily: no one stopped anyone from praying in London as far as he knew. Here, the danger was perhaps more that the praying would simply cease, wither away. The boys attended *cheder*, but he sensed that whereas they learned their Hebrew conscientiously enough, they absorbed English ways without even being aware of it.

Living daily with the ebb and flow of the war, they found the news from Russia curiously irrelevant: the workers' struggle intruded only peripherally into their lives and their workroom. In Europe the killing continued; more uniforms were needed.

By now Leah, too, was working on the uniforms, collecting finished garments, folding and packing. They were surrounded by a constant clatter: the hiss of the gas irons for pressing, the incessant humming of the sewing machines. The machines were usually loud enough to block out most noises from the street, but one afternoon Leah became aware of a steady droning from the sky. So loud was it that people were beginning to run outside and look up, shielding their eyes from the sun. She followed them out.

About twenty planes, flying low and in tight formation, were overhead. "It must be the Flying Corps," a neighbor shouted. "But why so low?"

When the bombs began to fall, tumbling lazily through the summer sky like black eggs, people were more astonished than afraid at first. "It *can't* be the Germans . . ." But it was. The sound of the bombs when they struck was no louder than the planes, already vanishing from sight.

Standing in the street, Leah frowned, shading her eyes. She, too, was more surprised than frightened, and she thought: *The bombs are several streets away, not near enough to do any harm.* Leah turned away, still thinking idly about the bombs. *They must have dropped several minutes walk from here, over there, over there where the infant school is.* As she began to run, she heard a curious noise, as of someone moaning, and realized it came from her own mouth. She clamped her lips together and began to pray, mechanically racing through prayers that she had not turned to for years. Everything else was blank. She would not allow herself to think. Others were running alongside her. No one called out or cried.

When she got nearer the school, she heard new noises: screams and groans and the crashing of timber. But here in this street, everything looked normal: no houses touched, nobody hurt. Surely it could not be different, just a street away? Her hands began to shake and she hugged herself as she ran, tripping and stumbling.

She reached the corner and stopped, hardly able to believe her eyes: the school was gone. What this morning had been a solid building standing among its fellows was now a gaping hole, a smoking, pulverized ruin.

She must have screamed, she heard a sound, then she hurled herself forward again, smashing aside a man who tried, kindly, to hold her back. All around the wreckage, children were lying, some motionless, some trying to crawl, calling out, crying. She went, crouching, from one to another, calling the three names over and over—"Emmanuel! Sarah! David!" She did not stop to help the children who were hurt, she dared not. She was blind to their bleeding, deaf to their cries. She was looking for her own. And, unbelievably, miraculously, she heard her shouts answered. From the other end of the playground, clutching each other, too dazed to run, Sarah and Emmanuel called, and Leah ran to them, grasping them fiercely, checking them for wounds, amazed, feeling their arms and legs, finding them whole, allowing the tears of relief to pour down her cheeks. She looked behind them, "Where is David?" she asked, knowing he was never far from Emmanuel, clutching his jacket or sleeve. Emmanuel stared at her, his face crumpled. Sarah had to answer.

"David stayed in the school when we came out to play. He wanted to see one of the picture books."

Leah looked again at the school, at the pile of rubble. "Stay here."

She pushed Emmanuel and Sarah against the playground wall and ran. Around her, people were running, some clumsily, panic-stricken, some purposefully, like the ambulance men moving gently but urgently. Firemen with hoses and axes had surrounded the building. The roof had caved in, and the dilapidated brick walls had crashed on top of it. Clouds of smoke and thick billowing dust made it difficult to see exactly what remained.

Leah was through the line of men before they could stop her, and she pulled frantically at a beam toppled crazily over some rubble. Perhaps she could find David in time, a child so small he might be sheltering under something. She was sure she heard a sound from beneath the wreckage. She began to scream his name, tearing at the rubble with her bare hands, unaware that they were bleeding. The firemen were strong, even though they were sympathetic. They carried Leah away from the wreckage despite her demented struggles. "Look, love: it's dangerous," one said, gripping her arms, holding her.

"My child is in there."

He shook his head. "You can't do nothing about it now. Our chaps and the ambulance men will try to get everyone out. You'll only slow us down. Be a good girl."

She sagged, realizing he was right. Slowly she went back to Emmanuel and Sarah, collected them and waited where she was told, while the men went in. Occasionally when her torn fingers dripped blood, she wiped them on her skirt. For a long time nothing seemed to happen. The men were clearing a path, tapping, lifting beams, shifting heaps of masonry. Slowly. So slowly. Then they began bringing out the small, limp bodies, handling them gently, as if it still mattered. More waiting. From where she stood the children looked as though they were sleeping, cradled in the men's arms. It took a long time. David was one of the last.

Everyone was going to a peace party; each street had its own. Bunting and flags were strung between the tall buildings; every window held a Union Jack or a brightly colored picture of the King and Queen. Trestle tables were carried out and laid with an astonishing selection of food. Chaim had agreed that the children could participate, but they sat at the kosher table approved by the synagogue —"At least we won't have to say no to the sandwiches on account of we don't know what's in 'em," commented Manny to Sarah. The other tables had pork pies and platters spread with tongue and ham and sausage rolls—wicked and forbidden fruit, all.

Sarah whispered to Manny, "I don't want none, not really, but I wanta know what it *tastes* like, that's all."

Even on the kosher table, alongside the rye bread and cream cheese, the smoked salmon, bagels, and egg rolls, there was fizzy lemonade to drink and a little handful of sweets for each child, wrapped in a twist of brown paper. Easily singled out, the returned soldiers, some still in their uniforms, were cheered and toasted with lemonade and cider. Jacob Fishbein was back—a corporal! His mother dragged him from group to group like a prize exhibit. "He was wounded, mine boy. But he's home, thank God. Doesn't he look a real *mensch* in his uniform?" Forgotten now were the threats she had used to try to stop him from enlisting.

The soldiers were begged for stories, souvenirs. Somehow the empty sleeves, the crutches, the dark glasses, added a heroic rather than a depressing note. "Tell us about the trenches, Jacob!"

The mud they drowned in, the poison gas, the coughing, and the shredded lungs were forgotten in a grand euphoria that was rounded to perfection when a military band struck up a march on the corner. Farewell, Verdun! So long, Marne! Peace was here again and things would be different now.

The table was crowded, not a chair empty. But for Leah there was an emptiness. She did not dwell morbidly on David's death; there had been, in any case, hardly time, too much to do. But she remained always aware that the group was incomplete. A part of her was missing. Now and again she would come upon some little reminder—a tiny garment, or one of the wooden soldiers a neighbor had given the child —and she would feel again that stab in her body, that leap of the heart— perhaps after all it had not really happened, perhaps she was just waking from a dream and she would turn and hand the soldier to its small owner. She would hold her breath for a moment or two, eyes squeezed shut, praying that it might be true. Then she would look around, and everything quickly became normal and she carried on with her work. Quite normal, except for an ache that filled her body, and an invisible creature within her who rocked and moaned, who mourned. Her early introduction to violent death in Peszno, later the shooting down of her parents in a Warsaw street—none of it had prepared her for this. To lose your child was different. The pain of childbirth was only a foreshadowing: the first of the agonies of motherhood.

Chaim, though mourning his son, was sustained by his faith. Leah resented his serene acceptance of God's will. Life did not strike her at all as the creation of a wise or logical God. But she did give thanks for peace.

Mendel, who saw things more clearly, did not. "Who will provide the work now? Who will need the uniforms?" he asked, and immediately got rid of the extra hands. He stayed on, seemingly a permanent fixture of the workshop with his squeaky bed and his sandwiches, his long nose forever dripping as though he had just surfaced from the seabed. "Peace will be worse than the war," Mendel said. And as usual, he was right.

The news from Russia, too, was disquieting. After the first splendor of the revolution, events seemed to be taking an unexpected turn. Could this be *the* revolution, the great proletarian victory they had argued about, marched for? Mendel, with his cynical eye, viewed the changes with detachment: "When the dust has settled, some will have, and some will have not. Just as always. Nothing changes."

Ruth was now thirteen and won a scholarship at school. Leah persuaded her to go on. "We'll manage. You shouldn't lose the chance of a proper education."

"What's the good of an education if there's no work?" Miriam asked, and quickly accepted a job at the fireworks factory nearby.

"The war is barely over and people are making explosives for fun?" Chaim questioned, appalled. But when work was available, no one turned it down. Everyone wanted work. The dockers rioted—for work. The miners marched to London—for work. And they straggled home again, defeated. A handful stayed on, earning a few bitter shillings by any means they could. Young Polanski's brother-in-law Ephraim was playing in a dance band for a few weeks, covering for their usual fiddler, who had influenza.

"All big stuff," he told Leah and Chaim. "West End hotels, dinner dances, charity affairs. Saturday night we did a ball—big hotel in Mayfair. The hostess is one of your smart ones—organizes a special cabaret: a bunch of miners, cloth caps and mufflers, the lot, to sing for the guests."

He had watched them from the back of the stage, the miners

clustered together in the middle of the dance floor, shabby and filled with hate. Ephraim knew the hatred that sprang from hunger and fed on condescension.

Afterward the miners were allowed to pass the hat around among the guests. The waiters, seeing their own tips jeopardized, were furious. "Bloody Welsh, bloody nerve, muscling in, taking bread out of our mouths. Why don't they go back where they belong!"

They were herded into the bandroom for beer and sandwiches. Ephraim passed them the ham sandwiches, and stood munching an egg and cress by the door. Floating back from the ballroom he heard a high-pitched, fluting voice: "Miners! Darling, how incredibly picturesque. Where did you find them? Something really ought to be done about them. I mean really."

Then the next dance band started up.

In the night Manny grew feverish and began to call out, delirious. Leah and Ruth sat up with him for the rest of the night, bathing his forehead and trying to cool him. His breathing became difficult and by morning he was barely conscious.

Leah sat with him day and night, giving him water to sip from a spoon, wrapping hot bricks from the oven in clean cloth and placing them near his feet when he began to shiver uncontrollably, soothing him with small tuneless noises.

Ruth said firmly, "We've got to get the doctor."

When he came, the doctor was brisk and unsurprised. "Influenza. It's everywhere. Best get him into hospital. If you can."

Shortly after midnight, the feverish mumbling stopped. Leah jumped up, alarmed, to bend over the bed. Manny's eyes were open and he smiled at her reassuringly. "Don't worry, Mum. I've a *shvartzeh g'vura.* I'll be all right, you just see."

He was out of bed for his tenth birthday and back at school a fortnight later. "I'm strong, Mum," he said, always with that encouraging grin. "You don't have to worry about me."

He was small for his age and stocky, with a round, serious face. But when he smiled the formless features broke into upward curves and chubby cushions with a disarming effect. "Remember," he insisted, "you don't have to worry about me."

But Chaim worried about Manny: "You do not study, Emmanuel. You are too busy with everyday matters," he said one afternoon.

168

"I come first in class."

"In school, yes. But what is schoolwork? Only a part of your studies. You do not spend time with the Torah. Schoolwork alone will not help you. You need God's help with the problems, the responsibilities of life."

Manny said shortly, "I go to Hebrew class, I say my prayers. But life is more than just studying Torah. I mean to make something of *my* life."

He had not intended to stress the word, but it emerged so, and Chaim flushed, aware of the implied criticism. "Do not imagine that success alone gives meaning to life," he said in a quiet voice. "That would be a sad mistake."

"And does failure give it meaning?" Manny asked recklessly. "Do patched clothes and worry give it meaning? Eh? I want to get somewhere, and I don't think I can leave it all to God to arrange."

It was the first time Chaim had been challenged by one of his children and he felt a shock of betrayal. He had always realized that Leah had ideas of her own, but he had somehow taken for granted that the old traditions, the old respect, would be accepted by the children, that the torch would be safely passed on, the word kept.

Manny stood, his short body tense with hostility. Astounded, Chaim blinked at him, embarrassed by this confrontation. He felt at a loss: he knew he was right, he knew that dependence on material values would prove treacherous. Yet it was hard to explain to a child that those who opened their shops on the Sabbath to grab more business, or those who failed to observe the Law in various unobtrusive but important ways, might be prospering briefly, but that ultimately they were to be pitied. Nevertheless he tried.

Manny listened politely. Then he remarked, "God asks too much of us." He wanted to say more, much more, but he hesitated to hurt his father, so he turned away, shrugging helplessly.

As he began to climb the stairs, he glanced through the open door of the kitchen: Chaim had turned back to his book and was bent over the kitchen table. He looked very frail, his thin, bony face almost transparent, his hair frosted with white. He looked like a tired old man. He was thirty-six years old.

Manny would have liked to say something to bridge the gulf between them, but he could think of no suitable words. For Chaim, obedience to the Law brought its own reward. For Manny, it brought increasing irritation. They had nothing to say to each other.

Chaim looked up for a moment and saw his son poised on the steps, but before he could speak, Manny had gone, his heavy boots clattering on the uncarpeted stairs.

Even Mendel had to admit defeat that summer. "You cannot get blood out of a stone and you cannot get work out of bankrupt customers."

Golomstok and Segal were once again living rent-free. Abbie had been accepted by the Jewish Orphanage, which meant that he got regular meals and wore clean clothes. Occasionally he came home on a visit, full of the institution's food and the fact that they had a whole bed each to sleep in. He was an amiable boy but Leah could see that he did not really enjoy his visits home. Life at the orphanage was more cheerful. Today though, he was bursting with news.

"We had a visitor last week, some lord, who gives money to the orphanage. He inspected us and asked the big boys questions. There was a young feller with him dressed in such fine clothes, a real gent. When I looked at him close to I saw that it was Simeon Abrahams. He's been studying in Paris. He asked how everyone was getting on and I said very well and successful. I didn't think you'd want him to hear how things are."

Leah had cooked a meat meal in honor of the child's visit, but he could still tell how things were: a child can tell from something as small as the muscles of his father's face how things are. If those muscles are slack, downward-pulled, the mouth pinched with anxiety, then the chicken on the table and the paper bag of sweets will not deceive.

The next morning when Chaim made his way down to the workshop he found Mendel's truckle bed bare. The bedding was gone and so was Mendel. A note scrawled on a page torn from an order book lay on the thin mattress.

> For many years I have planned to end my days in Jerusalem. I have decided to wait no longer. Goodbye and I wish you good luck for the future. Take my advice and find employment with a good work boss, you have no head for business.
>
> Mendel

A final line added, "The rent is paid to the end of the month."

Chaim was still staring, with mixed feelings, at the farewell note when Leah followed him down. She read it silently. Chaim said charitably, "At least he paid the rent to the end of the month."

"Out of the money he had kept from you all these years!" Leah snapped. "No wonder he can go to Jerusalem. He could *buy* Jerusalem. All through the war we worked like slaves, and who kept the profits? Mendel! And afterward, who made the economies? We did! Who ate at our table on Friday nights and festivals? Mendel! And who paid for the food? We did!"

"Perhaps the profits were not so great—"

"Perhaps pigs fly! He waited till he was ready, the thief, and then he went like a thief, in the night, may God punish him! May his ship sink to the bottom of the ocean and may his flesh be devoured by the fish!"

Chaim had a vision of Mendel at the bottom of the sea, fish mouth gaping while a stream of bubbles rose to the surface. Mendel among the fishes, casting off his greasy coat and revealing not limbs, but the flippers and fish's tail he had concealed all these years, swimming off to Jerusalem. Suddenly he began to laugh. "Under the sea," he said, "who would know if his nose dripped?"

They were both laughing when the others came down to see what was happening, and Leah thought hopefully, *Perhaps we can be more cheerful now; perhaps Mendel's absence will make a difference.*

The difference was soon apparent: they were even worse off than before. Chaim barely knew the names of the customers and the next few weeks were a nightmare, with Chaim running from one part of London to another, and working half the night to try to keep up with the meager orders they did have.

At the fireworks factory, as the pre–Guy Fawkes Day, high-selling season came nearer, the pace quickened. Miriam's deft fingers filled and sealed and packed the little parcels of explosives that would brighten the sky in a few weeks' time. They were supposed to wear protective gloves but no one did, since the gloves hampered movement and slowed down the work. So their fingertips gradually rotted while their lungs furred up with the poisonous particles they breathed in day after day. But on Friday night there was a pay envelope to bring home, and they gave thanks as the Sabbath candles were lit.

The workshop in Sidney Street looked busier than ever because the whole family was at work, at one time or another, during the day. Manny had picked up the machining and did his share after school, as did Sarah. She hated the smell of the machine oil, which made her feel sick, so she managed the pressing irons, her tiny wrists looking too frail to support their weight as she moved them on and off the gas rings, the blue flames popping and hissing gently. When she raised the iron and plunked it down, her stomach muscles contracted with the strain and her mouth curved downward, not only in distaste but in exhaustion. Every now and then she took her turn at the machine.

Chaim, coughing continuously, worked alongside Ruth, who was home from school with bronchitis. She lay on Mendel's old truckle bed so that Leah could keep an eye on her. Occasionally she raised herself on one elbow and tried to reach a glass of water. Leah or Manny would rush across and help her sip. Chaim seemed lost in a trance as he bent over his machine.

Not even Leah knew that in these last weeks, bitterness had entered his soul for the first time. He acknowledged to himself that he had failed his family: the two duties of a man were to obey God's Law and to protect his family. The first he had never faltered in. He studied the Torah and he taught the Laws to his children as it was commanded, but there were times when he stumbled over the familiar words, "Who is wealthy? He who is contented with his lot." But he was not contented with his lot. How could he be, seeing his family suffer? He had failed in his second duty.

The room was airless and cold at the same time. For a moment he allowed his eyes to stray from the needle shuttling in and out of the cloth. The faces around him were gray and joyless: Leah, bent over the clothes she was folding; Manny, sewing deftly, lower lip stuck out in concentration. Golomstok and Segal plodding wearily on, expressionless. Ruth lying on her side on the little iron bed, insubstantial as a wraith, her eyes two dark pits in her white glistening face. Sarah so withdrawn, lifting and banging down the heavy irons.

How amazingly good the old life in the old country now seemed. How full of color and good spirits—hours for study, then home to one of Rachel's fragrant meals, and Leah moving about the kitchen with her springy step and sparkling eyes. And the talk! The ceaseless cascades of talk and debate, the vitality of it all. What lay ahead here for any of them but poverty, dragging out their days until the very poverty itself helped bring it all to an end? Job called death the catastrophe that ends all catastrophes. . . .

He pulled himself together. This was blasphemy. It was written in the Midrash, he reminded himself, that "as a scarlet ribbon becomes a black horse, so poverty becomes the daughter of Jacob." But, treacherously, his heart told him to look at Leah, her hair already gray, her thin

172

face lined. He longed to be able to give her something more becoming than poverty. . . . The thread tangled suddenly in the machine, and he had to go back and do the seam again.

Leah stared at the unfamiliar figure on the doorstep: a well-dressed, heavily built young man with a mass of glossy black curls. She gave a cry of pleasure. "Simeon!"

He stepped forward to embrace her but she drew back. "No, no. Mind your clothes!"

"Never mind the clothes!" He hugged her affectionately.

She stood back and stared at him again. "How you've grown!" He wore a well-cut suit of smooth, dark cloth and shining leather shoes. The last time she saw him he had been wearing the corduroy suit and heavy boots from the Free School. He could never look elegant; his body was too shapeless, his head too large. But the good clothes improved him wonderfully. And even more than the clothes, there was something else: he had a confidence, a carelessness about the way he stood and moved that told you he was not afraid, not worried, he was his own master. *He is a man now,* Leah thought. Perhaps he had grown away from them, perhaps they would be ill-at-ease together. Or—worse still—polite with each other.

As though bearing out her fears he asked, conventionally, "How are you, Leah?" His voice had changed, had gained a resonance, and as always he spoke English to her.

"Terrible, thank you," she said lightly, trying unsuccessfully to laugh.

He flung an arm around her shoulders. "Come to the shops with me," he said. "I have a few things to buy."

He was shocked by the change in her, and to cheer her up he said, "Well: you're as slim as ever. No one would think you were the mother of five children!"

She shook her head. "Four children." And she told him about David. "A big boy for his age. Big, and with such a lovely smile—like yours. Such a waste." And then the tears came. After so long, to be talking about David made her realize that she had kept her thoughts of him shut away inside her. She knew it was not good to speak too much of the dead; life was with the living. But she felt sometimes that she wanted to talk about David, to remind herself that he had existed and still did in their memory, that he had not been blotted out that day at the school. Talking, she was comforted.

The shopping took some time and when Simeon and Leah returned, both were laden with packages. He pushed his toward her: "Now, prepare one of those magnificent meals I remember." The fact that the magnificent meal had probably been barley soup and a shred of herring in a roll did not detract from the truth of his statement. For Simeon, his snatched dinners at Leah's had been magnificent.

Leah had been fairly sure all along that the groceries were intended for her, but she now expressed amazement and reluctance in equal parts. "What? No, no, I can't accept . . ."

Simeon, who knew the form, repeated his gesture and added solemnly, "If you reject my presents you reject my presence . . . I shall have to leave!"

She began to laugh again. Simeon could always make her enjoy the English language, because he enjoyed it himself. She dropped her pretended reluctance, and he walked up and down the kitchen while she worked, questioning him. ". . . An officer! A poor Jewish boy an officer! How could you be an officer?"

"After four years of Charterhouse how could I be anything else?" he answered dryly.

"And then to volunteer," she said reproachfully. "You might have been killed and wasted all their trouble."

When the table was ready, she called the others but kept Simeon hidden behind the door. They caught sight of the banquet, and a chorus of exclamations broke out. Chaim was afraid for a moment that Leah might have lost her reason and stolen food from the shops. Then Simeon stepped out from behind the door.

More hugs and kisses. The younger ones did not know him, but Ruth, who was a little stronger now, greeted him warmly. Then Leah sent everyone to wash. In honor of the occasion she actually went upstairs and changed her dress, out of the drab everyday black into an equally old, but less worn dark blue one with a white collar.

Miriam came in smelling faintly of sulphur, which she tried to drown in carbolic soap, and they all sat down, even Golomstok and Segal. Chaim said the *Kiddush*, and they began the meal in bubbling spirits, considerably aided by the bottle of kosher wine Simeon had provided.

Manny whispered to Sarah, "See: if you've got the money, you can always have a good time!"

But Sarah was looking at the way Simeon held his knife and fork, immediately following suit. Noting the difference between the way Golomstok chewed his food and the way Simeon ate—slowly, mouth closed—she murmured, "Money alone is not enough. You have to know how to live." Then, louder, she asked, "Simeon, where do you live? Is it a big house and are you *very* rich now?"

Leah and Chaim glared reprovingly at Sarah but Simeon burst out laughing. "When I'm in London I live in a big house full of servants and I study law seven days a week. I have two new suits every year and go to the opera in the season and I have no money at all." Sarah's eyes were wide with fascination. "I've been to Paris and Italy and soon I'll be earning my own living. Morgenstern will be helping other boys."

"Is it never a girl?" Ruth asked, but no one took her seriously.

Sarah wanted to know about Lady Morgenstern. "Does she have ever so many dresses and have they got a big bathroom and a motorcar?"

"They have three bathrooms. And a car with a chauffeur."

"I shall have a car and a chauffeur, one day," Sarah said. They all laughed, except Manny, who had come to a similar decision himself.

The laughter and noise were so loud that only Golomstok heard the knock at the door and went to answer it. He returned, followed by a broad-shouldered gray-haired man in a shaggy jacket, holding a small boy by the hand. Chaim smiled politely, and the rest paused, staring at the newcomers.

Then Leah rose, agitated. "Mordecai," she said.

He came forward and took her hands, smiling. "But you look just the same!" he exclaimed.

Above the dark blue dress with its white collar, her face was flushed, the eyes sparkling, and in the animation of the meal her usually severe hair had loosened a little. With a shock, Chaim thought: *She does at this moment look young again. And no matter what the*

Midrash *says, happiness is more becoming to the daughter of Jacob than poverty.*

"This is my cousin Mordecai Shoobotel," Leah said to Simeon, in English. "The one I used to tell you about." Mordecai slapped Chaim's shoulder, kissed the girls, and ruffled Manny's hair. Then, like an afterthought, he pushed forward the small, silent child and said, "This is Jonathan. My son."

Leah looked down at the boy, so unlike his father. She looked at the silky brown hair that curled around his head, the fine curve of his face and slender body. *His mother must be beautiful,* she thought, and a long-forgotten pain twisted inside her, like the wrenching of an old wound. "Where is your wife?" she asked.

Mordecai shoved the child toward Manny. "Go and share a seat with your cousin. There is room enough for you both." Golomstok had brought in a chair from the workroom, and Mordecai dragged it up to the table and sat down. The scraping of the chair against the bare floorboards almost drowned his words, which were spoken in an undertone that was almost casual. "She died. I have no wife."

Leah heaped food onto his plate and they drank to his health, but something went wrong with the celebration after Mordecai's arrival. The mood changed. An air of anxiety seemed to hover over the table, and an odd watchfulness.

Simeon noticed how Leah carefully avoided looking at Mordecai too often. Simeon's own welcome had been very different—she had stared at him openly, touched his excellent suit, patted his curls. With Mordecai she appeared to be a little brusque, except when, passing him bread or wine, she gave him fleeting, greedy glances. Chaim was quiet, and the children, who had interrupted Simeon cheerfully, stared silently at Mordecai.

Then there was the curious matter of Mordecai's attitude toward Simeon. Mordecai kept looking at him in a rather suspicious way, and a couple of times when Simeon was speaking, he found Mordecai deliberately cutting across him to urge his son to take something to eat.

"When did you come from Peszno?" Chaim asked.

Mordecai laughed and shook his head. "Peszno! I haven't been in Peszno for years. I was in Russia for a while, and Warsaw, then Paris . . . and London." Suddenly he abandoned Yiddish and went into English, with a strong cockney accent, glancing almost triumphantly at Simeon. "I've been in London quite a while. I was in this very street, once, years ago. Pity I didn't know you was here, I was just a couple of houses away."

How natural, Leah thought, that Mordecai should have been mixed up with the anarchists. Another "new idea." Revolution, anarchy. He might have been burned to death in that house across the street and she would never even have known. And what now? Why was he here?

Simeon asked, as if reading her thoughts, "And are you staying in London now?"

Mordecai chewed energetically on a piece of fish before swallowing it. "Very likely. For a bit. I don't make plans. I have to be free to come and go."

"How convenient for you." Simeon spoke amiably, but he was looking at the child.

Mordecai said sharply, "The kid's always been taken care of." He put down his knife and leaned across the table to Simeon. "Of course we live very simply. When you got nothing, you don't need much to keep going. Not that you'd know about that, of course. Your sort—"

"My sort," Simeon said without rancor, "ate, slept, and lived four in one room, making slippers for a pound a week—in a good week. In a bad week the coal and bread and soup came with the compliments of the Board of Guardians."

Mordecai's expression remained hostile. "You've done well for yourself then. Got your own workshop have you? How many hours a day do your workers put in?"

Simeon reached into his waistcoat pocket and glanced at his fob watch. "Leah, I'm afraid I have to go. I shall be walking back—"

"The West End, I suppose?" Mordecai said provocatively.

Simeon smiled. "Oh, much grander than that. Mayfair."

Leah gave an exclamation. "You're never walking all that way."

"I enjoy it." He shook Chaim's hand warmly, patted the children, and kissed Ruth and Miriam.

Sarah said, in a rush, "Come and visit us again, I want to ask you ever so many questions."

Leah was accompanying him to the front door. Simeon paused beside Mordecai, who had continued eating. "Well, goodbye, Mr. Shoobotel."

Mordecai grunted, and Leah said brightly, "I expect you'll see each other again."

177

"Why?" Mordecai asked bluntly.

"Why indeed?" Simeon agreed. "We move in such different circles. Your life must be so exciting."

He went into the hall and Leah followed him, looking distressed. Two people whom she loved in different ways clearly disliked each other. She felt helpless and awkward and a little cross. As always, Simeon sensed her mood. "I'm sorry," he said.

"Why should you be? Mordecai behaved very badly. I can't think why."

"Well, my suit offended him for a start. A well-cut suit is tantamount to a crime in revolutionary eyes."

He took a small, leather-bound book from his pocket. "I have a present for you. Some poems by a man named Browning."

"I won't understand them."

"Try. Read them over and over. Listen to the sound. You may surprise yourself."

She turned the pages absently. "Why do you want me to read them?"

"Because he opens windows for the mind."

She slipped the little book into her skirt pocket. "I haven't opened many windows lately. Thank you, Simeon. I shall try, I promise. And don't stay away so long, next time."

He swung off down the street with his shambling but surprisingly fast stride. His allowance at the Morgensterns' was rather less than the scullery maid's wages, and he had spent every penny on the shopping expedition. But it was a fine night, and the walk, he reflected, would be pleasant.

Golomstok and Segal went to their room. Manny and Sarah went to sleep and Leah found a blanket and pillow for Jonathan to curl up in.

They sat around the table, quieter now, throwing up old names —Jochanan Minsky, young Slumkow, figures from their youth—and talking of losses and bereavements the way people do who have not seen each other for many years. Mordecai knew about Jacob and Rachel— "At that time, those soldiers were shooting down anyone— even children—if they made any sudden movements." He heard about David in the air raid. There were others, neighbors and friends in Peszno.

He poured out some wine. "I feel the links going, one by one.

Your parents, my brother . . ." he looked at Chaim, ". . . your father."

Chaim straightened in his chair and stared, shocked, at Mordecai. "What do you mean?"

Bewildered, Mordecai said, "But you must have heard. One of our men came over a couple of weeks ago at least, and mentioned it in passing."

"I have heard nothing. What has happened?"

"He was found in the cellar. He must have slipped on the stairs and fallen. No one knew for several days."

Chaim's face was twisted with wretchedness and remorse. Alone, old and frail, his father had died like a dog. Solomon should have been with them, cared for, protected. They had not done their duty—worse, they had not loved enough. Into his numbed brain floated the half-remembered words of a saying from his childhood: "An old man loved is winter with flowers." Too busy with the business of surviving, they had denied his father his winter with flowers. Chaim got up and left the room.

Ruth and Miriam soon went to bed. Leah and Mordecai were alone. For a while neither of them spoke. At last Leah said abruptly, "Tell me about your wife." Mordecai flexed his heavy shoulders and ran his hand through the wiry gray hair. He shrugged. "Lenin was organizing this school, in a place near Paris—"

"What sort of school?"

"A school for revolutionaries. There were classes on political economy, lectures, and so on. We met there."

He stopped and Leah waited, but there seemed no more to come. "And," she prompted.

"And then there was Jonathan, and then I had to go to Russia for the October uprising, and she came too, leaving the child with friends. One day there was street fighting . . ." His voice trailed off and again they sat in silence. But this time Leah did not prompt him. She felt a great weight on her chest, she felt hardly able to breathe, as she stepped for a moment into the skin of that unknown woman, Mordecai's "partner," who knew she had to follow him and leave her child, or else risk losing her husband. Mordecai was not the flashing, glittering boy she remembered, but the fire still burned in him, deep in his eyes. Any woman would have to brave that fire, be tempered—or be consumed by it—to gain his respect. But at what a price.

179

Mordecai stirred, shifting in his seat. "Well: you've done all right anyway. A workshop of your own, rich friends—"

From nowhere, Leah's rage flooded her. "We have survived. Don't ask how. Our workshop is a joke, a terrible joke. Simeon is not a rich man with a factory, he is a poor boy who was lucky enough to find a benefactor. Like you with Minsky! A good boy who remembers his friends. All this," she flung out her hand over the table, "is his doing. Do you think we sit down to a meal like this, even on a Friday night? Each new day is like a battlefield before us. We survive. So far."

He touched her hand gently, but she pulled it away. "Leah, I'm sorry. I have seen too much suffering. I see capitalist evils and exploitation all around me . . . sometimes perhaps when it is not there!" He smiled wryly. "But things will get worse, you know. There must be a revolution in this country. The workers—"

She looked at him, puzzled and angry. "I have not seen you for seventeen years and you have not changed *at all*. It's terrible! You still talk like a student. Don't you know about life? Have you learned nothing apart from revolution? Revolutions are for other people. Surviving is all we have the strength for, all that ordinary people have strength for."

"If you have the strength to survive, you have the strength to do something. If you had seen what I saw in Russia. . . . The unions here need organizing, more solidarity. If *enough* people strike we can do something."

Leah said, "Were you in London when the police went on strike?"

"The police?" he laughed in disbelief.

"Oh yes. Poor souls. Some were so penniless they had no clothes to wear, and did going on strike help them? Some of them are walking about now, still without work, starving. Did going on strike help the tailors?"

"Leah, if you went to Wales and saw the miners, how they live—"

"The Rubinsteins in Stepney, Mordecai, if you saw how they lived, in a week when no good friend called in with gifts of food—"

"You were never selfish, in the old days," he said reprovingly. "I see you have become infected with the Jewish preoccupation."

"Oh? And what is the Jewish preoccupation?"

"Marx says the basis of Judaism is selfishness—that the only thing that unites Jews is the conservation of their property. The secular culture of the Jew is usury, his God, money."

Leah gaped at him. "You talk like an anti-Semite."

"We must forestall the anti-Semites. We have these faults, Leah, and we should admit them and cleanse ourselves of them. If Jews could be emancipated from realistic Judaism, it could liberate them, allow them to mingle in the mainstream of humanity."

Leah's head flicked sideways, and she impatiently shook back a loose strand of hair. "Oh, dialectics . . ."

Mordecai said, "Everything is dialectics. People invent their own dialectic. There are people who can only exist, express themselves in very practical terms, but they can still arrive at conclusions which are dialectical conclusions. Each person can invent his own dialectic to carry out his or her personal revolution. You could have carried out yours— you still could. But you have to make a decision—"

Another flick of the head and she broke in: "I asked you about your wife and you told me about Lenin. I tell you about our life and you talk about Marx and dialectics. Are you human, anywhere in your life?"

She was leaning forward, staring at him intently, her face vivid, her eyes bright with anger. For Mordecai, the years rolled back like the parting of the Red Sea, and down the tunnel of time he saw Leah's face, tremulous and close—as now—that summer afternoon in Peszno; he felt the chafing of the splint on his broken arm and the moist softness of Leah's mouth. He longed to crumple into this woman's arms and give himself up to the comforts of the flesh. To let his mind spin free, dizzily, and just for an hour lose himself in absolute weakness. He blotted out the thought of Chaim, of loyalties, the fences of the Law, hammered into him for so many years as a child: "Thou Shalt Not . . ."

Should he talk of old times, their youthful dreams, the way her body responded in the secret corner of the timber yard in the heady sharpness of the resin-filled air? Or should he get up now and leave, before memory could speak? He reached forward and gently touched her neck, teased out a lock of her hair and tugged it, gently, in a gesture of unconscious intimacy. "Leah . . ."

Her mouth went dry; her throat tight with nerves, she looked at him, frightened. She wanted to say something dignified and profound that would hurt him and send him away filled with regret for what might have been.

But to her dismay she felt her eyes filling with tears. She thought of the seemingly endless drudgery of her days, of the pains and losses. Upstairs Chaim sat mourning his father. She should get up now, this instant, she knew that. But she knew too that she could not comfort

Chaim. He locked her out, he shut himself away in some private place that she could never share. She could not help him, and suddenly it seemed to her that she was no use at all.

"Leah? . . ."

She stood up. The workroom next door was in darkness, but the street lamp glimmered on the metal of the machines and threw blacker shadows against the dim walls. Mendel's old truckle bed was in the darkest corner of the cluttered room and Mordecai at first did not see it, until Leah took his hand and led him to it through the tables and the boxes piled beside them.

For a moment she faltered, remembering her wedding night, wondering whether again a fumbling awkwardness lay ahead. But if there was awkwardness, clumsiness, she did not know it. Mordecai's hands, his body, the warmth that sprang off his flesh, the faint sourness of his breath, were like a spell or a drug, and her own body fell under that spell. So this was how it could be. . . .

He was not a gentle lover; nor was he particularly tender. But she gloried in his confidence, in the sure way he held her, turned her this way and that to his needs, moving her about as casually as though she were a pillow, with a physical authority she found intoxicating. Outside a man clattered past the window on his way home, his footsteps gradually growing fainter, while Mendel's bed squeaked and shifted with their movements.

When Chaim came downstairs the next morning he found an extra person at the table.

"Jonathan is staying with us for a while," Leah said. "Mordecai has to go away and I said we could have him."

Another one to feed, Chaim found himself thinking despairingly before he guiltily repressed the thought. Instead he asked, "Does he not fear the boy will be contaminated by our bourgeois and theological ideas?"

Leah put a piece of bread on Jonathan's plate. "He has no choice. He will be in Spain for a while, working for the Party, building up its strength—"

"Building . . . destroying. . . . Words lose their meaning in the mouths of politicians," Chaim said bitterly. "If the child stays with us he will be brought up as I was, in the ways of the Torah. There can be no other way in this house."

Then Leah's sister Ruda, her husband, and Leah's brother Hirschl settled in Germany—soon after Leah left Peszno—they had faced the same problems as any other immigrants. Leah read between the lines of Ruda's optimistic letters and recognized the signs of struggle.

Later, things changed somewhat, and Ruda's occasional letters proved unsettling. As the older sister, she remembered that Leah had always been their father's favorite, indulged, spoiled, and allowed freedoms denied to Ruda, who had obediently followed her mother's wishes in all things. There was an unconscious tone of condescension in her letters, especially as her situation improved. She began to dwell on how good their life was, how everything was going to be all right in Weimar whatever might happen elsewhere, that everything in Goethe's garden city was lovely.

The bad times, the war and its aftermath, had been weathered, and it seemed that the future was secure. "We have had the house painted," she wrote. "The business is doing well, Hirschl is also doing well. . . . We hope you and the family will come and spend a holiday here soon."

Too proud to confess they could not afford the fare to Southend, let alone Germany, Leah tended to write back equally optimistic letters, saying that things were "rather busy" just then.

But as 1923 spun past, Ruda's letters, which arrived less frequently than usual, also became less complacent. "The Communists are causing trouble, it reminds me of Poland, always such troublemakers. This man Hitler says he knows how to control the Communists but I think he is just making noises to catch votes.

There were petulant comments on the difficulties to be endured. "A madness has descended on the money market. Shmuel and his partner, and Hirschl too, thank God, have taken certain precautions, but life has become very complicated all the same. A trip to a café is impossible:

if you order a cup of coffee, by the time you have drunk it the exchange rate has changed and the coffee has gone up in price!" Life in Weimar was still beautiful. But it was costing far more. "Things will get better. And in the long run I do not think we will suffer. We made a good decision to come here. Germany has a great future."

Leah had her own troubles to think about. Soon after she received Ruda's last letter of complaint, Chaim was soaked in a rainstorm while riding on an open bus top on his way to deliver a small order to a customer. Leah scolded him and made him change his clothes, her voice growing shrill and cross to cover her anxiety at seeing how tired he was.

Chaim sat down suddenly on the edge of the bed, his shirt half undone, and began coughing. She pulled his shirt off him and saw with a pang how his ribs stood out, skeletal against his white skin, and how his gaunt cheekbones cast a shadow onto his sunken cheeks. How frail he was! Nothing went right in their life anymore; it was like a misfitting garment that held them back from freedom, that chafed and irritated. But she loved him, as she always had, in the same protective way she had loved Danielsche, her little brother.

He went on coughing and Leah called to Sarah to bring some milk to soothe his throat. "You must stay in bed," she commanded. Chaim shook his head and struggled to his feet. "I will be all right at the machine." He tottered down the stairs and settled himself at the little table.

Reaching for the fabric that lay cut and ready, Chaim set the thread and pushed the material neatly under the needle. He realized that he had done all this without thought, without effort. He had become, God help him, a professional. Gone were the days when he took time and pleasure in the day's activity. Now his limbs moved without intelligence but with a repetitive skill. The treadle rocked, the fabric spun away from him smoothly; seam, turn, seam, curve. . . . So would a machine carry out its work—an automaton.

He was aware of feeling hot, but without comfort, and the old roughness in his throat felt worse, and then suddenly all order ceased, the fabric and the treadle began to behave in a disturbing manner—the cloth wavering and undulating, the needle slowing so that it rose and fell with the spiraling rhythm of a dream. Everything grew very large —the black enamel of the machine, the chipped gold lettering looming in his vision—and there was a soft roaring in his ears like the winter wind in the Peszno trees. As he pitched forward, he heard Leah shriek, "What are you doing? The dress is ruined!"

Leah saw Chaim slump forward across his machine and did not for a moment understand what was happening. She saw the soft green material, a teagown, jerk from his fingers and the needle plow across the bodice, stabbing and snagging the cloth. She leaped up, horrified at what it would cost, as Chaim lost consciousness and fell, his forehead striking the shaft of the sewing machine.

Manny, Sarah, and the others crowded around as Leah pulled Chaim away from the table, her stomach lurching with fear at the lightness of his body. She moved him easily, and with Manny's help laid him on the truckle bed.

For days he stayed there, too weak to attempt the stairs. Miriam brought him fresh milk, which he drank, but he ate nothing, his dry, almost scaly skin burning hot, his coughing growing worse. The doctor advised moving him to the hospital, but Chaim became unexpectedly stubborn and insisted on remaining in the house.

On Friday Leah was preparing to light the Sabbath candles when Chaim, stirring restlessly under the thin blankets, glanced across the room to see Manny starting another garment. "Emmanuel . . ." The voice was hardly more than a croak. "The Sabbath is almost in . . ."

Manny's round face grew red, but he continued to sit at the machine, and he set the treadle flying at a frantic speed.

"Emmanuel!" Chaim's voice was stronger and could no longer be ignored.

Manny stopped the machine and turned toward his father. "There's work to be finished. We need to complete this order by Monday. If I stop now we won't finish. God will have to understand. . . . There are times when He must—understand." He added, placatingly, "I'll pray at the machine." He went back to his sewing feeling shakier than he sounded.

Chaim turned his face to the wall and tried to pray, but he had no strength. From beneath the tightly shut lids, tears of weakness and grief slipped and slid their way along his cheeks and onto the gray pillow.

After a few days, Leah moved Chaim upstairs to the bedroom. The air of the workroom was clogging his throat and choking him, and his incessant coughing kept the others from working. He lay in bed, freshly washed and in a clean nightshirt, and for a moment he felt a sense almost of well-being. "Leah, do you remember that day we spent at Southend? We should go again, some time."

"Of course we will." She felt a chill as she heard the cheerfully reassuring note in her voice. This was how you spoke to children, to stop their worrying. She smiled brightly at Chaim: "I'll get you some broth. You'll feel better when you've had a little soup."

Chaim obediently drank a couple of spoons of soup and lay back, looking so peaceful that Leah's spirits rose. He should soon be strong enough to get up. Then they would get more orders and perhaps make a little extra. . . .

In the night she was awakened by the sound of his breathing: heavy, and with a rattle in the chest that frightened her. He seemed to be sleeping but when she looked more closely she saw that it was no normal sleep. There were flecks of foam along his lips, and in the lamplight his skin glistened yellow.

As she watched he gave a sudden movement, as if to throw off the blanket, and then he was still. She sat frozen, waiting. After a few moments there came one last grating sigh, then silence. She sat on, quietly, beside the vacated shell of Chaim, insulated by her exhaustion, knowing that presently she would begin to feel.

The mourners came and went, shaking their heads in real or ritual regret, weeping their tears. There were many who were genuinely sorry to lose Chaim's gentle presence. There were even some who came to repay little sums he had lent them unknown to Leah, who talked of his everyday kindness. But Leah still felt nothing. The occasional *shnorrer* came in with the rest, blowing his nose loudly and expressing noisy condolences. Manny and Sarah watched the visitors, unnoticed, from a corner of the kitchen.

"Look, look!" Manny whispered, pointing at an old beggar who had sidled up to Leah, shaking his head with immense sadness. Sarah saw the beggar wipe his nose and in the same smooth movement, using the handkerchief, scoop up the little pile of coins she indicated. "Such a pious man," muttered Manny. "He wouldn't touch money in a house of mourning, the ol' devil."

The mason, another excessively pious visitor, slipped his card into Leah's hand as he expressed his condolences. "Such a good man . . . a loss to the community . . ." He coughed delicately. "When the time comes for the stone setting, you won't find any better workmanship elsewhere."

Sarah and Manny crept out and wandered down the street.

The front door was half-open and Simeon, pushing it wide, cautiously stepped into the little hall. For once he was unsure of his words. On the way he had rehearsed various versions of speeches, none of which seemed right.

Outside the kitchen door he hesitated. Leah was standing by the table, looking very pale in her black dress, her face shadowed with fatigue. Beside her, leaning against the dresser, was Mordecai. He was talking rapidly, low-voiced, and she, head lowered, was listening intently. Simeon turned away. Clearly Leah had someone to look after her already.

He was on the front doorstep when Sarah came running toward the house with Manny. "Simeon! How are you? Aren't you stopping?"

"Actually, I'm in rather a hurry. I don't want to break in on Leah. . . . Just tell her I came to offer my condolences. I was sorry to hear about your father."

"Yes." She looked at him regretfully. "I wish you came more often." She watched him hurry away down the road and went back into the kitchen.

Mordecai finished speaking, gripped Leah's shoulder, and shook it gently. "I'll see you when I get back." He ruffled Jonathan's hair, picked up a heavy bag, and left.

When Mordecai went out of a room, Sarah thought to herself, it was almost like a big gust of wind sweeping through it: there was a sense of upheaval, disturbance, and then a gradual settling. "Where's he going?" she asked her mother.

"Germany. He says they need organizing."

Sarah had taken a dislike to Mordecai. "Oh well," she said, "I'm sure he'll solve all their problems. He'll probably fix them up with a revolution when he gets there."

When the visitors had come and gone; when the condolences and the pickled herring rolls were finished, Leah mentioned the stone setting for Chaim's grave. They must have a decent gravestone, she said; Chaim must not be disgraced in death.

"But we got no money," Manny protested reasonably. "How can we afford a posh stone?"

"We must save every penny we can," Leah said with a confidence she did not quite feel. "We must make economies. By next year we will have enough."

That night Sarah had a long, whispered conversation with Manny; she kissed Jonathan, and at dawn, before the others were awake, she slipped out of the house and hurried away, a thin, determined little figure in a bulky jacket, carrying a bundle under her arm.

When Leah stirred, Manny went in to her and sat on the edge of the bed.

Leah had never been a demonstrative mother—at least, not since David's death—and there had been neither time nor inclination for maternal cuddles in bed with the little ones. Toward Sarah she had always been rather sharp, perhaps because she recognized in those bright, narrow eyes something of the questioning, skeptical look she herself had possessed as a young girl.

But with Manny she had an understanding, a bond of sympathy. There was a curiously casual affection between the two of them, almost as though they were equals. And so she smiled at him questioningly, wondering if he had some favor to ask. "Well, what is it?"

"Sarah's gone," he said baldly.

Mrs. Bloom smiled down at Sarah, her widely spaced gray teeth jutting like a row of gravestones. "Yes, I was wanting some help in the house—Get my name from the baker's, did you? Put your bag down and come in here."

Mrs. Bloom asked questions, and Sarah invented a wretched biography, precise enough to sound convincing and vague enough for safety. She was hired.

The establishment was not quite what Sarah had expected of the outside world: the rooms were tiny; good taste and style were nowhere to be seen. The smell of fish filled the house, the sink was piled with unwashed dishes, and Mrs. Bloom's hands were ridged with the tidemarks of various hasty and inadequate washings. After Leah's immaculate austerity, it all seemed overpoweringly disgusting, but Sarah needed a roof over her head or the police might pick her up and send her home.

"You can do the dishes first, and then we'll see what next," Sarah's employer said, leaving her on her own.

In the middle of the afternoon Mrs. Bloom reappeared, magnificent in a full-length lilac gown, cut very low in the neckline, loudly urging her husband to get ready. "We don't want to be late for the wedding!"

She draped a slightly bedraggled fur stole around her shoulders and patted the mass of black curls arranged on top of her head. Sarah was given a pile of clothes to wash, to save her from boredom while they were out. Before the Blooms returned she was sound asleep on an eiderdown in a corner of the parlor—Mrs. Bloom had pointed out that as Sarah would be busy about the house so much of the time there was really no point in her having a room of her own.

The following morning, rising late, Mrs. Bloom handed Sarah a long flat box. "Whiteleys will be calling to collect this gown, Sarah; I had it on appro, but I telephoned them to explain it didn't fit right, so I shan't be having it after all." She retired to bed again. Sarah glanced at the cardboard box, lifted the lid, and moved aside the tissue paper. Inside was the lilac gown.

Two weeks later, with neither wages nor time off having been mentioned, Sarah asked for a half day off. Mrs. Bloom looked affronted. "What d'you want time off for?"

"To see my poor mother," Sarah improvised, "to let her know I'm all right."

Mrs. Bloom did not relish an anxious mother appearing on her doorstep, and Sarah was a splendid worker. Permission was given.

Half an hour later Sarah was sitting in Miss Walker's domestic employment agency, waiting to be seen. She had learned a few things during her two weeks in the outside world. Miss Walker's agency was both successful and respectable. She was used by the best houses and made sure that she sent them only the keenest applicants.

Miss Walker looked at Sarah. She certainly looked alert, sitting on the edge of her chair, thin face screwed up in concentration, funny slanting eyes fixed on Miss Walker. "You have experience of domestic service you say?"

"Oh yes."

"Whom are you with now?"

189

"Mr. and Mrs. Bloom. Golders Green."

"Why do you wish to leave their employment?"

Sarah felt instinctively that complaints about conditions would not be well received. "They're going on a cruise. Round the world."

"How nice. Well, you better let me have a written reference and we'll see what we can do."

Reference. Sarah had not thought about a reference. She nodded. "I suppose Mrs. Bloom will know what to write?"

"Of course she will, child. The usual thing: to whom it may concern, and then a few details about your work and character."

Sarah got home while Mrs. Bloom was still out shopping. She extracted a sheet of Mr. Bloom's paper from his office and carefully wrote a description of her duties, adding a few words about her hard work and honesty. *After all*, she told herself, *I am hardworking, and honest. Mrs. Bloom hasn't paid me a penny piece and I haven't pinched so much as a bit of bread.*

It was an excellent reference, but Miss Walker frowned at it unhappily. "Sarah Rubinstein. That's a Jewish name. Oh dear, are you a Jewish girl? I suppose you must be." She sighed. "I don't know . . . I've had problems with Jewish girls: that troublesome business with the food, what is it you can't eat, I never can remember. . . . And then Saturday being your Sunday, terribly confusing . . ."

"I'm not *very* Jewish," Sarah broke in "Hardly at all, really. Not so's you'd notice."

Miss Walker looked at her again. She was neat, intelligent, and apparently a good worker. "Well . . . all right. But don't let me down by singing any Bar Mitzvahs in your room at night or anything like that."

The Crawleigh house, one in a curving Georgian terrace, stood on a hill in Hampstead. Half of London seemed to be spread out before it. Sarah stared at the enormous front door, checked the number, and then, raising herself on tiptoe, reached up and lifted the vast brass door knocker. It slipped from her fingers and crashed heavily against the gleaming wood. Almost at once the door was opened by a tall, pale man in a black jacket. He peered down at the insectlike creature hovering on the doorstep.

"The agency sent me—" she began.

The pale man frowned. "Staff entrance. Basement." He shut the door quickly.

Sarah went down a flight of steps to a door in the basement. The kitchen entrance was small, the door flanked by a window opaque with moisture and thick steam. This time she was less nervous and knocked firmly. A girl even smaller than Sarah, her eyes dark and huge in her thin, greasy face, opened the door and waited for Sarah to speak. "The agency sent me," she began again.

The girl opened the door wider and jerked her head. Sarah stepped into the scullery to confront a large woman in a white cap, somewhat floury about the hands, who was busy at the kitchen table.

Sarah looked around the big room, taking in the scrubbed table loaded with vegetables and a huge pie ready for baking, the shining range and spotless flagstones, the rows of gleaming copper pots and pans on the walls.

The fat, floury woman placed the pie carefully in the oven, gently closed the door, and then turned to Sarah. "From the agency, eh? Well, once we've found you an apron you can get started on them potatoes." A mountain of muddy potatoes was heaped at one end of the table. "What's your name?"

"Sarah."

"Right, Sarah. Let's have your jacket and you can get down to work. Mary can show you your bed later."

It was nearly midnight when Sarah climbed the narrow back stairs, guided by Mary, the starved-looking scullery maid. Their room lay high up in the roof. The ceiling sloping almost to the floor and the two narrow beds pushed flat against the wall left little enough room for upright movement, even for two undersized girls.

"You're very lucky," Miss Walker had told Sarah. "This position has just come vacant, they need someone right away. You will have a half day off every week and your wages will be twelve pounds a year—you may pay me my fee when you receive your first wages."

Was it just this afternoon she had had that conversation? She felt she had been here for years, peeling, scrubbing, chopping, and scouring. Her hands were raw almost to the point of bleeding, and the skin over her knuckles was so rough and tight that as she unthinkingly clenched her fists it almost cracked open. She groaned and flopped onto the bed. Beside her, Mary was already stretched out. Eyes closed, she mumbled, "If you hear any scuffling in the night it'll be the footmen and the housemaids. They're at it like rabbits. Don't know where they find the strength."

A moment later Mary was shaking her shoulder, telling her it

191

was time to get up. Through the window the sky was a slaty black. "It's the middle of the night!" Sarah groaned.

"It's half past five. Come on."

Shivering, she pulled on her clothes, dabbed her face with icy water, and stumbled down the stairs after Mary.

First the grates, cleaning and laying new fires—quietly, without disturbing the sleeping household. Then the kitchen tasks: plates and glasses from a late supper. Then preparations for breakfast, with a pause for a quick kitchen breakfast. As with supper yesterday, Mary and Sarah ate standing, resting their plates on a mantelshelf, too lowly to share the table with the other servants, who sat around in some mysterious order of precedence. They were towered over by Mrs. Oliphant, wielding her vast brown teapot, and by Mr. Foster, graciously accepting plates of egg and bacon, cups of tea, and slices of bread.

Sarah wondered what to do about the bacon: should she swallow it bravely (and perhaps it was not too disgusting, when one actually got used to it?), or should she just say she didn't like the taste? The decision was not needed, for it transpired that scullery maids rated only a thick slice of bread with a smear of jam to go with their tea.

She listened to the conversation at the table. Lady Crawleigh's maid was French and seemed a cut above the other women, Sarah decided. In her black dress and with her hair very sleek, she looked like a lady herself. She was talking to another of the maids of a visit to the theater she had enjoyed on her afternoon off. "It was ex-trimly a-mus-ing," Sarah heard her say throatily.

Farther down the table two footmen were sharing a joke about the wine at last night's dinner and the game of cards that followed. Sarah felt she was almost within touching distance of the world she yearned to know—the world of beautiful women, well-dressed men, bright chandeliers, nights at the opera, silk and wine, and above all elegance and style. The mean little house in Sidney Street, the everlasting prayers and penny pinching seemed a million miles away.

"Right!" Mrs. Oliphant bellowed. "Let's get the breakfast dishes ready." Dish after dish of heavy silver—one for eggs, another for kedgeree, another for deviled kidneys—was lined up on the table, ready to be filled and placed over warming lights on the sideboard. *One day,* Sarah thought as she polished the lids, *I shall sit down to a breakfast as grand as this.* She held up the lid and looked at herself, nodding at her distorted reflection.

Glimpsing them occasionally through the window as they left

the house, Sarah decided the family was handsome: his lordship, stocky but well turned out, with bright blue eyes whose flash could be caught even from the basement; her ladyship, tall, graceful, with pretty hands and feet and wavy dark gold hair, her fine-boned face often wearing the slightly anxious expression of someone already late for an appointment; the children—the languid and beautiful card-playing Freddie, lately home from Oxford, and the two girls of about Sarah's age, usually dressed in pleated dresses and black stockings, their abundant fair hair tied back with ribbons.

"Sarah! The parsnips need doing."

"Just one more minute, please, Mrs. O.," Sarah implored, and was rewarded by the sight of the whole family setting off for church, colorful as butterflies. She began to scrape the parsnips.

Sarah had proved quick and deft, and Mrs. Oliphant used her more on the vegetables and simple preparations. Mary had to get along with the pans on her own. Sarah felt a pang of pity for the gray-faced girl forever bent over the copper pans, scouring and rubbing, but it was only momentary: someone had to do the pans.

When Mrs. Oliphant retired to her room for a predinner rest, Sarah was left in the kitchen to keep an eye on the simmering pans. For a while she enjoyed the rare experience of sitting and doing nothing. But she soon grew restless. Beside Mr. Foster's chair was a volume of Dickens from his complete edition—a present from a grateful past employer. She reached for it and idly embarked on *Oliver Twist*.

The conditions endured by the young orphan came as no surprise to her—indeed, there was a sharp familiarity about some of the situations. She knew that same grinding life, that hopelessness, that keen polishing of bowl with spoon to make sure no food remained undetected, uneaten. She realized though, with some surprise, that she had been rich in one possession: her home had been a poor enough place but it had been a loving one. She knew nothing of the cold, impervious cruelty of the institution soul. For a moment she weakened, put down the book and pressed her hands over her face to try to shut out the images jostling for attention—Manny's grin, narrowing his eyes into bright slits; the shimmer of the candles on the table on Friday night; the fragrant warmth that came from them, comforting to the fingers; her father's face like marble across the wavering flame. But that was no more. Chaim was a yellow shell now, in the earth, a shell to be decorated in due course with an expensive gravestone. She thought of Miriam, comfortable and easygoing, and Ruth with her daring ideas of changing the world, of living with a man's freedom. She thought of her mother with her bony face that just occasionally could light up in a smile as bright as Manny's, and the way she brushed and braided Sarah's hair after it was washed. Had she been right to reject them for this lonely, precarious exile?

She sniffed defiantly and went back to the book. After another page or two she suddenly stopped, blinked, and read on quickly, her heart pounding uncomfortably, her face reddening: "In a frying pan, which was on the fire, and which was secured to the mantelshelf by a string, some sausages were cooking; and standing over them was a very old shriveled Jew, whose villainous-looking and repulsive face was obscured by a quantity of matted red hair . . ."

Villainous . . . repulsive . . . Jews with their funny ways and problems about food. Always singled out as though unique in their villainy or ugliness. Even their piety had to be "different." This was what she feared and hated; this was what she wanted above all to get away from. She must be very careful. She did not want to be thrown out of this corner of the world where she had found shelter.

Mrs. Oliphant hurried into the kitchen, her cap crooked and her eyes puffy with sleep. From the main part of the house Sarah heard hurried footsteps and voices. "What's happened? What's the matter?" Sarah asked.

"Françoise has gone down with appendicitis, that's what," Mrs. Oliphant said with gloomy relish. "They're takin' her off in a stretcher now, using the front door if you please." Mrs. Oliphant had never liked the Frenchwoman. "Got it quite bad. Still, if they can catch it in time she should be all right." She sliced into a large slab of beef with her long, razor-edged knife, and a trickle of blood ran into one of the cracks of the scrubbed table.

Foster, looking agitated, swung open the kitchen door and banged the silver tea tray down on the table. He ignored Sarah and said impatiently to Mrs. Oliphant, "You'd think she could choose a better time! Typically French! So inconvenient, with the embassy ball tonight, and her ladyship *hates* last-minute upsets. And you have to admit Françoise is good with the needle." He noticed *Oliver Twist* open on the table. "Who moved this?"

"Sorry, Mr. Foster, I was just reading a bit." He closed the book firmly. "Is there something to be sewn?" she asked. "I'm good with a machine and with hand sewing too. I've got experience. Can I help?"

They stared at her as though a fowl on the table had suddenly got up and offered to do its own carving. Foster began to shake his head impatiently. Then he paused and asked, "How good are you? It'll cost us both our jobs if you muck it up."

"I'm good," Sarah said. "Look!" She pulled up her skirt a couple of inches. Foster flinched delicately, then allowed himself to bend over the leg she extended, to examine a neatly darned place on her thick stocking. The stitches were tiny, the sewing fine and regular.

"Wait here," he said, and vanished. Sarah took him literally and stood without moving until he reappeared.

"This way." Foster led her out of the kitchen, through the dining room and into the hall. The staircase curved before them, wide, shallow stepped, and with a banister of deeply polished mahogany. Sarah slid her hand up the banister, and beneath her fingers the wood was glossy as satin and smooth as glass. Even the air in this part of the house seemed finer, sweeter, with the smell of fresh flowers hovering about it. Sarah surreptitiously stroked the curtains as they passed a long window. The velvet was creamy and hung in shadowy folds.

Outside a pair of white-painted doors Foster stopped and knocked gently. Then he beckoned Sarah toward him and took her into Lady Crawleigh's bedroom.

Lady Crawleigh was lying on a day bed, her usual expression of faint anxiety deepened now into despair. She looked at Sarah and then Foster. "But it's a child!"

"She is an exceedingly accomplished seamstress, milady," Foster said smoothly.

Lady Crawleigh looked doubtfully at Sarah. "My dress is from Molyneux and the material is particularly fine . . . Françoise had unstitched the drapery to clean and press it—"

"I can do it, milady." Sarah's voice sounded husky and cracked against Lady Crawleigh's flutelike tone. She looked around and asked, "Where's the dress?"

Every summer the Crawleighs left the soot and grime of London for their place in the border country near Wales. There they had what they called a rest—"A taste of simple, rural life, my dear!" Lady Crawleigh said with a little laugh. To make sure they rested and enjoyed the simple, rural life to the full, they invited houseguests for weekend parties and organized balls and held dinner parties and paid visits to neighboring London families who were similarly engaged, so that when the summer drew to its close they could thankfully abandon the exhausting business of enjoying a rest and get back to the far less tiring round of London engagements.

This year, as usual, the preparations began with dust covers being placed over the drawing-room furniture and the potted plants being carried out to the conservatory while the rooms were shuttered and closed. But this year, one thing was different: Pansy and Daisy Crawleigh, having recently outgrown their nanny, were to have a maid of their own.

They were sorry to see Nanny Redditch go. "She was a ghastly bore, Daisy, but I do miss her tucking me in—the bedclothes get all muddled now, and I'm frightfully bad at drying myself after bathing."

But the rules were clear: "When a girl reaches the turning sign-posted Womanhood," Nanny Redditch intoned portentously, "she has no more use for a nanny."

"But Pansy hasn't—reached the turning," said Daisy, reluctantly adopting the old nurse's euphemistic label for menstruation.

"Her ladyship's made up her mind," said Nanny Redditch heavily. "And I have plans of my own."

"It does seem rotten," Daisy muttered to her still officially childish sister, "that just because I get the jolly old monthly visitor, things have to change like this." Nor were they enthusiastic when they learned that Sarah was to be looking after them. "She's smaller than we are—how's she going to be any good at brushing our hair?"

"She will stand on a chair," said Lady Crawleigh crisply, beginning to look anxious, as she often did when talking to her children. "I must go . . ."

At the door she added, "Do try to do something about the way she speaks. It's like a puppy worrying a bone."

Sarah had never seen the countryside before, and she was uncertain at first if she cared for it—all empty and green and prickly, and crawling with creatures of every sort, most of which bit or stung or scratched. But Pansy and Daisy were very much at home in the fields, climbing easily over stiles in their cool, pleated skirts, their neat boots protecting them from nettles. Sarah always seemed to trip over mole hills or bump into sharp pieces of wood.

Wearing castoff shoes and a dress from Daisy, weighed down by a picnic basket and traveling rug, Sarah plodded after the girls, sweating uncomfortably and longing to be back in the large, cool house where she could sew and iron peacefully, or even read a book undisturbed.

When the girls felt hungry, Sarah performed the duties Foster had trained her in: she spread out the rug, unpacked the picnic, and laid out the food and drink. She waited until the girls had sprawled happily on the soft plaid and then sat herself down a few feet away, trying to avoid the thistles. The girls chattered and munched, lying on their backs and squinting up at the sky. Their conversation was of no interest to Sarah, but she listened intently, hearing how they formed their words, the way their voices rose and fell, attending to the way they breathed.

"Sarah, I say, you haven't eaten a thing!" Daisy exclaimed. "Do have something—oh." She glanced at the tablecloth. "There's not much left. Look, here's a half sandwich hidden under this plate—"

"Oh Daisy, I was saving that! I'm *starving*," Pansy objected.

"I'm not hungry anyway, Miss Daisy," Sarah said swiftly.

"Oh. Oh well, if you're not hungry . . ."

On most days, Sarah felt herself to be comfortably invisible. She moved about the girls' room putting things in order, stitching or tidying, while Pansy and Daisy chattered on. As she brushed their hair or buttoned them up they talked over her and around her, and always she listened. And later, walking slowly out to the paddock beyond earshot of the house, she reproduced their words, vowel by vowel, trying to catch that special inflection, that effortless flow of phrase in which it seemed breathing played no part, so that the words cascaded out like music.

But her invisibility was soon to be removed. Lady Crawleigh announced that the girls were to attend confirmation classes every week— "You have been confirmed already I suppose, Sarah?"

Sarah shook her head. "No, milady."

Lady Crawleigh's expression sharpened. "Well, it's high time you were. You had better attend classes with Miss Pansy and Miss Daisy."

So the following Sunday, Sarah duly found herself undertaking a course of Christian dedication, learning questions and answers by rote, attending church and reading a new and quite different Bible. *Just like having a Bar Mitzvah, really,* she reflected. Much of it seemed vaguely familiar, except for what she referred to in her thoughts as "the Jesus stuff." At first she stammered so badly over the forbidden words that the vicar thought she had a speech impediment. But no thunderbolt crushed her, no plagues afflicted her. Her limbs moved, her life continued.

"What is your surname, my girl?" the vicar inquired kindly when she first appeared.

Sarah began to tell him, and then, in a panic, mangled the word. He leaned forward, "What? Robinson is it?"

"Yes, sir." *Of course.* "Robinson."

The confirmation classes were the turning point. Reading aloud, testing Pansy and Daisy, being herself forced to answer clearly, Sarah lost her shyness and her hoarse croak. Her quick, energetic manner returned.

"Sarah," Daisy said one day, "we wish to improve our tennis. You must send balls over the net to us."

"But why not play each other?"

"Then one of us loses and we fight and it ends in tears. If we both play *you*, you will be sure to lose and then neither of us will be upset. It's the perfect solution."

All this would have been enough to set Sarah thinking about the direction her life would take. But it was Foster who unwittingly made her aware of the possibilities of her present occupation. "You're a reader, then," he had commented, somewhat surprised, a few days after she had confessed to reading *Oliver Twist*. Most kitchen maids were illiterate. He realized that Sarah was not the usual type of skivvy.

His subscription to Mudie's Lending Library brought regular parcels of books to the back door, and occasionally he lent Sarah a novel he had found particularly interesting. *Middlemarch* he praised highly, but Sarah flagged and abandoned it after a few chapters. "At half a day each week, Mr. Foster, I'd be thirty before I got to the end," she said apologetically.

The next day he passed over to her a dark blue volume he had finished the night before. "A nice, light read," he said kindly, "not to be taken too seriously, of course."

Sarah had no chance to look at the book until late that evening when the girls had been seen through their baths, had had their hair brushed (one hundred strokes per head), their room tidied, and clothes put away. At last, her window open to the soft summer night, Sarah opened the covers. "Emma Woodhouse, handsome, clever and rich . . ."

Sarah read on, enthralled by the conversation, the dinners, the excursions, the games, and most of all by the tantalizing position of the "companion"—the girl from a modest background who could be taken under some generous wing and introduced to a life of ease and charm and elegance. The companion had to be worthy of the honor, of course. She had to be able to use her head, but if she was sensible and reasonably pleasing to look on, there should be no reason why she should not. . . . Sarah stopped, overwhelmed by the limitless horizons she sensed inching into her vision. *Emma* was no light read; it was a manual for self-improvement. She read on through the night, and when the book was finished, she turned back and began to read it again from the beginning.

After the confirmation classes there was usually lemonade and madeira cake in the vicarage garden, and Sarah's presence at the class led to her going on afterward with the girls. On one occasion Pansy and Daisy were drawn into a game of croquet with the curate, who proved to be a demon player. Daisy was not amused. "Here you are, Mr. Johnson!" she cried imperiously. "Sarah will take my turn—I'm far too hot and Sarah ought to learn how to play."

She handed her mallet to Sarah and fell into the hammock. Mr. Johnson stood aside politely. Sarah paused for a moment, holding the slim wooden handle of the croquet mallet, blinking slowly, almost sleepily, while through her body roared an ocean of excitement: she drowned and suffered a sea change; her past streamed off her like water—the workshop and the smell of the machine oil, the grime that no soap could dislodge, the scouring and scrubbing in the kitchens, the sand stinging the bleeding fingertips. The filthy Whitechapel street, the sound of Leah's voice scolding, the gabble in the crowded synagogue, the air steamy from damp clothing on wet days, the crying of children and the squalling of many cats—she soared free of it all.

With a smile so brilliant that the curate was startled, she stepped forward and with one smooth movement hit the ball—*click*. She was playing croquet on a sunlit lawn with a young gentleman who had been to Oxford. Her hands were white and smooth on the wood, feet narrow and neat in a pair of Daisy's shoes, mouth fresh with the taste of lemonade. The sun slanting down on her cheek felt warm, comforting.

She looked at the trees, really looked at them for the first time: the larches with their special, vivid green; the shiny beeches; the oaks deeper green with gold-tinged leaves. The laburnams dripped yellow onto the grass, and farther off the pink and white candelabra of the horse chestnuts glimmered in the blue gold air. Her eyes pricked with tears, tears of pleasure in this moment, rounded, perfect, when nothing but happiness and well-being enfolded her. In most lives she thought, there can be perhaps no more than a handful of such moments—when fleetingly, but unmarred, pure happiness is touched, and sometimes they can pass almost unremarked. Sarah resolved to make no such mistake. Her only error was in assuming that, pursued diligently, the fugitive moment of pleasure could be extended indefinitely.

"Freddy's bringing down all sorts of people for his wretched party," Daisy said as they walked back from confirmation class. "I *wish* I were two years older and could put up my hair and be treated as a grownup. It's not fair. All the best men will be off the market by the time I'm old enough."

"But there'll be others along by then," Sarah pointed out. "Men are like apples—there's a new crop every year."

"But they'll be *young* ones! I *loathe* young men. . . . What I want is a beautiful older man with shiny black hair and heavy eyelids who can dance the tango divinely."

"I suppose you'll marry someone like Foster, later on, Sarah," Pansy commented.

Sarah looked horrified. "Never!" She laughed. "I wouldn't marry a *butler*!"

Pansy misunderstood the inflection. "No, I suppose a butler would be a bit grand. Well, a footman then. There's one with rather nice eyes I noticed the other day. Would he do?"

For several days before the picnic and ball—the Crawleighs' final social event of the summer—the weather was gray and drizzly. Lady

Crawleigh went about looking haunted, murmuring that she could not conceive of what she should do if the rain continued.

The morning of the picnic was undecided, with a thick white mist and pearly sky, and, in the kitchen, boxes and baskets were packed without too much certainty that they would be put to use. Several cars were assembled to take the family and their guests to the valley road so that they could enjoy a modest hill walk before the picnic, while two footmen and two maids went ahead to set up a campfire and make the clearing ready. Large potatoes were set among the ashes to bake, and Sarah helped spread the blankets and the white cloths. She picked trailing ivy and decorated the tablecloth, winding the glossy dark leaves between platters of cold chicken and tongue, pies, hams, cheese, and mounds of golden apricots and pink and yellow peaches.

The picnic party could be heard long before they came in sight— groaning in weariness, straggling up the hillside, pausing to rest every few minutes, breaking into laughter at private jokes. From the top of the bluff, Sarah watched them arrive, the young men red-faced in their flannels and blazers, the young ladies looking cooler in modish frocks of sweet-pea delicacy, the more fashionable ones with startlingly short hair.

They collapsed onto the rugs, calling for champagne. No one, Sarah noticed, looked at the view. With her newfound delight in the countryside, she wanted to call out to them, "Look what you're missing! Look down there at the sweep of the hillside, that waterfall, the stream, the ruined abbey . . ."

And the flowers! Foster had a book, filled with illustrations of wild flowers, which he allowed Sarah to borrow—and she pored over the marsh valentines, butterwort, pimpernel, and yellow hill violets, learning to identify them. But of course the countryside had been on show to these people all their lives, and they did not need to remark on it.

At dusk, everyone wandered down to the waiting cars and slowly drove home while the staff cleared up the picnic, the men tipping bottles on end above open mouths to drain the wine. The white cloths were stained and crumpled, the dishes messy with leftover food that the servants quickly finished off, scooping up the crumbly bits and licking their fingers. Only the trailing ivy still looked as glossy and fresh as when Sarah arranged it. She gathered a couple of sprays and wound them into a wreath.

"Is that for me?" one of the footmen asked.

Sarah looked up. It was James, the one with nice eyes. She shrugged. "If you want it."

He stooped and she placed the garland on his curly hair. He had a well-shaped head and the ivy crowned him impressively. He grinned and turned to one of the other maids, striking a coy pose. "What do I look like?"

The maid giggled. "Like an idiot, that's what."

Sarah suddenly felt depressed and turned away, picking up napkins. Most of the others had started back toward the house, loaded with baskets. Behind a bush Sarah caught a flash of white and pulled aside a branch to retrieve another abandoned table napkin. She halted, appalled: the white object was not a napkin but the undergarments of one of the housemaids. The girl herself, skirt up and limbs abandoned to a quickening rhythm, lay beneath the curly-haired footman, gasping and groaning audibly.

Sarah let go of the branch and moved back, shaking and disturbed by the sight. She set off quickly down the hill.

The big, square house was dark and silent, while through the trees from the other side of the park there glimmered lights and floated the sound of a dance band playing "Yes Sir, That's My Baby," a song Pansy had been singing tunelessly over and over all summer.

Sarah followed the music and crossed the park toward the lake. Beside the lake was an eighteenth-century pavilion, rather Chinese in style, with white trelliswork screens and little alcoves and a covered balcony overlooking the water. A decorator friend of Lady Crawleigh's had brought in his men to adorn the pavilion with garlands of red and white flowers. At one end of the balcony a little fountain cascaded over an arrangement of fresh fruits—peaches and grapes, nectarines and pomegranates. Tiny lights edged the balcony and were reflected in the lake beyond.

Sarah grew restive, bunched in the side doorway of the pavilion with the other servants, and she wandered away along the lakeside, where the music sounded sweeter, carried to her on the still night air. She looked back at the pavilion, glowing with lights like a fairy-tale palace, shimmering with the movement of the dancers.

Nearby, a couple stood very close together at the water's edge. The girl broke away and ran back giggling toward the pavilion, her body a black shadow against the lights. Her companion—one of the red-faced young men of the picnic—noticed Sarah standing by the reed-fringed water. In the darkness, only her face was clearly visible. He came over. "I say, should you be standing so near the edge?"

"Oh, it's quite safe."

He peered at her inquisitively, at the narrow, pale face softly shadowed. The high-bridged nose and fine-lipped mouth gave her an almost haughty air. "I don't think we've met. . . . Spiffing affair, isn't it? Care for a jog?"

Sarah smiled faintly and moved forward so that a shaft of light coming from the pavilion showed up her clothes. "No thank you, sir."

He took in the dark dress with white collar and cuffs, frowned in embarrassment, and stepped back. "Oh. Ah . . . of course. Yes, well . . ." He cleared his throat. "A little liquid refreshment, I think. Yes." He walked away rapidly toward the lights glittering from the balcony and the tinkling music.

The surface of the lake was ruffled by a sudden chill breeze and Sarah shivered. Summer was ending. Next week they would return to London.

She went back to the house. Pansy and Daisy were in bed, but waiting for her to brush their hair and put away the clothes scattered about the room.

"Well, Sarah, what did you think? Weren't the men divine?"

She shrugged. "You won't do any worse by waiting for the next crop. This lot looked a bit green to me."

The girls shrieked happily. "Sarah, you'll *never* get married if your standards are so high!"

But they went to sleep consoled. "Actually," Daisy murmured, "I didn't see anyone with really shiny black hair and drooping eyelids except the bandleader. And he told me he was married."

The confirmation went smoothly. The church, already decorated for the harvest festival, seemed brighter than usual, with deep red apples in heaps, sheaves of corn and flowers and ivy twined around the pillars with glowing pumpkins at their base.

All three girls gave their responses promptly and were blessed by a quick laying-on of hands. Sarah had at first been secretly worried that something would give her away; some instinct would alert the priest to an awareness of the presence of an alien. But nothing happened. She had also hoped that perhaps she might experience something special as the hands were placed on her head. She had never felt much awe in the synagogue. A truly devout Jew could be an island in the midst of the noise and the movement, but she had found herself distracted. Here, however, in the hushed atmosphere of the little church with the sun filtering through the stained-glass window, the smell of stone and candlewax, and the echoing air, she thought something mystical might reach her. But it was simply a brisk little ceremony after all. Then Lady Crawleigh gave Sarah and the girls a new prayer book each, with white morocco bindings. The girls had new dresses, very straight and stylish—"Oh!" Daisy screamed. "I feel like a flapper already! *Can* I have my hair cut?"

Lady Crawleigh gave Sarah one of her own suits—"It's quite out of fashion, Sarah, but you're so good with a needle that I'm sure you will do something clever with it."

Foster was looking forward to London. "There's a novel by that Marcel Proust I want to get. Mudie's have promised me a copy."

"Any more Jane Austen?" Sarah asked.

"Maybe. But you don't want to go reading too much of that sort of thing, you know. It gives a very one-sided view of life."

Manny lifted the huge brass ring and let it fall against the solid mahogany of the massive front door. It banged, the sound reverberating deep within the fibers of the wood. He gazed nervously at the tall, narrow house, the dark rosy bricks, and the casemented windows.

Suddenly and silently the door opened and a tall man looked down at Manny with a dazed puzzlement, as though hardly able to credit the sight before his eyes. Manny took off his cap and tucked it under his arm and attempted to conceal his frayed cuffs by pulling down his jacket sleeves slightly, but the thin material gave under his fingers, sagging threadbare. The man seemed to consider speech unnecessary. He merely raised his eyebrows, at the same time drawing down the corners of his mouth. He also, slowly, began to close the door, clearly anticipating that their conversation could only be a short one.

Hastily Manny stepped forward, putting his foot in the door. "Hold on, guv'nor. I want to see my sister."

"Are you sure you have the right address?"

His manner was so magnificent, so altogether regal that Manny felt certain he must be at least a lord. "We had word she weren't well. Sarah. Sarah Rubinstein. I've come to take her home. She works here, don't she?"

The eyebrows dropped to their normal level. The brow cleared. "Downstairs. Staff entrance." The white-gloved hands moved. The door closed.

Manny went down the shallow stone steps and knocked at the kitchen door. After a minute the door opened and an enormously fat woman, her white apron stretched tightly over her vast bosom, her white cap pulled over her hair so that her pink cheeks bulged out, peered down at him.

"I've come for Sarah."

She nodded. "Family are you?"

"Brother."

She beckoned him in with a wave of a vast ladle and nodded him in the direction of a high-backed chair near the range. "We'll 'ave to fetch 'er down."

It was the biggest kitchen Manny had ever seen. When the cook opened the door of the oven he caught sight of a roast of beef that could have fed an entire street of people. The oven shut with a bang, engulfing him in a wave of unfamiliar, beefy fragrance that made him for a moment shudder with nausea. He was not accustomed to the smell of roasting, nonkosher meat, charged with the richness of fat and blood. Nevertheless he realized that in its way it was an appetizing smell, and it reminded him that he was hungry. The cook turned to him with an almost amiable expression.

"How is she?" Manny asked. "She didn't say much in her letter."

"She's been poorly of late. Mind you, she's been well took care of. Not like some houses where she'd of been out on her ear as soon as she couldn't work."

She paused, and Manny sensed there was more to come. Perhaps he was to hear something alarming, God forbid. Would she be able to walk? Should he have gone to the expense of a cab? There was no money for such things. But suppose she collapsed in the street. . . .

"Is she . . ." he paused, reluctant to raise with an outsider such a personal subject. "Is she in a bad way?"

The cook shrugged. "Oh she's over it now, really. But you'll need to keep 'er home for a bit."

There, Manny reflected, she spoke truer than she knew. Sarah might have gotten away with her rebellion once, but it would never happen again. After the tears, the lamentations, the searches, Leah had settled into an iron sternness. Sarah would not continue with her shameful life of domestic service with the *goyim*. She would remain in the bosom of her family, like it or not, until she got married.

Cook turned to the scullery maid who was standing slumped against one of the sinks, taking advantage of this brief interruption of work. "Nip up and tell Sarah her brother's come to fetch 'er home, and then get back to them pots, my girl. No dawdling."

Manny looked at the vast copper pans with dishes of sand and soap set ready for scouring, and he noted the girl's hands: raw and red. Would Sarah's hands be like that?

Cook leaned on the table, her black dress ballooning about her. "She's a clever one, your sister. She'll go up in the world, right to the top. A lady's maid at least. She's got the gentility for it, d'you see."

Manny could make no sense of this and merely nodded blankly.

She looked at his face, drawn and thin, the skin clinging flatly to the bones with no cushioning of flesh. There were shadows under his eyes and lines of fatigue pinching his mouth. "How old are you, lad?"

"Nearly sixteen."

"In work, are you?"

"Oh yes, I should say."

She heaved a wheezy sigh. "Thought you might be one o' them strikers. Fine carry on that was. Master Reggie and his friends had a good time driving buses, but will it do me any good? All the strikin' and fightin' in the streets won't get me a shillin' extra on me wages. I don't know what the country's comin' to . . . men fightin' their own countrymen in the streets, it's not like England, is it? Makes you think of them Bolsheviks."

Manny thought of Mordecai and his friends. Surely they weren't involved?

"*I* think it's all these foreigners," she said suddenly, as though reading his mind. "Foreigners coming in causing all the trouble—it's my opinion the Russians are behind it: they want to get another revolution going—got the taste for it now, d'you see. I'd round up the foreigners and put 'em all inside, *I* would."

She glanced at him again. "You look as though you could do with a bit o' nourishment."

What would his mother have said, to hear such a thing about her son! She had tried for twenty years to fatten up Chaim, give him a healthy look, and he had died thinner and paler than ever. In a terrible way Leah might have been consoled a little in her loss had Chaim gone to Abraham's bosom with a good color in his cheeks. It would have reflected better on her.

"How about a cuppa?" the cook said. "I was just gettin' tea ready anyway."

There was a silver tray on the kitchen table, its handles swirling into ornate curves. On it were cups and saucers and small plates of china so thin that Manny could see the light from the window glowing through one of the cups. There were tiny, rounded knives with pearly handles and queer, flat-pronged forks, and slices of bread and butter as delicate as the china of the cups.

The cook placed a fruitcake on a silver dish and filled the narrow milk jug. Manny watched all this as if in a dream. He almost remonstrated at one point—"Don't make yourself so busy on my account"—but by then she had filled the silver teapot, poured boiling water into a tall silver jug next to it, and he felt it would be churlish to protest. Besides, this was obviously their normal style. And in any case he was hungry. A bit of fruitcake must taste pretty much the same in any kitchen, even a nonkosher one. It certainly looked good. He could almost taste the moist richness, the currants, and the raisins of that cake!

The cook surveyed the tray, lips pursed. "There. I think we're ready."

"It looks a treat," Manny said heartily.

The big kitchen clock struck five, and through the door came the lordly man in white gloves. He found it unnecessary to notice Manny. "Ready, Mrs. Oliphant?"

"Ready, Mr. Foster."

He checked the tray, moved a dish a fraction of an inch, and then, with one smooth movement, picked up the tray and vanished through the doorway. Manny blinked. Had he imagined all the cook's words?

She turned back, rubbing her hands. "There. That's done. Now we'll have our cuppa."

She took hold of the gigantic kettle simmering on the hob and poured some boiling water into a plain brown teapot. As she brewed the tea and set out thick china cups, she glanced again at Manny. "How about a bit o' bread and dripping?"

Before Manny could answer, the scullery maid had slipped back into the room and returned to her scrubbing and scraping of the pots. Behind her, bumping and thudding down the wooden stairs, came a suitcase, held by Sarah. She entered the kitchen.

Brother and sister stared at each other silently. It was hard to find the right words. Manny thought: *If she gets any thinner her bones will come through her skin. She's a skeleton.*

Sarah thought: *He looks so tired. And so shabby.* She had a passing vision of the family, upstairs in the drawing room now, sipping tea. She did not begrudge them their ease; she simply wanted to share it.

"Hullo then," Manny said brusquely. "You got everything there?" He gestured toward the flimsy suitcase. She nodded.

He turned to the cook. "We'll be off then."

"Stop for your cuppa at least."

Manny looked at Sarah but she gave an almost imperceptible shake of the head.

"Thanks all the same," he said, "but we'd best be getting on."

Sara spoke for the first time. "Well, goodbye, Mrs. Oliphant." She did not approach the enormous woman. Manny had a feeling Mrs. Oliphant would have liked a more demonstrative farewell, a few tears perhaps, would have enjoyed cradling Sarah's head on her vast frontage, but Sarah spoke so coolly, was so obviously untouchable, that the cook merely shrugged a little helplessly and nodded.

"Goodbye then and good luck to you."

They were already halfway up the outside steps when Foster appeared in the kitchen entrance. "Sarah!"

She stopped and he came out. He spoke with slight embarrassment. "I never knew your name was Rubinstein. . . . That's a Jewish name, isn't it?"

Sarah nodded stonily.

"There are so many questions I'd have liked to ask you. . . . I read *Daniel Deronda,* you know."

Sarah had no idea what he was talking about. "Oh."

"Well. Good luck anyway. I hope what you've learned here will be useful to you. Here." He thrust a small package at her and hurried back into the kitchen.

At the top of the steps Sarah paused for a moment. She looked up at the house, to where a pale silken curtain could be glimpsed through the drawing-room window, and then she looked down at the kitchen, through the steamy window. Mrs. Oliphant, unseen, could be heard urging the scullery maid to "get on with them pans, my girl!"

Side by side they walked away from the house, Manny carrying her suitcase. "Well, Manny," Sarah said at last, "and how is everyone at home?"

He was upset by her voice. It was deeper than he remembered, and quieter, but the change went further than that. There was something quite . . . ladylike about it, he decided. He hoped Sarah hadn't picked up any bad ways in that big house.

She began to pull on a pair of thin cotton gloves as they walked down the long, curving street. He looked at her sideways, trying not to stare. Sarah was almost as tall as he was and she looked so different. She wore a brown skirt and jacket just like a picture from a magazine he had seen, with neat shoes and stockings that looked like silk. Her hair, most startling of all, was sleek and short. The last time he had seen her she had been a scrawny child. Now she was fourteen, and pale and thin though she was, she looked, he thought, almost elegant.

What Leah would say he could not imagine. She had wept when Sarah's letter arrived— "Bronchitis? She'll die of it without proper attention, her father had a weak chest!" And the letter did in fact say that the doctor advised rest and therefore Sarah could not stay on where she was —"Typical *goyim*!" Leah exclaimed. "Cold-hearted. Turn a sick girl out onto the streets!"

"She says they've been kind," Manny said, looking at the letter. "She says they aren't turning her out but now that she's a bit better she should go home to her family."

"And suppose she *had* no family? What then?" Leah demanded, and answered herself triumphantly. "The streets!"

She was expecting to welcome home a contrite daughter, who had learned her lesson. But Sarah had always had a generous measure of *chutzpah* in her nature. Manny could foresee clashes.

Sarah stumbled and he asked anxiously, "Can you walk for a bit? I reckon it's a hard life in them big houses, scrubbin' and cleanin'. You never should of gone, altogether. I hope you've learned your lesson."

She gave a faint, enigmatic smile. "Oh I've learned a lot."

"Well, you can rest up for a bit at home. We can manage on what Miriam and I bring in." He paused, hoping she would ask a question, but she continued walking along in silent composure. "Ruth's doing well. She's got a good head on her shoulders." Her silence exasperated him. "Why did you never write? Didn't you know Mum was worried sick? We all were. We thought you could be dead, murdered, fallen in with white slavers, anything!"

"White slavers?" She looked at him incredulously. "This is nineteen twenty-six, Manny, not the Middle Ages. There isn't any of that sort of thing now."

The buses were running again; the strike was over for most people and Manny reckoned it would not be long before the miners, too, went back. They caught one bus, changed and got on another, hardly speaking. Sarah sat with her head turned away, staring out of the window.

The streets grew busier, the pavements crowded with animated women gossiping over their shopping baskets, bearded men in black hats, boys wearing *yarmulkahs.* On one corner stood the old woman who sold bagels, the freshly baked rolls threaded on string like fat little wheels. Through uncurtained windows Manny could see, as they rode past, rows of sewing machines and figures bent over their work. Ruth had told him there were two thousand sweatshops in the neighborhood, and for a moment Manny pictured all those machines, those moving fingers, those bobbins spinning—he found it exhilarating.

"Nearly there," he said. She remained silent. He tried again. "I said we're nearly there, nearly home."

"Yes." Sarah's voice was barely audible. "I can tell. It's so dirty. We must be close to home."

"Dirty?" Manny glanced out of the window. "I suppose it is. I never noticed."

She looked at him in amazement. "You never *noticed?*" She gave a little laugh, but he saw that her eyes were very bright and glassy-looking.

"Hey," he said hastily, "you never opened your package."

She tore it open without curiosity. Inside was a dark blue book. Sarah felt a tremor of affection for Foster with his distant manner and his surreptitious kindness.

"What is it?" Manny asked.

"Oh, just a novel," Sarah said, clutching it tightly. "It's called *Pride and Prejudice.*"

It is hard to forgive injury; it is even harder to be denied the opportunity to be forgiving. Leah was ready to be magnanimous, to fall sobbing into Sarah's arms and wash away the bitterness in tears. But Sarah had learned an added reserve in her stay among the gentiles. She held herself back, failed to cry and hug, was polite. Leah felt cheated of her reconciliation and reacted by fault-finding.

"Come and eat. . . . Have some soup, a piece of bread. No coat? And you look so pale, like a ghost. Ruth, you know about such things, should a girl look like a sheet?"

Since Ruth had become a nurse at the Jewish Hospital, Leah turned to her for advice on all matters medical. Ruth exchanged an understanding look with Sarah. "No, Mum. But Sarah's always been pale. Anyway, she's been sick, hasn't she? Give her a chance."

Sarah took in the scene while Leah ladled out the soup: Miriam, looking scruffy, was rubbing ointment onto her sore fingertips; Ruth was assembling textbooks while she waited for supper; Jonathan sat, dreamy and composed, blinking through the glasses Leah had bought for him in Woolworth's after testing them by trying them out on her own eyes; Manny was cheerfully tearing himself off a hunk of bread. With her trim suit and short hair Sarah felt like a visitor. She sat down.

Miriam touched the jacket of Sarah's suit approvingly. "Lovely stuff, Sarah. Must have cost—"

"Well, you won't have much use for it here," Leah said sharply. "We don't want the neighbors thinking we've come into a fortune all of a sudden."

Sarah took a couple of spoons of soup, then suddenly stood up. "I'm rather tired. Can I go to bed?"

"You can have Golomstok's old room," Leah said, and Manny added encouragingly, "Sleep as late as you like, you won't hear the machines up there."

"I'll take Sarah up," Ruth said. "Don't everyone start getting busy. Where's the suitcase?"

Sarah climbed the stairs, her stomach contracting as she noticed the cracked and flaking walls, the worn linoleum on the stair treads, and she remembered with a groan that the lavatory was out in the yard.

"Listen," Ruth instructed. "Use the potty, it belonged to Segal's kid. You can't go trailing up and down all the time."

Sarah sat down abruptly on the narrow bed. Her legs felt wobbly. She touched the bedclothes: they felt flimsy and threadbare and slightly damp. The sheets were gray, not with dirt but with age. For the last two years she had slept in a hard bed, true, but one with firm white sheets and fresh blankets. There had even been a little runner of carpet by her bed, a spare piece left over when the stairs were recarpeted. It had a Persian design and the wool was warm and crunchy under her feet when she dressed. She looked around the attic despairingly.

She could hear the sound of rain against the window; in the street someone hurried past, cursing tonelessly; from next door there was the faint, continuous wailing of a child. The air in the room was dank and cloying.

"What did you *do* there, with those people?" Ruth asked, breaking the silence.

Sarah wanted to say, "I played tennis with rich young girls, I nearly beat the curate at croquet, I drank lemonade on the lawn and went for picnics and I watched the moon rise over the lake. And read novels."

"I'll tell you all about it," she promised, "tomorrow," and took refuge in a yawn.

For a few days Leah accepted the situation without comment. Then she exploded into questions prompted by anxiety. "Is it right that a girl should take to her bed night and day? A young girl? Hardly eating? How can she build up her strength? And silent! You can't get a word out of her, she's like a stone. I'm worried about her."

Manny, too, was worried. For he saw what Leah did not—that Sarah had no wish to get better. Had she been strong enough she would probably have run away again. As it was, she went away from them in her mind.

Leah did everything possible: she poured soup down Sarah's throat twice a day. She brought home a patent medicine, much recommended in the market. "See: 'Pink Pills for Pale People'! Well, she's pale. Read what it says: sores they've cured and bronchitis and rheumatism and burns. It's wonderful what they can do, the pills, and so they should at two and nine the box!"

What none of them suspected—how could they?—was that Leah concealed, behind her fussing and her endless exhortations to eat, a worry of a different kind: a personal guilt.

Could it be coincidence that everything started to go wrong suddenly? she asked herself. Chaim's death; Sarah running away from home, living among the *goyim* and learning bad ways; their own increasing poverty. It had all begun after Mordecai's visit, after her betrayal of Chaim's trust. Coincidence? Or a punishment on her? For years she had paid lip service to Chaim's God, preserving intact her own core of skepticism. But now she found herself carrying out the rituals with growing fervor; Jonathan was instructed ceaselessly in the Torah—Chaim himself could have done no better. The prayers that she had once endured patiently for his sake, she now inflicted on the family with genuine zeal.

Her own children, beyond a certain point, could not be manipulated, she knew. But Jonathan . . . "You have a good head on your shoulders," Leah had told him, "a good head and a good heart." So between his stints at the sewing machine he went to the *yeshiva* as Chaim had done in his youth, and he studied, swaying and rocking with the old men, chanting the old words, following the tenuous thread of knowledge that had brought Chaim consolation, and that Mordecai rejected so violently. And Leah, being a strong-minded woman, refused to face the question lurking at the back of her consciousness: Did she do all this to honor the one or to punish the other?

"For love is strong as death and jealousy is cruel as the grave," said the Song of Solomon. Perhaps even she did not know which it was.

The Pink Pills for Pale People may have cured neuralgia, St. Vitus's dance, anemia, and consumption, as claimed on the label. Unfortunately, they did nothing for Sarah, who lay, eyes closed, growing weaker day by day.

"She fades away before our eyes!" Leah moaned. "What is to be done?"

"Have you had a letter from Auntie Ruda lately?" Manny asked.

"Don't change the subject! I ask about your sister's health and you talk about letters from Ruda."

"I'm not changing the subject," Manny said. "I bet Auntie Ruda asked when we're going to visit her, didn't she?"

"You know she did. For years she has been asking."

"So this time we'll give her a different answer. We'll tell her Sarah is coming. For a convalescence."

"Where's the money coming from?"

"We'll find it." He grinned. "Come on, Mum: where's your faith? God will provide, won't He?"

And in the next day's mail there was a letter, with an American postmark, from Simeon, telling them about his professional adventures in Boston and enclosing a money order—"for Sarah's birthday. I'd like you to buy her something exciting and extravagant."

Manny said, waving the money order gleefully, "We'll buy her a ticket to Germany!"

Manny spent fifteen hours a day at the sewing machine, which paid for the rent and food, but not much more. Always racing the clock, always driving himself to meet delivery dates, he took his customers' completed orders around on Fridays, and on Friday evenings he gave Leah the money. Miriam brought home her wages from the fireworks factory, and Ruth contributed from her pitiful salary. "Nurses don't get paid enough," Manny said angrily. "Something should be done, it's not right."

"Yes, why doesn't your precious Labour Party do something then?" Miriam asked Ruth.

"They will, you'll see. It's early yet. We'll be looked after."

Miriam looked skeptical. "You'll need to go on strike before anyone takes you seriously. People like us, we don't matter, we're like flies: people only notice flies when they become a nuisance."

Miriam left for the factory as usual, straight after breakfast. Jonathan was already at the *yeshiva,* and Leah and Manny were at the machines when the hurried knocking at the door disturbed them.

"If it's that Mrs. Steen after a cup of matzo meal," Leah muttered, "I'll give it to her—over her head."

It was Mrs. Steen's daughter Deborah, a fat, good-natured slattern who worked with Miriam and planned to get married as soon as the marriage broker came up with someone who would have her. Deborah lived to gossip; she was incapable of leaving before the end of any story, and as a consequence was generally late for work.

"Shouldn't you be at the factory?" Leah said severely.

Deborah's face screwed into a grimace. She spoke shrilly. "There's been an explosion at the factory—"

Leah slammed the door, pushed the girl ahead of her, and began to rush, running and stumbling, toward the factory.

The girl was breathless and frightened. "I was late. As I got to the door it happened. There was this terrible noise, a bang—"

Leah suddenly had the feeling she was living a dream, repeating a nightmare. Lightning does not strike the same tree twice, it could not, would not prove to be really serious. Just fireworks. Just a bang. *Please God, no more.*

Running, she was running toward the school, the bombs, the children screaming, bleeding. *Please, God, haven't I been punished enough?* Running, running toward the factory, the school, the factory, gasping for breath, rounding the corner, the school gone, the ruins smoking, the factory . . .

The factory walls were flimsy. One gaping hole had already been blown out, through which smoke—brilliantly colored and evil smelling, was pouring. Girls, screaming and crying for help, were at the other window, and Leah rubbed her smarting eyes, trying to find Miriam among them.

The firemen were pouring water into the building, but every few seconds there was a new explosion. Bright, glittering flares lit up the interior, and thicker smoke—yellow and purple and green—billowed from the house.

The crowds gathered, watching the monstrous display as red stars and comet tails of purple and blue shot up toward the sky. Ladders were being moved to the upstairs window, but some of the girls—panic-stricken—had climbed onto the ledge to try to be first out of the burning building. Leah pushed her fingers into her mouth to stop herself from crying out as she saw the girls with their blackened faces and scorched clothes, standing precariously on the window ledge. There was another bang, a shower of golden sparks, and a sudden surge from within the room. The two girls on the ledge wobbled and clung on frantically. Then they fell.

It seemed to Leah that they fell slowly, so slowly that she could dash forward and catch them, cradle them in her arms, but before she could even move, they hit the pavement, almost together, with a terrible crack and thud, flesh and bone smashing into the flagstones.

Above them the wall began to give way, falling outward onto the firemen, carrying girls, masonry, beams, and blackened furniture

215

with it. Again that dreamlike sense of repetition, as Leah watched the building collapse. First, the curious bulging outward of the wall, almost as though it were being pushed from within; then the cracking and crumbling and the crash as the dust rose, choking them all.

Some of the girls were killed outright or hideously maimed by the fireworks, some crushed by the falling building; others suffocated inside. Miriam had been in the room where the first explosion occurred.

"Better that way, really," one of the policemen said gruffly to Leah. "You wouldn't have wanted her lingering on, suffering, would you? She was right there at the table, d'you see."

"Wasn't there a fire escape?" an onlooker asked angrily.

The policeman shrugged. "There *should* have been a fire escape, but these sweatshops, the bosses don't want to waste the money. They don't bother. Horrible conditions, I don't know why people put up with it."

"Because they need to work," Leah said bitterly, "to stay alive."

Now she was sure of it: God was punishing her. She had mocked him too long. Perhaps she was to lose everyone she loved; they would be taken from her one by one.

Sarah was out of reach in Germany now. Only Manny and Ruth remained. And Jonathan, she reminded herself. She could never admit that she was unable to love Jonathan. She cared for him, she worried about him, but when she looked at the boy, at the slender body and the clear eyes and the curly hair that fell around his pale face, she saw the woman who had been his mother. She saw Mordecai's partner, who had had the courage to tread the path from which Leah had drawn back. How much had he loved her? Had he mourned her, crazed with grief, or had he paid affectionate respects to a fallen comrade and moved on? Mordecai had always had a quality of ruthlessness about him; that, more than anything else, was what Leah had feared—that one day she would be weighed in the scales against some greater cause, and she would be sacrificed.

But seeing him again she had forgotten her fears and felt only the old, sweet, aching excitement. She was a wicked woman, she realized that now. She had sinned; she had put the weakness of her flesh above her loyalty. And, she added hastily, her duty to God. Probably she would spend the rest of her life in penitence for it.

So," Manny said firmly, "I've been thinking and I've made a few calculations and it's no good. We've got to have a bit more coming in."

"But we can't work any longer hours," Leah said hopelessly. "You know what will happen: one of us will fall asleep over the machine and spoil the cloth."

"I've thought it out," Manny said. "I'll get a job. Office hours."

"What kind of a job can you get? You only know the sewing."

"You'll see. There's plenty I can do. Something in the city maybe. I've got an appointment to see a man."

She looked at him admiringly. Manny was no taller than she was herself, but there was something about him: the square little body topped by that determined face in which her own eyes seemed to look back at her.

"I'll sponge and press your suit," she said. The suit had once been his best, his Bar Mitzvah outfit, to be worn only on special occasions. But what was a job hunt if not a special occasion?

While Leah carefully damped and pressed the serge, Manny went off to the public baths, his towel under his arm. It was a luxury, a penny, just for a bath, but worth it. He loved the steamy, cavernous building with its ornate Oriental windows and the slightly crooked sign above the vast wrought-iron and wooden doors: RUSSIAN VAPOUR (the final word, BATHS, having fallen off one day and never been replaced). Inside, it became a box puzzle, a maze of tiny cubicles, with voices floating and echoing over the partitions.

The attendant unlocked a cubicle with his long key, and Manny put his clothes on the wire rack while the bath filled. From the next-door cubicle he heard a voice—"More hot please, number five!" A woman's voice. Manny began to visualize her in the bath, her hair pinned on top of her head and her face shiny from the steam. Once,

217

when he was younger, made reckless by curiosity, he had climbed up the partition and peered over the top for his first glimpse of the female form unclothed. He hung there, palpitating with fear and expectation, and peered down through the steamy air.

The woman lay, pink and slippery looking, her breasts bobbing on the water like melons, her eyes closed. As he gazed down, she lazily rubbed herself with a bright blue bar of soap. The perfume of the soap rose to Manny's nostrils, dizzying him. This sinuous, glistening creature with ample bulges and mysterious jungle shadows was a revelation. He breathed unevenly, his mouth open, then, dry-throated, he swallowed with difficulty. At that moment the woman opened her eyes and looked straight at him. For a second she remained expressionless. Then, slowly, she smiled and parted her legs.

There was a tiny, involuntary noise in Manny's throat and he froze, hanging there like a mouse transfixed in a beam of light. The woman's hand flashed out of the water and a soaking sponge flew through the air and hit Manny in the face. His fingers, already greasy, slipped on the wall and he slid clumsily back, wrenching his toe painfully on the tap. He hopped about on one foot, shaking with excitement. *Fool*, he said to himself. Why hadn't he climbed over? She looked ready for whatever it was that had to be done. He tried to scale the wall again but there was no strength left in his arms and he leaned against the partition, pressing his forehead into the wood, cursing silently.

Now, a man of almost sixteen, he remained hardly more experienced—an occasional fumble with a Welsh girl on the common in return for buying her a cup of tea and a bun was all he had managed.

And behind that wall lay a woman, perhaps a lonely woman, who would also look up and smile in that lazy, contemptuous way. . . . But he must not delay. There was a job to be found. He picked up his carbolic soap and began to rub himself vigorously. The soap was so strong that it took a layer of skin off, but it certainly put an end to his thinking about the pink body slithering about in the next cubicle.

"Come in, come in!" The man at the desk looked impatient. "So you want a job?"

"Yes, reverend."

The man certainly looked reverend enough. He was peering at Manny closely. "You have had problems with employment?"

"Yes." Manny went into his rehearsed speech. "I want to work, I can get work. But only with *goyim* who open on the Sabbath and they refuse to let me have the day off, even though I am willing to make up the time . . ." He looked gloomy. "But my mother is not well and my sister . . ."

"Yes, yes." Pathos was wasted on the man. "We must try to find you something." He began fingering a greasy exercise book.

"Ah!" Carefully he copied down the address and gave it to Manny. "I knew your father. He was a good man. Remember the Sabbath Day, to keep it Holy, and we take ten percent of your first week's wages."

The Jewish Sabbath Observance Office was not as well known as its larger fellow-organization. Manny, however, had heard of their record and felt they were worth a try. He looked consideringly at the scrap of paper. "Bomberg's Bristles. Import-Export." It seemed as good a place as any to start.

Mrs. Bomberg looked at Manny with some suspicion. "You've done this kind of work before?"

"Similar," he risked.

"Can you use the typewriter?"

"Can I use the typewriter?" Manny laughed, praying she would not ask him for a demonstration.

"Well . . . come through."

The Bomberg Bristles Import-Export business occupied the ground floor of the Bomberg residence, and the curious smell of bristles "specially imported from China" piled around the office in sacks mingled with the aroma of kosher chicken simmering in the kitchen. The Bombergs obviously lived well.

There were two battered desks in the office. At one sat a clerk copying figures into a large ledger that could be locked with a brass clasp and key. He looked about Manny's age but thinner, with a pointed, ratlike face, dark curly hair, and alert brown eyes set very close on either side of his bony nose. He had a way of twitching his nose delicately and pursing his lips while he wrote, almost as though he disapproved of the figures. He glanced up at Manny and away again without speaking, and Mrs. Bomberg did not introduce them.

"This is your desk," she said, patting the piles of invoices, orders, and receipts waiting to be dealt with. "And here," she added proudly, "is the typewriter."

"Ah," said Manny. He had never, to his knowledge, seen a typewriter before. He looked at it closely. It appeared to be constructed of a thousand different pieces of metal, all linked in some mysterious way to a keyboard rather like a bunched-up piano, with letters on each disk.

Across the top of the typewriter was some faded gold wording: "Las Islas Canarias."

"That's a good machine," Mrs. Bomberg said firmly. "My husband picked it up on one of his trips," she paused, "abroad." She glanced at Manny. "I see you're looking at the shift bar."

Manny, who was not too sure what the shift bar was, tried not to focus on anything in particular. Mrs. Bomberg touched the shift bar protectively, as though Manny's silence had indicated criticism. "It's a good machine. You just need to get used to it."

The shift bar was weighed down by a large iron hammerhead, tied on with a bit of string, which gave it the weight to move along as the keys were struck. "You'll soon get used to it," she said, and went into the next room.

As soon as he door closed, the clerk threw down his pen, reached into his pocket, and pulled out some chewed-looking lumps of toffee. He handed one to Manny and began to gnaw on one himself. "What's your name?"

"Manny. Manny Rubinstein."

The boy nodded, his mouth full, and continued chewing for a minute. "They found the typewriter on a scrap heap somewhere. *He* fixed up the arrangement with the hammer. Well, you better get started. They listen for the sound of the machine."

"What's *your* name?" Manny asked.

The clerk did not look up. "Benjamin Disraeli," he muttered

"No, really?"

"Yes, really. It's my mother's fault. She said they *must* change their name, and it *must* be something English. Really English. Disraeli was the only Englishman she'd ever heard of. So . . ."

Benjamin's eyes gleamed with amusement. He smiled ruefully, and his small rodent face lit up into such an expression of merriment that Manny, too, began to grin in sympathy. "Mothers!" he said, shaking his head despairingly.

Manny touched a typewriter key with an exploring finger and the machine jumped noisily. "*Oy!*" he exclaimed.

"You'll get used to it," Benjamin said reassuringly.

Some time later the Bombergs went upstairs for their midday meal, taking the precaution of locking the front door so that their two clerks could not sneak in and get up to mischief. Benjamin and Manny stood on the pavement, shivering in the raw air.

"Know what I feel like?" Benjamin said. "A nice hot meal: fish and chips maybe, with peas, and a bit of apple pie to finish with. How about you?"

"Oh, I've only got enough for a cup of tea and a bun."

"Same here. Come on."

They hurried along until Benjamin found what he was looking for: a large, busy café, already half-full, the waitresses dashing from table to table, the air thick with the comforting smell of cooked food. "Go inside. Sit down at a table for two and I'll join you. But don't speak to me. We don't know each other, okay?"

Manny found a table and picked up the menu. A minute later, Benjamin wandered in, looked about vaguely, and sat down opposite Manny. As he unfolded a rather tattered newspaper which he took from his pocket, he remarked, "Order whatever you like and don't worry."

The waitress came over and looked at Manny inquiringly.

"Er—fish and chips, slice of bread, and tea, please."

"Right, luv." She took the menu and handed it to Benjamin.

Without looking up from his newspaper he said, "Cup of tea, roll and butter."

"Last of the big spenders," said the waitress irritably, and headed for the kitchen.

Manny's meal came and he gobbled it nervously, swishing the tea around his mouth to dislodge the last bits of fish. Barely moving his lips, Benjamin murmured, "Now go and pay, and wait for me at the corner." As he spoke, he casually pushed toward Manny his own bill, for tea and a roll.

Shaking with fear, Manny walked quickly to the cash desk by the door and thrust the bill at the cashier. She glanced at it languidly. "Tea and a roll—thank you." He almost ran out of the door, then waited, heart thudding, for Benjamin to appear.

He came sauntering up, grinning cheerfully. "But what did you do? How did you get away with it?" Manny asked.

"Simple. I called the waitress over and said, 'What's this bill? I've only had a cup of tea and a roll,' which she could see for herself. So she says, furious, 'The other chap's picked up *your* bill, the little bugger!' So I pay for my tea and roll and leave."

"But you must be starving!" Manny exclaimed.

"I am," Benjamin assured him. "So let's find another caff. Only this time it's *your* turn to have the tea and roll."

221

When Manny got home, Mrs. Steen was standing in the kitchen, cup of sugar in her hand, lamenting as usual. ". . . and his wife is going crazy, *nebech*."

"Whose troubles are we getting this time?" Manny asked Leah, after Mrs. Steen left.

"Fishbein. He got mixed up with some Manchester fellow in a deal with biscuits. And now he's got the front room filled with the biscuits and he's sick with influenza and the biscuits lie there."

Manny continued sipping his soup. "Where does he live, Fishbein?"

After he had eaten, he went out. He took a bus and made his way to Fishbein's place. He knew he had come to the right address because even at the door the mouth-watering smell of vanilla reached him.

Fishbein lay in bed, red-eyed and shivering.

"How do you feel?" Manny asked brightly.

"Feel? How do I feel? I feel like I'm two hundred years old and hot pincers are pulling at my chest. I feel like my legs have been broken and pepper is in my throat and my head is filled with banging—"

"Not too good," Manny agreed. "Listen, about the biscuits—"

"*Ach!* Don't talk to me about the biscuits! I never should have listened to that *momzer*. 'Biscuits like these, they'll sell themselves!' he said. So I stand in the market and freeze. The biscuits don't sell themselves. *I* can't sell biscuits. . . . My *wife* can't sell biscuits. . . . But that Manchester *gonif, he* can sell biscuits—to me!"

"I could help you out," Manny said. "I can't *buy* them, but I'll take them off your hands and share what I make, fifty-fifty."

"Fifty-fifty? But they're *mine* biscuits!"

"But you can't sell them. The rats will be after them soon and the cockroaches, and the bugs. The council will hear about your biscuits and send a man around—"

Fishbein groaned. "How do I know you won't just take the biscuits and I'll never see a penny? Maybe you can't sell biscuits either."

"Maybe I can't," Manny said, "but you can't for certain. You want to take a chance on me or let the biscuits rot there in your front room? They won't smell so nice when they start going sour."

Fishbein had one last try. "Sixty-forty. They're *mine* biscuits."

"Sixty-forty and they're *your* biscuits and *your* problem and they stay in *your* front room. Fifty-fifty and they're *our* biscuits. And our profit."

Fishbein looked at him with respect. "You don't talk like your old man, God rest his soul. He was a good man. Take the biscuits."

Manny wheeled them away on a handcart. He spent two whole evenings transporting them and stacking them in the workroom, to Leah's dismay. "They'll draw the rats."

"They won't be here long enough."

The next evening Manny decorated the boxes with symbols and slogans and a stamp that looked vaguely official. On Friday he went to see a man in the market and came to an arrangement.

He spent Saturday—his day off from the Bombergs'—in the market, surrounded by boxes, and throughout the day people not too concerned with Sabbath observance lined up and pushed and shoved to buy the biscuits and by evening all the boxes he had brought were empty. During the week he was at the typewriter. The following Saturday he was back in the market, and on Sunday night Manny took Fishbein his share.

The sick man almost choked as Manny handed him the stack of notes. "How did you do it? Hypnotize them?"

Manny shrugged. "People like something special. Biscuits they can buy anywhere. But *Chanukah* biscuits? For the festival? From Jerusalem? That's special."

"But they didn't come from Jerusalem!" Fishbein squawked. "They came from Manchester."

"Well, it's all the same once they're in the mouth, isn't it? And your *shlepper* was right, they're good biscuits. No one complained."

Leah stared at the money Manny put on the table in front of her. "You stole it."

"No, no. I earned it."

"How?"

"Buying, selling."

"When?"

He paused. "What's the difference?"

"You worked on the Sabbath. I don't want money earned that way. It's dirty money."

"You weren't always so particular about the Law. What happened, did the rabbi frighten you? You want clean money? I'll take the pound notes to the bathhouse next time, give 'em a wash. It was bad enough with Dad, but at least he believed." He stared at her angrily. "I don't know what it is with you, Mum. What happened to the thinking all of a sudden? To the freethinking and the arguments? You've turned so religious it sticks in my throat. We sit around observing the Sabbath and starving. Is that so wonderful? Well, not me. I'm telling you something, Ma: I'm going to the top and nothing is going to stop me. I'm not stealing and I'm not killing anybody. I'm just working."

He picked up the money. "And one day you'll take it. A few more deals, a few more years, and my money will be as clean as the chief rabbi's. Time makes all money respectable."

Mrs. Bomberg had been right. Manny soon got used to the typewriter. He learned to tap out the invoices and orders at a rattling speed, while the hammerhead carried the shift bar along, jumping and bouncing. During the morning there could be no gossiping: one or other of the Bombergs was always within earshot, primed to catch any exchanges between the clerks.

As Mrs. Bomberg locked the door behind them at lunch time, Benjamin seized Manny's arm excitedly and dragged him along the pavement. "I heard of a wonderful new idea! A feller in our street broke his dentures on a stone in the cabbage. The caff was so scared of the public health inspector they paid up on the spot for a new set of teeth."

"But I haven't got false teeth," Manny objected.

"So? Haven't you got any imagination?" Benjamin shook his head sadly and held out his hand: in it was a broken dental plate. "Come on."

In the restaurant, waiting to plant the stone that would break Benjamin's denture, they met Saul, a lugubrious youth with a long white face, a fixed stare, and big red hands hanging from wrists that stuck out from too-short sleeves. Saul was, he told them, in a brand-new trade: "Instant shoe repairs. It's a craze. People line up to have their shoes mended while they wait. You don't need to be a trained cobbler, nothing. You just have this rented machine and a room and you're in business."

For a man in such a booming enterprise he looked curiously unhappy. Manny asked keenly, "So where are *you* in business?"

Saul shrugged gloomily, "Just now I'm not exactly in business. The man who rented me the room decided to rent it to an auctioneer instead and kicked me out. I haven't the capital to put down for another room."

"You got the machine?"

"Oh yes. It's paid for till the end of the month."

"So where's the problem? We find a room," Manny said, "I pay the rent and we split your takings, sixty-forty."

"You want forty percent, just for finding the room?"

Manny shook his head. "No. I want sixty percent."

"But that's robbery."

"Okay. Forget it. But with a machine on your hands and premises in a busy neighborhood, forty percent of the take could bring you . . ." he shrugged. "Never mind. Forget it."

Saul looked uneasy. "If it was a really busy area . . ."

"I know just the place!" Manny exclaimed. "They buy biscuits, they'll need their shoes mended. It's human nature."

All week Manny typed his invoices. At night he spent a couple of hours at the sewing machine. On Saturday morning he went in to help Saul clear up the shoe-repair shop and collect his share of the week's takings. Saul was too busy to cheat him, and Manny had been proved right in his choice of neighborhood. Business was so good that after the second week they had to set up benches for waiting customers.

After the fourth week Manny told Mrs. Bomberg that he wanted to leave. She looked upset. "You're letting me down, Manny. It's a busy time . . ."

"Listen," Manny said, "I'd like to do you a favor. The invoices are up to date like they've never been, right? I'm a fast typist. I'll come in after work in the evening and do them."

She was uncertain. "You'll never keep up."

"I'm strong," he grinned. "Try me."

At the Labour Exchange the line of men waiting stretched around the block. But there was an occasional job, especially for a determined young man with extra drive.

Once more Manny found himself facing a new employer. But

he had moved up in the world. This was no Bomberg front room with a scrap-heap typewriter. This was a firm with a famous name.

The sales manager was tired. He had seen too many bright young men come into his office full of ambition and gradually tail off into disappointment. This boy looked intelligent and energetic but somewhat on the small side. "Do you know anything about vacuum cleaners?" he asked, without hope.

Manny had never set eyes on one. "A bit," he said.

"Well, you'll be selling vacuum cleaners so you better learn all about them. Housewives ask a lot of questions. You'll need to know the answers."

Manny learned about vacuum cleaners. He also learned something of the facts of a vacuum-cleaner salesman's life.

"For the first four weeks you get a salary of two pounds, ten a week. After that it's commission only, so it depends on you. The machine costs twenty pounds; the district manager gets fifteen shillings, the area manager seven and six, and the managing director gets a shilling for every machine sold anywhere in the country. I get thirty bob and you get three pounds, which, as you can see, is more than anyone else." Manny refrained from pointing out that no one else was actually walking the streets, selling the machine.

Carrying the unwieldy appliance with its wires and pipes and attachments in a large bag over his shoulder, he set off. The supervisor watched him from the window. *Enthusiastic. But on the small side,* he thought.

At the end of the day Manny had sold not a single machine. Nor had he at the end of the second day. He had demonstrated the machine, talked about the machine, spread its parts all over parlor floors, even enjoyed a cup of tea with a kindly housewife or two, but no sales. He moved on to another street. He was tired; it was late. He decided on one last try.

She came to the door with wet hair, shaking back the long, dripping strands and blinking at him. "I was washing my hair."

He went into his patter and she listened, watching him closely. When he had finished, she said, "Twenty pounds! You must be crazy! Why should I pay twenty pounds to sweep the carpet when I can do it for nothing with a brush?"

"Ah! But does the brush clean the curtains? Armchairs? Under the sofa?"

Her hair was still dripping onto her blouse and Manny found

himself staring at her breasts, almost visible as the damp white silk became transparent. She stepped back and said abruptly, "All right. Let's see what you can do."

Two minutes later, on the front room carpet, Manny did his best to show what he could do. But his inexperience went against him. She pushed away his suddenly limp body and buttoned her blouse. "I think I'll stick to my brush after all, sonny."

Manny had to concede that she had a point. Head whirling, limbs turned to jelly, longing to rest, he stumbled out.

At the end of the second week he was on the point of admitting defeat. The London housewife did not want a vacuum cleaner. Or if she did, he was not the man to sell it to her. Perhaps there was some mysterious path to her purse that a good salesman would know but of which he was ignorant. In other directions he had improved his skills; lonely housewives found him good value. But no improvement took place in his selling technique.

By the time he got home he was almost too worn out to eat. Leah watched him hunched at the kitchen table, nearly falling asleep in his plate. He had grown so thin that the bones gave his face a pointed look, like one of the modernist paintings she had seen in the newspaper.

There had been a coolness between them since the episode of the Sabbath discussion, which both found painful but impossible to dispel. His eyelids drooped for a moment, and she saw the lashes, dark and long, sweeping the shadowed eye sockets. Suddenly, like an end of winter thaw, Leah felt warmth rushing back, a sense of blood pumping through her. What kind of mother had she been, turning away from him when he was only trying to make life better for them? He was doing what Chaim had never been able to do: rise above the past. She smoothed his hair and felt how hot and moist his brow was. Nobody could work as hard as Manny, unrelentingly, such long hours, and keep his health. Anxiety pierced her, and remorse. She had lost two children already. She must never lose another.

"You're a good boy, Manny," she said softly. "Take a little rest now. I don't want to see you sick in bed. Tonight, just to please me, sit by the fire. We have enough to eat, so rest a little, by me."

Her voice, soothing and soft; the heat of the kitchen, the smell of the food, all swirled around him. He seemed to have lost the use of his limbs. He allowed Leah to lift him from the table and push him into their only armchair. For a moment, as she settled him in the chair, he wrapped his arms about her, as he used to so many years ago when he was a child . . . so many years ago . . . how many years ago? She held his head gently. Not so many years after all.

She put a cushion behind his head, another beneath his feet, and she sang very softly an almost tuneless old Polish song, one she used to sing to Daniel, as she led her little brother around the old square in Peszno, around the drinking fountain and the benches with their peeling blue paint.

Manny blinked, yawned, stretched, and fell asleep. It was his first evening of leisure since Chaim died. The sewing machines remained silent while Leah sat watching her son sleep, watching the lines of anxiety smooth out in his sleeping face.

On Monday morning, Manny's first housewife opened the door, took one look at the boy on the doorstep and began to close the door again. "I'm busy!" she exclaimed. "I have the whole house to clean, not a crumb should remain!"

Manny had forgotten Passover was looming. He was so little at home these days that the usual preparations must have escaped him. "How would you like to have the whole house spick and span for Pesach," he said quickly, "not a crumb of bread to be found, cleaned by the machine!"

She paused, suspicious. "The whole house? How long will it take?"

Manny shrugged. "You, it will take two days, at least. Me, with the scientific machine. . . . I could do it in a couple of hours."

He saw her digesting this and added, "Think how much extra time that's going to give you for the cooking and purifying the pots and pans." She opened the door wider and he added, "It won't cost much."

"How much?"

Manny was already unpacking the cleaner. "Look, I tell you what: you're my first customer. I'll do the job and then we'll talk about the price—I'll do a good job. So if I don't cheat you, you won't cheat me, right?"

He was taking a risk but it was worth it. As he worked his way from room to room, neighbors called in: the terrace walls were thin; the machine could hardly be called silent.

The women examined the dust-free floors and watched Manny speeding along. "Listen, come next door when you're finished here. I also could do with the machine. . . . You're not too dear, are you?"

That day Manny cleaned three houses and already had two women down for the following day.

The supervisor shook his head dolefully as he examined Manny's blank order book. "You'll have to try harder, son. I know it's not easy, and it's early yet, but if other people can sell 'em, so can you."

"Yessir," said Manny, and crawled home.

He called now only at houses with the *mezuzah* nailed to the door that identified them as Jewish, and all week he did Passover cleaning, leaving the houses not only dust-free but cleansed of impure crumbs before the Holy Days descended. And every day the shillings jingled in his pocket.

Things would be quieter next week, he realized, without the Pesach preparations to help him. Still: he could probably rent out the machine to a few women—maybe he'd let them clean their own houses for a cut price while he went and had a cup of tea.

On Monday he called in to the office to collect the cleaner. The supervisor had his coat on. "Right, lad, let's go."

Manny looked surprised. "You coming too?"

"Yes. Thought I'd give you a bit of moral support. Come on then—where's the first address?"

They reached the street and the supervisor paused by the corner. "I won't stand at your shoulder, lad. I don't want to cramp your style. . . . Anyway, they never like two chaps at the door: they think it's the police. Or Jehovah's Witnesses, and either way they don't like it. Off you go."

Manny knocked on the door and waited, very conscious of the supervisor hovering by the lamppost. What would he say? How many doors would it take to convince him that Manny was useless?

A large woman opened the door. Manny swallowed and began, talking very fast. "Can I interest you in—"

"Is that one o' them back-room cleaners?" she broke in. "Good. I've been meaning to come in and have a look at one. May as well do it now." She opened the door and Manny, throwing a glance of triumph over his shoulder at the supervisor, floated in to make his first sale.

Soon he earned enough commission to keep him at it. So it was as a promising new member of the sales force that he attended the firm's annual sales conference.

"You won't feel the same way about the job after today," promised the supervisor. "The old man can really give it to 'em. Inspiring it is. Does you good to hear him—the gift of tongues I call it—when he really gets going."

The entire sales force from all over the country was assembled in a big hired hall, each salesman in a tight blue suit and polished shoes, each with several pencils and a fat fountain pen tucked into his breast pocket. Manny had gotten himself a new suit shortly after joining the firm: it was a misfit from a local tailor and had cost only a few shillings, but Leah altered it so skillfully that one or two of the others were glancing at him enviously.

"I see the Jew-boy's done all right for hisself then," Manny heard muttered farther down the row. He sat up even straighter and flicked a nonexistent speck of dust off his sleeve.

The morning started with a song: "Only My Best Is Good Enough!" The words were in the little blue books the salesmen had been given, and everyone sang lustily, including Manny, who did not in fact know the tune. Then came area reports and sales tables and some grave figures on customer loss, followed by the presentation of the salesman-of-the-year awards.

At last, after another song, "Every Cog Is a Kingpin Here," came the high spot of the conference: the managing director's speech. And it was during this stirring call to arms that Manny became conscious of an almost overwhelming urge to stand up and shout rude words, words he had hardly been aware he knew. It had something to do with the faces around him, shining with sweat and earnestness, and the little blue songbooks, and the aura of paternalism hanging over the meeting and the unctuous tones of the managing director as he assured his boys that every last one of them was important to him, personally.

"Well, o'course we are, seeing that he's sitting back and raking in a bob from every cleaner we knock our *kishkas* out to flog," Manny whispered to his neighbor.

It was unfortunate that Manny, due to a gap in the seating, was clearly visible from the rostrum. And worse, as he whispered his comment behind a discreetly raised hand, the light caught his brand-new signet ring and flashed it into the managing director's eyes.

The old man paused. He looked in Manny's direction and said courteously, "I believe one of our salesmen has a contribution to make. Did you want to say something, young man?"

Manny intended to shake his head eagerly; he intended to murmur that he was just agreeing with the managing director, sir, and blend once more into the blue-suited anonymity of the ranks. But instead, to his horror, he found himself on his feet, hands wet with perspiration, mouth dry. "Yes. I've got a contribution to make. It's this!" Graphically he made public his feelings with a two-fingered gesture. "*That's* what I say to all this rubbish. We run our backsides off, and you sit there and pull in the profits." He looked around the hall, at the salesmen staring at him aghast, mouths slack with astonishment. "Make me sick, the lot o' you. Sit there like sheep, not an ounce of go between you. Well, I'm not going to beg for a bloody bone. Maybe I'll starve, but I'll do it on my own. I'll be my own boss!" He stopped, suddenly out of breath. The silence in the hall was painful, crackling with excitement. The supervisor was staring at Manny with amazement.

The managing director inclined his head, his interested expression unchanged. "I think perhaps if Mr. . . ." He leaned for a moment toward the supervisor who muttered something. ". . . If Mr. Rubinstein will permit us to continue, the meeting can proceed . . . ?" He paused, looking inquiringly at Manny, eyebrows raised.

"Bollocks!" Manny wanted to shout, and "Sod you all!" But he stumbled out without another word, tripping over various polished shoes, avoiding the gaze of his fellow-animals, most of them fearful or indignant, a few gleeful. Just one hand patted Manny's back furtively with a gesture of sympathy and encouragement as he passed. It almost finished him off. He did not dare look at the man; the tears of mortification were already building up dangerously behind his eyes and he only just reached the exit with dignity.

As he banged the door behind him, he heard the unhurried tones of the managing director saying, "And now, if I read my agenda correctly, we move on to the question of the new slot-nozzle attachment . . ."

Outside he began to run, clumsily, blinded with the tears he could no longer hold back, unable to see where he was going. Rage poured through him; rage at himself for not having the strength to carry off the situation like a man, instead of slinking out like a naughty schoolboy. Rage at the bosses, for their confidence and their easy callousness, and at the men for swallowing their dignity and their pride, for allowing themselves to be treated like cattle even to the extent of having pretty rosettes pinned on the winners. And Manny made a vow, standing outside the window of an invisible-mender's shop, staring

231

unseeingly at the scarred fingers of a woman sitting in the window darning a jacket. He vowed that he would never again be an employee, a slave, a jester singing songs to amuse the bosses. If bosses there were to be, then he would be a boss and call the tune.

At first Sarah was treated as a complete invalid: appalled by her emaciated, frozen-looking appearance, her aunt put her to bed and kept her there, feeding her on broth and chicken breasts, with small glasses of sweet wine to build her up. Later she was allowed to lie on a sofa in the drawing room, listlessly watching the trees swaying in the breeze outside the large windows, or listening to her cousin Siegfried practicing his Liszt and Chopin.

The drawing room was large, and to Sarah it seemed palatial, with its heavily swagged and draped curtains, its chandelier and ornate bracket lamps. Around the room were glass-fronted cabinets of walnut and maple holding porcelain ornaments and a silver tea set. A massive Buhl writing desk dominated one wall, inlaid with tortoise shell and topped by a silver inkstand and a framed photograph of Siegfried's older brother, who had not survived the Great War.

In Weimar, Sarah had absolutely nothing to do but rest. There was money, there were servants, there was style.

She could see herself reflected in the large carved mirror on the opposite wall: a small figure almost lost on the big chaise longue, with the window, framed in green velvet, glimmering behind her. There, in the mirror, she caught a glimpse of the piano and Siegfried, assiduously going over the Polonaise. He looked up and saw her watching him.

"Enough for today! We don't want to bore our cousin, do we?" A brisk eight bars of "Deutchland Über Alles" and he closed the piano. He wandered over to sit near Sarah. "You really are looking much better." He spoke German to her, as they all did.

When she had first arrived her aunt had instructed Siegfried to give Sarah lessons in German twice a day so that she could talk properly to them— "We never speak Yiddish here, that's ghetto jargon. We're Germans now, Sarah, and we talk German." Their names, too, had been adapted to the new country: Shmuel was now Sigmund, Hirschl had become Herman, and Ruda was Rosa.

Sarah understood their decision to belong, to assimilate, to lose their foreignness. Why not become one with your adopted country? Was that not exactly what she had wanted to do in England? So she worked hard at German, using her Yiddish as a springboard, abandoning it with relief.

During the first few months Sarah's fragile condition saved her from answering too many questions. Later she had to face them, especially when Leah's elder brother Hirschl, now Herman, and his wife came over for dinner.

Herman had married late, and at a time when his contemporaries were settling into prosperous middle age, ready to marry off their children, he was proudly bouncing two toddlers on his knee. "I'm a lucky man!" he shouted energetically. "They'll keep me young!"

No longer in pots and pans, Herman had gone into engineering with a German partner, and he was now a factory owner. Leah's description of her brother had led Sarah to expect someone rather like Chaim, a quiet, thin-faced lad. What she encountered was an expansive, smartly dressed man, almost military in his way of speaking.

"Pity about your father," he barked. "Mind you, I always thought he looked a bit sickly as a young man. Last time I saw him in Poland I said to myself, 'He's not got a strong constitution, that boy.'"

Rosa passed him a cup of coffee, adding, "And then, London: very damp . . ." Sarah could hardly believe this was her mother's older sister—she looked years younger, her face smooth and plump, her hands white, with rings on every finger.

Sarah's natural reticence and her reluctance to betray Leah's pride made her give answers that were as neutral as possible, and she realized that in fact they had no idea of the real conditions in Sidney Street. Leah had withdrawn from them for too long. "Things have been—very hard," Sarah admitted at one point.

They nodded. "Here too, of course. Inflation . . . unemployment. . . . It was dreadful, such hardship everywhere!"

Sarah sipped her coffee from the fine porcelain cup and managed not to smile. Their idea of hardship was obviously different from hers. "After father died we all tried . . . different kinds of work," Sarah said vaguely. She had decided to draw a veil over her own activities. "But Manny is doing much better now, I had a letter this week. He has a shoe-mending shop and he is starting some new business of his own."

Herman offered, "If he needs anything for this new business, tell him he only has to ask. What's family for?"

Rosa sighed. "Leah was always so proud. So independent. It's wrong. She could have come here, we could have taken her in."

The thought was kind; the wording patronizing. Sarah could understand suddenly why Leah had preferred to make her own way and her own decisions. She decided to change the subject. "Ziggy wants me to improve my tennis."

"Excellent!" her uncle exclaimed. "A fine game."

"Do you feel strong enough?" Rosa inquired. "See how you feel. You must not overtire her, Ziggy."

Siegfried was eighteen, as slender as Sarah, with lustrous gray green eyes and fine dark hair. He looked, Sarah thought, less like plump Rosa than Leah. There was something of the same long-faced, angular grace, a coiled, steely quality. She had hesitated, earlier on, to raise the subject of his music. Then curiosity conquered tact.

"Why did you not—" she was still feeling her way with German. "Why are you not a pianist, Ziggy? I mean a professional?"

"I trained for a while. But I was not good enough—not *quite* good enough. I could have been a respectable professional, yes. But I lack . . ." he shrugged. "I prefer to go into the furniture business and devote myself to the piano in my own way. I happen to be a very good furniture designer. I do not want to be a second-class anything. Certainly not a second-class pianist."

"I have no profession, no trade," Sarah said musingly. "What work can I do? I'm almost sixteen. I should do something."

"You are a girl, you don't need a profession. You will get married to someone splendid and give dinner parties and hold *soirées musicales* and I shall come and dazzle your guests."

She laughed. "I am not trained to be a lady of leisure."

"I shall train you. This summer we shall play tennis and go to dances and concerts and you will be altogether occupied. You will be *exhausted* by your social engagements."

The tennis club, the recitals, the dinner parties, and the Goethe readings did indeed keep Sarah thoroughly occupied. But after a year of it she felt she must raise the question of her future. Home—London

—meant not only the filthy street, the peeling paintwork, the endless economizing. It also meant living with worry: the worry that never left you, that rested like a small animal at the back of your mind so that you learned to behave as though it were not there. And then, while you were thinking of something else, the little animal would creep unnoticed into the front of your mind, growing larger, its eyes shining, and its face would fill your thoughts, pushing out peace and laughter.

In the public gardens of Weimar there was always the sound of children's laughter. She watched Herman's children playing now, clean in their sailor suits and white shoes. Stefan and Eva had a nanny; they had little half-sized beds specially made for them in Uncle Sigmund's furniture works; they had toys—lead soldiers, dolls, a monkey that clapped its hands by clockwork. She had never had toys as a child.

She remembered once, long ago, that Simeon had brought a little box of Meccano for Manny. It cost sixpence and Leah had been horrified at the extravagance. Manny had played with the Meccano once, spreading the pieces out on the kitchen table and screwing them carefully together. Then, suddenly anxious not to damage it, he had as carefully unscrewed it all and replaced the flat pieces of perforated metal in the cardboard box. He never played with it again, though he often took it out of the drawer, removed the lid, and touched the pieces lovingly. In time the cardboard grew worn, and the colored picture on the lid became faded and rubbed. But the Meccano inside was as bright and unscratched as on the first day.

Coffee cups. Sugar and cream. The fragile china raised to the lips and lowered. In a moment Siegfried would put down his cup and saucer and go to the piano. She said abruptly, "I have been thinking about the future." She refused to catch Siegfried's amused glance. "I realize that I cannot stay here much longer—" Rosa began to speak but Sarah raised her hand, determined to finish what had to be said. "But I do not want to go back to London."

Rosa said in her kindly, slightly condescending way, "We, too, have been thinking about your future, Sarah. There is no need for you to go anywhere. This is a nice town—"

"But I must find work."

"No hurry about that." Her aunt fussed with her pearls. "But there are certain things to be discussed. You should know that since we came here, we were . . . we wanted . . . we have been . . ."

"Baptized," Siegfried said cheerfully.

Sarah began to laugh, relieved to be able to talk about her own unmentionable activities. "I," she said ruefully, "have even been confirmed!"

She wrote to Manny the next day, unable to find the words to explain to Leah. "You may not approve, but I hope you'll understand. I feel at home here as I never did in London. I was never happy there. Dear Manny, it isn't just a question of the big house and the nice clothes—though those are very attractive, of course. It is that here I have begun a new life, just as a person, not a Jew."

Manny's reply was swift. He did not even want to discuss the reasons, but he wanted to tell Sarah immediately that her decision should be reconsidered: for some time now he had done well, very well. They were moving, "to Stamford Hill—imagine! A nice little house, double-fronted, with an indoor toilet, so don't think it's only in Germany you can live well!" He begged her to think again. She was with family, he knew that, but if she stayed in Germany Leah would feel she had lost another child. It would be terrible for her. "Dearest Sarah," he finished, "think of her."

She did not answer his letter. She put it at the back of the bottom drawer of her chest, where she kept the clothes she had brought to Germany—Lady Crawleigh's brown suit and the pair of shoes passed on from Pansy. It was a drawer she never used.

The summer of 1929 was like a ripe, scented pomegranate, too full, too tightly packed with sweetness, splitting open to spill out the seeds of delight. The factories were busy, the flowers seemed twice as large as usual, and the *Graf Zeppelin* flew around the world. Celebrations and festivities kept Sarah busily reviewing her wardrobe. No sooner had she borrowed Rosa's spare jewels for the reception to welcome home the *Bremen* bearing the North Atlantic Blue Riband, than she was closeted with Siegfried to work out their costumes for the masked ball, where everyone was to go as a Goethe character. In the end she gave in to his wish that he should go as Werther chewing grass, with Sarah as Charlotte, leading him in chains of flowers.

The local chamber of commerce was entertaining a party of foreign visitors, and Sarah, safe behind her black silk mask, watched the Englishmen with unaffectionate amusement. She had forgotten what knobbly, whiskery faces they had, what harsh voices. She intended to pause only for a moment and move away, but Sigmund, himself one of the hosts, noticed her and called her back to be introduced: "My niece . . ."

Sarah bowed slightly at the group, glancing along the faces—and with a shock of horror found herself looking into the incurious eyes of Freddy Crawleigh, who at once stepped forward and shook her hand limply. There was, of course, no trace of recognition in his eyes. Servants were never looked at, so she stood no chance of being found out, even without a mask.

"Don't speak your excellent language I'm afraid, but I find you're all so jolly clever I don't have to, what?"

She noticed that the smooth fair hair had coarsened slightly and the blue eyes, although as bright as ever, had acquired a slightly protuberant stare. Altogether he had a heavier, less appealing appearance now, and she smiled brilliantly at him, pleasantly conscious of her long, slim arms with a bracelet glittering on one wrist. She removed her white hand from his limp grasp, feeling suddenly exhilarated.

It was years since Sarah had spoken more than a few words of English, and she found it amusing to hear herself now. Her endless rereading of Jane Austen had given her English something of the formality of an earlier age; and to the carefully correct vowels she had so painstakingly learned at the Crawleighs' was added the unfamiliarity of speaking what had become almost a foreign tongue. She sounded not quite English, her voice low and quiet, with a tiny hesitation, an occasional pause like the shadow of a stammer, that was oddly beguiling.

Freddy was bored with receptions and balls. He was longing for a drink, and he realized that he could think of absolutely nothing to say to this extremely attractive girl. He grabbed frantically at a passing colleague. "Allow me to introduce . . . one of our party . . . John Middleway . . . er . . . " Having failed to catch her name, he slid away in mid-diplomatic mumble.

Sarah glanced up at a face as sharp and narrow as her own, with blue eyes that looked intelligent and amused.

"Fraulein? . . ."

"Robinson."

"Robinson? You're English then!"

"Yes." She glanced across at Freddy's departing figure. "Do you know the Crawleighs well?" she asked.

"Reasonably. We're related in some distant and complicated fashion."

"How are the girls?"

"Oh, you know them." John Middleway cast about desperately for something interesting to say about two of the most boring girls he knew. "They're fine. Daisy's engaged to be married."

Sarah looked delighted. "And has he got glossy black hair and drooping eyelids and great skill on the dance floor, especially at the tango?"

"I shouldn't have thought so. The Maulys are all carroty and pale-eyed, and at school Julian was considered outstandingly clumsy even by their standards."

Sarah felt a little sad. So much for the dark and steamy dreams of the nursery, the breathless expectations of romance entering with a Valentino glide. Poor Daisy.

The orchestra was tuning up for a waltz, and Sarah glanced toward the ballroom. "Do you waltz, Mr. Middleway?"

" 'Fraid not. Haven't got much of a gift for dancing."

A waiter with a tray of glasses skimmed past. "Well, do you like champagne?"

"Ah. That is an altogether different matter. I worship at the shrine of the Abbé Pérignon. For me the valley of the Marne is sacred soil—"

She saw Siegfried coming toward them and signaled him almost imperceptibly. John however, still noticed the gesture.

"So there you are!" Sarah called out. "I thought you had forgotten our waltz. Mr. Middleway? . . ." She nodded and moved away with Siegfried toward the ballroom.

John Middleway's answering smile was wry. He suspected he was dull in women's company and joked about it sometimes. But having the suspicion so noticeably confirmed was still a little dashing.

"What is all this? What waltz, miss?" Siegfried demanded in English when they were on the dance floor.

"Oh Ziggy, no waltz. Or rather, yes, *this* waltz, any waltz. I had just had enough of polite English conversation. Say something rude, or something dazzling. I want to feel . . . *extraordinary* tonight!"

"You are behaving in a very English way tonight," he said. "Well, Goethe should provide an antidote to that: '*Von Halben zu entwöhnen, und im Gauzen, Guten, Schönen, resolut zu leben.*' You could make that your motto."

Sarah looked flushed, almost feverish. "Not to do things by halves . . . yes . . . attempt life in its totality, beauty, and goodness. How right! How German! Oh Ziggy, I love Goethe, I love this country, I love my life here. . . . How wonderful it is to be alive and know that *anything* is possible!"

"Have you had a great deal of champagne?" he asked kindly.

"No. But I do feel drunk. Drunk with happiness." As she spun into the waltz she caught sight of the Englishman through the doorway. *Nice. But dull,* she decided.

Manny had always intended to move to Golders Green, the traditional steppingstone to paradise, but Leah liked the house in Stamford Hill, and he had to admit that with the clean air and the white paint, the neat, double-fronted little house was a palace compared to Sidney Street.

No workshop in the front room now. Instead, a brand-new three-piece suite. And in the kitchen: tiles and cupboards and every modern gadget on the market, except a vacuum cleaner. Not that Leah used any of them. "Fingers and forks and wooden spoons, that's all a good cook needs," she said, sniffing contemptuously at the modern appliances.

Meanwhile, Sidney Street had been put to good use and was now a busy factory. Manny was not an easy man to work for: he did not accept excuses for late arrival and he was rigid in matters of output. He knew from personal experience what a worker could produce, going at full speed, and full speed was what he expected.

Benjamin, who ran the shop which had once been a shoe mender's and was now Ladies and Gents Outfitters (HIGHEST QUALITY, LOWEST PRICES—WALK IN! SEE FOR YOURSELF!), sometimes suggested that Manny drove his workers too hard.

"They don't like it? They can leave. *I* worked—harder than they do! Why shouldn't they do a good day's work? Anyway, they're free to go any day they like."

"They're not. You know that. Times is tough. Work's not easy to find."

"So I'm doing 'em a favor. Lay off me, Benny. You're too soft. You want to manage someone else's shop all your life?"

Benny's sly, merry face was serious for a moment. "Manny, I'm not a real businessman, you know that. My dad's a barber, he's always been a barber, he'll always be a barber. You did me a good turn, getting me out of clerking. I'm happy. You have the worries."

Manny could never remain on bad terms with Benjamin. From their early days—the forays into the free-lunch escapades—Benjamin had been the one who had the bright ideas, Manny the one who slogged along and made something of himself. And Benjamin's twin deficiencies in tenacity and envy kept the relationship sweet.

"What you doing Sunday?" Benjamin asked.

"I thought I might take Mum to Hyde Park. She loves to hear the speakers."

"You took her last week. Why not come on a ramble with us instead?"

Benjamin's rambling group did not attract Manny, who could see little sense in walking when he could ride, and in walking without a purpose, no sense at all. He was about to say so when Benjamin added, "My sister's coming along."

Manny paused. "Sunday? Well, if it's fine, and if I have nothing else on . . . and *if* I feel like it . . . I might."

The ramblers assembled on Sunday morning under Findlater's Clock at London Bridge Station and took the train for the first stage of the journey. There were about thirty of them, looking sporty in Fair Isle sweaters and flannels, the more dedicated wearing heavy walking shoes—all carrying light haversacks full of sandwiches and fruit.

Benjamin greeted Manny and sat down next to him on the train. "You'll enjoy it, honest. And it'll be good for you, get your mind off business for a change!"

Manny grunted. "Where's your sister?"

"Oh, she didn't come after all. Dad needed some help in the shop and Mum wasn't feeling too good." He got up to talk to someone a few seats away, leaving Manny glowering.

The train stopped. "Everyone out! We're there!" Benjamin shouted with a cheerfulness Manny found distinctly depressing.

Outside the station the countryside spread away untidily in all directions. No order, no symmetry, that was the trouble with the countryside, Manny reflected. You knew where you were with towns. He grew gloomier by the minute while Benjamin opened maps and glanced about keenly. "How long, exactly, will this ramble be?" Manny asked.

Benjamin said casually, "Well, some people don't go the distance; they stop off and wait for us on the way back, but we're reckoning on twenty miles—"

"Twenty *miles*!" Manny was aghast. "That isn't a ramble, it's a forced march!"

Benjamin laughed unfeelingly and walked away, full of an organizing zeal that Manny found intensely irritating. He glanced at his watch bleakly.

The group moved off, laughing, straggling, chattering, and after a few minutes the station approach was silent and deserted. Then a figure appeared from behind the station building and walked briskly into the ticket office. "When's the next train back to London?" Manny inquired.

Benjamin's father was a good barber and his shop was crowded. Manny edged inside and looked around for Rebecca. She was busy taking money, giving change, entering the receipts in the book, and all the while talking—swapping amiable insults, teasing old regulars, jollying them along. Even several yards away her warm, confident, slightly strident voice could be clearly heard.

"Now then, Harry!" she cried warningly to one of the assistants. "Mind how you strop that razor—we don't want Mrs. Isaacs saying we've damaged her Monty's prospects!"

Roars of laughter. She glanced over and caught Manny's eye. "Yes? . . . Hey, you're our Benny's boss, ain't you?" She had called for

Benjamin once, at the shop, and Manny had met her. "I thought you went on the ramble."

"No, I skipped it." Manny was not usually nervous. He had brazened out too many scenes, pushed too hard, fought too much, and picked himself up too often to be shy. But suddenly with Becky he hardly knew what to say. She turned away to take some cash and he allowed himself to stare at her openly.

Becky was not a beautiful girl, but there was about her such an aura of vitality and good humor; a sense of boundless energy and generosity, that she gave an impression of beauty. Everything about Becky was vivid and highly colored: the black eyes snapped and glittered naughtily, the round cheeks plumped up like bright pink satin pincushions when she smiled, showing very white teeth and a clean pink tongue which she occasionally poked out saucily at overfamiliar customers. Her black curly hair shone and bounced as her head turned this way and that, her strong neck creamy and graceful. Below the neck her body was frankly on view—in itself a novelty for Manny, accustomed to Leah's and Ruth's shapeless way of dressing. Here, a tight blouse, an even tighter belt and trim skirt showed clearly the dimensions of Becky's figure: full in the breasts, unusually slim in the waist and distractingly curved at hip and thigh.

"Give us a brush-up, Beckela," requested an elderly man on his way out. She eyed him appraisingly. "I'd love to, Mr. Moss, but what would your old lady say?" More laughter, and then she leaned over the cash desk and whisked his shoulders with the clothes brush.

Manny felt his face go red with all this free talk: bawdy, light-hearted chitchat was never heard at home. Not that the house was quiet—sometimes he longed for a little peace, but it was usually enlivened by neighbors popping in for a gossip with Leah. His own limited free time was spent playing cards or looking in at one of the East End clubs for a social evening.

He realized that their home was rather narrow, rather old-fashioned. Leah talked a lot about the good old days in Poland; Jonathan seemed incapable now of discussing anything but Talmudic matters, and Ruth was so involved with her work at the hospital that when she was off duty they tended to get welfare lectures.

"Ruth's getting very political," Leah had confided apprehensively to Manny. "You know she's been attending those Socialist rallies at Vallance Road. I don't want her getting into trouble with the authorities . . ." She said this with such portentous emphasis that

Manny had a vision of Ruth being led away in chains to Siberia, like a Decembrist revolutionary.

Becky stretched out to shake hands with another departing customer, and Manny watched her blouse, fascinated by the way the material strained under her movements, watching the little creases and protrusions. She pushed her hair off her forehead and sighed gustily. "What a morning! I haven't stopped! Not for a second!" She wriggled in her blouse. "I'm really sweating, it's so hot today."

He thought of her flesh beneath the thin material, creamy and moist with perspiration. He swallowed and said loudly, "How'd you fancy dinner at Blooms?"

Becky looked at him in surprise. He was very young to be a boss, running a business and a shop, and she found it hard to take him seriously—so small and solemn-looking in his checkered suit and waistcoat. But she liked his eyes, and when he smiled, which was not often, she felt a pang of . . . warmth? tenderness? Something new. She laughed aloud at her reflections. "Okay," she said.

"I'll pick you up at six," Manny said, and smiled at her.

Leah knew Manny was restless. He was always out these days, and he appeared to be wearing his best suit a lot of the time. He also seemed to be somewhere else in his thoughts. She knew it could not be worry about the business. Even in these hard times Manny was doing all right. He was firm with the workers, kept them up to scratch, and the result was that they were managing comfortably.

But something was on Manny's mind. She decided to raise the subject after they had eaten. But Manny did not come home to supper that night, and when he did appear he seemed agitated. "Look at your meal—spoiled!" Leah exclaimed.

"Mum, I'm not hungry. Never mind the supper."

"But the waste! People are starving, and we're throwing food into the dustbin. It's wicked."

"All right. But forget the supper, I'd like to talk to you about something."

"And you'll be hungry later and you won't sleep and then tomorrow you'll be tired out—"

"*Mum!* I want to talk to you. Will you *listen?*"

"Listen? I spend my life listening. I listen to you, I listen to your sister, I listen to the neighbors—"

"Mum, I'm thinking of getting married."

He had silenced her at last. She stared at him. Then she nodded. "Of course. You should be thinking of getting married. You're a man now. No hurry, but it must be thought of, yes."

Leah certainly did not intend to be rushed. The choice of a daughter-in-law was too important to be left to chance. She knew several nice, quiet girls who could be trusted not to poison or neglect her son. But Manny was in an emotional state, the worst possible condition for any kind of sensible discussion. She must proceed calmly. Delay matters. She had an idea. "We'll call in the marriage broker."

He gaped at her. "The *marriage broker*? Mum, people don't use marriage brokers—"

"Since when? *I* had a marriage broker. So did my sister."

"I'm not having some old fool decide my life for me."

"Of course not. But no harm in hearing some professional advice. After all, there's no hurry."

Manny was about to argue. Then suddenly he said, "Okay. I'll get the marriage broker. I'll have him around tomorrow."

"Such a rush," Leah said, caught in her own ploy. "I'm busy tomorrow. Make it next week."

Manny opened the door and took the *shadchen*'s hat. "My mother is in the front room. Please go in." Then Manny went into the kitchen and began to make tea. He had a feeling it would be needed.

Leah said, very formally, "This is a very solemn moment for me, Mr. Rosten. My son, marriage, and with no father to turn to—"

"Of course." He blew his nose and took out his notebook.

"I have the particulars, of course . . . a very industrious young man—"

"A businessman, a success, Mr. Rosten."

"Of course. Ambitious . . ."

"A good son. Always thinks of his mother . . ."

"Of course. Of course. Well, I have a very nice young lady in mind. Nice looking, well brought up, a clever head on her shoulders, even a little dowry, and that's not always the case these hard times. A very suitable bride for an ambitious young man."

Leah said, "Nice looking, clever. So. What about the family? Does she come from a good family?"

"Very well thought of in the community. Solidly established." Mr. Rosten was choosing his words carefully. "A respectable family." He paused and plunged: "The father is a barber."

Manny heard Leah's scream through two closed doors. He picked up the tray and carried the tea into the front room.

"A *barber*? We would not have had such people in the *house*, in Poland. I'm surprised you don't suggest a butcher. Or a street sweeper. You come to me with the daughter of a *barber*. My poor son, he deserves better."

Mr. Rosten and Manny exchanged a quick glance as Manny handed him his tea. "Things are not what they were, Mrs. Rubinstein. These are strange times. A lot of young women are going to work outside the home, and young men are meeting and mixing with the *goyim*." A pause. "A lot of young men are . . . marrying out. Too many difficulties and delays and, who knows, you could find yourself with a *shiksa* for a daughter-in-law."

Leah glared at the broker silently. Manny said, "Listen, why don't we find out a little more? A barber's not such a terrible thing, after all."

"A wood chopper's not such a terrible thing, but I've never had one in the family," Leah said stonily.

Mr. Rosten put down his glass. "Lovely tea. Beautiful. Look, why don't we at least arrange a meeting? Just a preliminary . . . see what you think. No commitment."

At the front door as Manny and the *shadchen* shook hands, a banknote passed from palm to palm and Mr. Rosten pocketed it gracefully. "You did all right," Manny murmured.

The meeting proved oddly difficult to arrange. Leah had a cold and then she needed to clean the house and then her back began to trouble her as a result of scrubbing the cupboards. But finally one Sunday, with Manny in his best suit and Leah looking very severe and formal in her black silk, the Disraelis arrived for tea.

Leah had been working since dawn. "I don't know why you're going to so much trouble," Manny said. "He's only a barber."

She sniffed. "It's not for them. It's for me. For my self-respect. I don't want even a barber should think things are not as they should be in my house."

Mr. Disraeli shook Manny's hand warmly and began, "Well, Manny!" And then trailed into silence. Mrs. Disraeli, her face quite scarlet from the tight corset she was hooked into, said nothing but sighed a lot and looked around nervously.

And then there was Becky. Manny tried not to look at her too much and kept shooting her quick, consuming glances. He thought she looked very elegant in her black suit and pink silk blouse, her curls falling around her face in a shiny tangle, her bright eyes almost popping with the effort of being serious in view of the occasion. "What a lovely room! And such beautiful curtains!" she told Leah.

"They're not up to much," Leah said deprecatingly. "I made them quite quickly—"

"You never made them yourself!" Becky gasped and picked up a curtain to examine the stitching. "You'll have to show me how."

Leah had covered the food and tea things with white napkins, and when she removed them, Mr. Disraeli was quite overcome. "What a spread! You've been busy, you shouldn't have gone to so much trouble!"

"Trouble?" Leah said coolly. "It's just bits and pieces, nothing special."

Manny looked at the table with its lace cloth, covered from end to end with dishes of smoked salmon, bagels, pickled herring, cucumber, cream cheese, rolls, gefilte-fish balls, fruit salad, and cheesecake. He wondered what would happen if Leah *really* went to some trouble. . . .

Becky exclaimed over everything, admired everything, and her pink tongue curled over the edges of her mouth capturing stray crumbs with the speed of an anteater. She brushed the front of her suit where some caraway seeds had landed. The mood was reasonably amiable when Becky bit into her cheesecake, gave a sigh of delight, swallowed, and cried, "What cheesecake! Did you get it at Monnikendam's?"

"I made it myself, of course," Leah answered frigidly, "Does it taste like *bought* cheesecake? I'll throw it out!"

Becky said hastily, "But I meant it tasted lovely, we always have Monnikendam's cheesecake and it's ever so good, really delicious."

But it was too late. Leah turned away and said distantly, "Manny, why aren't you passing the biscuits? Where are your manners?"

She looked, Manny thought as he seized the plate, like a picture of Florence Nightingale in the Crimean war. The visit dragged on until, at a suitable hour, Becky's father took out his watch, examined it, and announced that they ought to be going.

Leah accompanied them to the door and shook hands with them all. As soon as they left she straightened her collar and turned to Manny triumphantly. "Out of the question! Low-class people. Out of the question. I knew it was a waste of time. A barber's daughter."

Manny said gently, "It's all settled, Mum. I've talked to Mr.

Rosten. Mr. Disraeli has been very generous. The wedding can take place next summer."

"What if I don't give my consent?"

Manny looked uncomfortable. "I'm sure you'll feel differently when you've thought it over. . . . I don't want to do anything that'll upset you."

They had always understood each other. She knew what he really meant was: I don't *want* to do anything to upset you, but I will if I have to. She knew that stubbornness; it lay within her too. So she nodded and said stiffly, "We'll talk about it." Maybe, she thought, they could put off the wedding a little, say a year. A good deal could happen in a year.

As they cleared the table Manny said casually, "Still, you must admit she's a good-looker, Becky is."

And it was only then, as she caught sight of an unguarded expression, quickly concealed, that the truth unfolded itself fully and plainly to Leah. How could she have been so deceived! She felt a sense of dizziness at Manny's duplicity. She said, wonderingly, "You arranged the whole thing, didn't you?"

He had never been able to lie to Leah for long. He looked guilty, then nodded. "Yes."

"Why?"

"*Why?*" He looked puzzled. "Well, I love her, don't I? Why else?"

Manny, falling in love unsuitably, had chosen for himself; *he* had marked out his companion, his partner, his wife-to-be. It took courage of a sort to decide what you wanted from marriage. Leah had decided—whether wisely or not, she would never know. Manny had decided differently. He would bring this bright-faced, crude young woman into the house and Leah would have to put up with her chatter and her fragrance lingering everywhere, her vulgar manners and her overpowering physical presence. The girl was amiable enough. Too amiable. She lacked taste. She lacked . . . a sense of proportion. A pickled herring would draw from her the same enthusiastic praise as a painting; she would respond as gratefully to a box of chocolates as to a diamond brooch.

It reminded Leah of a poem by Browning in the book Simeon had given her so many years before:

Too easily impressed; she liked whate'er
She looked on, and her looks went everywhere.

Oh yes, her looks went everywhere, and Leah would be sharing the kitchen with her.

At which point, tempted to express some of this, Leah instead did the cleverest thing possible, almost by accident. Small enough and insincere to boot, it stood in her favor, weighing against Becky in the many disagreements in the years that lay ahead. She said something that led Manny quite wrongly to believe that she had accepted his valuation of the girl and welcomed her. Leah said, "She's a very pretty girl, your Becky. And if you love her, then I shall love her too."

Your English beau is here again," Ziggy said, glancing out of the drawing-room window. "I thought he had gone back to London."

"I thought so too. I thought so last month and last week. He keeps putting it off for some reason."

"For some reason! Don't be mock-modest Sarah. He's mad about you. He's bewitched, he can't tear himself away from the siren song of your lovely voice."

"Seeing that like all Englishmen he's tone-deaf, that's hardly a compliment, Ziggy dear."

John Middleway heard them laughing before he reached the room, but when he paused in the doorway, Sarah's expression was, as usual, composed and amiable.

Ziggy got up from the piano stool. "I must have some exercise before dinner. John, you will excuse me? . . ." He shook hands politely and wandered out.

There was silence for a moment. "I've come to say goodbye."

"Again!" Sarah's smile took the edge off the words.

He laughed. "Yes, it *is* getting a bit like the opera singer's farewell performance, isn't it?" He looked wretchedly unhappy, and Sarah knew that she only needed to say something encouraging for him to speak more freely.

She chose not to say anything encouraging. "Well, I hope you have a good journey. And a lot of fascinating clients very soon. Shocking divorce cases and libel suits and that sort of thing so that we can read about them on the front page of the newspaper."

He continued to look unhappy. ". . . There will be other things on the front pages. . . . Things are in a bad way, you know."

"Yes, I know. Unemployment, and the cost of everything, it's awful—"

He glanced around the room with its Buhl desk, the fine carpet, the grand piano. The window looked over gardens and trees, more solid houses. It was very peaceful here. His fears would sound absurd. "I don't think you realize just how bad things are. I was in Berlin last week—"

"Oh, Berlin! They're always getting excited in Berlin. They *like* riots and demonstrations. Things will be better soon. This man Hitler—"

"This man Hitler is encouraging some very dangerous ideas."

Sarah said kindly, "It's hard for you to understand; you're an outsider. I read the reports of his speech to the industrialists in Dusseldorf and he seemed to talk a lot of sense. My uncle thought so too. The country needs some new thinking—"

"Herr Hitler's little group seems to me to be doing some very old-fashioned thinking—it's back to German romanticism and early Utopian socialism with some rather nasty undertones."

"Well, you surely don't want the Marxists to get any stronger, do you?"

"I don't like the Marxists, no. But just because Herr Hitler doesn't like the Marxists, that doesn't mean I have to like him, does it?" He got up and began wandering around the room in a distracted manner. "Look: if things became . . . difficult . . . if you found you had problems, you know you can call on me." He picked up a porcelain ornament and examined it closely.

Sarah did not often feel moved by other people's emotions, but suddenly, watching him now, she felt touched. She got up and took the ornament from him, replacing it on the table. Then she clasped his hands in both her own, gently. "I promise that if—whatever it is—happens—I shall call for help from no one but you."

She was smiling, teasing a little, but he remained serious. "You know where to reach me."

At dinner, Sarah announced gaily, "John was dreadfully serious and gloomy today. He seemed to think we were all heading for disaster!"

Sigmund said abruptly, "Maybe, Sarah, you should think of going back to London now."

She felt rebuked. "I'm sorry. I don't understand. Have I said something?" The very thought of returning to London filled her with panic. "What has happened?"

Sigmund said mildly, "We had a little bad news today. Your uncle's partner in the factory has got into some trouble. It will probably sort itself out."

"But what has this to do with me going back to London?"

"Life may not be the same here for a while. . . ."

"I don't care about that. If we have to work and make economies, I want to do it here."

He patted her head affectionately. "It is just possible that we may not be able to stay here. Still: nothing is certain yet. Ziggy, why don't you cheer us up with some music?"

Later, when Sigmund had gone to his study, Sarah pulled Ziggy over to the chaise longue. She propped up his feet and put a cushion behind his head. "Now. You better tell me the truth. I feel like some little girl who is being shielded from the big bad world."

He had always been frail, the fine bones making the green eyes seem even larger. Tonight, Sarah realized, he looked almost emaciated. "You read the papers," he began.

She shook her head impatiently. "Don't give me newspaper stories."

"Sarah, dear . . ." He looked at her consideringly. "We are facing ruin."

"Well, we all know that. It's what Hitler and his lot are always telling us."

Ziggy said patiently, "When I say 'we' are facing ruin, I don't mean the country. I mean us. We can't stay here much longer."

To think of leaving Weimar seemed inconceivable. Everything she associated with her new life was here: the house, the music, the elegance, the poetry. All now threatened.

Ziggy gave her the harsh facts of taxation: "They take fifty percent of our earnings. Now they've announced a fine of five percent for every two weeks delay in payment. The fine adds up to one hundred thirty percent a year, and so if you can't pay on time, you go bankrupt and the state takes the lot. No more factory, no more assets. It has an exquisite simplicity about it, really."

"But what about the house? Surely you couldn't just lose that as well? You could sell the house."

"Ah, the house. That's another beautiful trap. There's a tax on occupied houses, a stupendous tax. So no one wants to buy a nice big house anymore, not with so much tax to pay on it. We know people who have simply abandoned their houses rather than pay the government the tax."

So after all, the new life had been a dream, a bubble now pricked, sending her back into the grayness. She could still hardly believe it. "It all looks so solid, so permanent," she murmured.

"Money is never solid," Ziggy said. "It has a way of melting or burning or flying away mysteriously. Land used to be solid, property and land. But no more, not with the taxes. The middle class is doomed, my dear. We're on the point of vanishing. Between unemployment and taxation we'll just sink into the bog of the penniless proletariat. Not a prospect I look forward to."

Ziggy, having known only middle-class ease all his life, could view the future with a certain philosophical humor as a journey into the unknown. But Sarah, with only a recent taste of carefree plenty, felt the time running out as though it were her lifeblood. In this dreaming city she had learned to live easily, thoughtlessly. And now she had to leave it. Departure could no longer be delayed.

She wanted to say goodbye to the gardens, the park, the Belvedere Palace, gleaming in the autumn sunlight. Ziggy went with her and they walked quickly through the streets, sensing already, even here, a change.

At the tennis club, two people were playing, surrounded by empty courts. The white-clad figures danced lightly, like marionettes, as they sent the ball back and forth. Their voices floated across the sagging, unused nets around them: "Was that in or out?" "Oh, out, out."

Ziggy and Sarah paced around the wire-netted enclosure toward the clubhouse. "How can everything have changed so *quickly*?" she asked.

"It wasn't really so quick. We just didn't pay enough attention."

A workman was attaching a new notice to the entrance. The paint was barely dry, very shiny black on a white board. Sarah went closer to read it: NO JEWS ALLOWED. She swayed, overcome by a sudden panic, and reached out to steady herself. She gripped the wire netting hard, feeling it bite into her fingers. She stared across at the players, and for a moment it seemed to her that the wire netting was shutting her in somehow, though of course she was, as ever, on the outside.

They walked out of the gate, and the sound of the tennis

racquets hitting the ball, *Pock! Pock!* followed them down the road, carried on the crisp, still air.

When they arrived in Berlin the city was having one of its frequent demonstrations, the streets filled with banner-carrying crowds. Policemen seemed to be everywhere, bristling with guns and truncheons.

"Things can't be so bad if we can still take a taxi," Sarah said jauntily, as they got out and surveyed the slightly run-down street.

"There always has to be a last time for everything," Ziggy pointed out. "This was the last taxi ride. Come on, we better get the baggage inside."

The apartment smelled damp, and what furniture it contained was shrouded in dust sheets. By the time the rest of the family arrived, Ziggy and Sarah would at least have aired the place.

"It belongs to some people we know," Ziggy said vaguely. "They won't be using it for a while; they've gone on a visit to America."

He opened the shutters and they roamed through the rooms, letting in the already fading light, pulling the covers off the furniture. Ziggy's normally high spirits began to dim. "I better sleep in the sitting room. You can share the small room with little Eva and Stefan. That leaves the bedroom for mother and father—but then where will Herman and Hilde sleep?"

"*They* will sleep in the sitting room and you can have a bed in the hall."

"Nobody sleeps in a hall!" Ziggy objected.

"There's a *first* time for everything!" she retorted, "just as there's a *last* time!"

He huddled in one half-uncovered armchair, shivering with cold and dejection, the fine, rather long hair falling across his face. She sat down in the big armchair and put her arms around Ziggy's shoulders. "It won't be too bad, we'll find work, there must be something we can get. I can sew. We can live cheaply. Then, after a while, maybe we can go back to Weimar, when things get better."

He shook his head. "We'll never go back. I'll never see it again." Something in his voice chilled her more than the cold.

It was to comfort him, to distract him from the sad surroundings that she began, soothingly, to kiss his cheek and temple, brush aside his hair. Then Ziggy was pressing her against the back of the chair, and they were holding each other, half laughing, half crying, trembling with a combination of excitement and guilt. Astonished, Sarah stared at

Ziggy's shining eyes and intent expression. Suddenly she remembered something—a flash of white linen behind a bush; a girl, legs spread, beneath a man. She shook her head, frightened. "Ziggy . . ."

He placed his fingers gently over her lips to silence her. She still had on her gloves and she began to unbutton them hurriedly, fumbling clumsily with the tiny pearl buttons, her hands shaking.

Ziggy reached out and took her hand, putting the gloved fingertips to his lips, then inside his mouth, lightly clenched between his teeth. He sucked gently on her fingers, and Sarah felt, through the fine-close-fitting leather, the moistness of his mouth.

Then they slid to the floor, on to a heap of crumpled dust sheets, and the surroundings no longer mattered.

Sarah had been right: they all found something to do. She got work with a dressmaker; Herman and Sigmund went back to factory work—on the factory floor. And Hilde made cakes in the kitchen of a tearoom. Rosa cleaned the flat and cooked and took the children to school. Ziggy, who could never bring himself to perform in public because of his hatred of the second-rate, played the piano in a nightclub.

"I can't understand why you are all so cheerful!" Rosa said fretfully. "We are living like pigs; we have nothing to our name and you," she turned to Sarah, "are looking as though it was your birthday!"

"It's your wonderful cooking, Mother! There are advantages to not having servants." Ziggy and Sarah burst out laughing and disappeared into the kitchen carrying empty dishes. Out of sight of the others, Ziggy backed Sarah against the wall and began to nuzzle her neck.

She pushed him away. "Dishes first!"

The sound of their laughter carried out to the living room. Rosa might have noticed something odd about their almost feverish gaiety, but she had bigger things to worry about: Sigmund's exhaustion, his sleeplessness at night; the care they all had to take to remain safely anonymous at a time when even in a big city it was becoming increasingly difficult.

"And what did you do in school today?" Herman asked Eva and Stefan. The bounce had gone out of him, but he still tried to keep up a semblance of normality for the children.

"We sewed a flag and counted up storm troopers on the blackboard and the teacher told us a fairy story."

"Well, at least there are still fairy stories, then," Herman said.

"Father, what is wrong with the Jews?"

Sarah and Ziggy, coming in from the kitchen, heard Stefan's question and their smiles faded. The children, baptized and churchgoing, did not know their own background.

"Nothing is wrong, why do you ask?"

"Well, in this fairy story, the Nazi knight rescued the German maiden from the bad Jewish gnomes."

"Time for bed!" Hilde said brightly. "More about school tomorrow."

"But the teacher said," Stefan persisted, "that God created the white race and the black, but that Jews were the devil's creation and should be destroyed. She said that was Hitler's plan. There were these two Jewish children in the class, and she made them sit apart from us all. They began to cry. They didn't look wicked to me but the teacher said—"

"*Bed.*" Herman said firmly. Hilde swept them out, still protesting.

"It's all this being *different* that causes the trouble," Sarah said angrily. "Why don't they assimilate? Behave normally? These old-fashioned, orthodox ones are the problem. . . ." She reached for a newspaper lying on the sideboard. "Look at this—I found it on the bus today. It's Streicher's *Storm Trooper.*" She read aloud: " 'Whoever goes to the synagogues at Spital Square or in Essenweiss Street will see quite a sight at the beginning or end of the Sabbath, or on any Jewish holiday. To see these Jewish faces and figures all together is a sight that affronts any aesthetic sense . . . the way they begin haggling, jabbering . . . the way they stand around in greasy caftans with drooping curls at their temples—' "

She threw down the paper. "They're asking for trouble."

Herman said tiredly, "I wish it were as simple as that. But Herr Hitler is not going to be content with new business directories and separate schools. . . . When he says he wants to rid the country of the

Jews, he means *all* Jews, not just Jews in caftans and curls. They will want to see papers, know who your parents are, who your grandparents were. . . . The Gestapo is already busy with inquiries."

The realization had been a slow one, perhaps because she did not really want to face it, but at least it was plain before her: no baptism, no confirmation, no blue eyes or blond hair or playing of *"Deutschland Über Alles"* could save them. A piece of paper was already enough to lose you your job. How long before it lost you your freedom? How soon would it be before the prying bureaucratic fingers reached them, here in their safe little hideaway? And after that, what then?

She felt frightened, and despite Ziggy's tenderness and the exhilaration of their snatched moments together when the apartment was empty, she felt lonely. England seemed, for the first time, precious to her. People might make jokes about Jews in England but they didn't talk about killing them. Who cared about joining golf clubs anyway? You could still live safely.

Out of this sudden despair and homesickness she wrote to John, and his answer was a telegram: he would be in Berlin on Thursday.

She got to the station early in the morning, before the first train came in. John must not see the apartment. He still thought of her as part of his world; she wanted to preserve that shred of self-respect. For the same reason she dressed carefully, putting on her one good coat and a little hat of glossy green feathers, worn at the fashionable angle, tilted steeply over one eye.

It was past noon when she saw him walking down the platform, saw his beam of delight and amazement as he caught sight of her.

"How did you know which train to meet?" he asked.

"I met them all!" Sarah said gaily. "I didn't want to risk missing you!"

"You look . . . wonderful!" He took her hand and held it very tightly, and walked her rapidly toward the taxi rank. "Lunch first. And then plans. Can we go to the opera tonight?"

"Yes, if you want to. But it will probably be Wagner," Sarah warned him. "There's a lot of Wagner these days."

Wagner it was, but the excitement in the theater was not entirely due to the *Liebersverbot*. The sound of marching feet penetrated the auditorium from the street outside, and the audience's attention was divided equally between the stage and the guest of honor.

John peered through his opera glasses: "I don't think much of your *Übermensch*," he whispered to Sarah. She glanced over her shoulder, frightened. *How much we have all changed,* she thought, *when even a joke might be dangerous.*

They had dinner afterward and Sarah noticed that already, against the fine white tablecloth, her hands no longer looked quite so smooth and gleaming. She had creamed them and scrubbed the fingers with lemon before coming out, but the work at the sewing machine and helping Rosa in the flat was beginning to show. She kept her hands in her lap and hoped John would not notice.

"Well, I did as you said," he remarked. "I got the most sensational divorce case of the century."

"Who won?"

"Who always wins?" John said dryly. "The lawyers. Otherwise it was much the usual thing: a settlement that was less than she wanted and more than he would have wished." He paused as the waiter refilled their glasses with champagne. "On the way here I was thinking that it might be a rather jolly notion if you were to marry me," he went on conversationally.

He sounded as though he were joking but his eyes were serious. "I didn't feel too hopeful of my chances, as a matter of fact. Wasn't even sure I'd mention it. But then, seeing you at the station, hearing you'd waited all morning to meet my train—well, that must mean . . . well . . . something, must mean that, to an extent at least, you, well, care. . . ."

She was swept with remorse. Getting to the station early to protect herself from discovery, she had given him the wrong idea and now he would be hurt.

He saw her hesitation and said rapidly, "No need to answer now. Think it over. We'll just enjoy ourselves and you think it over and take your time."

Sarah sent word to the dressmaker that she was unwell, and for a few days floated once more on the tide of pleasure. The opera, dinner with John's favorite Dom Pérignon, even dancing—he announced that he had taken lessons and could now actually do the tango. "Pansy Crawleigh says I do the best tango she's seen outside the films!"

He insisted on delivering her back to her doorstep, and in the darkness she hoped the street looked acceptable. But each night she made excuses for not inviting him in: the apartment was being redecorated . . . Rosa was unwell. . . .

They were on their way to a new cabaret he had heard of when the increased disturbance in the street brought their taxi to a halt.

"There's been a fire at the Reichstag," the driver told them, after bawling a question at a passer-by. "Bloody Communists I suppose. Or Jews. Or both."

The next day John and Sarah had a farewell lunch. He refused to allow her to see him off at the station. "I'm getting the *wagon-lit* and you can't be out by yourself at that hour."

"You're looking worried and serious again," she said reproachfully, "which is hardly a compliment to my company."

He smiled dutifully. "I'm not asking you to decide about, well, us. But I wish you'd give some thought to leaving. Things are going to get difficult for everyone here. I know you're English and think you're all right. But you'd be better off out of it, Sassie." It was his special name for her.

She was frightened, she acknowledged that. But she was held to Germany by a dozen fine, strong threads. It was here that she had crossed the chasm that separated the "haves" from the "have-nots." It was here that she had joined the dance instead of watching from the outside. And Ziggy was here, still the joker in front of the others, but alone with her, increasingly wild, edgy, and in need of the comfort they found together. They took risks now, not always waiting until the flat was empty, as though time had to be snatched.

"I shall think about it, I promise," she told John, leaning out of the taxi window and waving goodbye.

Occasionally, in the next few weeks, Sarah had the fleeting impression that she was being followed. She told herself it was just her imagination, but little things—a movement at the outer edge of her vision, quickly stilled; a footfall; a car that dawdled or drove off if she paused too long at a curb—made her more and more nervous.

The street was, in any case, no place to linger. Demonstrations, broken shop windows, and marching troopers had stilled the commercial bustle. Stefan and Eva no longer attended school. There had been some awkwardness over papers, some questions of grandparents, so they did their lessons at home now, both very quiet, their faces closed. Even on summer evenings the family had tended not to venture out too often, and as the nights lengthened there was a feeling of settling in as though for some unmentioned siege.

Sarah hurried home, keeping to the outside edge of the pavement, away from the shadows. With her headscarf and boots, clumping along wearily, she looked like any other worker on the street. She came in sight of the building and unconsciously quickened her steps. One, two, three, four, key in the door, press the timed light switch, and if she counted uninterrupted to twenty on the stairs, there would be barley soup for supper. . . .

Outside the door she stopped, suddenly uneasy: why was everything so quiet? The children's voices, muffled but audible, usually reached her halfway up the stairs. She stood very close to the door, gripping her key, almost touching the varnished wood, and listened, straining to catch a sound. But all she could hear was her own heartbeat, thudding in her ears. For some reason she did not want to open the door.

The telephone. She could run down to the corner and telephone the apartment, and of course Rosa would explain that the children had simply gone to bed early, and scold her for being so silly. That was it. She turned toward the stairs, and, as she did so, she heard a slight creak on the landing below, the tiniest sound, as though someone had moved, someone patiently waiting had shifted his weight from one foot to the other.

The light switch clicked off.

Blinded by the sudden blackness, she fumbled for the keyhole: panic was rushing up the stairs toward her. Almost sobbing she twisted the key and flung open the door.

He was waiting inside, sitting quite still on the hall chair. She screamed, the terror flooding her body.

The man wore a raincoat and a hat with a snap brim, and the light from the street fell on him from the sitting-room window, illuminating his face harshly so that eye sockets and cheeks were black hollows, like a skull.

Her fingers flew to her mouth and she began to bite her knuckles to try to stop trembling. Where were the others? What was happening?

He rose and snapped on the light. "Good evening, fräulein. Your papers?"

She scrabbled in her handbag. She knew she should demand how he had gotten in, what he wanted, but she passed it over silently.

He noticed her hands shaking and barely glanced at the papers before handing them back. "British passport. Perhaps you should make use of it. This would be a good time to go home."

Sarah's mouth was so dry that she could at first get out no words. She swallowed repeatedly, trying to create saliva. "Where is the family?"

"They have been dispatched to a center for social and political reeducation. To train them to become useful citizens."

"Where?"

"Not far from their hometown of Weimar, I believe."

"May I visit them?"

"That will not be possible, at present."

She tried to organize her thoughts: "But the children, surely not the children—"

"Like the Jesuits, we believe in catching them young."

She could have questioned him further, asking the reason for the detention, the reeducation. But she knew the reason. All she could do was to try to hold on to the absurdity, the impossibility of a family being arrested and herded off to languish indefinitely in some detention center just because of a piece of paper in some file. They would be home, next week, next month. To hear anything to the contrary from this faceless intruder would somehow lessen the impossibility. The real terror of his presence was its ordinariness. He was no jackbooted, slavering madman. He was a drab official in a raincoat. His respectability was the true horror.

He gave a Hitler salute. "Consider making use of your passport," he repeated.

She closed the door very carefully and leaned against it. The shaking took possession of her now, so that she sank to the ground, legs wobbling, giving way beneath her. She found she was gasping for air.

It took Sarah some weeks to realize she was pregnant. She had never given much thought to the chances: there always seemed to be other, more pressing things to worry about.

After her employer twice found her vomiting in the lavatory she looked closely at her. "Are you expecting?" she asked crisply.

"I'm not sure. I think so."

Frau Hensel sighed impatiently. The girl was a brilliant machinist and finisher and they had some good Nazi wives who were waiting for their dresses. It was going to be a busy season, and she did not relish disappointing ladies who could be capricious in their ways. "You better go to my doctor. He'll look after you."

So well did he look after Sarah that a week later she was back at the machine, looking white and ill but working, nausea gone along with its cause. "You can pay me back out of your wages," Frau Hensel said amiably. "I'm in no hurry."

Sarah stayed on at the apartment, eating, sleeping, and worrying: hoping every day to hear something, fearful of what she might hear. There were cases of families who had been taken in for questioning and then sent on to some provincial town where they were permitted to scrape out a living unmolested. Any day she might get a letter. There were even instances of people being allowed to leave the country, to make a new start somewhere else. There were also the families sent to labor centers, and about these not much was officially said. But a family together and resourceful, surely she would get a letter from them?

Nothing for months. Then one night Sarah came home to find an envelope thrust beneath the door of the apartment. The writing was unfamiliar. The letter was unsigned. The writer had been an inmate of the reformatory or, as he called it, the "camp." He had promised her aunt and uncle to attempt to give her news if he was released. Now he was on his way to America and advised her to leave immediately. There was nothing to keep her here any longer.

She read quickly, skimming the lines: at the camp, wrote the unknown man, living in nightmare surroundings, worked beyond endurance, inmates succumbed daily to the typhus that flourished in the terrible setting. Her family, he much regretted to say, was among them.

The brief, flat sentences blurred. She swayed over a black pit that opened suddenly beneath her feet. She closed her eyes, shaking her head frantically to try to shut out images, to try to concentrate on just the facts, the last few facts about the only people she had ever allowed herself to love.

This then, was where it ended. In a place that had been a casually observed signpost on the road outside Weimar: in Buchenwald.

PART FOUR

Becky was understanding about the delays in arranging the wedding: she knew from family experience that these matters took time. So Leah's unwillingness to finalize the date bothered Manny more than his bride-to-be.

"Why don't we just slip into a register office and get married, get it over with?" he suggested.

Becky gave him a look of comic reproval: "You can't be serious! Mum's made out enough lists to fill every cabin on the *Queen Mary*, and Dad's looking at houses—"

"But we don't need a house!" Manny protested. "We got one. Mine."

"Yes, love, and it's very nice." Becky was tactful. "But it's a bit on the small side, when you consider the situation."

"What situation?"

"The situation of me having to share a kitchen with that old bitch," Becky wanted to say succinctly, but she smiled and nibbled his ear. "Well . . . there won't be just the two, I mean just the three of us forever, will there? I mean we'll be having a family won't we? We'll be needing more room then, don't you see?"

The association of ideas . . . family . . . Becky . . . he and Becky wreaking havoc on the bedsprings in the conjugal ecstasies he was still firmly denied, brought Manny out in a sweat of lust. "Well, I can't wait much longer."

"Talk to your mother then, lovey. See if she'll let us fix the date."

Manny took her advice. "If Hirschl and Ruda can't be bothered to reply, why can't we go ahead without them?" he asked Leah.

"And Sarah? Your own sister? Can you believe she wouldn't answer? Something is wrong. God knows what is happening over there. . . . You read the papers. And at such a time you ask me to think about catering and seating and dressmaking?"

When the letters were finally returned unopened from Weimar, even Manny had to agree all was not as it should be. They wrote to the synagogues in Weimar and received puzzling and puzzled answers. Leah was unable to shake off a conviction of disaster. There was something about the silence from Germany that reminded her of Poland. It reawoke in her a fear she had almost forgotten, something that was unknown in England: the fear of the knock on the door in the night.

Manny was in the kitchen with Becky, making tea and whispering, when the doorbell rang. Leah hurried to answer it, breathless, though without reason. "Yes?"

The streetlighting hardly reached the porch, and Becky peered at the young woman on the doorstep, unable at first to make out more than a shape. The visitor was thin, foreign-looking, fashionably dressed, her features mysteriously shadowed by a fine veil that swirled from a tiny green feathered hat.

Leah looked more closely; her heart jumped and she said, questioningly, "Sarah?" She drew her daughter—taller than she was, now—into the hall, pulling her head down so that she could kiss her.

Sarah tried to disentangle herself from the clutching arms and damp embraces. Her old dislike of maternal closeness came back to her. She stepped away involuntarily and almost collided with her brother. The hall, though immaculate, was tiny.

Manny gave a great shout of pleasure, hugging her cheerfully.

Sarah smiled politely. She was delighted to see him looking so happy and prosperous, but his clothes were appalling, the patterns too loud, the cut too sharp. Behind him hovered a plump, red-cheeked girl carrying a tea tray—the maid perhaps?

"Sarah, this is Becky, my fiancée—have you got a lot to catch up on!"

She took off her coat and hat and Becky exclaimed unselfconsciously, "Look at that figure! Such a waist! A model you could be in the magazines. Such an elegant sister you've got, Manny."

They led her into the front room, everyone talking at once. Sarah was astounded by the change in her mother: Leah was still slim; indeed she was almost scrawny. But even in the worst days she had had a certain grace and the vestiges of her girlish beauty. Now her face had settled into a droop of resignation and her mind seemed dulled. She had lost the look of poverty, and acquired a suburban conventionality.

Sarah had lived alone for some time now, existing daily with horror and hope, and it had had the effect of immunizing her against emotion. She had learned that to survive she must feel nothing more personal than hunger, cold, warmth. She sat now, listening to the bird-chatter of Becky on one side, the questions from her mother about her health, her activities. Manny's affectionate chaffing—"So why didn't you write? Don't you care that your beloved brother is entering into matrimony?"

"I never received any letters," she said. "I have been in Berlin."

Talking was an effort, not because she was unaccustomed to speaking English. She had, in fact, spoken a good deal of English lately, giving German conversation lessons to visiting Americans: they always seemed to want to spend at least part of the lesson talking their own language, perhaps to restore their self-respect after stumbling through the humiliations of foreign grammar. Rather, she was uncomfortable because these people seemed to her now like foreigners.

Then, from Leah, came the question Sarah had been dreading: "And Ruda? And Hirschl and the children? What about the family? Where are they?"

Leah knew she should not sit like this, brooding. But she felt stunned, suddenly very old. She looked over the half century of her life and saw nothing but shattered dreams and bitter memories.

Chaim was dead. She had no husband to turn to. Little David and Miriam dead—killed by the whim of falling bombs or exploding gunpowder, stupidly, uselessly, before they had tasted life. Daniel, still in her mind always the baby brother, taken for the Russian army, was probably dead too.

Until tonight though, she had lived with the hopeful illusion that she had a brother and a sister; that their children might comfort her old age . . . until Sarah—sitting upright and still as a statue, and talking in that flat, drained voice—had taken away her brother and her sister, their families, even the little children. Their lives were wiped out in a minute, in the time it took to tell it. How long had it taken them to die, infected, the germs eating their bodies?

The room seemed crowded with ghosts, noisy with unquiet spirits. Her life was meaningless; she might as well be one with them. She had done so little, just lived from day to day, meanly, exhausted by the little blows of survival, until the grand design—the noble aspirations, the excitements of achievement—grew dim, overlaid by the dust of daily existence, covered by the fluff of the cloth she had cut and sewn, the crumbs of bread that kept them going.

Mordecai, wherever he was (and perhaps he, too, was dead, shot in some foreign jail, purged in some new and necessary trial?) had rejected the small consolations for the greater glory. She saw now that she had sacrificed more than she knew—and for what?

She could not comfort her dead; she could not even help the living. She had become a thing. She ate and slept and wore clothes. Better not to have dreamed at all than to live and see her dreams become dust. When Sarah gave them the news she had wept, but now, for a while, she seemed unable even to claim the solace of weeping.

At last Sarah broke the silence. She said, gently, that it was time for her to leave; she had to meet someone in London.

"Is it so important that you have to go now?"

"Yes," she said, "it is important. As a matter of fact, I'm getting married."

They stared at her, astonished. Manny recovered first. "Well, when's the big day?"

Sarah hated what she had to say next, but she had made a decision and intended to abide by it. Her voice was deliberately hard. "It will take place in the country, privately. I have to tell you that I don't want anyone at the wedding."

Becky's mouth and eyes opened in amazement. Manny whistled, smiling to conceal his anger. "You've become a great lady, I can see that. This must be some big nob you're hitching up with and we're not good enough for you now." His face was sour with resentment.

She knew she could not explain, could not begin to tell them of her lifelong yearning for some beauty, some breadth in her existence. Of her desire for ease of mind and a style that would transcend her beginnings. They could not understand. So she shook her head and said in the calm, expressionless voice, "I have made a different life for myself, that's all. It's too late to explain everything now."

Leah got to her feet, her eyes blazing. "To be ashamed of your family shames *you*. In all the bad times, hungry, penniless, I never felt ashamed. We always lived right. We lived honestly. We were not thieves or *shnorrers*. But now I feel ashamed. Of my own daughter. Once I had a daughter, Sarah, a princess, a child I loved. But she is no more. I have no daughter but Ruth now. You have disgraced your family. You are dead to me." She went slowly out of the room and up the stairs. They heard her bedroom door close.

"It's none of my business," Becky said. "I'm an outsider here, but I'd have said a family was too important to chuck out like bits of bread at Pesach. People you love, you want to keep with you, you don't want to lose them."

"You can't always do that," Sarah said. "You can't keep people with you if they're taken away. Loving people doesn't save them from anything."

Mrs. Middleway looked taken aback. "I must say, John, I find this most . . . unsatisfactory. You arrive late for dinner, and now you tell me you contemplate marriage to someone your father and I have never even met. It won't do, I'm sorry, it really will not do. We're not *quite* Bolshevik Russia yet, you know."

Humphrey Middleway muttered gloomily, "A foreigner to boot."

"She's not German, she's English. I told you: she lost her people and went to live with some relatives by marriage—"

"Lost her people, yes." Mrs. Middleway sighed. "Most unfortunate. One simply never knows where one is with people who have lost their people."

"She *is* a friend of the Crawleighs. She has stayed at their country place, knows the family . . ."

"That does sound . . . encouraging." Her frown lifted slightly. "Well, where is this girl of yours, John? I suppose we ought to meet her." Mrs. Middleway was consulting her diary. "Ask her to come next weekend, how would that be?"

Sarah had spent a lot of time and thought preparing her London wardrobe. Frau Hensel had allowed her the use of the machine in the evenings and had sold her cloth at trade price. She had been sorry to lose the girl, but she could see the sense of returning to England. "Perhaps everything will turn out well. You will get married and come to Berlin for a holiday. Perhaps I shall make you some dresses. Now . . ." she had studied the magazines spread out on the worktable. "Chanel is bringing in the waist, still soft, just indicated, and you could have a suit like this, with piping in the front, and perhaps a blouse with a jabot to go with it. And for evening . . . these Molyneux overblouses are perfect for your cold English houses; we shall find a silky fabric with a little weight to it, you'll need to line the cuffs so that they fall right."

Arriving at the Middleways, Sarah allowed herself to feel nervous: like stage fright, she knew that a certain degree of concealed fear would lend conviction to her demeanor. This was the sharpest test: if Mrs. Middleway sensed a social gulf, then all would be over. Sarah did not see herself as the Wallace Simpson of the Middleways, shattering John's prospects and family unity. She wanted life on her terms, and that included social acceptance.

Mrs. Middleway greeted Sarah with an exquisite balance of warmth and reserve. The girl was certainly attractive in the modish, skinny way. Lovely eyes. Good bones. Very pale, foreign-looking almost, must be something to do with living in Germany. "How lovely to meet you, John has told us . . ." not much, after all. ". . . You know the Crawleighs."

"I was so sorry to miss Daisy's wedding."

"It was quite charming."

The conversation languished, and Mrs. Middleway said at last, "I expect you would like a rest before dinner?"

"Thank you." Sarah took a careful breath and asked, with what she hoped was a charming smile, "Could one of your maids press a couple of my things, d'you think? I'm hopeless at packing for myself."

Mrs. Middleway looked considerably reassured: a girl who was hopeless at doing her own packing could not be altogether beyond the pale.

After dinner John went to the piano and began to play, rather badly. Mrs. Middleway turned to Sarah. "Do you care for music, Miss Robinson?"

"Very much. Particularly Chopin. This nocturne is one of my favorites . . ."

Artistic, Mrs. Middleway thought. That did explain a certain amount. Artistic people were notoriously vague about their affairs. She would have made further inquiries but Diana Crawleigh was in America. She recalled that her son had always had a worrying streak in him; his father had caught him reading Baudelaire once, in the holidays—for pleasure, he said. It was the only time she could remember seeing Humphrey really angry with John.

The wedding was set for June. The guest list was small—just family and John's closest friends. The Middleways had been graceful about Sarah but they could not pretend to be overjoyed. So many of their questions led to dead ends. "Lost her people . . . lost her money in the 'twenty-nine crash . . . it don't sound well, my boy." Mr. Middleway said, "You're set on this marriage so we'll have to make the best of it—peculiar marriages seem to be the thing this year—but I can't say it's ideal."

In the little gray church in the village near the house in Kent the Middleways gathered for the wedding.

"We don't often see you in here apart from Christmas and Good Friday, Mr. Middleway!" the vicar said jocularly.

"Well, you hold your doings at such deucedly inconvenient times," Humphrey responded crossly.

The choir sang, their voices blending in a head note just short of shrillness that spread out and was lost in the dimness of the ceiling. Dust flecks floated through the air, shimmering in the slanting sunbeams.

Sarah's dress, a real Molyneux this time, gleamed and rippled as she moved down the aisle. Afterward, in the soft, diffused light of the little striped marquee on the lawn, her heightened color and the pearly reflection of the gown gave her a glow like an Ingres portrait.

Mrs. Middleway, far from delighted originally by her son's eccentric choice, had to acknowledge that the girl was graceful and knew how to stand. So many modern girls slouched about the place like stable-boys. "Humphrey, you better make your speech," she murmured. "Do keep it short. And remember: no jokes about the Germans, please."

"And when you make your speech," Leah said to Manny, "keep it short, and no jokes about the rabbi."

One hundred invitation cards—"deckle-edge, and with glitter-frosting," Becky instructed the stationer—had been sent out and replies received. Frockcoats and top hats were shaken free of mothballs on every side of London and dressmakers were kept busy on shiny, brilliantly colored outfits. The bridesmaid and pageboy wore pink and mauve to tone in with Becky's bouquet, and a tiara of pearls and near-diamonds was chosen to top her black curls. The hired car, too, fitted the occasion. It was large and glossy—"You'd take it for a Rolls Royce, honest," said a neighbor enviously.

The wedding canopy had been erected in front of the Ark—a cloth of blue velvet covered with silver embroidery, supported on slender, decorative wooden poles. In his top hat and formal clothes Manny looked very solemn and absurdly young. The cantor sang the blessings, they sipped the wine, and Manny slipped the ring on Becky's finger, then rather gingerly stamped on the wineglass, prudently wrapped in a napkin. The noise level rose sharply with cries of "*mazel tov!*" and generous weeping from the guests in their silk dresses and draped turban hats.

The congregation poured out of the synagogue into the gray London street like a flock of birds of paradise released from a cage. Their plumage shone and glittered—hot pinks and vibrant blues; fiery greens and singing purples; rings on fingers and diamonds around necks—or what looked like diamonds, at least. With a cheerful calling and chattering from one to another, they climbed into the cars, and the morning-suited top-hatted menfolk in their somber monochrome merely intensified the brilliance, like black velvet in a jeweler's window.

Leah, in truth, had little spirit for all this festivity: there was a dark heart to her life these days: a family lost in one breath, as though scythed down by a cosmic hand. An obscene end for innocent souls. And a daughter vanished into a world of gentile strangeness, apparently untouched by affection for her own blood kind, or by remorse for her betrayal of them. On her own part, a guilt she was still unable to face, the guilt of her attitude so many years before: morally superior, despising the harmless pleasure her brother and sister took in worldly goods that she could afford to disdain since she could not afford to enjoy them. In this mood the flamboyant gathering around her struck an even more jarring note.

She was flashing a glance of barely concealed disgust at Becky's mother, who was poised with a smoked salmon roll in each plump hand, when she felt someone touch her shoulder.

"Your feelings are showing," a voice murmured in her ear.

She turned. "Simeon!" The sharpness of her expression melted into a welcoming beam. "You look so well!"

The boyish heaviness had been replaced by a rugged sturdiness that helped a little to balance the large head. His expression was as she always remembered it: one of amusement and gaiety. "What have you been doing? We thought you weren't coming."

"I've been in the Middle East for a while . . . a few dramas. Where there's oil there's trouble, sooner or later."

She nodded. "I always knew you would be a success."

"Of course," he said, "I do it all to gain your admiration really." They both laughed. "Your son looks very happy," Simeon commented.

"He's easily satisfied," Leah said thoughtlessly, and then added, filled with quick self-reproach, "but she's a good girl."

"She's a bright girl," Simeon observed. "She has the same energetic drive as Manny. She'll be a great help to him."

Leah looked surprised. "Really? You think so?" She looked at Becky more hopefully. *Things could be worse, then*, she said to herself.

Lunch was announced and the sluice gates opened. From the kitchen the waiters poured into the banqueting hall, so many boats on a flood tide, laden with dishes and plates. The noise mounted to a crescendo that obliterated the musicians dutifully sawing, scraping, and plucking away on the dais.

The food was demolished swiftly, the tablecloth bearing the debris of chopped liver, plaice, chicken, apple pudding, and fruit salad. The pace slackened; the musicians took heart and plunged into a syncopated Yiddish melody. Free at last to enjoy the music, the guests applauded heartily.

Manny loved the noise and bustle and the abundance of it all. Becky in her stiff silk dress was as pink and shiny as a china doll. The black eyes winked knowingly at old friends, the head waggled comically, the pink tongue curled around the deeper pink lips. He leaned toward his mother and said "Pretty good affair, eh?"

271

Leah was aware of Becky laughing shrilly at some joke, heard her confident retort, the voice strident, and thought again: *Is this the best he could have done?* But she heard the tentative note in Manny's voice, the small anxiety underneath his expansive laugh, and she squeezed his hand reassuringly. Anyway, Simeon apparently saw some merit in the girl. "Such a big man now, a married man, you won't have time for your poor old mother now you've got a pretty wife."

He roared with laughter and glanced proudly at Becky. She *was* pretty. *Ah Becky,* he thought longingly, *When all this is over, will I really be allowed to touch you properly, do all the rude things you joke about so freely but don't permit?*

Leah broke into his steamy reverie: "You'd have thought Ruth would at least manage to get here on time."

Manny shrugged good-naturedly. "You know how she feels about these bourgeois customs. She had an important trade-union meeting—she'll come when she can."

How unsatisfactory children were, Leah reflected. They never lived up to what was expected of them. They went off and started living their messy lives, marrying the wrong people or wasting time talking politics, when what life was really about was . . . what was life really about? She knew, once. It was about trying to change the world, wasn't it? Later it was about love and responsibility. Finally it had narrowed down to survival, and when she next raised her head she found it had emptied of everything but the price of bread and coal. She had no fine thoughts now, no arguments over theology and free will. There was time, yes, but she had nothing to say on the matter.

Mechanically she acknowledged the greetings of the guests, a sharp-faced, angular woman in a dark silk dress, with only an occasional lowering of the eyelids over her long, almond eyes betraying her absolute boredom.

Still replete, the guests moved off lethargically, to go home and change for the dinner and dance. Manny was carried off by Becky's parents, and Leah found herself alone. She rode home in the big, hired car, relaxing in the comfortable leather seat, and encouraged the driver to chat. Being alone was strange to her.

But the drive was short, and in the house silence waited for her in every room. Without realizing it, she had grown dependent on noise: first children, then sewing machines, later on Manny and his friends with their card games, and now Ruth with her modern ways, bringing home odd people, smoking cigarettes, everyone shouting and interrupting. If she could only be content with the nursing, Leah thought, but she had to go trying to organize strikes to change things, when the truth was that nothing changed, really. Leah had said as much, once, and Ruth became very angry and talked passionately about the labor movement and workers' control. It reminded Leah of Mordecai and the bright young days in Peszno.

Were there still couples walking by candlelight along that cobbled street on their wedding day? How innocent they had been then, how green in the ways of the world. . . . She changed for dinner, brushing her hair, the black streaked with white here and there, and coiled it onto her neck. Decisions . . . how could you ever know where your decisions were taking you?

"Gracious host and hostess, happy bride and groom," roared the master of ceremonies, "dinner is served!"

Manny and Becky were led in, still in their wedding finery—a little crumpled now at hip and hem. Jonathan sang the grace before the meal, his warm voice mellow, his expression benign. *What a good boy he is*, thought Leah. She had brought him up strictly, with a sort of perfunctory affection, and he alone of all the children had never caused her a moment's trouble. Ceremonially he sliced into the huge challah loaf and sat down. Chaim would have been proud of him.

A waiter hovered at Leah's table: "Horses doovers?" he inquired.

"You wonder where they put it all!" Manny marveled, undoing his top trouser button and pulling at his increasingly tight collar. Despondently he awaited the speeches. They were as numbing as he expected.

"I remember Becky when . . ."

"Manny won't remember this, but I . . ."

"I recall the occasion—on the day of his Bar Mitzvah as a matter of fact, when . . ."

"A lovely girl . . ."

". . . All the happiness in the world . . ."

"Mazel tov!"

The speeches dulled Leah into an overfed torpor. The music and the chatter swirled around her. Someone was saying "Mother!" and she turned to find Ruth at her shoulder, wretchedly dressed as usual, with her hair all over the place.

"So you finally managed to get here. Congratulations." Leah was furious.

273

Ruth grinned unrepentantly. "It was an incredibly good meeting." She paused. "I hope you don't mind, I brought someone along."

Leah turned and looked behind her. It was Mordecai. His hair, white now, was as wild and thick as ever, his clothes neater, more citified than they used to be. He looked less foreign, she thought, almost smart. He smiled at her and grasped her hands with an odd nervousness.

"Leah!"

"Mordecai. What a surprise. How wonderful." She turned to Ruth. "Fetch Jonathan over, tell him his father is here." Leah suddenly looked glowing with vitality. "What a day to come home! Where have you come from?"

Mordecai waved his arms. "Scotland. I was in Spain and Russia and then Germany. I've been in London for a bit, union business . . . I meant to get in touch before . . ." his voice faltered slightly, ". . . but I didn't have your address, and there was always so much to be done!"

She smiled. Still full of the great ideas. No wonder he seemed so young.

Ruth was leading Jonathan over to them. Mordecai stood up and stared at the slender, rabbinic figure coming toward him.

"*Shalom*, Father."

The two men embraced awkwardly. "Well . . . Jonathan . . ." Mordecai laughed, pulling a long face. "So you've joined the opposition! What are you trying to do to me?" He managed to give his genuine dismay a note of humor.

Jonathan said without irony, "I could always try praying for you. You might find it useful one day."

Mordecai stood, shaking his head slightly, for once lost for words. Jonathan, who like Chaim had the gift of tranquil silence, smiled at his father without bitterness, teeth white against the darkness of his beard.

Leah said brightly, "Well, are we to have the honor of your company for a while, or are you already late for a revolution somewhere?"

He roared with laughter, almost naturally, and flung an arm across her shoulder. "Oh, you'll have to put up with me for a while."

Across the room Simeon noted the new arrival and his carefully casual warmth. And Leah's radiance. His neighbor was asking about the Middle East question: "What I want to know is," he repeated, "is this good for the Jews? Or bad for the Jews?"

Is this good or bad for Leah? Simeon wondered.

The imperatives of the wedding ritual interrupted the group: the photographer, threatening to lose all self-possession, was flapping about the camera, sighing and waiting to get on with the family portraits. Leah was needed.

"Sit down and eat," she urged Mordecai. "We'll talk presently."

It was only as she was posing, her smile wide, before the camera, that she wondered how Ruth had met Mordecai. At the union meeting, she presumed.

Becky surveyed the hotel bedroom with approval. Private bathroom. Fur rug. Silk lampshades. "Very nice, Manny."

He beamed. "Well, I thought: may as well have a spree. You only have one honeymoon, eh?"

She flashed him a smile. "It's lovely."

She opened her smart new suitcase and began to unpack her things. Watching her greedily, Manny was struck by how composed she seemed, placing dresses on hangers, underwear in a drawer. Perhaps she was pretending, trying to appear calmer than she felt? He himself was sweaty-handed and shaky, constantly clearing his throat. He was experienced enough: there had been the housewives for whom the vacuum cleaner's performance was not all they wanted demonstrated; there had been workers at the factory, not all of whom were ugly and most of whom were willing. But Becky was his first and only love. Getting her was like winning the sweepstake. He could still hardly believe his luck.

She shook out a night dress: black chiffon with mauve and purple bows on the shoulders. The bodice was tiny, amazingly low-cut. "Like it?" she asked.

For a moment he visualized the flimsy garment filled by Becky's flesh, her limbs gleaming through the almost transparent veil. He began to speak and had to clear his throat again. "Yes. Very much."

She took off her costume jacket, then undid and slipped off her skirt and blouse. Manny stared, dazzled at the rounded succulence of her; the curvy, plump legs poised on high-heeled patent-leather shoes, the white thighs bulging slightly above the stocking tops. She wore no petticoat and her brassiere was quite inadequate for the mammary splendors it supported. She glanced across at him, smiling, pleasantly conscious of him staring at her. Then she sat down on the satin bedspread and cocked one silken leg over the other to remove her shoes.

The undulations, deepening cleavages and strains on flimsy garments this produced were too much for Manny.

He groaned and rushed toward her. Becky rocked back with the force of his embrace as he began to reach for her still-hidden delights.

"Hang on then!" she cried, giggling encouragingly and at the same time holding him off while she finished undressing. Manny gasped, rolling on to her like a swimmer plunging into the creamy surf. While he floundered breathlessly Becky removed his clothes and they wrestled together, creasing the satin bed cover—two moist, plump creatures, buoyant as dolphins, brimming with energy and excitement.

Then Becky unobtrusively took charge. As far as Manny was concerned, his wedding night was glorious—Becky saw to that. A generous girl, she knew how to give, as well as receive, satisfaction.

"I must say, Sassie my dear, that you run your establishment well." Mrs. Middleway was, reluctantly, impressed.

The house overlooking Hyde Park gleamed in every corner, and those items of furniture that were not family pieces had been selected with discretion. True it was a little overfurnished, perhaps, in the Germanic manner, but quite acceptable. Her daughter-in-law appeared to have a good eye for choosing servants, and it was clear that a firm hand was on the reins.

The season was already half over and Sarah had survived almost unscarred. There had been some awkward moments—her total lack of experience in horse riding, her ignorance of dogs and their complex pedigrees, the question of schools. These had called for skilled fencing. On the other hand her fluent German won compliments at diplomatic parties and receptions; Germany was much in the air.

The most dangerous moment, the long-dreaded encounter with Lady Crawleigh, caught her completely unprepared one night as the lights came up for the intermission at Covent Garden.

The Crawleighs were in the box adjoining theirs. They had obviously come in late, after the opera began. Humphrey Middleway greeted them with surprise. "Heard you were still in America. . . . You know our daughter-in-law, of course!"

Freddy Crawleigh caught Sarah's eye. "Rather!"

Lady Crawleigh gave her most minimal smile, in which the lips stayed closed but a modicum of cordiality was expressed by a brief upward pinching of the cheeks. Clearly Freddy knew this young person, and there was, to be sure, something vaguely familiar about her face. But she had no recollection of ever meeting her.

Sarah smiled brilliantly and plunged. "Good evening, Lady Crawleigh. I hope Pansy is well?"

Lady Crawleigh's face cleared. That explained it. This must be one of the seemingly endless succession of young things who swarmed over the house at the invitation of her daughter. These casual modern manners made it so difficult to keep track of people's names. Her smile gleamed. "Pansy is extremely well. You must come and see us very soon."

The coronation set the mood: the Middleways, like everyone else, were caught up in a flurry of weekend house parties, dinners, balls, and other diversions. *Lost Horizon* at the Tivoli had to be seen sooner or later, even if the *Daily Telegraph* did call it a synthetic utopia for a synthetic world. The wholesome Englishness of the gardens and countryside at Glyndebourne even disarmed the general suspicion of Mozart.

It was a busy season, until Sarah became pregnant. It was not in itself a bar to normal activity, but in her case a giddy, nausea-racked three months was followed by a miscarriage.

The obstetrician was dry in the Scottish manner: "You have not looked after yourself, Mrs. Middleway. This is not, I would say, the first miscarriage you have suffered, and if you take my advice you will rest for a few months. Some women can ride to hounds throughout their pregnancy and shrug off the birth over a stirrup cup. You will need to be more careful next time."

Being careful with herself was a new occupation for Sarah and one that quickly palled. She lay on the sofa and read three novels a week, though she found she could not warm to Mrs. Woolf's disturbing people as she had to Jane Austen's waspish and essentially practical characters.

She was roused from a deepening depression by Lady Crawleigh's invitation—her first to the young Middleways—to a luncheon for a "promising politician," a British Fascist. Pansy had visited Germany on a finishing tour and was much taken by the uniforms and blond good looks of the German officers.

"Shall we go?" John asked.

Sarah thought carefully. She hated what she had seen of the new party so far, and Lady Crawleigh's candidate was unlikely to be much different: modeled on the German pattern, tinged with the same anti-Semitism. But Lady Crawleigh was an important figure, not to be lightly turned down. Was this not the goal she had set herself—the very center of the world to which she had aspired? Surely at the center things were most stable. And was it not stability that she craved more than anything? Safety and high style. That had been the idea. "I think it might be amusing," she said, "and I'm feeling so much stronger."

Lady Crawleigh's promising politician was an accomplished luncheon guest. He gave good value in wit, charm, and fiery idealism. His pronouncements had a nice ambiguity that allowed each listener to draw the conclusions they wished.

Sarah, eyes watchful above her neat smile, took care to avoid greeting Pansy until both Lady Crawleigh and John were out of the way for a moment. Then she employed her new technique of the judged plunge. "How lovely to see you, Pansy, after so long. Your mother has been telling me about your German trip."

Pansy's smile was uncertain. She knew this person's face; they had obviously met before. But she could not place her. "Germany was divine," she said enthusiastically. "Do you know it at all?"

Sarah nodded. "Oh yes. I was there at the same time as Freddy. Yes . . . Germany can be divine."

She noticed John coming toward them. "John dear . . ."

"Sassie?"

Sarah had from the beginning adopted John's name for her. It seemed more of his world, and using it freed her finally from her old identity. "You know my husband, don't you, Pansy? John Middleway."

"Oh. Oh yes," Pansy gasped with relief. That must be where she had seen Sassie Middleway before—at one of her mother's ghastly parties.

"John knows a great deal about Germany, so you must tell him all about your visit, bring him up to date." Sarah left them together and moved on serenely. Another dangerous corner navigated.

Lady Crawleigh had been slightly put out by some of the reactions to her political sponsoring. She recognized it as a mixture of apathy and chauvinism, but could not help finding it irritating. She said fretfully to her husband, "Freddy and Daisy are being *most* tiresome at the moment. They both seem quite taken with Mr. Churchill's doom warnings. They even refused to come to luncheon today." Her face brightened as she caught sight of an elegant figure across the room. "Ah, Sassie my dear . . ."

In the game of social snakes and ladders it is sometimes quite trivial matters that advance or wreck a move. Sarah looked both intelligent and charming. The bias-cut, feminine drapery of that season's dresses flattered her bird-boned figure; the severity of her features was modish. And she actually looked as though she were enjoying herself. Lady Crawleigh decided to take her up.

"What a success you are!" John said admiringly from the doorway. Sarah stood checking the angle of her hat in the drawing-room mirror. He dropped his briefcase on a pale silken chair. "Going out?"

"Mm." She nodded, still adjusting her hat.

"A woman came to see me about her divorce today—and spent half the time talking about you."

"*Me?*"

"Yes. She went on at inordinate length about the 'terribly good work' you and the Crawleigh women are doing for charity. You are quite celebrated."

Her face bloomed pink for a moment, then faded to its usual pallor. He looked at her closely. "You aren't doing too much, perhaps?"

"Perhaps," Sarah said gaily, "but it is so amusing!"

She smiled at him and he took her hand for a moment. "You feel chilled." He rubbed the slim fingers, then almost casually raised them to his lips and kissed her fingertips. She stopped smiling and stared at him for a moment, her lips drooping. Her eyes were filled with tears and she blinked rapidly. "I think I may have a slight chill . . ." Pregnancy, she thought, must be making her overemotional.

She began to hunt in her handbag for a handkerchief and he handed her his own, neatly folded. "Shall I see you for dinner?" he asked.

"Oh I imagine so. This is just a charity tea dance."

"In aid of what? Undernourished German officers?"

She tapped his hand reprovingly. "That's all Pansy's nonsense, you know. This is a real charity. African children. Or perhaps Indian widows. Did you know that an Indian widow is supposed to throw herself on to her husband's funeral pyre?"

"Only Hindus, actually. Yes." John took back his now crumpled handkerchief. "Well . . . if someone you loved very deeply were to die I can imagine feeling that life had no further meaning, can't you?"

She looked at him quickly. "I think someone's at the door."

A moment later the butler announced that Lady Crawleigh's car was waiting.

"I must fly." She brushed a light kiss on his cheek and was gone, the front door closing behind her with a faint thud.

He stood for a moment in the darkening drawing room, listening to the laughter and greetings on the pavement, the slamming of the car door, and the sound of the engine as it pulled away. Then the silence established itself, filling the room like a fog.

There was nothing he could say in any case, even if Sarah were here. She might think he was not quite himself. Nor could he speak openly about the urgency of emotion that surged through him even at the thought of her. The way he found himself impatient to get home, hurrying, quickening his pace until he was actually running up the front steps, almost breathless, just to catch sight of her a moment sooner. To see that cool, pale, pointed face, the narrow-boned completeness of her, the repose. The way she moved, each separate action graceful in itself, and flowing into movement equally graceful. To be with her.

He had been brought up by people who mistrusted emotion. The heart was better left undisturbed. His childhood hunger for love had remained unassuaged. Respect, compatibility, harmony: these were the cornerstones of a relationship. His was an idyllic marriage then, by normal standards. Was it only in stories that flame was joined to flame? Isolde, Guinevere, Helen, Cleopatra—was their ardent spirit dead with them? Did women no longer have the desire, the ability, to feel tempestuously? The world well lost for love.

He rang for tea.

Political meetings! That's all I'm short of! On a working day!" Manny gulped his tea impatiently. "I got a new shop opening next week and an order waiting for delivery now. What am I? A dogsbody?"

Leah went on, as though he had not spoken. "It's the blackshirts I worry about. Bully boys. Fascists. Up to no good. I just want that Ruth shouldn't get hurt. It won't take all day. You can do your deliveries first."

Manny and Becky exchanged glances, and she poured him another cup of tea. The new house was at the better end of Golders Green —practically Hampstead—double-fronted with mock-Tudor gables and quite large enough for them all, including Ruth and baby Deborah. But the pressure of Leah's presence cramped them increasingly.

Ruth did not in fact spend much time at home; she seemed so occupied with her political meetings, and now with Mordecai elected to the union council she was even busier with administration.

Becky, whose amiability did not stand in the way of common sense, knew that sooner or later Leah would have to move out. She herself could shrug off the criticisms, the sighs and murmurs of disappointment—"Becky, who's your butcher? A thief—he's sent you a bird you can't feel the flesh on it. And Becky, I don't mean to criticize but these matzos are soft, limp as a piece of rag, old stock they must have sold you."

But the problem was more complex than mere criticism. Leah composed their encounters with the precision of a sonata, finishing her last phrase as Manny appeared on the scene so that all he heard was Becky retorting in exasperation, "All right, so I'm a no-good shopper! Is it such a tragedy if the matzos are soft? Put 'em in the oven for a minute. Or throw them out!"

Then Manny would grow red-faced and stamp about the room

᎗ 281

and say to Becky later, "Why do you have to get so upset with her? She's only trying to help, to give you the benefit of her experience." Sometimes the ensuing conversation grew loud in argument until it ended in tears or slammed doors.

Becky had talked about it to Ruth one day. "We all act so bloody stupid! All this argument about curtains or lamps or *lokshen* soup. Who cares? *I* don't, really. I don't think she does. So why do we do it?"

"I came to the conclusion once," Ruth said, "that somewhere we all have a caricature of ourselves waiting—like a sort of Platonic idea gone wrong—and gradually we grow to fit our caricature. Look at Mum, she grows more Yiddisher-mama every day. I think she must pick it up in the shops or something. You wouldn't believe how different she was once. When I was a kid she read books, she sang songs, recited poetry—the first English poem I ever heard was Mum reading something from Simeon's schoolbook. She could talk about all sorts of things. She had such thoughts in her head—it was hearing her talk that first set *me* thinking about things.

"We all have the possibility of escape, but most people's lives are so exhausting that just living takes all their strength. They haven't any left to be themselves, which requires an extra effort."

"Oh that's rubbish," Becky protested.

"Is it? You'll finish up the same way, just like Mum. You may not think so now, you may not want to. Inside you may even be thinking your own thoughts and dreaming of something different, but you'll be waving your arms just like she does and shouting about the quality of the chicken, and no one will think it's strange because by then they'll all be doing their own caricature routine too. Sad, isn't it?"

Ruth looked at Becky sympathetically. She was still pretty, though overplump. Ruth was like a younger version of Leah without the beauty: her eyes dominated her bony face, but the black hair was pulled back uncompromisingly, her nose was too long and her skin was sallow. Becky was all creamy flesh. But in one respect Ruth knew they were alike: like puppets they would walk and talk and wave their lives away, falling into the automatic response, the easy reaction, until nothing else was possible, neither originality nor daring nor discovery. Was that why children always seemed so free and astonishing? Because they had not yet given up, were still themselves?

"What do you want out of life, Becky, really?" Ruth asked.

Becky's curls bounced as she shook her head. "I never thought about it much. I just lived from day to day, it seemed enough. I don't have deep thoughts like you do. I just worry about today. Maybe that's wrong, but I never could work out what you gained, worrying about all the rest. I mean, what do *you* want?"

Ruth laughed. "Freud asked the same thing. Well, I wouldn't mind a retroussé nose, a rosebud mouth, and blond curls . . ." She shook her head. "Oh, I don't know . . ."

"I can't see you as a Yiddisher-mama."

"Oh I agree there. If I got married to a nice Jewish boy, his dad would give us a house; in no time at all I'd have a couple of kids and a good relationship with a kosher butcher. I'd be buried under the wall-to-wall carpet, and no one would even notice I'd disappeared. It would be the end of me. No. I don't think I'm the marrying kind." She looked at herself in the mirror and wrinkled her nose. "Just as well, really."

All this Becky remembered now, at the breakfast table in the big, shiny kitchen. She heard Leah tell Manny he should go to the political meeting, to keep an eye on Ruth, and she was about to disagree, to say the opposite. But she made an effort. She thought about what Leah was really saying and decided that just this once Leah was probably right, and she said so.

Manny knew when he was beaten. "Where is it—Vallance Road?" He sighed noisily. "My customers can wait. They only supply the food we eat, the clothes we wear, the holidays we take—"

"Manny!" Becky said warningly.

"I'm not arguing!" he shouted. "Am I saying anything? What's the use, does anyone give a bugger what I say or think anyway? So why should I argue? I'm not saying a thing!"

Becky drank her tea calmly. Manny shouted on. She could feel compassion for him, because she realized it was the caricature shouting. Manny, the real Manny, was somewhere out of sight, worrying about something quite different. Important worries you kept to yourself.

Sarah did not know the location of this particular charity bazaar but the details were unimportant. She had provided generously for the white-elephant stall and would now attend and buy equally generously, laying up store for future white-elephant stall donations. The convoy of large, gleaming automobiles swept through London, heading east, the occupants chattering brightly, warmly wrapped in rugs and security.

Lady Crawleigh had organized everyone into attending, and Sarah was not entirely pleased to find herself ferrying Pansy to the bazaar. The girl had grown increasingly vivacious in the last year, and her manner now verged on the hysterical as she enlarged on the "simply divine" notion of the super-race.

As Pansy chirped on, Sarah glanced idly out of the car window. It was a long time since she had been this far out of the West End, and her stomach turned at the squalor of it all. It looked more wretched, more derelict even than she remembered. There were children clustered on doorsteps as there had been in her childhood days; white-faced, with big, shadowy eyes that dominated their features, and clumsy, handed-down boots that looked enormous below their sticklike legs. Some lacked even this protection, and their bare feet were raw and blue with cold.

At streetcorners men lounged apathetically, their necks pale and scrawny above their collarless shirts, arms folded against the biting wind. The leisure of the unemployed, the workless—"the existenceless," as Hitler had referred to them once, she recalled, in one of his earlier, saner speeches.

She saw a woman, young but furrowed and grayed into premature age, drag a child indoors, scolding drably. She shivered. Pansy said solicitously, "Are you chilly, Sassie? Have my rug."

Manny unloaded the boxes and signaled to Cyril to come out and help carry them in. Cyril was a good boy, a brother of a friend of Jonathan's, but he had to be told. Honest, but lacking in initiative. Still: for a manager, Manny had concluded early on, you wanted someone straight, but not brilliant. "If he's clever he'll try and be too clever and end by robbing you blind," he told Becky. Cyril had a cheerful, open face and guileless eyes. Manny's only fear was that the customers might rob *him*.

It was already late, and Manny looked—and felt—disgruntled. Was it asking too much to be left in peace to get on with his work? He never bothered anyone, but people seemed incapable of extending the same courtesy to him. If his *meshuggeneh* sister wanted to go off and shout at political meetings, good luck to her. That was her business. Now it seemed it had to be his business too. He sighed.

The shop was small, but well placed, with a window onto a busy street. Manny glanced around: shop number three. *Not bad*, he told himself, spirits rising, *for a boy who started out typing invoices on a broken typewriter and selling leftover biscuits.*

He was at the back of the shop checking stock lists when the man came in: young, neatly dressed, with a stiff white collar, brown suit, and a very short haircut.

"Can I help you?" Cyril asked politely.

The man looked around the shop, smiling pleasantly. "I may be in a position to help *you*." He did not notice Manny behind a rail of clothes. "Do you own this shop?"

"No."

"Ah. I thought not. Look, why don't you come along to our meeting this afternoon?" He handed Cyril a leaflet. "Not far away, Whitechapel. I think you might find it of some personal interest."

He pointed through the half-dressed window at a shop a few doors away, across the street. "You see that shop? Jewish-owned. *And* the greengrocers farther along."

Cyril stared at him, puzzled.

"It's time something was done. British shops should be British-owned. There's too much alien influence about. Why should you have the bread taken out of your mouth by Jews and foreigners? That's something we intend to take care of."

Manny came toward him from behind the clothes rail, a slow rage gathering, like a thickening in the blood, within him. "Oh yes? You'll take care of it, will you? How? Like your Nazi friends? Give me a for-instance how you'll take care of it, mister."

The man took in Manny's small, plump figure, his dark, rosy skin, and the look in his eyes. He backed casually toward the door. "It's nothing personal, you understand. But this is a small island. There's not enough room—"

"Oh I understand. Nothing personal. Well, you listen to me: *this* is personal. If I catch you sniffing around here again I'll give you a kick in the *tochis* that'll stop you sitting down for a week!"

The man had reached the door and he snatched it open. "You yids better watch out. You'll get your windows broken first and then your beaky noses!" He slammed the door and was gone.

Manny was breathing heavily, unevenly, and his face was scarlet. "Shut up shop, Cyril, for today. I don't want you here on your own."

Ruth came out of the hospital carrying a satchel stuffed with pink leaflets. Mordecai met her and they fell into step, walking fast and talking briskly. They were early for the meeting, but already people were gathering and they had to slow down. The crowd spilled off the pavement into the street, bringing traffic to a crawl. At one point Ruth shouldered her way through a knot of earnestly arguing Orthodox Jews, faces solemn beneath their black hats. She handed one of them a leaflet. He looked at it suspiciously, then threw it back at her. "Politics! We are not concerned with these matters!"

"You will be, brother," Ruth said warmly. "You just wait."

They walked on and she laughed suddenly as she saw Manny's stocky figure trotting toward them farther along the street. "There's my big brother. Mum insisted he must come along—to protect me!"

Mordecai, massive beside her, looked irritated. "She doesn't think much of me then. Wouldn't I be able to look after you?"

"Well," Ruth said honestly, "you might be so busy addressing the crowd that you wouldn't notice I'd been trampled underfoot."

He laughed, not altogether pleased. "You're not a damsel in distress, you're a modern woman. A worker. I expect more of you."

"Quite right," she agreed, her voice cheerful. But she glanced at her reflection in a shop window and flinched at the wispy-haired, baggy-skirted creature striding along so mannishly on her flat heels. In the shop window the dummies were sleek haired, with outrageous eyelashes. They wore brightly colored, clinging dresses of silky-looking material, and their legs, above their flimsy shoes, were silky too. She thought they looked vulgar and cheap and female. The last word took her unawares. They looked female. Their flesh and blood counterparts would smell of perfume and hang on their escorts' arms, pouting and giggling. She had passed some girls once who wore tiny bells on their garters that tinkled invitingly as they walked, drawing every man's eyes and thoughts to their thighs, their perfumed flesh.

She looked at the women in the street around her: grimy-handed, shabby, a vertical worry line etched permanently between their brows. That was reality. People living in hunger and fear; mothers unable to feed their children properly, even by going without food themselves. She felt reassured suddenly, and ashamed. How could she yearn—even briefly—for pampered femininity? The price was too high.

Mordecai led the way, pushing through toward the parked cars from which the speakers would emerge. There was a burst of cheering and some boos as a group of hard-faced young men surrounded the temporary platform, and then the first speaker appeared, acknowledging the cheers, his eyes flicking over the people to see where hostility was likely to come from.

At first the talk was innocuous, dwelling on unemployment, the economic crisis, international problems, America, the shortage of jobs for men eager to work. Gradually the tone changed. British workers were starving while foreign elements enjoyed the cream. Immigrants with powerful friends were infiltrating. Communists were undermining the very fabric of society. He spoke more plainly: "Communists and Jews, that's where the danger lies! Communist spies are everywhere, they want to destroy our way of life. They want to change Britain. They want to take over Britain for the Communists, and I ask you this: who was behind the Russian revolution? Jews! Karl Marx, Trotsky . . . look behind the Communist red flag and you'll find the Jew lurking. Pulling the strings. . . . You let one Jew into your business and before you know it, you'll be out of a job and his friends and relations will be in. These people are not British. . . . Just as Herr Hitler in Germany is doing so much to help the German workingman, so we want to help our people. Help the *British* workingman . . ."

Mordecai and his colleagues were at the front of the crowd by now, hemmed in by hundreds of agitated, shouting East-Enders. Manny stuck close to Ruth, who was yelling abuse at the speaker. The noise rose in a great jumbled roar; the heads bobbed and waved like a troubled sea. Manny was pressed so hard against a big, angry-faced man that his chin was scraped by the other man's coat buttons. Pandemonium, waving, jeering; rattles and placards and flags, and then someone threw a brick.

To Manny it seemed as though the brick had been a signal, for without warning a squad of military-looking young men appeared from somewhere and burst through the crowd like trained troops, striking out at hecklers, using knuckle-dusters and swinging heavy-buckled belts.

The crowd surged back from them in alarm, flinching, stumbling. There were screams; some men hit back. Ruth was shouting, "Filthy Fascist murderers!" when a fist crashed into her face, blood began to pour from her nose and she collapsed into Manny's arms.

"I'm sorry, Madam," Timms said, "there's nothing we can do. We're stuck. There's a ruddy meeting ahead, begging your pardon."

Pansy clapped her hands in delight: "Oh Sassie, can't we get closer? I'd love to see what's happening."

"I think we shall soon see what is happening," Sarah said dryly. "They seem to be moving this way."

The Bentley was at a complete standstill, in a line of traffic that extended to the corner and beyond. The rioting crowd surged back from the swinging fists of the unofficial keepers of the peace, mingling with hastily summoned policemen who were hampered by not knowing just who was fighting whom and therefore often getting hit by both sides. Surrounded by struggling figures, the cars were banged, jostled, and rocking dangerously as the mob gained a self-perpetuating fury.

Pansy was in an ecstasy of excitement: "This will really make the government take the problem seriously. Something will be done!"

Sarah gripped the grab handle beside her and felt a slow-rising nausea and faintness. *Something will be done!* She remembered the night of the Reichstag fire, and Goebbels—"Now we have to act!" She felt perspiration break out on her forehead and begin to trickle down her temples. Was she in London or was she in Berlin? Who was being hunted now? Was she safe, even in her steel car, her furs?

The fighting was all around them now, and one of the mob, catching sight of Pansy's rapt smile from within the gleaming car, turned and hurled something at them that crashed messily against the window. Sarah cried out in alarm, but Pansy said, "It's just an egg— the glass hasn't even cracked."

The angry faces, the hostile eyes, the shouting mouths were pressing in on them. The car was buffeted, bouncing from side to side on its chassis. Sarah gasped for air, not daring to open the window.

Thrusting inch by inch, using his head like a battering ram, Manny dragged Ruth through the crowd, half carrying her, astonished at her lightness. Around them the noise and the yelling still surged, and Ruth's face, covered with blood, was pressed into his shoulder. *And just today,* he thought, *I had to go and put on my new suit.*

If he could get through the traffic jam, on the other side he would be able to find a shop doorway, somewhere to let Ruth rest for a moment. He hauled her along, edging past one of the cars with a uni-formed chauffeur, a right *klutz*, at the wheel. Manny was stuck for a moment, slammed up against the warm, gleaming radiator. Two women were bouncing around in the back of the car all done up in fur. One was grinning like an idiot. The other was his sister Sarah.

There was time only for an amazed glance, and then the impetus of the crowd carried him on, toward the pavement. He shoved aside one burly laborer with a force that sent the man crashing into a lamppost. He needed suddenly to get away; his lungs were bursting.

Sarah reached for the door handle. She tried to call out, but as she sat forward she felt a stabbing pain low in her stomach, and the familiar sharp ache draining through her. "Timms," she began, and then Pansy saw the blood trickling down Sarah's legs, seeping onto the pearl-gray carpet beneath their feet.

"Oh, God, Sassie," she squawked, "your shoes will be ruined! How frightful!"

Leah shrieked, "She's dead!" as Manny helped Ruth in.

"Mum, she's walking. How can she be dead? I took a cab all the way. She'll be fine when we get her cleaned up a bit."

Without pausing in her exclamations of despair, Leah set out bandages, antiseptic, and hot water in a bowl and began to bathe Ruth's face and head. She had a cut on her scalp and a badly bruised face. Her nose was tender but not broken. "Hooligans! What do you want to go getting mixed up in political meetings for? It's your own fault, foolishness! You should be ashamed!"

Ruth had not spoken since she came into the house, but now she looked up at Manny and tried to smile, wincing as her split lip began to bleed again. Both of them were thinking of a faded photograph they had seen, years before, of a young, proud Leah, striding in a bunchy, long dress at the head of a ragged procession, holding a banner made out of her own red skirt.

"Such nonsense! Next time if you'll come back with your head broken or your teeth missing, don't expect sympathy from me!" Leah cried.

When the doorbell rang, Manny went to answer it and Mordecai pushed past him and into the kitchen without even a greeting. He looked at the basin of bloody water and Ruth's white, bruised face and then dropped to his knees. "I'm sorry—"

"What for? I should have taken better care of myself."

Clumsy in his bulky jacket, Mordecai held her hand. "I want you to go away, have a rest for a few days. The country—"

"I'd rather stay."

They talked with an odd intensity that made Leah and Manny feel uncomfortable. The front door slammed and Becky's clear, cheerful voice called, "So where's everyone? Debbie and I want some tea. It's freezing out!"

"Suppose I said I'd come too?" Mordecai said.

Ruth laughed. "Oh, something important would need your attention."

289

"Look. You're going to rest and that's an order."

Leah said harshly, "Mordecai, you may be an important man in the union, but you have no right to give Ruth orders."

Becky was in the kitchen doorway, taking off her rabbit-fur hat, her face glowing from the cold. Behind her, Debbie sat cosily in her pram. Becky looked at Ruth and Mordecai, and then at Leah. "Oh for heaven's sake," Becky said briskly, "they've been sleeping together for years now. That must give him some right!"

"Becky!" Manny was deeply shocked. In his entire life he could not recall anyone referring directly to sexual or bodily functions in Leah's presence. He avoided looking at his mother.

Leah had her hands in the hot water, squeezing the cloth. She stopped, frozen for a moment, and then mechanically went on squeezing and squeezing until the cloth was bunched tight and hard between her hands. She looked down at it in a kind of surprise, as though wondering what it was doing there. She looked dazed, almost stupid.

"I'm sorry, Mum," Ruth began, but trailed off as Leah's eyes flashed at her.

She put down the squeezed cloth on the kitchen table, emptied the bowl into the sink, watching the crimson water swirl around the white enamel. Then she dried her hands on her apron and walked out of the room without a word.

"Becky, you shouldn't have!" Manny muttered.

"There's too much hypocrisy in this house," Becky retorted. "No one ever wants to face up to the truth, and it seemed about time to let some in."

Ruth said, "She's very old-fashioned. I don't think she understands—"

"She's had five children hasn't she? She must have had some understanding somewhere along the line!" Becky gave a shout of laughter. "You give me a pain in the *tochis*, the lot of you. Now I'm going to have some tea."

Becky said, "You *volunteered*? Are you crazy?"

Leah added, "What do you want, you want to be a hero? Is that it? You want to get yourself killed? Go ahead, volunteer, be a dead hero, don't think about us."

Manny sighed. "I volunteered. But they wouldn't let me join up. I'm too valuable. I can make uniforms for other people to wear." He sounded miserable, and Becky, now that she knew he was safe from the call-up, felt a rush of sympathy. It was like a wedding invitation: you knew you'd hate the party when you got there, but if you didn't get invited you felt left out.

"Listen, love, it's not just the troops that win wars. If they say you're more valuable doing what you do, they know best. I mean, what do you know about fighting? Eh? But does anyone know more about the garment business? You'll give them the best uniforms they ever had!"

He smiled. "That's right." But he was deeply mortified. He had so wanted to do something, something direct, something physical to help. He was not a particularly brave or idealistic man, he knew that. But this country had taken his family in and given them safety. Nothing more; they had had to fight for a living, but the safety had been genuine. His mother's brother and sister had gone to Germany in the same spirit of trust and hope and their bodies had fattened the worms.

This is my country, he thought. *I was born here, I belong by right. I didn't even have to ask, like Mum and Dad, signing papers, worrying. I'm British.* Hitler must be stopped, and Manny had wanted to play a personal part in the stopping. But it seemed he was not needed.

"Volunteered? Oh John. Wasn't that a little—impetuous?" Mrs. Middleway looked reproachfully at her son. "The whole thing will be over by Christmas and you'll find yourself stuck somewhere quite frightful and won't get home for weeks."

"Too late now, I'm afraid. I'll be pushing off as soon as they give me the word. Anyway, I thought if you could keep an eye on Sassie . . . see she doesn't overdo things or get too wretched on her own . . ."

"My dear boy, we shall all be pulling together and so forth. At any rate your father will be pleased to hear what you've done. He's never really been happy about the Armistice, you know. I think he'll feel you're carrying on the good work where he left off. Not that I go along with him on that. Don't ever tell him, but I've always found the Germans perfectly charming, socially."

"I don't suppose I'll be meeting many socially, Mother."

"I suppose not. But John, could you try not to kill anyone—*personally*, I mean? It will all be over soon and really only governments win in these matters. It's rather like the law isn't it? You always say only the lawyers win every time. The soldiers seem to me to be the losers, whatever happens. Not that you'll be doing any actual, as it were, fighting, I hope?"

"I shouldn't think so," he said reassuringly. "Not as it were, personally."

When he was ready to leave, he and Sarah stood in the drawing room like people on a railway platform waiting for the train to leave, filling in the last moments that are too short to say anything of purpose and too long for silence.

"Will you be allowed to write?" she asked.

"Oh yes. Just chitchat, you know. We have to be careful not to say anything that could give away information. Even a remark about the weather can tell the enemy something under the right circumstances."

"I can see it's going to be an enthralling correspondence," Sarah said ironically.

"Personal comments are allowed. So I'll be able to tell you I love you and all that sort of nonsense."

"I shall enjoy that."

"And you," he said, smiling, "could say the same sort of nonsense to me. If you feel like it."

Sarah's dark eyes took on the flat, unfathomable look he knew so well, and he went on hastily, "And let me know how the garden's looking and so on. Tell me if the floribunda is up to scratch. Well . . ."

He kissed her formally on the lips, and then, unable to hold back, he began to kiss her eyelids, her brow, her throat, the corners of her mouth, with quick, gentle kisses, as though with each fleeting contact he would remember it the better, like a man drawing a beloved face in his mind by touching every hollow and curve before leaving it.

With a final kiss of her fingertips he went out, and Timms drove him away, and she found to her surprise that she was crying.

Afterward, when people talked about the war, Sarah found that their memories were quite different from her own. She was dimly aware of burning buildings and shattered streets, air-raid sirens and planes overhead, but she seemed to live out the months in a state of almost hallucinatory calm, waking fully only now and again for some particularly vivid moment, as when John came home for brief weekends, spoiling her and taking her out to five-shilling lunches at the Savoy.

John's parents tried to persuade her to join them in the country, but she insisted on staying in London. She was alone in the house now: Timms had gone, volunteering, then apologizing—"I hate to leave you in the lurch, madam." Then the other servants had been called up, to factories, or landwork, or the services.

She was aware of a creeping sense of dread, a feeling of apprehension that at first she could not define. Then it came to her that her life was going backward, like a cinema film run the wrong way. The discomfort was part of it: the appalling inconvenience of everything. No traveling, no servants, no gaiety, no Ascot or grand balls or amusing house parties. Worse, no *style*. Panache could belong only to the soldiers now, but that, too, was romanticism; battles were no longer fought with trumpets blowing and proud standards flying in the wind. And if the war were lost. . . . She saw herself, alone and naked, wandering the streets, a yellow star painted on her back that could be used, perhaps, for target practice by the occupying forces. There was no sure refuge after all. No stone to hide herself beneath. Like the rest she would end by dying as part of some perfectly rational plan. It would have been quicker to have gone to Buchenwald and ended it then. In Berlin she had begged the faceless men behind their desks to take her too, but quirkishly they had pushed her out, telling her to go home, to England. For the moment it had suited them that she should survive.

She took more and more to living in the basement, sleeping on a divan in the corner of the big kitchen. She brought down from the hall the big carved mirror that she had taken from Weimar to Berlin, and borne home to London, the only possession she had held on to to remind her of Ziggy and the family, a memento mori. The mirror was propped against the divan, and when she lay sleepless at night, her hand reached out to touch the smooth carving, as though to check it was still safely there.

She had never learned to drive, and there was in any case no petrol, but sometimes she curled up in the deep leather seats of the Bentley, wrapped in a rug, and dreamed she was on her way somewhere green and peaceful. Like the Crawleighs' place near Wales with the steep little hills of lush grass that looked like fields standing on their sides, and small sheep grazing calmly, leaning inward on the slope to keep their balance. Croquet on the vicarage lawn, sun through the beech trees, glittering on the shiny leaves and the feel of the smooth wood under her fingers, *click!* and the sense of being absolutely and totally happy.

Most nights she drank a large glass of whiskey so that she would sleep, for a while. There was a line in a Noël Coward song—"We can feel our living past in our shadowed present" that she heard on the radio, tears dripping into her whiskey glass while she listened. Oh, how her past lived, or rather those moments of her past that she permitted herself to remember.

She was not frightened. Even when the bombing was at its worst, night after night, unrelenting, she felt no panic. Death dropping out of the sky and striking at random seemed to her quite in accord with nature's larger cruelties. It was far less terrifying than lists drawn up by men, marked names, knocks on the door, and transport to places of detention and death.

She began going out by night, in the blackout, feeling her way through the crowds, enjoying a curious sensation of being part of a teeming, termite universe operating blindly, part instinct, part obedience to a general law. She had cut herself off from friends. Clothes no longer mattered, or food. She said as much to John's mother who had come to see her: "How could we possibly have spent all that time dressing and undressing; changing for dinner and worrying about the right gloves and shoes?"

Mrs. Middleway had looked at Sarah anxiously. She was thin and sallow and her clothes looked crumpled and dusty. She was not coming through all this very well. That was the trouble with bringing outsiders into the family: you never knew how they would behave under fire. "Well, dear, I know it seems very frivolous in some ways," she said, "but there is a certain discipline in keeping up standards. Even now, even with the shortages and the clothing coupons and everything, it is perfectly possible to keep oneself looking smart."

"I'm not interested in looking smart. I just want to be left alone."

It was in order to be left alone, to avoid even the minimal social obligations, that she had volunteered for war work. The man from the ministry was brisk: "Splendid! What can you do?"

"Well . . . I can use a sewing machine."

"Yes. Unfortunately, or fortunately, I should say—the factories turning out uniforms, parachutes, and so forth are fully manned at present. I'm afraid it looks like munitions."

The first morning she arrived at the factory neatly dressed, hair bundled inside the turban everyone wore now, and the foreman showed her where her smock was kept and where to sit. "You'll need to cut your nails. They'll get in the way. The belt moves at quite a lick."

The noise was bad—not just the clatter of the machines and the chatter of the women, shouting cheerfully to each other, but the radio blaring "Music While You Work" at them, an unrelenting stream of melody as mechanical as the conveyor belt grinding past. But worse than the noise was the smell. Sarah became aware that from every side, as the day progressed, the heat and movement released body odor that eddied round her almost visibly, like a yellow fog. She tried breathing through her mouth but began to imagine she could taste the smell as the stale air coiled down her throat.

The next morning she had a stiff whiskey before leaving home and drenched a scarf in eau de cologne, tucking it around her neck.

Each day it grew harder; the whiskey wore off more quickly. She sat, glazed and sickened, watching the large, steel spokes spinning toward her, each cradling a shiny container of death. As the belt moved past her, she just had time to tighten the screws, locking in the deadly contents before it moved on.

She tried to abstract herself from the scene. The women were alien to her; they laughed jovially and chattered and joked and slipped out for illicit smokes in the lavatory. For most of them, the life was no worse than they would have known in peacetime—better for some. "Gets you out," one said perkily. "You're not stuck in the ruddy kitchen all day."

Sarah watched them with a kind of hatred, despising them for their acceptance of what she had fought to escape from—a life confined to the basics of living—despising their sturdy lack of concern about the refinements that had come to mean so much to her. She did not feel *better* than they. She suspected that they were stronger and in some cases braver and certainly more honest than she was. Indeed she despised herself, but she knew with shaming certainty that their physical presence was deeply offensive to her.

"Workers' Playtime" on the radio. Break for lunch. Nausea in the canteen. A smell of urine and cheap tobacco in the lavatory that had her retching. The whistle for the afternoon shift.

The steel spokes spun, revolved, lowered their cases one after the other. Sarah's hands, covered with grease, moved automatically, the nails clipped short and black-rimmed. If she struck one of the shells with her wrench, would it explode, she wondered, hurling them all to the ground, blinding them, filling the air with the acrid smell of gunpowder? Would it kill her as it had her sister Miriam?

Gunpowder smelled better than stale sweat and damp tobacco and the metallic meaty odor of reheated food that rose from the canteen. In the kitchen, long ago, when she was scouring the pots, she had one day seen a scullery maid plunge her hand into boiling water so that she could escape the drudgery for a few days and enjoy the privilege of medical treatment. It had worked: the girl was put onto light duties—tea trays and flower vases.

She looked about dimly. They were all tied to the machine. If the machine stopped they could rest, go home. She no longer remembered her absurd desire to play some part in the war effort—that the machines meant the difference between fighting and losing, and what losing meant. The machine, the smell, and the noise, they were the enemy.

If, she thought dreamily, she were to thrust her hand into the spokes, surely that would clog the works for a minute, cause the machine to shudder to a halt, blocked with flesh. . . . Before she could think further, her hand holding the wrench shot out and into the twirling, skeletal drum.

Shriek of a whistle, scream of interrupted machinery. Silence. Everything black. Sarah returned to consciousness and a numbness that shattered abruptly as she attempted to move. Her hand was wrapped in dressings, and pain stabbed up her arm.

The welfare officer gave her a small glass of bitter liquid and went out of the rest room. The foreman stood by the door looking puzzled rather than angry. He was an elderly man with wispy hair and spectacles. He stood very straight, tapping his hand against his overall pocket. "You're very lucky," he said severely, "lucky this is a modern plant. That sort of accident could have cost you your hand. The emergency brake saved you. You can thank the emergency brake for saving your hand."

Bravo, emergency brake. Hand: thank emergency brake. She looked serenely at the foreman. "I suppose the machine will take a while to put right?"

He laughed. "Machine? Don't you believe it. It wasn't hardly stopped. Just for the minute while we got your hand out, and the wrench—*that's* badly bent," he added reprovingly.

So the machine had simply spat her out and carried on, barely interrupted. She felt tears trickling down her cheeks and wondered why. The foreman cleared his throat noisily. "Hurts a bit, I dare say. The doctor'll be here presently, give you something to help."

The doctor had black rings of exhaustion under his eyes, Sarah noticed. He had probably been up most of the night with bomb casualties—people in real trouble, not self-indulgent weaklings. Sarah began composing an apology, and noted that the doctor's hands shook slightly. *God, I'd hate to be having an operation now,* she thought, and laughed.

The doctor looked at her sharply. "Have you anyone at home who can help you? Your hand will be in plaster for a while."

"I can manage." Her head felt clearer than it had for weeks. She heard, faintly, the machine rumbling on.

Becky had tried sleeping on the Underground platform, wrapping Debbie in blankets and taking tea in a thermos flask, but it was not a success. "I like my own roof, even if it comes down."

When a roof two doors away did come down, they decided to leave London for a while. Leah, however, refused to join them. "No, thanks. I'll stay where I am. I know the shops."

"The shops!" Manny exclaimed. "What are you, a wholesale supplier? Who cares about the shops? Suppose you get bombed?"

"I don't like running from place to place. Hitler can't scare me with his bombs. He wants to make us run, the *momzer*, but I'm not running. It's different for you. You've got to think of Debbie."

So Manny and Becky and Debbie moved to Potters Bar, Leah moved into an apartment, and Manny went to London every day, to the factory. "At least keep an eye on Mum," he said to Ruth. "You've got a whole hospital you're practically running, and you're nearby."

"She won't talk to me, you know. She's never forgiven me."

"Ach!" Manny rubbed his head crossly. "Becky was crazy, telling her—"

"Anyway, it's all over now. Not that Mum'll ever believe that, of course."

Manny asked cautiously, "You never thought of getting married?"

"To *Mordecai*? Don't be daft. Mordecai cares too much about The People. Capital *T*, capital *P*. There's nothing left over for individual frivolity."

"Well, I'm asking him to keep an eye on Mum too."

"He's only an A.R.P. warden."

"No harm in dropping a hint, is there?"

Manny had a forceful way with a hint. Mordecai put the word out that he was to be notified at once if anything happened. He was just coming off fire-watch duty a week later when he got the telephone call. By the time he reached the scene, the local firefighters, ambulance men, and A.R.P. men were digging their way through the smoking rubble.

"Flying bomb," one said tersely, and carried on digging. One floor of the building had collapsed completely, crashing down into the story below. Mordecai joined the diggers. Clambering over great jagged shards of woodwork and mounds of broken bricks, he made his way toward where he knew Leah's apartment ought to be. He worked fast but efficiently, his face becoming blackened with soot and smoke.

Leah, crouched under her kitchen table, a saucepan still clutched in her hand, heard vague noises through the rubble that sealed her in; scratchings and scrapings, like rats behind walls. Her eyes, ears, and nostrils were clogged; her brain seemed filled with dust. She stayed very still, expecting at any minute that the table would give way and crush her.

The thought flitted across her mind that this time she was inside the building, that beyond those collapsed walls others were staring, running, digging. She might be about to die—like David, the life forced out of his small frame. Like Miriam, exploding in a sheet of flame. Someone would find her and lift her out. It hardly seemed to matter anymore. She felt herself slipping away, sensation growing fainter. Breathing was difficult; she seemed to be floating.

The light, flooding in through a hole in the wreckage, blinded her. She crouched like a mouse, bleeding, bruised, covered in a thick layer of white dust. A hand reached toward her, grasped her, and she moved, coming out shakily, the glare still dazzling her. When she saw Mordecai with the lights shining behind him, silhouetting his stocky figure, gleaming on his tin helmet, for a moment her heart leaped as it had when she watched him making his speeches on the bench in Poland. She tried to run toward him and found unaccountably that she could not. She fell forward into his arms, her eyes closed tightly to shut out the ruin of her home and the reality of her life.

Someone shouted, "Get her out, quick!" But there was no time. From behind the wall there was a rumbling, a vibration that grew louder. With a splintering crash the wall bulged and split. Mordecai heard the sound, but, before he could move, the masonry was hurtling toward them, chunks of wall torn out and sent flying by the pressure from above.

He had time only to swing Leah around, away from the wall, and fling himself over her—a human shield. Then the wall came down.

Comfortable in the hospital bed, Leah watched Ruth's authoritative progress down the ward with an amazed pride. She had made a decision: the past was the past. There were many episodes in life that were painful to think about. Some should be ignored, had to be ignored, if life was to continue. Ruth had much to be ashamed of, but Ruth was, after all, her daughter.

"That's my daughter," she told the neighboring patients, who were too ill to care.

Ruth grinned briefly when she reached Leah. "The doctor says you're doing fine. You'll be out of here in a couple of days—we need the bed."

"The bed you can have!" Leah retorted. "The way they tuck me in, what are they trying to do, make a parcel for posting?"

"Well, you'll be more comfortable in Potters Bar with Manny."

Forestalling protest she added rapidly, "We all have to do our bit. Don't you know there's a war on?" She moved away to the next bed.

In the entrance hall, a nurse directed Sarah to the ward: "Up the stairs—turn right—through the arch—along the corridor—second on your left down the ramp—you can't miss it."

She missed it. Peering hopefully through a glass porthole set into wooden swing doors, Sarah heard footsteps clicking past behind her and looked around. Ruth glanced up, checked her stride, and said, incredulously, "Sarah?"

They were uncertain how to greet each other, whether or not to embrace, and in the end the moment passed and they stood, not touching. The nurses hovered. Ruth handed her clipboard to one. "Carry on. I'll catch you up."

The little convoy moved on. Ruth studied her sister. "You look incredible. What is it—is it money, that makes you look so good?" The tone of genuine interest took the sting out of the words.

"Having one's husband home on forty-eight hours' leave does wonders for the grooming. You should have seen me last week!" They fell into step together. "How is she?"

Ruth shrugged. "Driving the nurses mad. Demands to see her own charts, takes her own temperature. She's fine. How did you know about it, by the way?"

"Manny phoned."

They reached the ward, and Ruth pushed the doors open. "Oh God, you've got a mass gathering I'm afraid."

Grouped around Leah's bed were Manny and Rebecca, an anxious-looking rabbi, and a well-dressed, gray-haired man. "Who is that, on the other side of the bed?" Sarah asked quickly.

"Oh, Oedipus, home on a visit." Ruth looked guilty. "That wasn't very nice of me. God knows, we've all got our funny ways." She raised her voice as they reached the bed. "Here's another visitor for you, Mum."

Leah stared at Sarah. Sarah waited, smiling, the tension sending a flood of color to her face. So often, in the past few years, Leah had envisaged some future meeting when Sarah would come begging forgiveness, falling to her knees, weeping. And Leah would raise her up, and forgive her, merely reminding her in passing that she had broken at least one and possibly two of God's commandments and that Leah hoped she had learned her lesson—a brief but forceful lecture that she felt would not be out of place. And now here was Sarah, slim as a boy, her face glowing, wearing a fashionable outfit, with box-pleats and square military shoulders, her legs shimmering silkily and her crocodile shoes matching her handbag.

To her surprise Leah saw that her daughter was beautiful. What she did not see was how like herself, when young, Sarah was. The narrow, imperious head, the wide brow, the heavy-lidded eyes, the coloring. A line from a poem came into her head: "The faint half-flush that dies along her throat." Never had she seen it in real life before, the delicate stain of a blush fading to paleness and ivory. *She looks like a queen!* Leah thought. Tears of pure pride welled up in her eyes and she held out her arms.

"Don't cry, Mother, please."

Leah's arms enfolded Sarah, stifling her, knocking her hat askew, almost crushing the breath out of her body. With difficulty she disengaged herself, straightened her hat, and smiled at Manny.

"Hullo, Manny . . ." She realized she had forgotten his wife's name, and she smiled apologetically at the plumply pretty woman. Becky was modeling herself on Betty Grable at the time, with a bang of frothy curls on her forehead. The nipped-in waist of her jacket was strained, emphasizing her slight tendency to overweight.

"You remember Jonathan, of course!" Leah said.

Sarah looked at the rabbi in amazement. He smiled and blinked at her shyly from beneath his black hat. He was her own age but he seemed to belong to a different century.

"How is your father?" she asked.

Jonathan's kindly smile faded. "I believe he is progressing well."

Manny said hastily, "Mordecai was injured, helping get Mum out—if it hadn't been for him, she wouldn't be here now. He's got a broken shoulder and cracked ribs."

Jonathan broke in, "I have to go back . . . people to visit. . . ." He nodded at them vaguely and went off, his black coat flapping.

"He's a good boy," Leah remarked without enthusiasm.

Becky said brusquely, "He works so hard, always helping after air raids, he's ever so brave really."

"Mordecai should see him." Leah's voice was severe.

"Mum," Manny said reasonably. "Mordecai is a committed atheist. You bring up his son to be a rabbi and then expect them to be inseparables?"

"No, but still . . . he could show some affection."

"He hasn't the time," Ruth commented dryly, and then there was an awkward silence.

Becky said, "We brought you a banana. I couldn't believe it—the greengrocer wrapped it in tissue for me." She laid it on Leah's bedside table and eyed it longingly.

The gray-haired man had walked away to the other end of the ward to put some flowers in a vase. Now he wandered back, and Sarah recognized him.

"Simeon!" Her voice was warm.

They shook hands, his slow smile broadening. "You remember me then. How very gratifying."

Ruth patted Leah on the shoulder. "Lucky thing. . . . Family and friends all around you. Well, I must go. I'm late for my round."

They watched her striding away down the ward, erect, confident.

Becky smoothed her tight jacket down over her hips. "We should go too, we mustn't make you tired."

Sarah looked again at Leah. She was very thin and her face was bruised and lacerated, but the long eyes were as glittering and lively as ever. Her hands, which Sarah remembered as slim-wristed and grace-ful, had suffered over the years. Almost as though reading her thoughts, Leah moved them quickly, placing them under the bedclothes.

"What are you doing, Simeon?" Sarah asked. "Something fright-fully important, I'm sure."

"Quite right," he said gravely. "Certainly far too important to talk about!"

"It was wonderful of you to find the time to come!" Leah was too fond of Simeon to find it the least bit surprising that he should bother to keep up the old friendship. He took her hand in both his own, for a moment, and then stepped away slightly. Leah hugged Manny and allowed herself to be hugged by Becky.

"Can I give you a lift somewhere?" Simeon asked Sarah.

"What! You've got petrol?" Becky exclaimed.

"It's an official car. I am, in fact, on my way to a meeting . . ."

"That would be lovely," Sarah said, "as long as I don't take you out of your way."

The goodbye ritual was as awkward as the arrival. Manny in-stinctively respected Sarah's reticence, simply giving her arm a quick, affectionate squeeze. Becky floundered between resentment and admiration. Leah said, optimistically, recklessly, "Don't be a stranger." Simeon led Sarah out as Manny gave Leah another farewell kiss.

In the car Sarah said, "Look. I ought to tell you, today was special. I thought. . . . Well, anyway, I came. But for future reference, Simeon, I have no family. They are strangers to me. It's best to let it stay that way. That's how I want it to be."

He nodded, the heavy jowls screwed into a wry grimace. "A pity in a way. I sympathize, of course. I couldn't bear my own family. They seemed to personify everything I disliked—most unfortunate!"

"There you are then!"

"And yet . . . you cannot ignore. . . . There's something in the blood. The blood link is like a piece of elastic that is infinitely stretchable. You move away, or they move away, you build your life, you rise, you forget them, deny them, and then when you least expect it, snap! You're jerked back, involved."

"That may be so for you. You're nicer than I am. It won't be like that for me, I promise you."

She tapped on the glass division and the car stopped. The driver got out and opened Sarah's door. She took Simeon's vast hand. "I always admired you so much. You were so brilliant. You rose above it all."

"*On doit se défendre*, my dear. When one looks as I do, to be brilliant is the least one can do!"

She got out, waved, and the car moved on.

Alone, Simeon slumped in the corner of the seat, his face sagging into a scowl of depression. He moved in influential circles and was at the center of events, but he had never achieved a simple act of heroic daring. Not for him the snatching of the heroine from the burning building or the killing of the dragon. No romantic broken shoulders for him. If *he* had tried to rescue Leah he would probably have tripped over a beam and fallen flat on his face.

The car appeared to be crawling along. At this rate he would be late for the meeting. He pressed the switch of the glass partition, intending to snap irritably at the driver. But habits die hard. "George, my dear fellow," Simeon said gently, "if I wanted to get there a little early, do you think you could manage that for me?"

George beamed. "Right, guv." He pressed the accelerator. *A lovely man, Abrahams*, he thought. *Never a cross word.*

Manny tried to keep the worst of it from Leah by hiding newspapers, switching off dangerous broadcasts. But she learned the facts, like everyone else. She learned the names of the death camps, the methods of extermination, the numbers murdered. Appalling but distant facts to most people. Not to those, however, who could see themselves behind that barbed wire, feel the weight of those emaciated corpses pressing down their own bones. Chance had dictated their various paths, one leading to an island sanctuary, the other to a barbed-wire en-closure, a cattle truck, a gas oven, a mass grave.

"It could have been us," Leah said.

Even Manny's irrepressible optimism faltered in the face of the evidence. Like these people, he had committed the offense of existing. Unlike them, he had survived. This time. But the danger the next time, where would it come from? And how should it be faced? There was no real safety anywhere.

In England, with its small social cruelties, its cultivated wariness of foreigners, there was at the same time a sense of fair play that to Manny seemed in no way paradoxical: if a man put his energies, his brains, and his loyalty into the country, he was allowed, albeit grudg-ingly, to become a part of it. It would take time and hard work, but he felt that the weaving together of the strands had already begun.

"Nuremberg?" Sarah asked. "You're going to Nuremberg?"

For her the name meant mass rallies, the decrees for the protection of German blood and honor, Hitler's voice screaming over the radio. But Hitler was dead, and Nuremberg, supreme irony, was ready for the day of judgment, for other voices to be heard.

She had barely grown accustomed to peace, to the beneficence of John's presence, the shy humor that hid behind the assiduously culti-vated blandness of his public personality, before she learned that he

304

would be gone again, and to Nuremberg. Curious to think that without knowing it he would be helping to avenge her dead.

Even now she still remembered the exact moment of opening the letter. Often at the edge of sleep, or engaged on some mundane task, she would find herself reliving the moment—tearing open the envelope, heart thudding, looking for and finding no name, the thin paper rustling under her shaking fingers in the stuffy little Berlin hall. She had the letter still, folded and unfolded so often that one day it fell apart in her hands. Piecing it together she could still read the slanting, hurried writing of the unknown man, the lines sloping crooked down the page— ". . . Your cousin taught a Polonaise to the two children and told them that when they were frightened, they should sing it inside their head, over and over, whatever was happening. I saw them last in what is called the hospital hut. On a good day it holds about seven hundred people, on a bad day nearly twice that number. The dysentery is very bad, and there are operations—" Here, some words scratched out, the ink splattering. "There is another hut, behind the hospital, and, since the typhus, each night the bodies are moved out so that the cremation cart can take them away in the morning. Each day perhaps a hundred die, but always there are new ones to take their place. . . . Through the wire it is possible to identify some of the bodies . . . I tell you these things so that you will know there is nothing, no one to keep you in this country, this country that was so fine, so great."

All of them gone, rotting with typhus, into the hut, the cart, the cremation pit. But in Nuremberg, now, the crime would be answered for.

In London life slowly returned. The scars of the city began to heal. In Nuremberg, the stench of death hung over the drab courtroom as the files were opened and the festering places gave up their secrets, in simultaneous translation.

The chief American prosecutor's voice was unemphatic, flat, ". . . national socialist despotism equaled only by the dynasties of the ancient East . . ." A chair scraped, men shifted, someone blew his nose. ". . . At length, bestiality and bad faith reached such excess that they aroused the sleeping forces of imperiled civilization."

John wrote daily to Sarah. Before he went to bed, at the leather-topped desk, he tried to empty his mind of the searing details of the day's evidence. They were dealing in statistics of degradation and inhumanity that seemed at first unbelievable, then unendurable, even in the listening. He wrote to Sarah about the view from his window, or a bird seen behaving absurdly in the hotel garden; a bare tree caught against the sunset, or a snowfall.

She wrote back with unexpected news: "I am pregnant! Astonishing. I had not expected another chance after the last episode. The doctor —a new man—says with delightful originality that I must take care of myself!!! Do you suppose they have a phrase book of suitable things to say to expectant mothers? Don't worry, I shall take care of myself. I would rather like to have this baby. Wouldn't it be a nice welcome home for you? I wonder if you know how much I miss you. . . ."

Now his letters were sprinkled with advice about watching out for loose stair carpet, avoiding hot baths, heavy parcels. Each day the tribunal reached further into the files of the Third Reich, the subjects of the inquiries: domination, death. And at night, John scribbled to Sarah about calcium in the diet and the importance of resting with the feet higher than the head. He renewed acquaintance with life.

The dangerous weeks passed with no miscarriage. Sarah's pregnancy reached its final weeks and she packed a suitcase as instructed, ready for the time her contractions would begin. There were servants at Stanhope Terrace again; people came to tea. Life seemed normal, and Sarah felt unworried. The labor would be painful of course, but as her gynecologist pointed out, "Pregnancy is not a *disease,* Mrs. Middleway."

A week before the arrival date, she woke in the night to find the bed soaking, and in the darkness she lay for a moment of horror, unable to move, thinking she was bleeding. But it was only the water breaking early, and she telephoned the hospital to say she was on her way.

She had read books on self-help in childbirth and found to her surprise that the breathing exercises that had seemed so absurd practiced in her bedroom did help. Her response to the sharpening discomfort was confident; she surprised nurses accustomed to noisier reactions.

"Is this your first baby?" one asked. "I'd never have known it, you're being so good."

She pushed when instructed and did her best to fulfill her part of the proceedings. At midnight the child was born—a girl, delicately formed, with silky dark hair. She lived until morning.

Manny yelled into the telephone, "It's a boy! Becky's fine, everything's fine! Listen, Benjamin, tell everyone at the factory they can have the rest of the day off. . . . Well, there's a good half-hour left, isn't there? With my compliments!"

He began dialing another number, puffing happily on his cigar.

Becky waved her hand protestingly, and Leah at once stepped in. "Enough! Go home, make your phone calls somewhere else. Becky needs to rest."

Becky, radiant and slightly complacent, was looking through estate agents' leaflets. "Manny, here's a house in Finchley with a swimming pool. What d'you think?"

"Certainly! The children will drown, I'll rupture myself clearing out the leaves, and three times a year it'll be warm enough for us to have a dip. Swimming pools. Great idea, you got any more like that?"

The baby lay asleep in a cot at the foot of the hospital bed. *A thin baby*, Manny thought. "You'll need a bit of fattening up, Joseph my boy. I don't want to worry about breaking your bones if I give you a bit of a *klop!*" he said, pinching the baby's cheek.

Not that there would be any real fights, of course. Not with his son, his flesh. Neither God nor any other idea would come between him and his son. His son would grow up to be . . . better than Manny; he would be proud to have the child surpass him. It would be good to have an ally, a strong arm, a son who would know things that had been beyond his own reach.

"Hey, Becky," he said from the door, "shall I put him down for Eton?" He went out, chuckling with delight. Next week, the circumcision, the formal covenant with God—all very nice. But his own covenant with the child was already made.

It was Benjamin who bought the first building: a dilapidated house in Shepherd's Bush. Then he offered Manny a half share.

Manny was baffled. "Okay, it was cheap. So you're offering me fifty percent of a *cheap* disaster. What d'you want to do, ruin me?"

"Have I ever been wrong?" Benjamin demanded. "When we started with the shops didn't I say we should increase the factory? And wasn't I right? I'm telling you: I have an idea."

"Ideas are ten a penny, Ben. Every day I throw away more ideas than cigar butts. An idea has to *work*."

Benjamin showed him the map: "Here and here and here. Streets full of old rubbish, half of them bomb-damaged, ready to fall down if you sneeze. Nobody wants them."

"You amaze me."

"Listen. We buy up the old rubbish, house by house. Dirt cheap. No competition. Then we start sneezing. Demolish. Develop. And wait."

"Go on."

"That's it. What happens to everything in the whole world? It gets more expensive. We just have to stay ahead of the rise."

"I'm in the clothing business, Ben. Not the building business."

"You're in *business*."

"What do I know about buildings?"

"What did you know about shops? About factories? About fashion? Did that stop you? You employ experts. They know. All you have to know is how to raise the money."

Manny looked at the map again. He drove around London. He looked. He asked questions. He did sums. Then he went back to Benjamin. "Okay, we're in business. But you can't maintain a fifty-percent share, Ben. You haven't got the capital. Who are you trying to fool?"

"I wondered if I'd get away with it."

"No chance. But you'll do all right. I'll look after you."

The buying program was launched: a house, two houses, a street. . . . Manny began sleeping badly; he suffered from indigestion now, and stomach cramps. He got shingles. He was landing himself progressively deeper in debt in the expectation of a growing demand. Suppose there was no demand?

The first building was completed, a toothpaste-tube carton standing on its end. Economical, unimaginative, ugly. It was snapped up at once. Customers clamored for the next. The slow upward spiral had begun.

One Friday night Manny opened a bottle of champagne—"I asked for the sweetest they'd got, so it should be good."

"What are we celebrating?" Becky asked.

He clinked glasses with her. "We're celebrating our future. Becky my love, we're on our way. Time you got yourself a better mink."

What d'you want for your birthday?" Manny asked. "A camera?"

"I've got a camera, thank you," Joe said.

"Well what about a radio?"

"Can I have an outing?"

Manny gave an approving shout of laughter. "He's eight and already it's the social life. All right. Saturday will be Jo-Jo's day. What d'you want to do?"

Breathless with excitement, Joe whispered, "A day in the country."

Manny looked disappointed. "Wouldn't you like a proper treat—lunch in a good restaurant, then a film or—"

"A day in the country!"

"Tell you what—"

"A day in the country!"

Rebecca gave Manny a look that said, "You and your big mouth."

Manny shrugged. "Well, if that's what the boy wants—"

"Yes, yes!" Joe begged.

"Right. A day in the country."

It started badly, with a low, gray sky threatening rain. "Maybe we should make it another day," Rebecca suggested, but Manny saw Joe's face go tense and said heartily, "No, no. Let's get on with it—it'll probably brighten up later."

They packed into the car and set off, Deborah looking bored. Manny was driving the car himself, to give the day a family intimacy.

"I thought we'd have lunch in High Wycombe," he said, swerving to avoid a keep-left sign.

"Where Disraeli made his speeches?" Joe asked.

"Was it?" They drove on.

"Is this the country?" Joe asked.

"Well, of course it is—it's all country around here, can't you tell?"

"I hope we won't get back too late," Deborah muttered. "I'm expecting a telephone call."

"Oh?" Rebecca frowned. "Who from?"

"A friend."

"What friend? Do we know this friend?"

Manny roared, "Will you stop that! How can I concentrate on driving with you bickering in the back? Relax! Enjoy the scenery!"

Joe looked out at the scenery: the road was very wide. What green could be seen was almost gray from the dust, and everywhere there were glimpses of houses and other roads. "When do we get to the country?" he asked.

"This *is* the country, *boychick*," Manny assured him. "Look at all the trees and bushes! Cows, sheep, what more do you want?"

"I thought we'd stop in a field, have a walk . . ."

"Right! We'll pull in somewhere—"

"Manny, I don't want to go getting my shoes muddy—" Rebecca said.

"It's okay. We'll stop somewhere dry. Don't get so worried."

He drove on, looking for somewhere to park. After about twenty minutes he saw it: a lay-by, dry gravel, and next to it, fields with trees at the edge and even a stream running along one side. He pulled in and braked violently. Cars never seemed to behave properly with Manny at the wheel. It must be something to do with coordination, he decided.

"Right. Here's your countryside, Jo-Jo."

"Can we go for a walk?"

Deborah groaned, and Manny said placatingly, "I'll take him. You can stay in the car with Mum and listen to the radio. There's a box of chocolates in the glove compartment."

They got out and walked over to the field. Manny struggled with the gate for a moment or two, getting red and impatient.

Joe said, "I think it's fastened here," and undid it. They set off, following the stream around the field.

"Look at that tree!" Manny exclaimed. "What a size, what a color!" He was determined to get into the spirit of the thing.

"Yes. It's an elm."

"Is it? How d'you know?"

"I've got a book." Joe stopped and knelt down, peering into the stream.

"Don't go getting your trousers dirty or Mum'll never forgive me," Manny said, not altogether joking. "What are you looking at?"

"Just the stream." There was a fish, lying close to the bottom, motionless, blending in with the sand and the pebbles; Joe watched him intently and swished his fingers through the water. The fish seemed barely alive—by his stillness, the way he took on the texture of his surroundings, he became almost invisible. A good trick.

With his face very close to the surface, hardly breathing, Joe felt as though he were a part of the stream. Was he watching the fish or was the fish watching him? As he gazed down, crouching, very still, he seemed to enter the stream, touch each frond, feel the ripple of the water flowing over him, cool. . . . He became stream and fish and pale pebbles. . . .

310

Manny glanced at his watch. He coughed, then glanced again at his watch. "Well . . ."

Joe got up at once and they walked on. They stopped for a moment when Joe came upon a trail of ants and squatted down to examine them, but this time Manny had had enough.

"You're not going to stand there looking at a bunch of ants! Ants we have at home in the garden; you can see ants any day. What's special about ants?" They walked briskly around the field in silence, Manny restlessly jingling the small change in his pocket.

Rebecca said, "Well! You took your time."

"The boy wanted to see some countryside, didn't he? Okay Jo-Jo, can we go now, have you seen enough of the country, can we have a bit of lunch now?"

Manny spoke cheerfully, but somewhere inside him there was a tiny spot of desolation. He could not say what had caused it, and it would go away in a moment, but for a fleeting instant he recognized it as a sense of disappointment.

Joe's small face was expressionless. He nodded. "Yes, thank you," he said politely.

Life is a series of deaths before the final day's dying, Manny had read somewhere. He felt now, as he glanced quickly at the boy's closed face, a tremor, a death in the heart.

The school was a rambling, Georgian country house, swagged with wisteria and climbing roses. Against the white-painted casements its rosy brick was almost velvety, with a faintly sooty patina.

Joe stood waiting with his classmates for the bus to the railway station, the gray uniform giving him the stereotyped neatness of the prep-school boy: socks unsagging to the knee, tie precise, shoes polished, blazer buttoned, and, under the school cap, hair cut and brushed to seal-skin smoothness. The group of boys chattered and whistled and hopped from one foot to another, jiggling, fidgeting. They tugged aimlessly at each other's clothes and caps, constantly shifting and bobbing like small pink-and-gray birds.

"What are you doing in the hols, Joey?"

"I think we'll be in Cannes for a bit. We usually are. You?"

"Oh, Devon as usual. I loathe Devon. I hate the beach. I detest swimming, and I can't bear sunbathing. And they still pack buckets and spades for us. It's pathetic. I have tried to tell them, but they don't seem to hear me. Have you found that?"

"Oh yes. My father's awfully good at that. It's very trying."

"Parents are ghastly on the whole. Still, one only has to put up with them in the hols, and at Christmas there's all the grub and presents and so forth—so one mustn't grumble, I suppose."

"I suppose not," Joe agreed.

On the train he pondered the holidays ahead. Summer was the worst: weeks and weeks to be gotten through. He gazed out of the window: soft greens and browns and curves everywhere, rising and dipping, not a piece of concrete in sight. He would miss all this, during the summer. At school the country was all around him. If he climbed up onto the roof above the dormitory (strictly forbidden, of course), he could turn a full, slow circle, and see nothing but trees and fields, unbroken sky above.

School had its cruelties, its bigotry and harshness, but not all the time, and at school he felt himself the hub of a green universe, a spinning, soothing wheel with him at its center. But during the holidays the wheel was abandoned, and the world became angular: England shrank to a web of streets, and even France, glimpsed mistily from the plane window, was reduced to grand hotel architecture and the geometric formality of beach umbrellas, striped mattresses, and deck chairs.

He could read of course. He always did. But between books he would have liked someone to talk to, someone to listen.

Rebecca was at the railway station to meet Joe with the car— "Aren't you dying to see the house? Aren't you excited?"

"Yes," Joe said politely. He patted the leather upholstery. "New car, I see."

"It's just for running around, shopping, you know—" She glanced at him as she put the car into gear: he was looking well, though pale. But she felt uneasy, as always, when they were alone together. She never knew what to say to him. When she spoke, she felt her voice was too loud; when she introduced a subject, it was like playing ball with someone who kept pocketing the ball and walking away: You were left standing there with your hands out. And yet he was a nice boy. Not spoiled, nor a whiner like some children she knew. But she wished they were closer. She regretted yet again that she had been so busy when he was a baby, that she had had to leave him so much, but things were tough after the war, with Manny having his hernia operation, and after that there was Palestine and raising money for the refugees—all the excitement and hope. How vivid those days seemed, even now, full of possibilities, working day and night to help the ones who had come back from the dead.

And then there had been the bitterness, Mordecai going off grim and angry—"The bastards aren't going to let us just step ashore and make ourselves at home, you know. Our people are going to need organizing, need a little strong-arm assistance."

"God almighty, more fighting?" Manny had groaned.

"Who knows? In an ideal world the British would keep their promises, and the Arabs would treat us like brothers, and we could sail into Palestine singing the *Ha T'ikva*. But as it is . . ." he shrugged. "I'm prepared for anything." Soon after that he got a broken arm from a British soldier's rifle butt.

"Again broken bones," Leah said flatly. "First the Czar, then the Germans, now the British. Is there never to be any peace? Any safety?"

Rebecca had listened to all the talk, and for the first time she began to think about a larger design to life, about how things were and why they should be so—about yesterday and tomorrow. She wanted, ached to be part of this new stream she felt herself drawn into. But there were others with more to give—all Rebecca could contribute was her energy, her enthusiasm. So gradually it became a matter of charity dinners and raffles.

Beside her in the car she became aware of Joe winding the window down a few inches, trying out the handle. "All right, Jo-Jo?"

"Fine," he said, with a reassuring smile. He wished he could think of something to say to her. He had heard other boys chatting away to their parents—there must be something wrong with him. He seemed to live inside a glass bell that sealed him off from them. He could see them, even hear them, but he felt nothing. He supposed they could sense this and it made him feel helpless and guilty.

"We've done so much to the house—we put in a proper drive and a new front door and we knocked two rooms into one so there's a bit of space to breathe, and the kitchen—"

"What's the garden like?"

"Very nice. We laid down a lovely patio at the back, and there's a barbecue pit. There was a great big tree but it shadowed half the garden so we had to cut it down."

Even though he told himself nothing could surprise him, Joe was taken aback by the new house.

"We brought your grandmother over and d'you know, she cried!"

Joe had not suspected Leah of such good taste.

"She cried like a baby," Rebecca said affectionately. "She said it was like a dream come true . . ." She looked at the ormolu clock on the mantelpiece. "Darling, I have to dash, I'm due at the hairdresser, I'll hear all your news at dinner."

Manny was on the telephone until they were all seated at the table. Joe could hear him shouting instructions, and he looked irritated when he came into the room. He hacked himself off a piece of rye bread and looked at Joe, his expression softening. "So what's your news, Jo-Jo? How's school?"

"Breast or leg, darling?" Rebecca asked Joe.

"Leg, please."

"*I* want the leg!"

"Deborah, pass your brother the gravy and don't carry on. To-night he'll have the leg." She glanced at Manny. "You were on the phone long enough."

"That *shlemiel*! I employ accountants and have to do their thinking for them!"

Joe stared down at his plate, drawing gravy pictures with his knife.

"Jo-Jo! You're so quiet. Aren't you glad to be home? What d'you think of the house, not bad, eh? So. How's school?"

Joe shrugged and waggled his head, but he was saved from having to reply. Manny was already asking Rebecca what *her* day had been like. And not listening.

As Joe had predicted, they went to Cannes, staying as usual at the Carlton, which Manny said offered a very nice class of beach. They arranged themselves on their mattresses, neat as sardines in a tin. The beach attendant made sure Manny and Rebecca were fully shaded by the umbrella; tilting it to just the right angle, he pocketed his tip and strolled off. Joe noticed him pause and move two mattresses a few inches, to bring them into line with the rest.

"Ah . . ." Manny lay back and closed his eyes. "Peace . . ."

Farther along the beach a young boy in white shorts and T-shirt was loping, weighed down by a bag holding newspapers. He called, tonelessly, *"Express . . . Telegraph . . . Daily Mirror . . . Express . . . Telegraph.. . . Daily Mirror . . ."*

Manny leaped up. "May as well see what's happening, eh?" He waved at the boy and wandered over, jingling his coins. Joe watched him buy the paper, glance at the headlines, and then stop, reading intently. After a few seconds he hurried back, stepping over beach sandals and bodies while he continued to read.

He threw the paper down in Rebecca's lap. "Look at that! Marvelous, isn't it! There's going to be trouble now. Big trouble. They'll have to do something."

Rebecca read the front page. "I never trusted him anyway. Still, it may not be so bad—"

"What d'you mean, 'not so bad'? Of course it's bad. Nasser has nationalized the bloody Suez Canal. Don't you see what that means? With him in control of the canal, where does that leave Israel?"

He flung himself down on his mattress, all holiday ease gone, and continued the argument. Joe read the front page over his shoulder. Well: whatever else Nasser had done, he had certainly enlivened the holiday.

". . . I'll tell you where it'll leave Israel," Manny barked. "Up the creek! And Britain too if we don't do something. If Eden lets them get away with this we'll be finished. A laughingstock."

The bright gold sunlight poured down onto the beach, glittering on fashionable sunglasses and gold chains around the necks of the bronzed young Frenchmen who were casually leering at Deborah's exposed opulence. But for Manny, Suez had cast a shadow over the holiday, one that prevented him from relaxing. He heard Joe explaining the headline story to Deborah, accurately, but in the elaborately phrased style the school inculcated. He found it gratingly pompous. Already in bad humor, he cut in crossly on Joe: "What d'you mean, 'propinquity'? Why can't you talk normal English like anyone else?"

Without waiting for an answer, he added, "I'm going in for a swim. It costs a fortune to come here and then we all lie and look at the sea and no one goes near it. You coming?"

"I rather think I'll stay here and read, thanks, Dad."

Joe watched his father trot the few yards to the water's edge and stand, staring down as the clear, tideless water nibbled his toes. Manny was wearing a pair of striped swimming trunks, and the paunch he was already developing strained the firm material. Joe suspected that for his father the anticipation, the planning, the *idea* of a holiday were the best part. After that, it was all anticlimax.

Having gotten his feet wet, Manny was unsure what to do next. In fact he did not particularly feel like a swim, but, having made the statement, he could hardly get out of the action without looking like a fool.

He stared at the sea. Once, a long time ago, he recalled going to the seaside in England with his parents. He had few tender memories of his childhood, but suddenly he was flooded with the remembered sweetness of that perfect day. They had gone to . . . Southend, that was it. In the train, green and gold countryside sliding past, amazing him. And his sisters had splashed and paddled and laughed. And Chaim, for once not frowning over the sewing machine, not bent over a book, had laughed too.

Had they built a sandcastle? Certainly they had sat on a bench and had a picnic. . . . A girl passed him, wearing a skimpy bikini, licking at an ice-cream cone which melted, glistening, in the blazing sun. Manny smiled. That smell of vanilla, that was part of it. They must have eaten ice cream too. What a day that had been! August Bank Holiday 1914. . . . He had been three and a half years old. Suddenly he remembered the date of the trip, and what it meant: of course—the next day war was declared. Funny, he couldn't remember anything about that at all.

He waded into the warm sea, his feet displacing the fine, soft sand. He could not actually swim, not properly, not out of his depth. But he felt it was only right to use the sea, enjoy the amenities. He looked back at the beach. Rebecca was now reading the *Daily Express*: in the black swimsuit she looked very shapely, her hair carefully swathed in a chiffon scarf. Deborah seemed to have fallen asleep, and Joe—what was Joe doing? Manny narrowed his eyes to see more clearly. Joe was looking through his binoculars, out at the water. Not, as Manny could see for himself, that there were any interesting ships or anything to look at—just a small, green island.

Apart from missing the countryside, Joe preferred St. Paul's in London to his boarding school. He had approved of it the moment he caught sight of the warm red brick, the lawns and trees. He felt reassured by the place: the spirit of those long departed still populated the corridors and odd corners. It radiated a casual, crowded well-being. It also accommodated a healthy minority of Jewish boys who appeared to thrive on the vegetarian lunches they were allocated to avoid any dietary problems. There were Jewish prayers every morning, and there was also something called Jewish gym that took place while the cadet corps drilled and marched and acquired military skills, but this was a quite unofficial name, since not all anticorps boys were Jews—"Though," as one of them pointed out, "all Jewish boys do seem to be anticorps—it's individualistic obstinacy, I expect."

Each morning the chauffeur dropped Joe at school and collected him at the end of the schoolday. "How was it, then?" Danny inquired one afternoon, passing him an apple. "Did you get them equations sorted out?"

"Yes, I suddenly got the hang of them."

"Course you did. Just takes a little time. Concentration, that's the thing to remember. Concentrate your mind. One thing at a time. Half the failures in life are what they are not because they lack the talent, no: they lack the concentration. You can't do two things at once."

"But Danny, you drive and you listen to me."

"Yes, and I'm a bleedin' failure, ain't I? Proves my point."

They rode in comfortable silence. Joe enjoyed Danny. He was restful, he only gave advice when asked, and he actually listened. Joe wondered what Manny paid him. Danny was easygoing, and while Manny would never deliberately cheat anyone out of anything, he saw no reason to pay more than he needed to.

The following day in English there was a new man in the classroom. "Standing in for Whiskers, apparently," Joe's neighbor informed him. "He's gone down with mumps, poor swine."

"You're reading *Brighton Rock*, I believe. Will you," the master nodded at a boy, "carry on." McEndrick began to read: "Mr. Colleoni came across an acre of deep carpet from the Louis Seize writing room, walking on tip-toe in glacé shoes. He was a small dark Jew with a neat round belly—"

"Sir," another boy said, "my copy's different. Mine just says 'a small dark *man*.'"

The master raised his eyebrows. "Really? I suppose it's a different edition. Anyway, it's just a description. And it's obvious the man's a Jew."

Joe asked mildly, "How is it obvious, sir?"

The master looked nonplussed. "Well . . ." he looked hard at Joe, and reddened. "Well, the *name*," he said firmly.

Joe looked increasingly interested. "But Colleoni—isn't that an Italian name, sir?"

The master was feeling hot and uncomfortable. He was extremely glad this was a temporary appointment.

"Yes, sir," piped up another little horror, "over the page it says, 'his Italianate features'—"

"Oh sir, mine doesn't, mine says 'his *semitic* features'—"

"Shall we move on? Did you note that awfully good bit of description about how Colleoni 'clinked as he walked. It was the only sound he made.' Isn't that excellent? Doesn't that conjure up exactly that sort of . . ." he paused, ". . . *moneyed* person?"

Does it? Joe wondered. He thought it could conjure up different things to different people. Manny had a way of jingling coins in his pocket; it was a mannerism he had. Did that give him the "clink" of a moneyed person quite obviously to be despised? But if Manny had no coins, he jingled his keys—he had even been known to rattle pebbles in extremis. Joe found it irritating, but he had never thought of it as sounding "moneyed." Anyway, surely no truly moneyed person would carry anything as small as coins in his pocket? Would it not be all fivers and check books? A really moneyed person would surely rustle?

No doubt the author knew all about his characters, and this character must exhibit his proper warts, but Joe decided that, while Graham Greene was marvelous at Catholics and atheists, he was not too good at Jews. He asked himself, *am I overreacting? Am I being oversensitive?* And then thought: *No, I'm not.*

Afterward, during the break, a boy from his class wandered up to him. "Isn't your old man Raeburn the property developer chap?"

Joe nodded. The boy was slender and fair-haired, with slightly supercilious, attenuated features. The voice was confident, languid. "Jewish, aren't you?"

Joe nodded again.

The fair-haired one smiled pityingly, and sighed with a certain theatricality. "My life!" he drawled. "Have you got problems!"

"Look—"

"My dear chap, relax. I'm a member of the club. My mother made me have a nosejob when I was twelve. I must admit I do look prettier now, but she forgot I'd been circumcized, of course, and in the shower who looks at noses?" He shook his head sadly. "Poor Mother, she does worry so. I think she'd have a seizure if she knew I attended Jewish prayers at assembly time."

"Why do you?"

"Oh, I don't know. . . . It's all a lot of rot, isn't it, but I find I can keep a marginally straighter face addressing Jehovah rather than *le père et le fils et le pigeon*, like the young man from Dijon."

Joe gave him a lift home that afternoon: "Danny, this is Hilary Punter."

There were Hebrew textbooks lying on the car seat, and Hilary picked one up. "At least I'm saved all this. How d'you manage, what with French and Latin?"

"Oh, I know chaps who do Greek as well. Tend to say everything four times over to keep up their vocabulary. Does slow up the conversation a bit. . . . Still, it'll be over soon."

"Ah, the great occasion. Your Bar Mitzvah."

"Want to come?"

"Love to. I'll tell mother I'm going to a confirmation."

Without knowing quite why, Danny felt sorry for the two boys: he glanced at them in the driving mirror, one with his golden hair and surgically elegant features, the other so pale and insignificant except when he smiled.

"Don't forget," Hilary was saying, "Mary was a Jewish mother: can't you just hear? 'Where d'you think *you're* going? Dinner's almost on the table.' 'I'm off preaching,' Jesus says. 'I must be about my father's business.' 'Oh well,' she says with one of her sighs. 'Go ahead, you go out and have a good time, enjoy yourself doing conjuring tricks for your friends at picnics. Don't think about your mother. . . .' Poor bastard—which, technically speaking he was of course—no wonder he left home."

Bouncing about, never still, the two boys chattered ceaselessly. ". . . Anyway," Joe said, "she finally made it to the posh country club, dipped her toe in the swimming pool, and screamed, '*Oy veh!—* whatever *that* might mean!' "

They began to giggle, growing wilder, building with a sort of spontaneous combustion of humor until they were both yelling with uncontrollable laughter, falling about, tears running down their faces.

"Abraham Lincohen . . . ."

"Rabbi Burns!"

Danny realized it was the first time he had ever seen Joe really laugh.

"Go on, laugh," Hilary said, sighing hugely, "I don't know what your poor grandfather would have said, God rest his soul."

"But that," Joe said, "was in another country, and besides, the *mensch* is dead!" He rummaged about in the glove compartment and found some chocolate biscuits.

Joe looked at the guest list. "What is this—is Dad floating a new company or is it a charity gala?"

"That's for your Bar Mitzvah."

"Don't be ridiculous. There must be two hundred people on this list."

"Two hundred and thirty."

"I don't want two hundred and thirty people at my Bar Mitzvah! I want the absurd business over as quietly and quickly as possible."

Rebecca looked shocked. "D'you want to kill your grandparents? Mum and Dad and Leah, they're all expecting it to be done properly. We can't let them down."

"I don't want to let them down. Let them come. Let the whole family come. But who are all these other people?"

"Friends of the family, Joe."

"And there's another thing: I'm not making this speech. It's appalling. 'For all the gifts bestowed upon me'—"

"The rabbi has always written the speech for the Bar Mitzvah boy," Rebecca said, looking upset, "It's the tradition. Rabbis know what has to be said."

"But not how to say it. It's not even English—and I'm not talking about the Hebrew bits!"

"Show some respect!"

Manny, trying to run through a company report against the sounds of the growing argument, gave up the struggle and called Joe into his study. "Shut the door."

Joe shut the door and stood waiting.

"Look at it this way," Manny said. "You think it's a terrible speech. All right, it's a terrible speech. Two hundred odd people, that's an awful lot of people. All right, it's a lot of people. So it won't be fun. But how much will you suffer? Will they stab you? Beat you? For them it'll be a wonderful day, a proud day, a day they'll remember. For you, it'll all be over in a few hours and you can forget it. Do it as a kindness. What d'you say, Jo-Jo?"

"Ladies and gentlemen, pray silence for Joseph Raeburn, your Bar Mitzvah boy!"

Applause. Two hundred and thirty pairs of hands clapping, palms moist, collars tight, mascara smudged, girdles biting, faces smiling.

Joe looked around the hotel banquet room, at the expectant faces, at the rabbi sitting waiting for the compliments to come his way and for his dreadful speech to have its airing.

Joe's pockets were stuffed with envelopes—fivers and checks, thrust into his hands by guests. He realized that he rustled as he moved. A really moneyed person today. He felt like laughing. Or crying. Or running. He could just turn and head for the door and he would be through it before they knew what was happening.

The long table was covered with presents—gold fountain pens, gold tiepins, silver wristwatches, gold cufflinks, books, fountain pens, a gilt-rimmed diary, silver-backed brushes, another fountain pen, gloves, a rare prayer book, yet another fountain pen.

Friends, Romans, countrymen, lend me your fountain pens . . . My beloved parents, grandparents, sister, relatives and friends, Rabbi . . . today I am a fountain pen, Joe wanted to shout.

The synagogue that morning had not been at all bad. His name called, the lonely walk to the *bima*, up the steps to read the portion of the Law, the blessings, the old men shaking his hand, welcoming him into their ranks. Childhood's end. Here began the first day of old age. At thirteen you put away childish things. So you did not say, "Today I am a fountain pen," which was an old joke for young boys.

He looked around the room again, at the faces: shiny, plump, wrinkled, gaunt, fine-boned, knobbly. All different, but all waiting confidently for the traditional words, for his dreadful speech.

Earlier they had descended on him in turn, ruffling his hair until he felt like screaming; pinching his cheeks sore, telling him how he had grown, all the while slipping him envelopes. He envisaged their shock, their horror, their bewilderment, when in a moment he launched into the speech he intended to give: truly appropriate to the occasion—destructive, rejecting, realistic.

Now the faces were all turned his way, like marigolds following the sun. He was their source of light and energy and hope. And he must play his part, put away childish things.

"My beloved parents, grandparents, sister, relatives and friends, Rabbi: Today I am a man . . ."

Manny handed Rebecca his handkerchief precisely at the instant her sniffs finally dissolved into tears. He always carried two handkerchiefs on such occasions, and he mechanically transferred the spare from one pocket to another.

The huge room shone, every surface reflecting the light: silver, candlesticks—even the white tablecloths dazzled. Manny's own Bar Mitzvah in the little East End synagogue had been very different, with the vestiges of the old *shtetl* customs lingering on—the women showering nuts and raisins from their gallery, little boys rushing forward to pick them up. And afterward, the *Kiddush* in the kitchen at home, just a little wine and cake, with Leah's lace cloth gracing the kitchen table.

Leah, on his other side, was crying now. Resignedly Manny gave her his second handkerchief. "A lovely boy!" Leah sobbed. Manny nodded and patted her shoulder. He began to sniff. Three handkerchiefs on future occasions, he decided.

Joe was plowing on: "I want to thank my parents for their hard work in giving me a good Jewish upbringing. I would like to thank the Rabbi—" his eye caught Hilary's and for a moment his voice wobbled, "for all his hard work in teaching me . . . thank my relatives and friends for being with us on the most important day of my life, and for all these beautiful gifts which you have . . . which you have bestowed upon me."

Simeon Abrahams, like an amiable but watchful old bear, moved across the room to Manny. "Congratulations, Manny. You must be proud."

"Proudest day of my life, Simeon."

"I hear you pulled off something of a coup in the city the other day."

Manny shrugged. "Fell into my hand." His voice grew enthusiastic. "You should come and have a look at the new complex. We're really making progress now that little bit of bother with the strike is over."

"Manny, are you planning to cover the *whole* of London with your office complexes?"

"Why not? Supply and demand! Wren built churches. To me, my buildings are beautiful. Not decorative—you've got to remember the economic necessities. But they're solid. Secure. They rise and we all rise with them. This is a great time to be alive! And one day, before too long, Joe will take over the business and then it'll have someone with *education* to look after things. You're lucky, Simeon. You've got status. The respect of the world. You had an education— that's always been a regret of mine. Still, no matter. Joe will put things right. The man at the top should have an education."

Simeon noticed Joe cross the room, making his way toward a slender, fair-haired boy. He watched them turn away from the room to conceal their mirth. "Does Joe want to take over the business?"

"Of course he does! Why shouldn't he?"

"I don't know. Have you asked him?"

Manny turned and nodded a greeting as Jonathan Shoobotel joined them. It always surprised Manny that, with so little success in his life, Shoobotel could look so cheerful. He was a good man, who had probably never had a bad thought in his head. Lucky for them all that there were such men about. He wondered why, since they had been brought up as brothers, there was so little closeness between them.

"*Mazel tov*, Emmanuel."

"Thank you, Jonathan."

"Soon it will be the turn of my son, Isaac. Not such a grand occasion, of course, but I hope you'll enjoy our more . . . modest celebration."

323

Holy men, Manny reflected, *have their own ways of hitting below the belt.*

Hilary dragged Joe into a corner of the room. "That was divine! I thought I'd expire. How did you *do* it? I wouldn't have missed it for worlds. Now: I want to meet the Rabbi. Go on, introduce me."

Joe led Hilary over and made the formal introduction. The Rabbi smiled benevolently. "I must say, sir," Hilary muttered, "that was a most excellent speech you wrote for Joe."

"Well, my boy," the Rabbi said, allowing himself a trace of complacency, "I have had some experience in that field."

Rebecca nudged Manny. "See: he's introducing his friend to the Rabbi. Isn't that nice? Oh, Manny," she heaved an enormous sigh, "this is the happiest day of my life!"

He tried not to be ashamed of them. He told himself how snobbish, discreditable, and egocentric it was to be ashamed of one's parents.

And every year, as school open day came around, Joe wished them elsewhere—stricken by some temporary but prostrating disease, too busy, too far away, cruising on a luxury liner—anything that would save him from the moment when they climbed out of the Rolls in front of the school.

Not all the boys had his problem: Joe looked enviously at friends escorting anonymous, almost invisible parents through the building. The fathers were suitably bland, the mothers satisfactorily colorless. Walking wallpaper, discreet, attracting no attention.

Next to him, his mother's electric pink silk coat and matching turban hat seemed to light up the entire corridor. She also wore a bright smile that remained in position whatever she looked at. He tried to shield her from the eyes of passing boys, but she was considerably plumper than he was, and simply could not be concealed.

324

Becky's feet, in the narrow pink shoes, were killing her. She longed to sit down and have a cup of tea somewhere away from all these cool, expressionless people. As she plodded along corridors she felt increasingly unhappy. But she was determined that Joe should think she was enjoying it all.

The afternoon wore on. The sun hung a little lower in the sky and the long shadows slanted across the grass. There was an edge of regret to the usual nostalgia, for everyone was aware that soon the school would be moving to new premises. The old building was headed for demolition. Joe, who loved the cathedrallike splendor of the glowing, red-brick pile, was not looking forward to its modern replacement. Meanwhile, the day went on, tea was served, and soberly dressed boys conducted families and friends on a relentless tour of inspection.

"Well," Manny said heartily, "what do we look at next?"

They moved on, to the geography project. Manny, astonished into rare silence, stood before Joe's town-planning project, a minutely calculated and deftly executed scale model. As a developer he personally would never have approved the use of space and resources allocated to pedestrian precincts and leisure areas. But he could admire it as a piece of work. He stared and nodded slowly. "Good. *Very* good."

Joe said casually, "Oh, it's neat enough. Look, there's something in the next room you might like to see."

He led them into a classroom where a number of folders were laid out in rows on various table tops. On a desk apart lay one folder, dark red, with his name on the cover and a printed card above it: "Literature Prize. J. Raeburn." He pointed toward the desk. "My essay."

His father opened the first page and recited the title: " 'The English Poet: A Study in the Contrast of Metaphysics.' "

"Well!" Manny said, and leafed through the folder quickly, without reading a line.

Joe, unable to hold on to his aplomb, muttered, "It could make a university thesis later if I wanted to extend it."

When they got home, his father could hardly wait to get out of the car. He strode about the room, excited, talking feverishly, waving his cigar. "Joe, you've got talent. You've got it in the fingers and the head; you get it from me. But you can do what I never had a chance to do: get yourself properly qualified, be master of a trade. You're a born architect. My trouble was I had a living to earn. But you'll be a big architect. One of the biggest!"

325

Joe's mouth went dry and he stared at his father anxiously. "But I don't want to be an architect."

"What then? Have you other ideas? Let's talk about it. I don't want to force you, I just think you have talent and it's a pity to waste it. But let's talk: what do you want to do?"

"I rather want to write."

"Write? Write? So write, who's stopping you? I'm talking about qualifications! Write whatever you want to. And study architecture."

It was settled.

Friday night at the Raeburns'—as in so many other similar households—had deteriorated gradually into a largely culinary activity: a passing of plates rather than a meeting of minds. Manny, like most of his generation, was sentimental about Sabbath night. It might be a sterile social cliché for his oversophisticated son; a bore for his daughter. For Manny it was still a point of renewal, and on Friday evening he usually arrived home in a particularly benevolent frame of mind.

"Thanks, Danny. Have a nice weekend." He watched the chauffeur guide the Rolls into the garage. It was his favorite car. He would never exchange it, even if they brought out a revolutionary new model. This was the way a class car should look, and he cherished it. Pride of ownership entered into it of course, but it was also a matter of respect, of admiration for its perfection. He smiled and went into the house.

A few minutes later a small white sports car turned off the busy main road, and Joe drove slowly along Bishop's Avenue. Next to him Hilary gazed affectionately at the housefronts along the spotlessly clean street. "You've got the wrong approach, Joey. It's an art form, all this. I love it. Why didn't my parents buy a house here? They've deprived me of my patrimony."

There was a certain style to Bishop's Avenue—even Joe had

to admit that. Manny and Rebecca, like their neighbors, had started to transform the house as soon as they bought it: acquiring it had been the realization of a dream, as Leah said. In the East End, praying aloud "Next year in Jerusalem," like their fellow-immigrants, they silently added, "Or if not Jerusalem, then Bishop's Avenue." It was their panache, their plume of triumph, evidence that another battle had been won. They put carriage lamps on the gateposts, hung gothic oak gates beside them, and put in ten-foot-high front doors of wood so highly varnished that it looked like plastic. They built columns and a balcony and loggias, and draped the windows in an extravaganza of snowy nylon net flounces. They filled the rooms with tightly upholstered furniture and glass cabinets full of ornate tea sets and silver candelabra. Into every room they put thick wall-to-wall carpeting and bright chandeliers and lamps, and they lit up the façade of the house and then sat back happily, secure in the knowledge that the ghetto had been left behind —blithely unaware that they had brought it with them and were flood-lighting its very walls.

Unlike Hilary, Joe looked at Bishop's Avenue with an unforgiving eye, forgetting—never in fact having known—what inspired it. He had been to Beverly Hills once, and in the fairy-tale craziness of that Californian garden suburb, with its sunlit follies set in smoothly barbered lawns, he had recognized the same unreality—as on a film set of apparently solid housefronts behind which lay emptiness.

He swung the little car into the long, curving drive of the Raeburn home. Behind the Morgan, a large Daimler rolled up to the house and Joe's older sister Deborah, her husband Michael, and two children got out. Deborah called a querulous greeting, while Michael looked over the new car. "So this is the birthday present? Funny-looking car if you ask me. More like a toy. I'm surprised Manny bought it for you."

Becky made a brief appearance to light the Sabbath candles and vanished into the kitchen. Joe moved restlessly around the sitting room. Even filled with people, it looked unlived-in—no magazines or papers lying about; no stubs in the ashtrays, no dust, no squashed cushions, no scratches on the paintwork, no books.

Manny chewed carefully on a large green olive from one of the silver dishes and automatically switched on the television.

"Must we have that on?" Joe asked.

"There's something good in a minute." Manny extracted his olive pit. "I'll turn the sound down till it begins." He took another olive.

They all sat around watching the blue white screen. Even without the sound it dominated the room, the mouthings and grimaces gaining in portentousness through their very lack of meaning. To break into the silence became impossible. Joe capitulated. "Oh, turn the sound up, Dad. I can't stand the suspense."

Manny shrugged and turned up the volume. At once they all began to talk, pitching their voices to drown out the noise of the program.

After a minute the room was pandemonium, Deborah shouting at Scott, and Manny tickling Jeanette, while Michael yelled questions at him. The children were smartly dressed like little dummies from a shop window: Jeanette's white socks dazzled, her patent shoes gleamed. Scott's suit was a diminutive version of his father's, with a spotted bow tie at his collar.

Hilary and Joe sat observing the scene. "Listen to that orchestration! The ebb and flow," Hilary whispered. "Positively operatic!" He lay back, the mop of golden hair bright against the maroon upholstery. "It's so quiet at home, I never get any of this. We've acquired true gentility."

Becky called them into the dining room. "It's all ready!"

Still talking, Manny leaned forward to switch off the set. He gave an exclamation of disappointment. "It's just finished."

"So?"

"That was the program I wanted to see. With all your chatter I've missed it."

They straggled into the dining room, settling themselves at the table. As the meal progressed, the noise level rose to new heights. Deborah leaned toward her brother. "I haven't seen you for weeks, Joe. Now: tell me what's new."

He was saved by the arrival of Maria with a huge platter, on which rested two splendid chickens, their skins glistening dark gold. Deborah turned away, toward the food. Becky, knife poised over the chickens, said, "Now the phone will ring."

Manny snorted. "You're always looking for problems."

The telephone rang.

"It'll be your mother."

"Why should it be?" Manny demanded.

It was his mother. "Hello, Mum, how you feeling?" he asked mechanically.

Leah sighed. Manny could interpret his mother's sighs the way a seismologist analyzes squiggles on a chart in terms of movements of the earth's crust. So as he heard the sigh (about Force Eight, he judged), he cut in quickly. "Mum, we're just sitting down at table."

"Then I won't keep you. Enjoy your dinner."

"Right. Why don't I ring you back?"

"If you like. I'm an old woman. Who wants to bother with an old woman?"

Heat began to rise in Manny's brain as the chicken cooled on his plate. "We'll talk later, Mum." He replaced the receiver before she could turn the farewell phrase into a philosophical debating point.

Dinner over, they tottered back to the sitting room, replete. Manny switched on the television set.

"Must we?" Joe asked again.

"The news is on in a minute."

"I've got to find someone to open a charity bazaar next month," Becky shouted. "They want a big name."

"How about the Beatles?" Hilary suggested.

"They're not Jewish, are they?"

"They're talented enough to be," Hilary said.

"It's all right to joke," Manny said sententiously, "but talent is a very Jewish thing."

Michael pursed his lips in agreement. "Look at the writers, look at Proust. And Heine, greatest lyric poet Germany ever—"

"Heine was baptized a Christian," Joe said, "and Proust—"

"What about Meyerbeer and Mendelssohn—"

"Wagner!" suggested Hilary.

"*Wagner?*"

"That's why he was so noisy. Covering up, like Hitler."

"On the other hand, he did look like Charlie Chaplin."

"Who?"

"Hitler."

"But Chaplin never said he was Jewish."

"Neither did Hitler."

Manny began to scratch his bald patch. "Look at the painters! Chagall, Pissaro, Modigliani . . ."

"I was reading somewhere," Becky said, "that the proportion of men of distinction in the Jewish community outnumbers those in the outside world by fifteen to one. The only things we lag behind in, it said, are the hereditary nobility and the church."

"And that's just a matter of time," Hilary said, getting to his feet. "Lovely meal, Mrs. R. Sorry, I've got to go."

329

Without Hilary's complicity, his mischievous companionship, Joe withdrew into himself. Sitting here among the family, he felt like a visitor from another planet, untouched by their narrow preoccupations, like the endless game of spot-the-Jew or list-the-Jew or justify-the-Jew. Couldn't they for once, he had asked, in a bitter clash with his parents, just *forget* the Jews? Weren't there other things in life to discuss? The fact that their forefathers had been high priests at the court of kings when ancient Britons were running around painted in woad, had the appeal for Joe of an Eskimo history lesson: interesting but of small personal relevance. Sad though it might be, he felt no connection with the past—*their* past, that is. Their past was another country.

Manny was telling a funny story about some coup in the city, and the others laughed comfortably, nuts and chocolate mints vanishing into receptive mouths. The laughter hovered like a barrier of sound, shutting Joe out. George Eliot had said somewhere that a different taste in jokes is a great strain on the affections. Joe had repeatedly learned the truth of that statement.

Ironically, they all shared a sense of history, an awareness of long perspectives, but they were looking through different telescopes. England was Joe's universe. He could dwell on the Elizabethans as though they were neighbors, using a language he delighted in. To open a page of Donne was to pick up a message from a bottle floating on the sea of time. He began to murmur vague excuses about schoolwork and said a general goodnight. Scott and Jeannette, who were kneeling on the carpet, noses to the television screen, did not reply. Halfway up the stairs, Joe glanced back and caught his fathers' gaze, the long, almond-shaped eyes gleaming in the fleshy moon of his face.

Manny, watching his son, felt the tiny shock of a long-forgotten moment reasserting itself. Like a shutter flying up in his mind, another Friday night, another meeting of glances between a father and son came back to him. He must have been about ten, going up the mean, cramped staircase of the little house in Stepney Green. He had looked back, and through the open door had seen his father at the kitchen table, covered as usual after Friday night supper by a threadbare velvet cloth with bobbled edges. Bent over his book, the Hebrew lettering difficult to decipher in the dim lighting, skullcap on head, beard almost touching the page, Chaim looked like a model for a romantic painting of a religious old man. Manny only now realized that in fact his father had been a young man still—frail and worn, his eyes sunk in his head with exhaustion, but young.

Chaim had turned from the page for a moment and met his son's eyes. For Chaim, who spent six days a week slaving over the sewing machine he had painfully taught himself to use, it was more than a duty, it was a blessing, a *mitzvah*, to study the holy book on the Sabbath. Six days he gave to the needs of the body, the demands of the world. He was not prepared to donate God's portion. "Remember the Sabbath Day, to keep it Holy . . ." And in truth, in obeying the Law he found the only relief from drudgery that he could afford.

But to the young Manny it was all a tragic waste of time: to pore over a volume of irrelevant Hebrew when your family was short of food; to strain your eyes unraveling ambiguities of ritual when there was work lying waiting. What had one to do with the other? Rather, he concluded, you should study an English textbook, improve your chances of getting on in the new country. Not that Manny had ever felt it was a new country: it was his country, his language, and he would make his life the English way. Chaim had gone back to his book, and Manny continued on up the stairs, his scrawny, undernourished frame casting a goblin shadow on the grubby walls, his head whirling with ideas, possibilities, determination to order his own life differently.

Joe had reached the top of the wide, thickly carpeted staircase. Brilliant lights softened with pink pleated shades flooded the hall with a cheerful glow.

But Manny felt the chill of the little house in Stepney fall on his spirits. He called out suddenly to Joe, and his son stopped and looked down at him, waiting. "Don't read too late, don't damage your eyes," Manny said helplessly.

On Sunday afternoon, Danny parked the Raeburn Mini outside Solly Slumkow's little suburban house in Edgware and carried a large cardboard box to the front door. Mrs. Slumkow took the package without comment, and in her kitchen unloaded several flat packs of smoked salmon and boxes of Davidoff cigars. She had been hurt and insulted by the advance guard the first time it happened. Now she accepted it as normal. As Becky said when they were alone once, "He likes his smoked salmon from a man in Orkney who does it specially for him; he gets regular consignments, he's accustomed, now. So isn't it simpler for me to send along some—he'll be happier, you'll all be happier. With his cigars he's also particular. Don't be offended. Nothing personal."

By eight-fifteen they were all assembled, the air thick with cigar smoke. Solly's front room, carpeted in a pattern of red, beige, and gold, was brilliantly lit and furnished with the appropriate bulging armchairs and sofa. There was a square, walnut-veneer table in the center. Later there would be food, but for the moment the table, covered with a crimson chenille cloth, carried only boxes of cigars and packs of cards.

Besides Solly, a dozen men were present, some old immigrants like "Jock" Minsky and Aaron, young Polanski, who was white-haired now, and others whose parents had come over and who were themselves British born, like Manny, Fishbein, and Cohen (the partners everlastingly locked in hostility), Segal with his dress house and Saul, who had a chain of shoe shops. And then there were a few whose arrival had been brought about not by the Czarist pogroms but by the events of 1940–45, like Sam, a jeweler, who had thought of Poland as his home until rudely disabused of that fantasy by the arrival of the Nazis.

Manny looked around the crowded room, nodding greetings to familiar faces. The old ties, the old roots still clutched. These men had built entire lives inside a few square miles of London—their fortunes had been hammered out on British soil—yet their imagination was still fired by thoughts of an old way of life in a ghetto that would have buried them all had they stayed on. Health and business commitments permitting, they gathered in one another's houses every couple of months to play cards, gossip, and plan fund-raising functions for the charities they supported.

"How's Joe?" Sam asked.

Manny looked long-suffering. "He's fine. He's in his second year at Cambridge."

"So he's almost finished."

"Don't make me laugh! To be an architect, Sam, you start young,

and why? Because it takes so long. The college, and the 'year out' they call it, working with an architect, and then the college again and again a year out. Then he gets the letters after his name."

Solly handed Manny one of his own cigars. Part of the ritual was that the true source of the supply was never referred to. Manny smelled, checked, and approved the pale, slender tube.

"Has Simeon been on to you about this idea of his?" Sam asked.

Manny gave an impatient shrug. "I told him, he's *meshugge*."

"Well, I'm not so sure." About the same age as Manny, Sam had an emaciated-looking frame and sharply drawn features. "I was thinking the other day: I've got a lot of lovely stuff in the shop—silver, precious stones, valuable stuff, very nice. But what gives me the most pleasure? I'll tell you: the miniatures and the cameos. You pick one up, hold it in your hand. It's a little bit of the past and it's survived."

"When I talked to Simeon, I had a funny feeling that's what he's after—a bit of the past, to show our children and grandchildren. He doesn't need to do this book; he's got enough stuff to publish without messing around with Peszno."

"If I know Simeon, he's probably got some charity to underwrite the print costs— He's no fool," Fishbein cut in dryly.

Sam ignored the remark. "How many of us are still here who remember that little town, the way it was, the streets, the houses? What became of the people, the ones who stayed, and the rest of us, the ones who left?" He was touching on disturbing ground. Mortality was not comfortable. Smoke poured from furiously puffed cigars.

Manny, who already knew that they would end by doing what Simeon wanted, said irritably, "Listen, what are we here for, are we here to talk history or to play cards? So let's play!"

Manny collected Leah from her Maida Vale apartment and they drove slowly toward Mayfair.

"Danny's dropping me off at the office and then he'll take you to Harrods."

"How are you, Danny?" Leah asked. "Have you been a good boy?"

The chauffeur shrugged his massive shoulders. "I'm kept too busy to be anything else, Mrs. Rubin." He grinned at her in the driving mirror. Leah continued to reject the Raeburn metamorphosis. To change her name once—from Rubinstein to Rubin—that she had regarded as a fair tribute to her new country. But enough was enough.

"What is a name? Is it a fur coat that you change a little here, a little there, shorten, refashion?" she had said.

She rested like a round cushion on the back seat of the Rolls. It was warm, but she wore her mink jacket. Her legs were thin as sticks, but her feet had suffered over the years and even the handmade kid shoes could not disguise their lumpy shape. Through the crepy mask of her flesh, her bones recalled the narrow-featured slenderness that had vanished: the nose still arched firmly; the lips, no longer smooth, could still curl in scorn. And the long, dark Pharaoh eyes had not lost their brilliance.

She said fretfully, "Simeon called me about some nonsense he's thinking about . . . some book. Hasn't he got anything better to publish?"

"I thought you'd enjoy it. You love talking about the old days."

"Talking, that's something else. That's a comfort. But to put it down in some book for everyone to read, that's not a nice idea. Anyway, nobody will buy such a book. Nobody is interested!"

"But you just said everyone would read it."

"In a manner of speaking. It would be there *for* everyone to read. That would be upsetting. But no one would buy it. So it's foolishness. I shall tell Simeon next time I speak to him."

"He was hoping you would—"

"I know, go searching through my trunks, he asked me. It will be no good to him. Everybody remembers things differently. It will just cause a confusion."

Manny opened his mouth to make a comment, and she cut him off sharply. "You know nothing, Manny. You're a cockney. You know nothing about the way it was."

Danny had pulled up outside Raeburn House, and Manny patted Leah's hand as he got out of the car. Through the open window he said, "Don't worry. I'll tell Simeon not to bother you—you probably don't remember much about it anyway; it was a long time ago."

She went stiff with resentment and rolled up the window of the car without thanking him for lunch. Abruptly she sat forward, wobbling slightly with the movement of the car. "Danny, drive around to Victoria Station. It won't take long, will it?"

"Five minutes. But I thought you wanted to go to Harrods."

"That can wait." She looked up at the slim column of the new Hilton hotel towering above them. She liked it. Why were these journalists always making trouble about new buildings? They wouldn't be so attached to the old ones if they had had to live in them.

"Here you are," Danny said. "D'you want me to get you a timetable?"

She shook her head. It was a long time since she had really looked at Victoria Station; when a train was about to go there was neither time nor inclination for contemplating the scenery.

The whole area, she realized, was a mess: a muddle of grimy buildings, tatty shops, peeling notices, and flaking paintwork—a jumble of taxi ranks and bus stations, and, on every side, litter-filled gutters. Victoria Station in 1966 was a shambles.

Hard to believe that the first time she had seen it Leah thought it was the most elegant, prosperous neighborhood she had ever set eyes on: horse-drawn cabs and ladies in long dresses . . . great houses shrouded in a foggy winter gloom. Now the air was clean, but everything else seemed dirtier. Had London changed so much? Or had she? She felt very old and wished suddenly that she had not come. These days she confined herself to the more pleasing areas of London—the parks and better shopping districts. Now she felt depressed. This is what came of poking fingers back into the past. The past was better forgotten.

"Forget Harrods today, Danny. I feel a bit tired."

He took the hint. The dividing glass slid into position, sealing her off into silence.

The apartment, overlooking a busy Cambridge street, was very large, with a first-floor balcony beyond open French windows. Joe leaned on the stone balustrade, balancing his wine glass on the broad ledge as he watched the traffic below.

The evening was still light and sunny, and all the cars seemed to be driven by men in shirt sleeves listening to their radios with the windows unrolled. Through the muted roar of the traffic he caught the occasional wisp of melody: the Rolling Stones' "Paint It Black" giving way to something classical as the next car approached. Undergraduates on battered bicycles wove their way among the cars. Frank Rosen and Nicky, with whom he shared the flat, came out and stood on either side of him, also looking down into the street. Frank's dark, sharp-cut good looks gave him, even in his open-necked shirt and jeans, the urban neatness of a Peter Arno cartoon character. Nicky, blonde and creamy to a point just short of plumpness, waved an empty glass for more wine.

Frank reached for a bottle to refill their glasses. "When I was a kid," he said, "I remember walking round town, staring up at balconies like this and brightly lit windows with people holding glasses and girls with bare arms laughing, and I used to think how fantastically privileged they were, the lot of them. And here I am, a goddamn glass in my hand, looking at the poor sons of bitches down in the street . . ."

"I never had any experiences like that," Joe said ruefully. "I'm afraid I was always one of the people on the balcony. You had a lot of advantages, Frank: lack of money, deprived childhood. Look how motivated it's made you—coming over here flashing your scholarships and erudition in all directions. And now hurtling back to the States to make your fortune. You can't fail."

"Kidding apart, I do appreciate your old man's introduction to these people in New York—"

"He's a generous chap, my father. He does a lot for other people, gives a lot to charity. How d'you think he got the knighthood?"

"Nicky," Frank flung an arm round her shoulders, "are you going to look after this poor kid when I'm gone?"

"He has an open invitation. Come and stay with us any weekend," she said to Joe. "Come next weekend if your family will let you out of their clutches."

It would be odd, Joe thought, living alone next year, in London, with none of Frank's exotic bottles of aftershave, preshave, and cologne cluttering up the bathroom shelf, and Nicky's sludge-colored Mary Quant underwear hanging above the bath. He knew that it was not so much that he would miss the other two personally: what he would really miss was the evidence of living they supplied.

The term was almost over; already he felt an interloper in a city on loan to tourists. In a few days he, too, would be gone, cases packed, books cleared, away to London for a year. An awkward hiatus, but fortunately temporary. On the less temporary awkwardness he would have to face later—when Cambridge was finally finished with and decisions were demanded of him—he would not allow himself to dwell.

So this was Buckingham Palace. Manny glanced about keenly and tried, unsuccessfully, to look poised and at his ease. He also attempted to remember all the instructions he had received about the forthcoming procedure. His head began to hurt.

Crowded at one end of the enormous ballroom on spindly chairs, those about to be honored were allocated the front rows, while their families were ranged behind them. Manny was already aware that all the other men seemed to be at least seven feet tall and slim. They could stride confidently, kneel gracefully, and bow with assurance. He waited his turn—lips dry, armpits moist with a growing awareness that his collar was strangling him.

There seemed to be a banging in his ears, through which, faintly, he heard his name called. He scrambled to his feet and began to head for the dais. He found it difficult to place one foot before the other in the usual way: his thighs seemed to have grown huge, so that they bumped awkwardly against each other as he walked.

He tried again to remember the instructions: bow and kneel, was that it? He knelt, his knees cracking like gunshots, and realized suddenly how very tightly his trousers were stretched. Why had he not thought to practice kneeling at the tailors? He felt the nervous perspiration prickle through his pores. The next movement could do it: an extra bend of the knee, even a shift of balance, and there would be a terrible sound of rending cloth and his buttocks would be revealed to the world . . .

"Rise, Sir Emmanuel . . ."

He was rigid, unable to move. Stone. The tiniest quiver of puzzlement creased the Royal countenance. Then Manny, with the calm of despair, pushed himself clumsily to his feet. He heard some threads give—tiny, snapping sounds, but he was safely upright, stomach churning, deafened by his own heartbeat, and wringing wet from neck to ankles. He smiled gratefully in the general direction of the Royal blur, and backed away.

He found his way to his little chair and collapsed into it, while the rest of the Birthday Honours were handed out—nearly two hundred in a little more than two hours. He admired the efficiency.

At last everyone jostled out, families attaching themselves to their honored member like iron filings to a magnet. Manny paused for a moment in the entrance. The transport arrangements, too, were efficient: no waiting.

"Sir Emmanuel Raeburn's car . . ."

Manny endured the embraces of his mother, his daughter, his son-in-law, and the slightly ironical congratulations of his son. He sank gratefully into the back of the Rolls, avoiding Becky's sunray pleats. The soft leather claimed him with a sigh, the door closed, and almost silently the car moved around the side of Buckingham Palace and out of the great wrought-iron gates.

"Drop Mrs. Raeburn—"

"*Lady* Raeburn, d'you mind?" Becky interrupted.

"Drop *Lady* Raeburn at the Dorchester, Danny."

Becky looked regretful. "You're sure you've got to go into the office right away?"

"Yes, yes. I've got an urgent bit of business to attend to. Joe can come with me. I want to show him something."

"Well, I'll just pop into the Dorchester and see that everything's ready for tonight."

The doorman outside the hotel helped Becky out of the car and saluted Manny through the window. The Rolls moved off. Danny had the ability, common among professional drivers, to take in his passenger without, apparently, removing his eyes from the road. "Well: how's it feel then, being a knight of the realm?"

Manny scratched his bald patch until it glowed pink. "I'm starving. I've got a splitting headache. I want a smoke and I need a pee. That apart, I feel great."

There were a number of well-proportioned, sunny offices in Raeburn House. Isaac Shoobotel's was not one of them. He had a small room in the worst lit, least accessible corner of the building. It had probably been a maid's room when the original owner, an earl, had occupied the building. Now it held a clumsy desk, a filing cabinet, and a small table on which stood teapot, electric kettle, and tall glass. Isaac made his own tea, morning and afternoon, not from personal preference, but because the tea lady always forgot him. He also collected his own paycheck from accounts on Fridays because the pay clerk never remembered to call in on him, and for some time now he had been dusting his own desk and cabinet because the cleaners seemed unaware that the office was in use, despite the notes he left for them.

He was not an ambitious man, nor a man of strong feelings of any sort, and he did not resent the size of his office or the size of his salary. He was, however, a little worried by the work he had just been assigned, which seemed to have little to do with Raeburn Development and even less to do with bookkeeping. Collecting and sorting material sent in from Manny's friends about an insignificant Polish town, that he himself was delighted never to have seen, was slow work. Looking at the stuff still unsorted, it sometimes seemed to him that, like Moses, he would spend his life on the journey and hand on to someone else the uncompleted task before expiring.

Two floors below him, Joe, just returned from the investiture, was being shown the office he could use in the coming year. It was a huge room with an Adam fireplace and decorated ceiling. "Do I need all this? I'll have to be over at the architects' place most of the time—"

"I want you to be comforatble, Jo-Jo. I know you're only in London for a year, at the moment, but I'm looking ahead. Who knows, you might decide one day that you'd like to come into the business. What d'you think?"

Joe's shoulders rose and fell in the smallest of shrugs. "I've told you, Dad, I'm not sure."

Manny's color deepened. "A man twenty years old and he doesn't know what he wants to do? You're spending seven years getting letters after your name as long as a menu and you're telling me in the middle of it you still don't know!"

He sprang up from his chair, too agitated to sit still. "I've raised a *putz!* I never forced you into anything! If you came to me and said, 'Dad, I want to build mud huts for savages,' I'd say, 'Go right ahead, kid, someone has to build 'em . . . I suppose.' But this . . . messing about. 'Not sure!' Okay, if there's nothing better, come into the business. You might even come up with a new idea or two, with all the expensive education you've got."

"What new ideas? New ideas for better ways to squeeze more square feet of letting room out of a shoebox block? Better ways to cut the cost of building the shoebox so that the return will be even more spectacular? Ideas for gearing up the finance to the point where *all* the capital can be untouched while new assets are raised?"

The unfairness of it made Manny physically dizzy—to say this to a man who had probably given away a quarter of his fortune to charity, and not all of it ostentatiously; who had, in the early years, given money to neighbors in need, money he never expected to see repaid, and who indeed was seldom disappointed in that expectation. Business was business, and he'd driven more than one competitor into bankruptcy. But in his life Manny did not love money for its own sake. His intention had always been to make a success of himself, get to the top and enjoy the view. And he did enjoy it, he enjoyed it all: the power, the decisions, the exhaustion, the risks, the competition, the rewards. While he was wheeling and dealing he was living.

But he had spoiled his son. He saw that now. He had created an empty vessel, a house with dark windows. There was in this boy no love of life, no joy in the cut and thrust of the marketplace, and what was the world but a marketplace? Joe was a dreamer, impractical and unfitted for responsibility. Worse—he was a drifter, a dreamer cut off from the source of his dreams. As Manny's son he could never be described as unfortunate. But his father saw that there was no flame in him. He was no better than that *nebech* Shoobotel upstairs.

Manny stood at the window, staring out, jingling the small change in his pocket. The boy would get nowhere. A *putz.*

The waiter paused at Manny's shoulder, a dome of *cassata sicilienne* at the ready. Manny waved away the ice cream and eased out of his seat. He beat his way up the banqueting room, tacking from table to table, a handshake here, a patted shoulder there.

"*Mazel tov,* Sir Manny!"

The mirror-clad walls reflected the crowded room, the dinner jackets, bare shoulders and jewels. He wished the younger generation looked less untidy: he knew that it was the fashion, that the King's Road dictated the way the kids looked, but he would never be able to accept it.

He decided to avoid the cabaret. A bunch of West Indians playing their homemade instruments was Becky's idea of helping the immigrant community to integrate. He passed the musicians lined up, waiting to make their entrance: colorful, garishly clashing clothes gave an impression of gaiety belied by their liquid, watchful eyes. He felt uncomfortably aware of them.

In the cloakroom he relaxed and washed his hands with a leisurely, almost voluptuous enjoyment. He gazed down at the white oval of soap slipping like an ivory egg between the pinkness of his small, plump hands, creating a snowy lather. His hands were neat, the nails manicured, the skin of the fingertips smooth, fine-grained. Soft hands, the hands of a man who used his head to earn a living. Hands fit for a title. On one finger was a modest gold ring. There had been many occasions when he had been tempted to improve on it, but he never had. The ring was a tangible reminder of the day he vowed his hands would never work for him again. It helped him recall the way his fingers looked in those days: nails always black-edged from the East End grime that nothing would wash away. The soap they had used for scrubbing was as hard as stone; it left his skin dry and scaly, with a papery feel to the touch.

They used to buy their soap from old Polanski. His son was sitting at one of the tables in the banqueting hall now, and his hands, too, were smooth and white. Old Polanski had been the neighborhood soap-and-candle man in Peszno, so Leah naturally patronized him when he later moved to London. But she had never been able to accept Polanski's rise to riches, his vast cosmetic empire. "Face creams? Perfume? Beauty masks? But he's a soap-and-candle man!"

In the mirror, reflected next to his own blank, dreaming face, Manny realized there was another face, a face he knew. "Simeon! I didn't see you inside. I thought you were at some book fair."

Manny offered him a cigar as they strolled back toward the banquet hall. Simeon lit up slowly. A familiar figure was threading through the tables, heading for the exit, and Manny's mouth turned down in a scowl. He was still smarting from the afternoon's exchange with Joe.

Beneath the throbbing West Indian music, Simeon sensed rather than heard the exclamation Manny stifled between clenched teeth. Simeon glanced at him and then across the room at Joe's retreating figure. "Problems?"

"Problems you wouldn't believe. He's going to grow moss on his backside sitting thinking about the ethics of architecture. Great."

Simeon steered Manny gently out of the hall and into one of the adjoining anterooms, talking soothingly. The barman brightened as they approached, but they walked on and he relapsed into lethargy. He hated Jewish functions: the bar was a dead loss. Cigars, yes. Raffles, yes. Drinks, no. They just didn't seem to like the stuff. They were probably knocking back the orange juice as if it was the Gobi desert in the dining room, and not a gin and tonic among the lot of them.

Despite the late night following his investiture, Manny was, as always, the first person to arrive in his office. In fact, he was the only man in the firm who knew the night security officer personally. By

7:30 A.M., winter and summer, Manny was at his desk, cigar clamped into position and in-box empty. The notes made in his diary, which he kept by his bedside, had been fed into his dictating machine; incoming trans-Atlantic calls recorded during the night had been played over and replies dictated. He was ready to face the day. There was no need for him to be in at that early hour—it was a hangover from the days when a panic order from a wholesaler might come through and mean the difference between red and black in the books. Today, he had already got through those sections of the newspaper that concerned him and smoked his second cigar before the telephone rang. He tilted the padded swivel chair almost horizontal to get comfortable. The day had begun. . . .

As he put down the phone, his secretaries arrived. As usual, Manny glanced at the clock and as usual, found they were on time. "Morning, girls."

"Morning, Sir Manny!"

Molly, gray-haired and neat, who had been with him for more than fifteen years, called him Manny when they were alone but was formal in the presence of outsiders. Jilly, whose father was a peer and whose salary barely covered her bills at Harrods, was definitely an outsider in Molly's book. But the conspicuous attractions of an upper-class secretary were all part of a vast display, lovingly constructed and designed to show off the style of Raeburn Enterprises. Like the Raeburn-endowed orphanage in Hackney, the mansion in Bishop's Avenue and the diamonds around Becky's neck, the display showed the world that Manny Raeburn was somebody. It was his *laissez-passer* to the Top Table.

Molly made his tea and brought it in with two plain biscuits. She had made Manny's tea in the days when they shared not only an office but a single telephone, and she still made his tea.

He sipped, and studied the diary. A busy day. Once again Becky had talked him into a cruise, and there was much to clear up before he left: at 10 A.M., a meeting with the accountants to go into the details of an overseas project that had unexpectedly failed to do what was expected of it; at 3 P.M. a meeting with a man from the *Financial Times*; at 5 P.M. a planning meeting; and at 6 P.M. a private viewing at some art gallery in aid of yet another of Becky's charities. Between meetings, correspondence. A crusading journalist wanted to stop him from knocking down a useless artisan dwelling block and had devoted half a page to a violent attack on the Raeburn empire.

That would require a letter to the editor, and he loathed writing those letters.

The bright boys downstairs always altered his rough draft, and he had a feeling that they laughed at his grammar while they corrected it. Not that there was anything wrong with his arguments, ever. The smart alecks downstairs had letters after their names—they planned the logistics and discussed implications and were aware of nuances in the subtext and a lot of cobblers like that—but ultimately it was they who were working for him, not the other way around.

He looked at his watch: 9:59. The door opened and Molly ushered in the accountants.

"Morning, Sir Manny," they greeted him.

Manny looked grim. He came straight to the point: "Do we have to pay the bastards or can we fight this one?"

Cardboard boxes stood empty on Isaac Shoobotel's filing cabinet, their contents stacked in untidy piles on his desk. "I'm trying to arrange them in families, where possible," he told Joe. Isaac hated the deferential note that crept into his voice when he spoke to Joe, but though he despised himself, he could not control it. Joe was, after all, the boss's son.

Joe gazed down at the mass of paper in amazement. "Didn't any of them ever throw anything away?"

"Doesn't look like it. Real magpies."

Magpies? Surely not. Was this, Joe wondered, the most glittering collection they could manage—scraps of paper, old cuttings, letters, recipes, diaries, documents, and creased photographs?

"All the Yiddish is being translated for you," Isaac said, "so you can read everything later on."

Despite Isaac's respectful manner, Joe sensed the condescension of one who had, unlike Joe, kept true to his roots. He nodded. "I'll let you have my grandmother's stuff. She's dug out a whole heap."

He went back to his own room, glad to get out of the cramped stuffiness of Isaac's box of an office. On his desk stood Leah's cardboard box, full of more creased and folded papers, more mottled photographs.

As he picked up one, a cheaply mounted portrait of a smiling baby and a thin, dark-haired girl, a small batch of newspaper clippings fell onto his desk. He picked them up and began to read them. . . .

PART FIVE

As soon as Joe said there was nothing to worry about, Leah knew somthing was wrong. She gripped the telephone anxiously. "What has happened?" she asked.

"Nothing. Don't worry."

"You've had an upset with your father."

An upset. Joe could still see Manny's face, congested with fury, hear him shouting, "I'll make it plain. I pay your bills, I pay for everything. So I'm not bloody asking, I'm telling. Don't see the girl again."

Joe broke into his grandmother's flood of words. "I must go."

"At least tell me where you're going," Leah said quickly.

"Israel. I'll be—" They were cut off.

Joe put down the phone. A few yards away, in the airport lounge, Samantha waited. Joe picked up their bags, his own, heavy with Leah's papers, tipped straight from the cardboard box. He no longer felt angry; he felt exhilarated. The world was suddenly a place where the unexpected could happen, where you came to a decision and acted on it. He took Samantha's arm. He was beginning to enjoy life.

Leah could not reach Manny in his office. She put down the telephone and went slowly back to her armchair. The television beamed blue white light into the room. She sat, eyes closed, trying to blank out thoughts that led into a past she flinched from, now. Old people, she reflected, lived in the past because they thought it was easier: the past was like a worn shoe, comfortable, its contours known, effortless to slip into. But the past was *not* an easy place; the past was full of deaths and departures, and bright hopes that gradually lost their shine and became drab. Dreams that were once a consolation chafed as their impossibility became more obvious.

Old people had selective memories. The past was the country they chose to revisit; its landscape and its history could be endlessly changed to fit the mood. But Leah knew that when you returned to the present you faced the consequences of that past—the dead child did not live; the daughter who rejected you remained a stranger. The loneliness was the reality.

Each morning as Becky woke, before the bustling and the routine took over, she allowed herself a moment to prepare for what she might hear that day: a sort of bracing against an awaited shock. She was a busy woman; there were meetings to attend, decisions to be made. But fleetingly, like a spider casting its fine thread, searching for something to latch on to, she offered a prayer.

She knew Manny worried as much as she did, but somehow they had lost the means to share their anxieties. Somewhere along the years, always busy, always striving, they had stopped reaching each other, and merely talked now, the words impersonal. Once there had been so much to say that a lifetime hardly seemed enough to contain it. Now they eked out their communications, placing them strategically between the silences. And sometimes even the words themselves were merely noisier versions of a silence. And so to her surprise she found herself attempting a dialogue of a different sort.

Her ancestors, surrounded by danger and hostility, had prayed like this, daily. It had been natural for them. But danger and hostility had been strangers in Becky's life for a long time. It was only now, faced again with anxiety as the months passed, that she rediscovered the need for those regular conversations with the deity. Joe was in Israel. And Israel was vulnerable.

So when it came, the news seemed already familiar. She was well rehearsed in dread. At daybreak the Egyptians had launched a heavy artillery barrage on the settlements of the Western Negev facing the Gaza Strip. It was June 1967, and Israel was at war.

Leah telephoned as soon as she heard the news on the radio. "What can we do?"

"Nothing," Becky said, "except maybe raise some money."

"The way they're outnumbered—"

"Yes."

"Joe's still there?"

"As far as we know."

"What can we do?"

"Nothing." Except pray.

The rumors, the fears, the preparations, the endless preparations, crystalized now into action. The Israelis poured their youth into the mold of battle and produced a fighting machine. What would once have seemed absurd—Jews fighting, Jews militant—now became the standard of their Jewishness.

"What an army! What an air force!" exulted a fellow fund-raiser. "They'll win. They know they have to, to survive."

"They'll win," Rebecca repeated. "They have to." But not everyone would survive. Young men would die in the sand, bullets in their bodies and brains; mangled inside their tanks. Young men would choke on their own blood or fall out of the sky, burning—winners and losers alike.

The newscasts relayed the confidence, the bravado, the determination. Who was counting the cost, the deaths? Rebecca knew who was counting the deaths. You cannot win a war without losing soldiers. And soldiers were just another name for sons.

She tried to get news. She telephoned Mordecai and bullied her way past two officious secretaries to reach him. "I want to know where Joe is . . . is he all right. For God's sake, Mordecai, have I ever asked you a favor before?"

Sarah telephoned no one. She barely spoke. The radio remained on all day and she sat quietly, reading the newspaper reports of the war, hearing statistics in terms of Samantha's existence. "The Arabs

349

have vowed to drive the Israelis into the sea . . . to annihilate them . . . this is a Holy War . . ." The old terror, the old smell of fear, washed away by the years, was thick around her again. The voice she had heard screaming over the loudspeaker in Germany and later in the streets of the East End echoed in her head. Once again extermination. Once again the Jewish problem was being solved. And her own guilt tormented her.

John left her alone, trying to keep intact a surface normality that was as thin as a veil of ice. But alone he found himself embarrassed at his own weakness, putting in a polite word with God, who must be awfully busy at the moment, but if he had the time, if he could see his way to it, there was this small matter of Samantha's safety. . . . Samantha, who seemed to him, despite her coming of age, barely out of the egg, with her short-sighted stare, her slight body. He had never been ambitious on her behalf, never planned glittering marriages or impressive careers, though both were possible. Unwanted herself, she had been entrusted to them, had filled their emptiness. Adoption was an ingenious way of circumventing nature's malice. She had made them happy. He had wanted no more than that for her. It was only now that he realized that life itself might be enough—too much indeed—to ask.

Stunning in its brief ferocity, the war surprised everyone by its ending, as it had by its beginning. After six days it was over, and while Manny and Rebecca sobbed tears of relief, Sarah poured herself another drink and sat quietly in the drawing room, aware once again of the cool pleasures of the green-and-gold walls, the high white ceiling, and the view of Hyde Park through the bay window.

She and John were together in the library the evening of the cease fire when the telephone rang. Sarah picked it up quickly, hoping it was Samantha.

The line was fuzzy and she could not at first distinguish the words. "I'm sorry, I can't hear you. Can you speak louder? Who is speaking?"

"Lady Middleway, this is Joe Raeburn. I'm afraid I have some bad news for you."

"Samantha's dead," Sarah said.

"How did you know?" he shouted, above the crackling.

John got up from his chair and came around to Sarah's side. She held the telephone slightly away from her ear so that he could hear Joe's words too. "Please tell me what happened."

"We were bringing some wounded troops back to hospital. I

was in front with the driver, Samantha was in the back of the truck. There was a bad corner and the truck ahead of us went out of control. Our driver slammed on the brakes but there was a truck close behind and oil on the road . . .''

"Did she die at once? Quickly?"

"Yes." Joe paused. "I wanted to ask you: what do you want me to do? Do you want Samantha brought home?"

The line crackled and buzzed. Then it cleared, so suddenly that Joe feared they had been cut off. "Hullo? Lady Middleway?"

Sarah's voice was very clear. "Samantha should be buried in Israel. Tell them her mother is Jewish and has placed you in charge. Will you do that? And come and see me when you return. Please."

She put down the telephone and sat with her hands in her lap. There seemed to be no words left in her head. What could there possibly be to say? What malign fate had ordained that of all places on earth Samantha should go to Israel? There was a slow-grinding inevitability about it all that numbed her—the way the past had come full circle. Her people, unknowingly, claimed her child from her as she had once wrenched herself free of them. You could not fool the Furies.

Her own recurring guilt, the evasion of her role, the betrayal of her dead through denial—all this circled in her mind. John rubbed her chilled hands, her shoulders, equally unable to find appropriate words.

"When she was a baby," Sarah said suddenly, "I was always afraid of her getting killed. Falling out of a window, or under a bus. Being run over. Even at school I thought she might fall off the swings or be injured on the playing field. I was frightened at the wrong time. . . . Of course it's my fault. This is my punishment."

He registered the dangerous tonelessness of her voice. "Rubbish! It's not something that's anyone's fault. It's something that just happens. It's the bloodiness of life."

"If you build a life on lies, you're guilty." She turned her head toward him, a movement of drooping exhaustion. "I'm sorry, John. I should have told you everything, at the beginning."

"Listen, old girl," he said, moving his weight from one foot to the other, a big man suddenly clumsy. "Did you really think I didn't know? Did you really imagine I could leave you in Germany, then, without taking some precautions to see you were all right? I knew a chap at the embassy. A weekly telephone call checking on the welfare of a British subject was—reassuring." He smiled apologetically. "Naturally it meant I became aware of certain things. Changing your name doesn't really change much, you know. It was the only way of making sure you were safe, d'you see?"

Her eyes were red and sore-looking. "I wasn't in love with you," she stated harshly. "I married you for safety. For security."

"Yes. But I thought it would do—for a start."

She swayed, suddenly dizzy with weakness, and John grabbed her to keep her from falling. As the loss of Samantha seeped into her, she felt the dark pit opening again and clung on to him, desperately, her eyes closed, shaking her head in a confused way, as if trying to dislodge the pain.

He stroked her hair, comforting himself by comforting her, though for both the comfort was pitifully inadequate.

"Oh John. What a waste. . . . What a waste."

The butler let Joe in and showed him to the drawing room. Sarah was waiting, standing by the fireplace. They shook hands formally.

"Good of you to come," she said. "Would you like a drink? Coffee?" It was a parody of a normal social call.

"No thanks."

There was a silence. Sarah began to pace up and down the dark green carpet. Up to the window, turn, pause, down the room again. "Has your father told you about me? I assume you know the facts."

"He didn't need to. I'd figured it out by then. I was packing Samantha's things before coming home and I saw a picture that I thought was of my grandmother as a young woman. Then I realized it was you, taken at your wedding."

He looked at Sarah now, seeing afresh the resemblance that had nagged at him when he first met her: the imperious turn of the head, so like Leah; the almond eyes he had himself inherited; the arched nose; the broad brow.

"There was a photograph of two children among my grand-mother's things: The boy died. Later I realized what had happened to the girl: she had become Sassie Middleway and ceased to exist."

Perhaps it was his own crushing sense of guilt over Samantha that made it easier to dislike Sarah. To him, the completeness and efficiency of her identity change denoted a ruthless character and an ambitiousness that overrode softer feelings. Her strength had been for self-preservation. His feelings showed in his face.

"I don't expect you to sympathize, but you have no way of knowing what it was like. Your father saved you from having to find out. We were all obsessed with the desire to escape from it. All of us. We chose different ways: Ruth put her faith in politics, to try to change the world. Your father fought his way up out of it. I ran. I admire your father's guts, but I didn't have his strength."

How different it all sounded, Joe thought, as she told it. She talked, without emotion, of the filthy streets, the foul-smelling alleyways, the fear of something worse happening each day. It was a childhood filled with hate, with none of the gaiety, the glee that Manny brought to his own recollections. In Sarah's memory they were all prisoners: hungry, sore-fingered, worn-out, trapped by their poverty. Her bitterness, her blind loathing of those days summoned up strangers with familiar names who had nothing to do with the well-fed complacency that had always surrounded him.

"You have no way of knowing," she said again, "because of the way things are today. In the thirties it was rather offensive to be a Jew. The thought might be delicately expressed, but you couldn't miss it: the amusing little sneer, the condescension, the faintly distasteful nuance. . . . You couldn't pick up a book without facing it. I didn't mind too much about people like ghastly old Buchan and his nonsense, but there was Ezra Pound's raving, and Eliot writing things like, 'The red-eyed scavengers are creeping from Kentish Town and Golders Green . . .' It was part of everyday life.

"To be Jewish was to be irredeemably second-rate; always the *arriviste*, always the social climber, the outsider trying to join in the laughter in the next room."

"But you played into their hands!" Joe protested. "You acquiesced in your own destruction: to accept the stereotyped definition of oneself is to abandon all possibility of dignity."

"Oh, you're all right." Her voice was weary. "You've grown up in the age of Jewish chic. Leading playwrights: Jewish. Prize-winning novelists: Jewish. Top pianists: Jewish. Nobody even comments. In the fifties, as recently as that, I can remember young Jewish writers agonizing all over the page about how difficult it was for them, at odds with their philistine backgrounds, and torn between ancient loyalties, and so on. But that's not even relevant any more. Today you can afford the luxury of indifference. It just doesn't matter what your parents were. Jewishness is just another trendy asset."

"Not everywhere. Not if your frontiers are surrounded by hostile Arabs."

"Israel is a nation now," she said. "It has the problems of any nation with hostile neighbors. It must define its own future."

"I don't think it can do it alone," Joe said. "There's a small question of survival involved. I don't think we can opt out of that."

But from disliking her, he began to understand her a little, as, despairing in the loss of her child, she acknowledged almost carelessly her own identity. "I'm not a demonstrative person. I find it rather hard on the whole to express emotion. Perhaps because I taught myself for so long *not* to feel, or rather to feel only determination to change my life. Which I did. Well, you know what Wilde said," she gave a sad smile, "about that particular item, about achieving one's greatest ambition."

"I left some things in the hall—just some personal things . . ."

"Thank you."

"You might like to know that Samantha once told me something you said about having a happy childhood—"

"Oh yes. Hardly matters now."

"It matters more than ever. She said you gave her a childhood without a shadow. Like a fairy tale. You said, 'Whatever happens you'll have had that.' You were right. You gave her the most perfect time of her life."

The social training carried her through. She managed a brief smile and walked him to the door. "Are you staying in England now?"

"Yes. I've got two more years at Cambridge and a year of practical work to catch up on."

At the last minute her calm crumpled. She caught sight of Samantha's small zipper bag, containing her things, placed beneath the large, carved mirror in the hall. "I want to hate you," Sarah said. "She wouldn't have gone without you. But I realize it's all part of a larger retribution. Perhaps after a while you'll come again."

He was amazed that she did not see the guilt he felt branded by, the self-rage that he alone had survived. For staying on in Israel had been his idea. An opportunity to sacrifice himself. Make a grand gesture. . . . "If you want me to," he said.

He crossed the road, smelling the freshly cut grass from Hyde Park, seeing the deck chairs, people sleeping the afternoon away, children playing. Warmth lapped around him, laughter floated across the park. The scene was very peaceful.

In Israel peace was an odd affair—more a temporary state of nonwar, while the streets were cleared, the dead buried. It was the first war Joe had known, and the strangest part about it, at the beginning, had been the weather. In films and books, old newsreels and photographs, war was a winter thing: a time of lowering skies and churning mud; rain on tin helmets, breath steaming on air bitter with cold.

But in Israel the sun shone on guns and glimmered on barbed wire. The blue sky was too clear; the heat shimmering off the desert made death seem improbable—but did not prevent it.

And soon enough it all looked as it should: the sudden bursts of gunfire blackened the blue sky, the smoke and grime blanked out the sun. The gaiety of the young soldiers—girls and boys alike—hardened into professionalism and, for some, ended there in those littered streets. And what was the point, after all? Now peace, soon again war. An old game. . . .

He felt the old hopelessness stealing over him and resisted it, setting off briskly along the pavement. He had to make his way home.

The snow flurried against the windows. Looking out, Joe could see the lights of Manhattan winking on, block after block of tall, narrow buildings glowing into life, golden honeycombs studding the darkening sky.

Through the open door to the next office he could see Frank Rosen pouring coffee from a jug. "You want some, Joe?"

He wandered in, took a cup, and helped himself, settling comfortably into one of Frank's huge armchairs. The year in New York was proving a success: an old Cambridge friend for a boss, and responses from all over the country to his letters and classified ads. Someone had a theory that all Jews were in some way related. After reading the dozens of replies he had received to his inquiries, he began to think there was some truth in the idea.

He had located Peszno people in Miami, San Francisco, Detroit. There was a fiddle player in a Philadelphia orchestra; a doctor in New Jersey; a couple of rag-trade hustlers in New York. A sad, failed academic who put no return address on his letter had said that there was little sense in their meeting. "Reunions are for two purposes—congratulations or charity. I am in the market for neither."

Joe was still surprised by what seemed like the infinite variety of humanity that had scattered from that small town and replanted itself. He no longer knew what it was that he was pursuing—a search for a pattern, a place into which he fitted? It had become a quest in its own right—an existential journey.

"You still planning to go to Washington tomorrow?" Frank asked.

"Yes."

"Weather looks pretty bad. Can't you make it some other time?"

"I don't want to disappoint them." The truth was he did not want to disappoint himself.

The snow falling past the windows was sparse, whirling lightly through the air. But on the ground it lay hard and thick, masking sidewalks and steps, the surface evil and glassy.

"I'll be sitting in my nice, warm apartment watching the ice float down the East River. I'll think of you."

The air was so cold that as Joe stepped from the warmth of the office building he gasped, breathless for a moment, his lungs burning. People walked up and down, clumsy with cold, a few of them dashing through the moving traffic at the sight of an occasional cab. Joe decided to walk. He turned away from the street.

The snow crunched under his feet and the Christmas lights were reflected up at him. Across the street a store blazed with electric promise, and the glassy pavement reproduced its brilliance, as though another glittering store had sunk beneath the ice and lay there, submerged, with all its lights shining from below the surface.

He had to be in Washington the next day. There had been other journeys, disappointments, but this time he was sure: he had checked and doublechecked: one particular Peszno trail led to a suburb of Washington, D.C.

During the night it rained and froze hard again, and in the morning the planes were grounded. He would have to take the train. Washington was only three hours by rail; he knew people who did it all the time.

The coach was crowded but Joe managed to find a seat. "Welcome aboard Amtrak, folks . . ." The train slid silently out of the station and the suburbs spread out to the horizon.

Two breakdowns later it had become a four-hour journey. "Sorry about that, folks," drawled the easy voice over the loudspeaker. "We're just having a little trouble here on account of the snow . . ."

Joe lined up at the bar and ordered a vodka and a sesame-seed roll with hot roast beef. The vodka came in a neat glass with plenty of ice, but the roast beef had to be thawed out, its plastic envelope dunked in boiling water, and the sesame-seed roll was flabby, like a damp rug. He chewed doggedly.

The scenery, when they began to move again, was enough to put even delayed travelers in a better mood: small, chaletlike houses, chocolate-box pretty towns and villages with neat gardens and hedges, the snow covering everything with a snug blanket of sparkling white. Streams cut through fields and lay like silver filaments in the snow, but the Delaware River coming suddenly into view was a rich, dark yellow as it raced past, and Chesapeake Bay looked bleak and stormy, the gray water heaving angrily in the wind.

The picture-book country suburb in which Joe arrived seemed an unlikely setting for a bunch of Polish immigrants. This all-American landscape was studded with small, pretty churches and garish parking lots for automobiles used and new. Where were the Jews to be found, he wondered. Would they have blended, conforming, into the population, with only their absence from Sunday services to distinguish them? Or would they suddenly show themselves, a bizarre, highly colored Oriental thread among the homespun?

In a drawer in his apartment lay Leah's collection, neatly filed and docketed now, dates and names cross-indexed, knots of mystery gradually unraveling, the Yiddish translated by a girl Frank had put him on to.

Joe had seen Sarah again before he left London for his year in New York. They had walked across the park as she talked, reluctantly, of the past. Once, as she told him about her first employer, Mrs. Bloom, with the tide-marked hands and the gray and yellow teeth, Joe began to laugh, and she had laughed too, seeing for the first time the absurdity of those wretched days.

She wrote to him occasionally, and Joe looked forward to her letters: in their correspondence Samantha still lived—Sarah talked of her daughter's childhood, and Joe recreated for her their time on the kibbutz, before the Six Day War. Occasionally she turned inward, in self-examination. She had looked at the world, she wrote once, as though through a shop window, her nose pressed to the glass, always outside, gazing in at the good things. Unable to reach them. When the whole shop, later, was hers for the asking, she found, unaccountably, that she still sensed that barrier. "Are some people destined always to be outsiders wherever they are? Is there no way to live unselfconsciously, in the present? You're young, you should be able to."

They were very alike in some ways, he and she. Both observers, both holding back, unwilling or unable to join the stream. Could they ever do so? It was perhaps also to answer that question that he carried out this endless investigation into the past—not so much investigation as resuscitation, an attempt to bring to life the unawakened heart.

The banquet room was large and crowded and in some ways reminded Joe strongly of every charity dinner he had attended with his parents in London. The combination of familiar event with unfamiliar voices, coupled with his exhaustion after the six-hour journey, lent a dreamlike quality to the scene.

"Welcome to Washington!" Jacob Lanski, fine-boned and dapper, rimless glasses flashing, took him through a throng of well-preserved matrons, shiny-faced girls and swarthy, bright-eyed men.

"Now, Joe: you wrote me about Peszno, and like I told you, I think we really got something for you. Tomorrow you get to meet a senator whose old man was born there, and when he gets here, I'm going to introduce you to a guy who actually came from Peszno himself."

The Chanukah dinner was underway: waiters whirled around the tables serving the meal; the band played, speeches were made, and generous responses called for. The raffle draw took place, and in a moment, Jacob promised, their special guest would be arriving. Meanwhile the fund-raising went on.

"I donate one thousand dollars!" called a large man from the next table, "anonymously!"

"One thousand dollars donated by Mr. Westbaum—anonymously!" roared the master of ceremonies.

Dinner was almost over when Jacob sprang up and hurried over to welcome the awaited guest, a girl who paused uncertainly by the entrance before being escorted in by a large, bald-headed man. She was dark-haired, short and sturdy, so that she gave an impression of being compact rather than slender, though she was in fact slim. She wore a high-necked blouse and shapeless skirt.

"Ladies and gentlemen, our guest has arrived—much delayed by the weather—Miss Galina Goldberg, whose escape from the Soviet Union we have all been reading about in the newspapers. Galina has flown in from Israel specially to play her violin outside the White House as a human-rights protest, as a protest against the inhumane treatment of Jews in the Soviet Union—in particular those Jews dismissed from their jobs, harassed and imprisoned for no other 'crime' than the desire to go to Israel. We hope to see as many of you at the demonstration as can make it."

He led her about the room, and when they were introduced, she shook Joe's hand, unsmiling, and nodded as she studied his face. "*Shalom*, Joe." Her own face was round, saved from plumpness by delicately chiseled lips and a neat, pointed chin. Her hand in his was cool; her green eyes were large and clear like a cat's. "You come to demonstration tomorrow?" she asked Joe.

"Of course."

"Good."

Jacob touched her shoulder tactfully, to move her on. She smiled at Joe. "Goodbye for a little."

He found he was still holding her hand and released it, nodding. "Till tomorrow."

Galina was introduced to the next group of guests, and then Jacob came back to Joe with the big, bald-headed man who had brought in the Russian girl. "Here he is, Joe. I told you we had a real Peszno guy. Dan Lever."

Joe's hand was crushed in the enveloping paw of the huge man. He was solid, not gone to softness. Only his white eyebrows gave the clue that he was more than middle-aged. Joe looked up at him as he removed the vast cigar, looked past the cloud of cigar smoke into a well-fleshed, dark-eyed moon of a face.

"Hi," Dan said, shaking Joe's hand vigorously.

"How d'you do." The unexpected familiarity of the face made Joe forget the regular form.

Dan, predictably, guffawed. "You British, you don't change, do you?" He slapped Joe's shoulder, his eyes narrowing to humorous slits as he grinned.

"I'm not sure I can tell you much about Peszno, I wasn't more'n a kid when I left town. I was in the Russian Army—*that's* the kind of thing you remember. They nearly killed us at the beginning, and I tell you, there were days when I wished they would. It was worse for the Jews, of course. If they caught any of us praying—or even *looking* as if we might be praying—they'd beat us, to discourage us a little."

He shook his head. "What they never figured out was that it was the praying that gave us the strength to go on." He roared with laughter again.

"Dan," Joe began, but the big man was in full spate.

"This is a fine community we got here. We like to think we maintain the traditions. At the same time I think it's wrong to hold ourselves apart. I campaigned—this was a long time ago now—to get the country club desegregated."

"They barred blacks?"

"They barred Jews! But no more. I've been a member for twenty years—I'm on the committee. I have a good social life, a lovely home and family, and I run a good business. We produce objects connected with religious ceremonies. There's been a great revival of interest in

Orthodox matters, Joe. In observance. And we're catering to that revival. For instance, we do a very beautiful folding *succah* in rustic-finish plastic. You just open it up and you have this roomy hut, kind of a gazebo, light trelliswork, you could lift it with one finger, but you can put it out on the patio or wherever for the festival. Close it up afterward and it hangs on the garage wall till next year. That's proved a very popular line. Of course we do the decorations to go with it—fruit, vegetables, we even produce *lulav* fronds and *esrogs*, the whole bit, all in washable, lifelike plastic."

"That's amazing," Joe said.

"You're right, Joe. It *is* amazing. There is so much scope for modern thinking here. Like for instance, Passover cassettes, to play at the Seder, and then Chanukah bushes! Our kids always gave us a bad time around Christmas. They see all their little pals with the Christmas trees and the stockings, right? So we do the Chanukah bushes—plastic, no mess. Electric menorahs have been big this year, people don't like wax candles burning in their homes—you got the fire risk, problems with young children, babysitters can't be trusted . . . this way you combine the traditional rituals with safety, right?"

"Right. Dan, about Peszno—"

Dan put his hand on Joe's shoulder. "I'm glad to see you're interested in the old country, Joe. I can tell you that traditional values have never been more needed: currently between ten and fifteen percent of Jews marrying in the U.S. marry non-Jews. The problem is serious, parents are worried." His smile broadened. "I'm okay as it happens: four daughters and all happily married to good Jewish guys. And don't think luck had anything to do with it, I don't leave things to luck. I wrote to all my suppliers and I told them, 'From here on in, the salesmen you send me need two qualifications: one, they gotta be single. Two, they gotta be Jewish.' They got the message. The girls are happy, everyone's happy."

He beamed at Joe, a sleek, well-nourished old man with youthful eyes; an older version of Manny. He looked contented and prosperous. A solid citizen. Respected member of the community. And this was the end of the Peszno line in this particular corner of the world: Danielsche, the baby of the family, Leah's younger brother, left behind and missed so desperately by the sister who had been like a mother to him.

How odd, Joe reflected, *that a man should lose a lifetime of dignity in the instant of his rediscovery.* Daniel, the little brother mourned for dead or lost to the Russian Army, was a tragic figure, a speck of helpless humanity at the mercy of powerful forces. Dan found, was a joke: a big man with small ideas. The irony of it was irresistible.

"Shall I tell Gran, or will you?" Joe asked. The connection was very clear and he heard his father sigh.

"I will," Manny said. "I'll break it to her gently. Then you call her and give her the details."

Manny phoned Leah. "Listen, Mum. Your little brother Daniel, your baby brother you thought was dead—"

"Danielsche, ah . . ."

"Well, he's alive and well and living in Washington."

She shrieked and began to cry. He shouted irritably, "So why the tears? He's alive!"

Joe began *his* call cautiously: "You've heard the news, Gran?" "Yes."

She sounded calm enough. He relaxed. "Wonderful, isn't it?"

"Yes." She began to cry.

"Gran . . ."

"Is he well?"

"Very well."

"He didn't lose an arm or a leg in the army?"

"No. He's fine."

"How does he look?"

"Splendid. He looks a bit like Dad, only bigger and heavier. He's pretty bald, but it suits him. And I told you he's doing very well— Why are you crying?" he yelled. His head was beginning to hurt.

"My baby brother, so little, so gentle, with the big dark eyes, he used to suck his thumb and now you tell me he's a big fat man with a bald head. It's terrible!"

Joe felt the old dizziness descending. He pressed on. "Gran, I have to go now. I have photographs of him and his grandchildren—"

Sobs.

"And he plans to go to London for a holiday very soon so you'll see him."

Sobs.

"Well, isn't it all splendid?"

"Yes." She went on sobbing.

The White House demonstration began quietly. The sun shone on the snow and on the placards held by the demonstrators. In the brilliant light their dark clothes against the whiteness gave them the look of statues.

Galina, in a baggy fur coat and hat, began to play her violin, surrounded by men with black armbands on their sleeves.

Standing on the outskirts of the crowd, Joe listened as the pure notes rose in the crisp air and melted into silence. A television crew was filming the event, and the reporter moved in close to interview Galina as she began to put away her violin in its case. At that moment the demonstration ceased to be solemn and orderly. A small mob, edging in from across the street, surged forward and began to rough up the demonstrators, making sure to remain in camera range. Shouting, punching, and pushing, they sparked off a response that in seconds had the entire crowd brawling. Propelled into its midst, Joe was punched in the face before he could even get his hands out of his pockets. A press photographer's camera knocked him on the side of the head and he was hurled back against the railings. He felt the iron thud against his skull.

"Peace!" he heard someone shouting faintly, and "Jewish troublemakers!" from another throat.

The planes were taking off that afternoon, though the countryside dropping away below was still an unbroken white. The plane hummed, and the engine noise was soporific. Joe unfastened his seatbelt and stretched tentatively. A burning sharpness stabbed at his spine and he grunted in pain. From the next seat, Galina glanced at his bruised face and grinned cheerfully. "Well, Joe. You see what it means, to be music lover."

Joe mumbled indistinctly, his lips swollen.

She touched his arm sypathetically. "I invite you to dinner. I owe you. For this." She placed her fingertips lightly against his bruised mouth.

Joe had noted the rubbed cuffs of her dark blouse, her thin shoes. He also knew what dinner could cost in New York. "Why don't you have dinner with me?" he suggested.

She laughed. "I understand your motive. Listen: beautiful charity pays. Charity pays everything. They bring me from Israel for demonstration. They organize television, arrange everything. I have Cadillac at Kennedy Airport to take me to hotel. You are my guest, okay?"

He nodded.

"Good." Her voice was deep and husky with an accent part Russian, part American, a touch of Garbo in *Ninotchka.* Joe wanted her to go on talking, just so that he could listen to her voice.

"What was that you played this morning? It sounded like a requiem."

"Wieniawski violin concerto, slow movement." Galina grinned. "I am thinking: Wieniawski was greatest violinist who ever lived, practically, and he was Jew. Why not remind Russians?"

"Appropriate."

"Much so. Wieniawski had motto: *'Il faut risquer.'* I believe same thing. Necessary take risk. When I got out of Soviet Union I thought: maybe I fail, maybe they catch me. But must take risk. For important thing."

But how important is important? Joe wondered. *What should be risked, and whom?* To risk yourself, that was easy, but where was the line drawn? At what point did the grand gesture become the selfish one? A narrow street in Israel, a truck suddenly sluing, the street tilting, the world exploding. He, absurdly, unhurt. Samantha, guiltless, pointlessly sacrificed.

The Cadillac was indeed waiting and swept them deftly through the evening traffic into the city. The hotel was discreetly luxurious, and Galina's shapeless coat was noticeably out of place. Cheerfully she sailed across the lobby and into the elevator with Joe.

"Now. We order dinner." She flung open the door of the suite: "You like?"

The rooms were opulently furnished, with large baskets of flowers and fruit arranged on low tables. She wandered about, reading the messages, sniffing critically at the flowers—"No perfume, terrible!"—

and eating the grapes. She pressed one of the service buttons and vanished into the bedroom, calling through the open door, "You like dry martini Joe, or should it be rather vodka?"

She reappeared, a white terry-cloth bathrobe wrapped around her, and threw her blouse and skirt onto a chair. Joe's expression went wooden. Perhaps Russian women were more accustomed to taking the initiative, but this no-nonsense approach left him feeling at a distinct disadvantage.

He was uncomfortably aware too, that since Samantha, his sexual encounters had become increasingly unsatisfactory: a matter of routine processing, uninvolved servicing. He did not want another such mechanical nonevent to take place now.

There was a knock on the door. "Ah!" Galina let in the bellboy. "Room service. You have these cleaned right away please." She handed him her clothes.

She flung out her arms happily. "I love room service. Makes everything simple. And charity pays." She looked at him, her head tilted. "I think you do not approve, Joe. But I do not ask them for money, and they have so much money, and they love expenses! Always they ask, 'Do you want car? Do you want food? Drink?' I did not ask for such a hotel, such a suite. But they insist. So I make them happy. I enjoy. Enjoy with me a little, why not?" She glanced at his suit, rumpled after the journey, and asked hopefully, "You want clothes cleaned, maybe?"

"No thank you."

"Okay. We order dinner now. Maybe caviar?"

Dinner arrived, wheeled in, and they ate sitting by the window, watching the gray city sparkle into beauty as the night crept in on it.

"Beautiful city. You live long in New York, Joe?"

"Almost a year now. Soon I'll go back to London."

"We'll meet there maybe. Maybe charity will invite me to London. I shall see Queen Elizabeth Hall and I shall have Oxford marmalade for breakfast and Earl Grey tea to drink and also Bath Oliver biscuits and Stilton—"

"Not for breakfast, I hope. How do you know all this?"

"Ah. I am quick learner. Someone told me you're architect."

"Just about. I've spent seven years turning into one. I just need a final bit of paper now, which will make me much more expensive to employ."

"And then?"

"Ah, that's the difficult part isn't it? How do you ever know what you'll do next? When did you plan to leave Russia?"

"I didn't. I didn't know I would go to Israel. There was friend of mine, cellist. One day he comes to me and says, 'I want you to have my piano. I'm leaving for Israel.' I am amazed. I say, 'Why you want go to Israel, you're sixty years old, why change life now?'

"But he goes. And he gives me piano. My mother is not pleased. We have so little room. Every day I look at piano and every day piano gets bigger for me. I'm starting to think about Israel. I go to library and find Hebrew book. Librarian gets angry: why I want read Hebrew? I begin to look for synagogue. Pretty soon I'm trying to teach myself Hebrew. Maybe it is because they forbid that it becomes important. Because I must hide what I do. I don't know. But I decide I must get out, to be where *I* can decide what I read, who I speak to, maybe what music I play. Where I can breathe."

"Didn't your parents want to get out of Russia with you?"

"My father is dead. My mother does not wish go out. She is not Jewish of course."

Joe looked at her incredulously. "Your mother is not Jewish?"

"No."

"But—" he began to grin. "Does the charity know this?"

"Why should they? Who cares?"

Joe looked at her incredulously. "Your mother is not Jewish?" not officially. You must know that."

She began to laugh. "Then I am imposter! Don't tell charity!" Laughing, her ivory face flushed with warmth, she seized his hand, demanding complicity. Joe smiled, and she was startled by the change in his face—a brightness that for a moment transfigured his normally commonplace features. She let go of his hand and looked at him more carefully, and saw that in fact his features were far from ordinary, but that he assumed a sort of cloak of blandness, a camouflage that veiled him from casual observation.

The waiter returned to take away the dishes. He was a small, voluble Italian, quick on his feet, his arches not yet fallen in the service of his trade. He noted Galina's instrument case on a chair as he left the room. "Violinist, huh? I heard an old story about violinists—before a concert they won't, and afterward they can't." He threw a glance of commiseration at Joe. "Well, have a nice evening anyway."

"Do you have to go straight back to Israel?" Joe asked.

"Well, quartet has commitments of course—" She stopped. "Why you ask questions all time, Joe? Talk all time about me? Of course I like, it's nice, talk about self. But what about you? Let's talk about you, Joe."

"I don't like talking about myself, and anyway I'm far more interested in hearing about you. Tell me about violinists: is there any truth in that old story?"

She was stretched out on the sofa, bare feet crossed at the ankles. She untied the belt of the bathrobe. Her small, rounded body was silken, amber and cream and brown against the rough white cloth, sensuous as Goya's *Maja*, glowing with life.

"As music lover," she said, "maybe you should find out for self."

The following morning Galina had a press conference. After that Joe took her to lunch and they walked through the streets of Manhattan, thawed and filled with a thousand tints and colors, vivid after the blanketing whiteness.

"Being musician is a little like being refugee," she said. "Always a suitcase and always a strange city." She looked at her watch. "Soon I must catch plane. Will I see you again, Joe? Will you come maybe to Israel?"

He had thought Israel could never be revisited. It was the center of his guilt; Samantha's grave marked the fiasco of his attempt at self-determination.

Surprising himself, he said, "Yes. I could come to Israel." He took her hand, firm and cold, and tucked it protectively inside his overcoat pocket, holding it tightly. "You should wear gloves in weather like this."

She laughed at him, teeth gleaming against her rosy skin. "Fuss, fuss!"

They crossed the street. The Miës van der Rohe Seagram Building on Park Avenue rose before them like a vast mirror; in its gleaming façade the New York sky, full of scudding, rain-filled clouds, was reflected, the copper tones giving the sky an out-of-season, autumnal glow. As they walked toward it, the whole building seemed to be on the move, drifting sideways with the clouds.

Frank said in astonished tones, "You're telling me that you have persuaded this charitable organization to put up the loot for a musicians' center in Israel?"

367

"Provided I do the building."

"Joe, this isn't like you at all. This is like me. *I'm* the hustler, the mover, the guy with the get-up-and-go. How come you're suddenly so motivated?"

"I found there was something I wanted."

Galina met him at the airport. "See: in Israel, too, we have cars to meet important people at airport!" She waved Joe to a small and battered saloon. "Why should it be necessarily a Cadillac?" And she drove him to the apartment she shared with two members of the quartet.

She put salad and cheese on the table and poured him some Israeli wine. "Something to drink—why should it be necessarily vodka!"

She was thinner than when he had last seen her— "Army food, my dear. We have to do military service. Khaki uniform, metal hat, heavy rifle. I patrol valley. And then, such luxurious sleep in so-romantic tent. 'Clean your rifle!' they are shouting. I try, but not well. 'Can't you clean rifle? What are your hands, precious?' 'Yes,' I say, 'my hands are precious.' Must I damage hands even when there is no fighting? After all, I want still be able play violin!"

He looked around the small, sparsely furnished room, her violin propped against a rough table on which the meager meal was spread. "Not as luxurious as New York."

She waved her arm toward the window. "Where I am does not matter so much. I'm alive. I'm breathing, enjoying freedom. Small freedoms, big freedom. Inner freedom. Is necessary. And soon you will put up beautiful building for us, and beautiful charity will pay. And we are together again."

It was different, this time, in Israel. He was constantly experiencing what he came to think of as a sort of kosher Crispin Day connection: the casual allusion picked up, the reference caught, and the building contractor or the girl at the drawing board in the office would recognize him as a fellow-survivor from the Six Day War. He might disregard all other bonds, deny links, reject ties, yet that one experience united them in a miraculous brotherhood.

He stayed away from Samantha's grave, trying to keep the past in its own box. But one night in a restaurant they encountered David and Moshe, friends from the old kibbutz, who roared a greeting, embraced Joe, and talked without embarrassment of Samantha.

Afterward Galina asked, "She was English?"

"Yes."

"How she died?"

He told her.

"I think you are blaming self," Galina said when he finished. "This will not help. So much guilt already, half world drowns in guilt. Try *use* your life. Don't waste."

Easy words, but he sensed a danger. He had never cared about his own life, a futile episode on the journey toward the void. But Galina was not to be wasted.

At last he visited Samantha's grave. This was where ultimately all battles ceased. Death was a necessary end, man's life a very shadow. What seemed stable, permanent, melted like ice into nothingness.

The skepticism that had seemed so obvious provided no defense. Among his grandmother's papers he had found a bit of Browning, copied out in her faint, spidery writing:

> All we have gained then by our unbelief
> Is a life of doubt diversified by faith,
> For one of faith diversified by doubt,
> We called the chessboard white—
> We call it black.

Black or white the chessboard remained, still had to be crossed. You had to create your own reason for the journey. Standing beside Samantha's grave, Joe tried to remember her as she had been in life—not that last day, trapped in the wreckage, among a heap of wounded men. Finding her, he had thought for a moment she was unhurt—merely stunned. Until he touched her, and her head rolled sideways and the dark hole in her throat pumped blood that soaked his arms as he held her.

He tried to obliterate that image—to think of her filled with the innocent enjoyment she brought to everything, working on the kibbutz, scrubbing pans in the kitchen—"I've been goosed by the chickens again!" she had laughed. Examining a book or a picture very close up, myopic eyes wide behind the tinted shields, filled with life—"Joe, could I be psycho-Semitic?"

He dwelled on what they had shared, rather than its cutting off. The perfect childhood she had been given, followed by a time of gentle happiness. How should a life be measured? In terms of moments spread out, sparsely, to cover the gray years? Samantha had died with her happiness still unrationed. He should give thanks for that. Thank who? Black or white, you were faced with the same chessboard.

"*Or ever the silver cord be loosed, or the golden bowl be broken or the pitcher be broken at the fountain, or the wheel broken at the cistern . . .*"

Well, what then? The ancient chroniclers at least, were in no doubt: "*Then shall the dust return to the earth as it was; and the spirit shall return to God who gave it.*"

Meanwhile there was a site being readied, ink on paper to be translated into concrete. Building to be done.

London looked dirty. New York had its squalid streets, and two years in Israel had accustomed Joe to litter, but London looked distressingly dirty, like a seedy old woman.

The Bishop's Avenue house was, however, as immaculate as he remembered. Becky fussed over him and apologized for the untidiness. "Such a mess!" He looked at the gleaming room, the bright brasswork, the flawless tabletops and unmarked armchairs. "Shocking. I don't know how you live in this pigsty."

"You can joke, Joe, but your father's always leaving things spread around. Lately he's been bringing home half his filing cabinets, telephone calls through the night, papers everywhere—I ask him, 'Why don't you relax, give yourself a rest?' but there's always something that has to have his attention now, right away. Maybe you can persuade him to take it a little easy."

She picked up a copy of the *Investors' Chronicle* from a chair and put it in a drawer. "That's better. . . . You *will* stay home for a bit, won't you, Joe? We haven't seen you for such a long time—New York and then Israel, you're never here!"

"I'll stay for a bit." There was a good deal to be done, no time to waste. He had to raise the subject of Galina with his parents before she arrived in London. She had a few more concerts with the quartet and then she could leave. Meanwhile he would organize the final paper at Cambridge and then—

Joe sat down rather suddenly on the sofa as the room began to revolve around him. "It's ridiculous how tired I feel. Flying doesn't usually affect me at all."

She looked at him carefully. "It must be all that sun, you look quite yellow. As yellow as a guinea. It's the sun." But she called the doctor.

"It's hepatitis," the doctor said, "Lot of it about at the moment. Bed. Rest. Bland food. No alcohol. You can't take risks with it, could turn nasty."

"I won't come too close," Manny told Joe apologetically. "I don't want to catch anything. I hear things worked out very well in Israel."

"Amazingly enough, given the circumstances, they seem to like it," Joe said dryly.

"Listen: don't imagine they'd have been happy whatever it was like. Charities and relatives—the worst type of client. Nit-picking, not sure what they want, but knowing they can take advantage of you. And a charity *with* a relation . . . ! Anyway, it's not just them. There's a bit in the *Times* about it." He dropped the paper on the bed. "Some chap's had a look at it, talks about its human scale and warmth and goes on about ziggurats and identifiable vernacular, and a lot of cobblers I can't quite follow. Anyway, it certainly looks . . . unusual, in the picture."

Manny was being tactful. He seemed tired, standing by the door, jingling his small change in his trouser pocket, and for the first time Joe realized that his father was an old man. He was sixty-two, and the lines of strain made him look more than his age. Joe wanted to say something reassuring, but exhaustion got in the way of the words. He closed his eyes.

"Rest a little now," Becky said anxiously. "Presently I'll fetch you up some soup. *If* the cook's got it right. They just have no feeling for it, these people."

Becky, inevitably, was busy planning a charity affair. Leah, unlike Manny, had no fears of "catching something." She arrived the next day and announced that she would look after Joe.

"You'll do as you're told and you'll get better quicker. I brought you some soup in a jar, and after that you can have some grapefruit." She tucked him in firmly.

371

He grinned, defeated by her confident authority.

"You want something to read?"

"I'd like you to talk to me," he said.

She looked surprised. Her soft, round body was almost weight-less as she sat on the edge of his bed. She pursed her lips thoughtfully, the wrinkles radiating from her mouth like gathers in fine fabric. "What about?"

"Tell me about Poland. About when you were a girl."

"Oh you don't want to hear about that, it's very boring for young people to listen to us old ones talking, you have your own lives to lead. Of course when I was a girl, it was different. Then, we had respect for old people . . ."

He made himself comfortable. Curious: terrified of the boredom she could inflict, he had spent years heading off and avoiding this old survivor, blocking her out. Now, rising to the unfamiliar challenge of a question, she trawled her past for long-sunken treasures to offer him.

On Yom Kippur the family went to synagogue as always, fasting. Joe lay in bed and fretted, bones aching, head throbbing. Without Galina he felt as though a part of him were missing. He was still very shaky and the slightest effort left him breathless and dizzy, but the worst effect of the illness was the depression and lassitude that hung over him like a cloud. No wonder "jaundiced" had entered the language.

Unable to concentrate on reading, he switched on his bedside radio and came in halfway through a news broadcast. He could not at first understand what the news reader was talking about. "Stiff fighting . . . surprise element . . . Egyptian and Syrian assaults launched simultaneously."

"I'll just recap on the headlines." The voice was jaunty, almost cheerful, as he repeated the facts.

Israel was at war again. And Galina was in Israel. The wrench of fear brought Joe to his feet, staggering. But even as he reached for his clothes, his knees were buckling under him. Sick and shaking he crawled back to bed. He still found it hard to believe. Today was Yom Kippur. Wars didn't start on Yom Kippur; it was inconceivable. But this one had, the country caught unawares, all work stopped and the pulse of life slowed. He had no need to use his imagination—he could visualize the action from his own experience: the swift change of gear, the mobilization, the shift to a war footing; tractors, desks, factory lathes abandoned. For a while peace, now again, war. Galina would be in uniform. He could hear her husky voice—"Heavy khaki, metal hat, heavy rifle . . ." Even now she was on some dusty road or barricaded street, her violin left behind, her hands tuning an instrument of war, eyes scanning not a score but the skyline. In her world there was no longer a place for a fiddler on the roof. That was where snipers lurked.

Attempts to telephone were useless. His skin itched, his head burned as he lay safe in London, tensed against a faraway bullet. He could do nothing. Don't drown in guilt, Galina had said, but this Yom Kippur was, indeed, a day of atonement.

The following afternoon he had a visit from an old friend. Hilary Punter, now a doctor, ignored Joe's illness, briskly unsympathetic in the medical fashion. "Listen, I'm leaving for Israel. This time I might get there before it's all over."

"What about your parents? They thought they were grooming you for a life with the *goyim*. Won't they be upset?"

"Actually, they've been incredibly decent. Even mother was no trouble. Said she understood. Which is more than I do. Why do I feel this need to go rushing off to foreign parts? I'm English, this is my country."

"The roots that clutch?" Joe suggested. He had always resisted the emotional pull of Israel. Going there, he had assessed the state's chances of survival rather than celebrating it. Faced with its casualness he had behaved with stubborn English formality. He had found the Israelis' pride tactless, their manners graceless, and the place itself awesome in a quite impersonal way. He had been astonished, but not drawn in.

Two years had done much to change that. Gradually, without polemics, he had gained an understanding. In the barbers', on the arm of the man cutting his hair, a tattooed number. "Yes," he said, embarrassed, "Auschwitz. I always meant to have it removed, but then I thought, it's part of me." The mark was just another sign of that determination, that obstinacy to go on living that had shamed Joe. Now, away from it all, he was with them.

"*Then will he strip his sleeve and show his scars . . .*" A tattoo, also, was a scar. But this was not Crispin's Day. The despair, the deep dread that lay over that faraway country gathered him within its bleak folds.

373

Galina sent a typical telegram. OKAY I BROKE FOOT BUT LUCKILY NO ONE HAS WRITTEN SONATA FOR LEFT FOOT.

The official ceasefire seemed like an interim measure. And Joe was acquainted with that overlap between war and peace, the no-man's time. He left for Israel.

He sensed a new mood as soon as he landed: no jubilation; rather, gratitude for a breathing space—a weary gathering up of strength for the next time it was needed. In the dazed eyes of those he passed in the street, he saw an awakening from the dream of invincibility induced by the Six Day War.

The Israelis sowed crops and planted oranges and avocados, but no dragons' teeth could have sprouted a deadlier harvest. For every new war, new warriors. And after every war, new dead. In a country so small, few families were now complete. The homeland, it seemed, extorted a sharp toll.

Everything here was a monument to survival, and for the first time he allowed himself to wonder at the variousness of its forms. He had tended to think always in terms of the difference between himself and others. For the first time he dwelled instead on what was the same: the common factor beneath the superficial differences.

He shared with these people not only the present, but a past, a path to this present that he had never wanted to explore beyond a certain point. It was a past cluttered with symbols he had rejected. Perhaps what he felt was the existential depression that the rootless creature suffers in place of the faith he is unable to accept. *Ubi sunt* . . . etc. The weight of generations past pressed on him, their mysticism, their prayers—and what was prayer after all, but a habit?

The tracks led back through the years, beyond the Holocaust to the ghetto where they had thought themselves safe enough, creating a tiny world within a world, cast out when it suited their hosts. Moving on, fighting to adjust, families like his, disparate and fragmented, were held together by a thread that tied them, struggle how they might. He, too, was bound, lightly but inextricably. Always the thread led back into the past. The present re-created that past just as the past created the present. Israel was a vulnerable homeland, but there was another homeland that had proved hostile—*der Heim*, Poland—that someone once told him meant "rest you here" in Hebrew. They had rested, built lives, families, dreams. It took a millennium to establish roots and then wrench them up.

Leah's stories of her little town, her odyssey to the land not of milk and honey but of silk curtains and soft carpets. . . . The thread spun, clung, held. The life passes, the world endures. Could he recapture that life, gain life from its renewal? Absurd and pointless, this searching; there was never any going back. But was it, strictly speaking, for him a going back, or a going forward?

He drove Galina to Tel Aviv, snatching at least the traveling time to be with her. "Quartet is giving concerts all time, Joe. In hospitals, military camps, all over. I must stay while I am needed. What will you do?"

The train was still rolling through a landscape of factories and apartment buildings, although according to Joe's calculations it should have been nearing Peszno.

They had already been held up for six hours by a switch failure, so it would be night when they arrived. He was disappointed. He had looked forward to the approach to the town, the sweep through the last few miles of field upon field, the whistle of the train—so often described by Leah. Now he would see nothing.

Joe had deliberately chosen to come by train, to trace the footsteps of Chaim and Leah, to see what remained of their departing tableau: the track across the fields outside the town, the high train looming above the crops, drawing to a steaming, reluctant halt at the shelter. Well, there would be a station now, and the train was diesel, not steam, but he still felt a thrill of anticipation, visualizing that horizon of curving earth, bleak and frosty, the untouched countryside through which the steel had cut so long ago.

Then the train was slowing and the small man sharing the compartment, who looked like a commercial traveler, was getting his suitcase down from the rack.

"Peszno?" Joe asked, sure that it could not be.

"Peszno!" The man nodded, beaming. He looked at the label on Joe's case. "English?"

"Yes."

He nodded again, still smiling. "Peszno important town. Very big engineering works. High productivity. Good export record."

Joe looked through the window as the last of the sprawling buildings gave way to the station. "I thought the station was outside the town—"

The man snorted impatiently, frowning, "Outside? How, outside? Station is very central, of course. Necessary to have central station in important town with industry. Station is in center, of course."

"Of course." Joe joined the people hurrying off the train and then stood, trying to get his bearings. Nothing looked remotely like the town whose stories he carried inside his head.

This was a bustling modern city, sprawling as far as the eye could see, bristling with industrial chimneys and busy with delivery trucks loading and unloading at the station.

There were taxis outside the station. Joe headed for one and gave the name of his hotel. It proved to be disconcertingly international, and he wished he had gone somewhere smaller.

After dinner he went for a walk, flinching against the cold as the swinging doors released him from the faintly stuffy warmth of the hotel. He walked, briskly at first to keep warm, and then more slowly, trying again to establish some pattern to the streets. There were cafés and wine bars and a sense of nightlife going on for those who knew where to find it. After a few minutes a small car cruising past pulled up, and the driver rolled down the window, stuck his head out, and asked a question.

"I don't speak Polish."

"English. Ah. You want go place?" He made a female shape with his hands. "Good time."

"Oh. No thanks."

"Okay. You want lift some place? Cheap fare."

Joe would have preferred to walk back, but the man had an appealingly jolly face, and he felt it would be mean-spirited to deprive a hopeful moonlighter of some extra earnings. "Okay. Hotel." He gave the name.

Back in his room he checked the time and put through a call to Galina. "How was the concert?" he asked her.

"Good. How's the hotel?"

"Depends what you want. I had beef stroganoff for dinner and the wine waiter was patronizing. Then a local offered to show me a good time—"

"I thought this is small town—"

"So did I—"

"Hullo, who is speaking? Please give name." They had a crossed line plus crackling noises.

"I miss you," shouted Joe.

"What? Who is speaking?"

"I miss you."

"I'll call you tomorrow."

The next morning the streets were crowded and people rushed past Joe as he made his way across town. They looked prosperous, the women more fashionable than he had expected. Only the high-cheekboned, sharp-eyed faces retained an East European stamp. At a large crossroads he stopped a middle-aged man. "Excuse me, do you speak English?"

A nod.

"Can you tell me in which direction is the river?"

The man sucked on his mustache and pursed his lips. "Well, not near here . . ."

"But the direction?"

"In that way is general direction," he paused, "but it is not the best part of town, of course."

"Thank you."

Joe walked on through a network of streets, with buildings tall and thin on either side. There were billboards advertising Chopin recitals and concerts and a large poster announcing a competition for young pianists. No baked beans or cigarettes writ large, though he did spot a sign reading COCA-COLA.

He skirted a large square planted with formal flower beds. On all four sides, massive buildings, bulky and official looking. There was no bandstand where Chaim once listened to the waltzes, marches, and mazurkas that followed "Long Live the Czar." Could this be the main town square? Hard to tell, but, taking it on that basis, he turned down a steep, hilly street and began to descend gradually toward the lower end of town.

Flimsy-looking gray high-rises dominated the streets, offices occupying the lower floors. The district was clearly shabbier as he walked on. It was, as the man had said, not the best part of town. But then it never had been.

Walking steadily, Joe had covered more ground than he realized, for suddenly he was heading out of town, the houses thinning out and then, rounding a curve, he came upon the river, looping away to his left.

He turned and followed its bank. The river, too, had changed: the green, glinting water the young girls had strolled by was frothy with pollution from the chemical factories lined up like aircraft hangars on the opposite bank. There was a bridge, newish but already stained and cracked, and the old stone bridge—the one they had hung over, gazing down into the river, trying to spot fish—was barricaded, no longer safe to use.

Still, he must be very near now, and he found himself hurrying, giving in to a sense of urgency, pulled along almost, summoned. There was a chapter in *The Wind in the Willows* that used to bring him to the edge of tears as a child—the bit where Mole, without knowing it, approaches his old home on a bitter winter day and is suddenly assailed by a summons, a powerful current: "Home! That was what they meant, those caressing appeals, those soft touches wafted through the air, those invisible little hands pulling and tugging, all one way!"

Dulce domum. But he had no abandoned home, no roots here, no reason for a sudden ache as from a long-forgotten wound. He had Leah's father's address on a piece of paper, which he held out to a woman passing by. She stared at the street name, puzzled, and shook her head. Two streets farther on an older woman nodded vigorously and began to gabble.

"Do you speak English?" Joe asked hastily, "French? German?"

She spoke German badly, but well enough to explain. There had been a road-widening after the war, she said. (*Which war?* Joe wondered.) The street no longer existed.

He was unprepared for the intensity of his disappointment. He had built up the street, house by house, in his mind: the little iron balconies at the first-floor windows, the dusty cobblestones. Some houses, he had known, would be gone. But for the street itself to be gobbled up in the maw of time—he had not expected that.

The woman smiled sympathetically. There had been others coming in search of their beginnings, their hopes dashed in the same way. She told him to take a left turn, then a right, and he would be where the street had been.

378

Left and then right, past a shoe shop where a small line of customers sat immobile, waiting to be served, past offices and a shop filled with refrigerators. Past a butcher with another line of patient customers and a carcass hanging in the window bright red and gaping, like a Soutine still life.

He found himself at the bottom of a broad avenue lined by large apartment buildings. The street curved slightly, and as he began to walk, a sudden chill wind caught his coat and wrapped it tight against his legs. A fine spray of icy sleet stung his eyes. The weather, at least, had not changed with the years.

There was no point in continuing to fight his way up this anonymous boulevard against the wind, and he turned aside to explore one of the streets running off to one side. Easier walking here, sheltered from the wind. He hurried on and came out suddenly into an open space, a little square. People and shops gave it a bustle, and there were still some small, old buildings holding the high-rises at bay. There were slender lime trees to shade the square in summer, bare-branched now. There was a drinking fountain. There were benches, their blue paint faded and peeling, and a café behind whose steamed-up glass doors people were gathered, drinking tea and schnapps.

He wandered around the little square. So many possibilities had been discussed here, so many dreams had died. And the square remained. He went into the bar for a drink.

His foreignness was an immediate conversation starter, and a couple of English-speaking locals were pushed forward, with encouragement and interruptions from the rest.

Yes, he was from London, Joe told them. But his grandparents and their parents had come from this town. Exclamations, a toast to his family, a toast to the town.

"Of course," he went on, "they left a long time ago, but I recognize everything in this square from my grandmother's description—even the benches."

Translated, this was greeted by roars of laughter. "After war, square was ruin. New benches. New drinking fountain. New trees."

So nothing was as it had been. Even the trees. He saw now that they were young, too young to have sheltered the Esperanto classes and the chess-playing old men. The paint on the benches was faded and cracked because it had been done cheaply; money had been scarce after the war. So much for the little tugs and murmurs and the summons: *dulce domum* was a figment of his sentimental imagination. But still:

the square lay where it had; people drank tea in the bar that had been Slumkow's café. The blue benches were blue.

They drank to each other, the schnapps glowing through them like fire. One man, white-haired and gnarled, who had said nothing, suddenly spoke, in English. "I remember procession you speak of. We marched with red banner."

"My relatives were in that procession. My grandmother was one of the leaders," Joe explained.

When they heard the family name there was a pause. The synagogues were gone, they said. Bombed like so much of the town. They began to drift away, huddled into their coats, shoulders hunched against the wind, visible for a moment when the glass doors opened, and then blanked out by the steam of condensation.

The white-haired old man, still crouched over his drink, said blearily, "Cemetery was not bombed. You want see Jewish cemetery?"

He hobbled quickly through the bleak, almost deserted streets, Joe hastening to keep up with him. Then they came to a brick wall, crumbling, with weeds and moss growing in the cracks. The old man jerked his head toward the broken gate, nodded at Joe, and limped away.

The gate was secured with rusty wire. Joe climbed cautiously through a gap in the wall. Inside, the cemetery was a wilderness of weeds and broken gravestones. On the far side, the wall had been demolished, and Joe could see that preparations were underway for clearing the area. Soon, where he stood, another superstructure would rise.

He picked his way through the debris, rubbing the soot off an occasional gravestone, trying to read the names. He sensed someone watching him and glanced about. High above him, in one of the buildings, a woman was leaning out of her window, her huge arms resting on the ledge. Expressionlessly she stared down at him. He turned away and continued to wander slowly around the graveyard.

Somewhere here was Jacob's mother, Hannah, who had organized them through the night of the fire; Medel the blacksmith, old Golomstok, and so many others. Here, brushing the grime from their gravestones, he felt their fingertips touch his. He sensed that he had, unknowing, been in their company for a long time; that, finally meeting his past, he had known it all along.

When Joe came back from Poland and announced he was getting married to a girl named Goldberg arriving any day from Israel, Becky and Manny prepared to be delirious with joy. It was when Becky began to talk about invitation lists that Joe realized half-truths would not do.

They took it as well as could be expected: a brief bout of hysteria from Becky; Manny shouting a bit.

"It could have been worse," Joe said. "At least she's *half*-Jewish."

Becky said sadly, "I never thought to see a register-office wedding in the family."

"It could have been worse," Joe repeated. "It could have been a church." He forebore from pointing out that the family had, in fact, had one of those already.

The wedding was quiet. No *chuppa*, no glass stamped underfoot, no cries of *"mazel tov!"* no top-table dramas. Not like a wedding at all, Becky decided.

"Lunch in a restaurant, what kind of a reception is that?" she said in the car, trying hard to produce a few appropriate tears. She watched Galina and Joe climb into the car in front of them, the girl dramatically elegant in white fur coat and Cossack hat.

"It's a very good restaurant," Manny said placatingly, "and I think it's very nice, a family group around a table, a real family celebration."

"If you get through this," Joe warned Galina, "the family around one table, without losing your cool, the late Beethoven quartets will be a stroll."

Against the dark wood paneling of the restaurant, the family faces stood out like a Rembrandt portrait. Leah seemed lost in thought, silent, her eyes blank. She thought: *This girl Joe has chosen will be a partner.*

"It could have been worse," Manny whispered in her ear, echoing Joe's words. "It could have been a church."

"God forbid!" Leah exclaimed, reaching for a roll.

Months passed before Manny decided Joe could no longer be kept in ignorance of the situation.

"How serious is it?" Joe asked.

"Oh . . ." Manny shrugged, waggled his head, pushed out his lips, going through his repertoire of dismissal. He looked at Joe and embarked on a smile without quite achieving it.

"It's about as serious as it could be. It's been a bad time—the miners, the three-day week, then on top of that the Labour Government with their bright ideas. Community Land Act! Slow murder. Of course the house is in your mother's name and I made a few . . . contingency plans early on, but bankruptcy is never a bundle of laughs, however you look at it."

Joe was stunned. He had always taken for granted Manny's ability to make, hold, and increase money. It was an ability he had never prized highly, but he had acknowledged its existence and its relative rarity—and Manny's wizardry at it. But now Manny was telling him the magic touch had failed; the Midas gold was losing its luster.

His father said defensively, "It's a bad time all round: a lot of the old *machers* have been hammered—in the bankruptcy court these days it's like running into a committee meeting."

"Why didn't you tell me earlier?"

"When? At the beginning? Things might have got better. Why worry unnecessarily? Later? When you were ill? Terrific. When you were getting married maybe? It's not easy, finding the right time for bad news. Look, I'm not so worried, I can start over, there's always opportunity—"

"Dad, it's not the same anymore. Thirty years ago, after the war, things were wide open. Not now. Developers aren't needed, the world's changed—"

"So I'll change. What kind of world is it that doesn't need something! You just find the need and you supply. I hear they're cutting down the civil service, that's a good sign: they'll need more office space. Have you noticed whenever there's a cutback they end up needing more offices in the civil service? Law of life."

Joe forced a smile.

"Don't worry, my boy. Bad times have a way of providing. I remember after the war, suddenly there's a stop on uniforms and what with clothing coupons and shortage of material, nothing is happening. And then I have to go into the hospital for a hernia operation and Becky's on her own. And she was wonderful! There I am in the hospital and Dior launches the New Look. Overnight every woman is out of date. It was a real panic. There wasn't a woman in London who wouldn't have killed for a New Look outfit. You know what your mother did? She called everybody in the factory together and she took all the short dresses and found trimming *shmattes* and added bands to the hemlines—grosgrain, taffeta, contrast, anything. They worked day and night, they never even went home, and forty-eight hours later we had the Raeburn New Look collection ready while other people were still biting their nails and looking at their stock lists.

"Some of the things looked a bit funny, terrible really, a mess, but nobody minded: they were the latest thing. A woman put on one of those midcalf, swishy skirts and for the first time since before the war she felt like Cinderella at the ball. We could have gone under, then, if it hadn't been for your mother. You were still a baby, but she got out, she shoved samples in taxis, she *shlepped* them round London in the worst winter we'd had for two hundred years—the bloody birds froze to the telegraph wires—and she's out there forcing her way into wholesalers and stores like a pro. I've never forgotten that. She's a brave woman, your mother, that's why I know we'll be all right. Whatever happens."

Manny's round face had grown very red. He got up suddenly and began to walk up and down the office. "This book you've written. It's not what Simeon had in mind when it all started, is it?"

"That was two wars and several years ago, Dad. Nothing's quite what it was then. Simeon always said there was more than one way of doing it. I found *my* way. I haven't falsified anything."

"I know, I know. But people see things differently, looking back. They have a way of rewriting history. Your grandmother has already denied most of it. 'Why does he have to write about such things?' she asked me. 'Bedbugs, cockroaches, what is he, an insect specialist? Is it interesting to read about such things?' and so on. But then she's always been hard to please. Listen: you can't please everyone. It's like minutes at a meeting: put in everything and you'd have something the size of a telephone directory. Don't worry about the *kvetching*. I'll deal with it."

Still walking up and down he said casually, "I see that Israeli musicians' center of yours has won an award . . ." He paused, jingling the coins in his pocket loudly. "I'm very proud of you, Jo-Jo." He blinked, standing there, embarrassed, suddenly able, after so long, to find the right words.

"You were the one who said I should be an architect, remember."

Manny looked surprised. "Was I? Well, I was right, wasn't I?"

"I suppose you were. Pity about the recession though: most of the chaps my age in the business are either out of work or doing other things and praying for the wind to change."

"What will *you* do?"

"Oh, I'll tread water, see what happens. I've got a working wife, haven't I? And I've got the offer of another book."

"Maybe it'll be a best seller and solve your problems."

"Hardly likely. Simeon's dug up and dusted down an obscure nineteenth-century novelist and wants me to do a biography of the old boy. Then, hot on its heels, they'll splash a new edition of his ineffably boring works. Simeon says that's what's called using your backlist intelligently." It was a new experience, this: talking to his father, an exchange, in place of the old pattern—paternal monologues and guarded nonresponses.

"I'm sorry if the old people are going to be upset by the book," Joe said. "They're your friends, after all."

"Don't worry. They just need time to get used to it. Simeon's invited them to the publication party next week. I bet you they all accept."

"It'll be just like my Bar Mitzvah—without the speeches!"

The hotel penthouse suite had a view that extended far across London's rooftops to a low line of hills on the horizon.

The room was filled with people—friends, family, and members of various charity committees Simeon belonged to. On a table stood a stack of Joe's book, white covers lustrous with a silver sheen. The design was of a prayer shawl with a deep blue thread running above the fringe, and the title, *Winter with Flowers*. Next to it, a group of elderly men were leafing through their copies.

"Well, I tell you frankly, I don't know what to make of it. Some of it's a bit peculiar—know what I mean? Here—listen: 'Always, beneath the surface, hardly discernible, lurking like a patient shark, lay suspicion,' etc., etc. And the stuff about the scent of blood and so forth. I'd have thought the people who read this book won't want to know from sharks and psychology; they want to read about their old man, about the *bubeh,* the flavor of the pickled cucumber and the sound of the *chazzen* in the *shul*. They want a reminder of *der Heim*. Sharks they don't need. Sharks already—and the town not even on the coast!"

A few yards away, Joe stood with his arm around a very pregnant Galina, talking to Simeon and Manny.

"Did you see that thing in the paper?" Manny demanded angrily.

"You simply must not let it upset you," Simeon said mildly. "Newspaper columns of that sort are nourished by malicious innuendo; it's their lifeblood."

"But it wasn't even accurate! All that rubbish about Zionist backroom boys pulling pursestrings and defending frontiers with golden signatures!" Impatiently he waved away a waiter hovering with a tray of drinks, and his eyebrows rose in surprise as he noticed a new arrival threading his way across the room toward them. It was Mordecai. Manny thought to himself that for a man who once regarded grooming as a bourgeois irrelevance, Mordecai was looking remarkably dapper. The well-cut suit was a far cry from the shaggy jackets of his younger days.

"Hobnobbing with the capitalists these days?" Manny inquired.

Mordecai shrugged impatiently and ran stubby fingers through his thick white hair. "I knew you'd all be here, and I wanted to have a word." He turned to Simeon. "Sorry to break into your little party."

"What's so urgent?" Manny asked.

"It may have escaped your attention," Mordecai said irritably, "but last week the United Nations passed a resolution—"

"—Condemning Zionism. I know. I read the papers. But you can't take that seriously, it's just Arab pressure—"

"I take Arab pressure very seriously indeed."

Simeon said, "I have to agree with Mordecai, for once. But it isn't just the U.N., Mordecai. Your friends in the New Left aren't helping. The whole spectrum of Communist and Third World sympathizers are defining a political philosophy that favors the anti-Zionists—"

"And what about your pals in the city? Big business? All of them?" Mordecai retorted. "Arab money talks. Loud and clear."

"What is so beautifully ironic," Simeon murmured, "is that the early Pan-African pioneers held up Zionism as an inspiration for their own ideals. However, this is not a political meeting and we mustn't keep Joe from his signing duties—"

"Look," Mordecai broke in, "the reason I came, with all due respect to you, Joe, was not to get a copy of your book signed for posterity."

As Mordecai spoke, Joe glanced at the swing doors, thinking he had heard a shout from outside. Then Mordecai tapped him on the arm, and he looked away from the entrance for a moment.

"You mark my words," Mordecai went on. "There's going to be trouble." Joe looked back at the door. Three men were standing in the entrance. Two held back the doors with their shoulders; the third stood slightly behind. Two of them carried machine guns, the other, a heavy revolver.

Only those nearest the door had seen them so far and were edging away as unobtrusively as possible, their eyes fixed on the weapons. Then the high-pitched chatter changed to cries of alarm that cut off abruptly into ragged silence.

One of the men with machine guns moved his weapon slowly across the room like an antenna. His dark eyes were wide, feverishly bright. Every few seconds he jerked his head as though trying to shake sweat from his brow.

The bearded one called sharply, "Yusuf!" and he fell back a little, so that his machine gun was covering the elevator and staircase.

Joe looked around the room: waiters stood gripping trays, open-mouthed and terrified, but not spilling their load of drinks. People remained frozen in midstep or midgesture, like players in some deadly game of musical statues.

One of the men took a large sheet of paper from his pocket, beckoned the nearest waiter, and placed the sheet of paper on his tray. Another pressed the button for the elevator. With a soft pinging sound it arrived, and the waiter was pushed inside. Taking care not to move too quickly, the waiter cautiously put out his hand and pressed the button. The elevator doors closed.

By the entrance, the two terrorists stood poised, eyes flicking over the people in the room. The bearded one, who had been addressed as Mahmoud by his colleagues, stepped forward. "All right, listen. You can sit if you want to, but no sudden movements. Keep it slow. And listen: we have certain demands in the name of the Palestinian people, and, until those demands are met, we hold you hostage." His English was fluent, with a slight American delivery.

"We shall be here certainly for a little, so we should organize. The toilet can be used, one person at a time, after permission, but door must not be closed. If you have a question, raise your arm."

Mordecai, across the room, raised his hand. "Who are you—P.L.O. or what?"

"We speak for ourselves," Mahmoud announced. "For the Palestinian people. It is up to each one of us to carry the battle forward. We speak independently for Palestine."

There was a pause, and then Jonathan Shoobotel's dark sleeve waved for a moment. His eyes behind the steel-rimmed glasses looked anxious, but his voice was firm. "These demands you speak about; what if they are not met?"

"You had better pray to your God that they are."

For a while people stood about uneasily, watching the terrorists closely. Some of them glanced often toward the doorway, anticipating perhaps a rescue attempt. Others moved carefully to the end of the room farthest away from the weapons.

After some hours and a whispered consultation among the Palestinians, Mahmoud announced that any non-Jews could now leave. For a moment no one moved. Then some of the waiters began to sidle cautiously toward the door.

Joe touched Galina's arm. "You too," he said.

She shook her head. "They would never believe."

Another hour dragged by without any response or sign of activity from below. The very silence was unnerving, but there was a bizarre calm about the room now: exhaustion was creeping over the hostages, and people began to try to make themselves comfortable.

"Can we get our coats from the cloakroom?" someone asked.

"No. Too complicated. No going outside."

From huddling together like a herd, the crowd began to break up into families or groups of friends. They got cushions from chairs to use as pillows, found corners or convenient walls to support their backs. After a while a primitive instinct to attempt to form some kind of nest took over. A woman stood up and reached for one of the curtains.

"What are you doing?" Yusuf asked roughly, his machine gun twitching toward her.

"Trying to get comfortable, you fool!" she snapped, weariness stronger than her fear.

She tugged, tugged harder, and the curtain came away from its glider rail. She wrapped it around her and lay down on the carpet, her face shadowed by a small table. At once others began to follow her example: a rug was hauled away to a corner by an energetic old man who simply seized one edge and politely requested those standing on it to remove their feet. No one questioned his right to appropriate it. Initiative was the imperative.

Joe watched the scrabbling and the pulling at cushions and curtains and was dismayed: he hoped no great demands were to be made of them all. He did not feel confident himself to play the title role in some new version of *A Hero of Our Time*, and these others had perhaps already played their parts, been tested too greatly long ago in one arena or another and would no longer have the resilience. Others again, bred in ease, might have no understanding of the scenario being enacted.

Silence established itself. Now and again someone would cough or get up, speak to the man with the gun, and walk slowly to the bathroom. Then the gurgling of the water closet refilling would provide a soothing noise for a minute or two. The elevator had not moved for hours, and there had been no response to the Palestinians' note of demand.

Once, during the night, Yusuf, who was guarding the staircase, heard a tiny movement around the bend in the flight of stairs. Without even moving, he sent a burst of gunfire down the stairs. There was a frantic scuffling, then silence once again.

As the early morning light came through the windows, disheveled people staggered to their feet from creased curtains and flattened cushions to stretch cramped limbs. Despite the many windows the air was stale—they did not in fact open, and the air conditioning was proving inadequate.

Bleary-eyed and hungry, the unwilling guests stood or sat about, complaining in whispers, speculating. All yesterday's dapper grooming and immaculate coiffures had gone: stubble-jawed men, their suits wrinkled and sagging, were fit company for the women with their ruined makeup and crumpled dresses. The conditions created a weird intimacy: never before, Joe realized, had he slept in the same room as his parents or seen Becky asleep, her restless eyes closed, her muscles slack. Seen thus she seemed much less invincible.

To try to cheer up his mother, Manny said, "Well, you always said you hated soft beds."

"Don't treat me like a baby!" she rapped, eyes flashing.

Leah looked at Simeon and Mordecai, both of them bulky men, though Mordecai retained even now a certain athletic grace of build, while Simeon, years younger, slumped, all chins and jowls like an untidily wrapped parcel. How they had disliked each other when they first met! For a moment Leah saw them again, facing each other across the kitchen table in Sidney Street, antagonism and mistrust sharp in the air. Now they seemed like old friends. Probably, she thought, surprised, they *were* old friends. She was the one who had become irrelevant.

She supposed that she should be feeling frightened. She merely felt tired. For herself she wanted nothing but rest. Long ago she had wondered where it would come from, the danger next time. The older she got the more she saw hopes dashed and dreams shattered. If she had died last month she would not have lived to hear Zionism branded as racism. Death now could only save her from further unhappiness and disappointment. But for the younger people, she feared. And those to come. The grandchild. She would like to see Joe's child.

The ping of the elevator stopping seemed very loud, and everyone scrambled up, inching forward for a look. The door slid open. Inside was a cart laden with coffee and rolls.

The tall Palestinian hauled out the cart and looked quickly for some message. There was none. He slammed the cart back into the elevator, upending the coffee container so that the dark liquid cascaded over the white cloth in a boiling, frothing tide, soaking the rolls. He pressed the ground-floor button.

There was a low groan of dismay. The smell of the coffee filled the room and heightened the hunger pangs of those inside. The rolls had looked crisp and appetizing.

The guerrillas were angry: "We are not happy with this situation. We have certain demands, and we must have an answer. Perhaps they do not understand this. We did not want to harm anyone here, but if we have to, we are prepared to sacrifice every one of you—and ourselves."

They spoke rapidly together, and then Mahmoud, the bearded one, raised his voice. "We must be sure your government understands our serious intention." He nodded his head toward the table with its neat stack of gleaming white books."

"The author of this book, come forward, please."

Becky cried, "No!" and tried to hold Joe back. Leah did not move but sat shrunk into her chair, her face as closed as a carving. Galina held Joe's hand very hard. She made a tiny movement as though to go with him, but he put his hand on the mound of her belly and shook his head. He kissed her on the forehead and went toward the terrorists. It seemed to take a long time to cross the few yards between them.

Farcical, really, that it was the book after all that had trapped him. Yet there was an absolute rightness about it. He had shrugged off the book at the beginning, until, insinuating its way into his head, it had forced him to an identification, a decision—until, embarking on a sentimental journey, he had taken his first step to this moment.

But even as he thought that, he knew it was untrue: the first step to this moment had been taken long before he began the book, before he was born even. The journey had been long and slow. A bullet can take a lifetime, and only in the instant of impact is its destination certain. But it was always coming.

Manny said, "Wait—" but he, too, was pushed back by the machine gun. Behind him, Joe could hear the sound of someone weeping. Mahmoud led him to the entrance and closed the swinging doors behind them. Would it be now, here? Would they call for the elevator and send down a mute ambassador to the police waiting below?

Joe's voice sounded faraway in his own ears. "I thought your leaders had decided to try more reasonable methods—"

"Leaders can talk to leaders. Sometimes those they represent can prove an embarrassment, when the time for action passes, or is not yet. Everything turns into politics and economics. Compromising and bargaining and rapprochement. But we have nothing to gain from their rapprochement. They begin to make speeches and sit around conference tables and we rot. Because we have nothing to bring to the conference table except our predicament. So we don't want diplomacy. Only through violence can we make our voice heard."

Mahmoud spoke softly. "We are desperate men. We are past being reasonable, too tired to be reasonable. If we are not taken seriously, there will be killing and more killing until we get justice."

"Until you get what you want, you mean. Are you sure that *justice* is what you are seeking? The Jews too, ask for justice. Terrorism is no way to get it."

"No? No?" Mahmoud thrust Joe against the wall and shoved the revolver hard into his abdomen. Joe felt the circle of steel press into him and his body went numb. With difficulty he forced himself to mutter, "Murder remains murder."

"You're wrong! Today's killing is murder. In ten years' time it is remembered as nationalist action. The world is full of national leaders who spent their apprenticeship in British jails. The killers of one generation are the pioneers of the next."

"There can never be justification for murdering men, women, and children whose only crime is their existence. That does not change with time. That remains murder. You cannot use people's lives as an argument."

The dark eyes blazed down into Joe's. "Yes? Listen: I was a child six years old when the Israeli terrorists came to my village. They came with guns, they bombarded our homes, leaving us homeless. Then our land was taken. And you say terrorism is no answer?"

"Most people were not terrorists, they did none of those things. Most people were just trying to cling onto life." Joe tried to steady his breathing and his voice. "You have no way of knowing how those people felt. What would you do if you had been condemned to death, penned in the death camps, waiting to be murdered like the rest, and suddenly found you were reprieved, had a chance of freedom, the homeland you had actually been promised thirty years before—the original homeland of your people? And then, when you reach it, you're told it's all a mistake, go back where you've come from, go *back* to where the barbed wire is still standing, where the grass hasn't even grown over the graves yet? They came to the country their ancestors had lived in, filled with hope and possibilities. They were met with suspicion and hostility. It was not the Jews who began the killings, the wars. They wanted peace. In their position, wouldn't you have fought, for life?"

Mahmoud's eyes were wide, and his hand gripping Joe's shoulder clenched it to the bone. A sense of pain flowed between them, so forceful that without knowing he did it, Joe gripped Mahmoud's arm. So they stood, locked for a moment.

A stranger, seeing them, might have supposed them comrades saying goodbye. Then the heat died out of Mahmoud's eyes. He stepped back. "You will speak to them." He gestured toward a wall telephone a few feet away. "Tell them if we do not have some kind of answer within one hour we will start shooting."

From behind the doors, Yusuf added, "Your family first."

"My family. Why?"

"We know all about you. You're big Zionists, all of you."

Joe had no inclination to laugh. "I'm not a Zionist, you know, not the way you mean it." He lifted the receiver and at once a man's voice said clearly, "Hullo?"

"I am speaking from the penthouse. I have been told to say that unless the Palestinians' demands are met they will start shooting in one hour."

"Anyone injured up there? Has there been any—"

"No. But they are getting impatient."

"Listen carefully." The man spoke in a fast monotone. "Try and string them along. Say we're waiting for instructions. Try and keep them as calm as possible, no trouble, right? The longer you hold on, calmly, the better. Got that?"

"Yes," said Joe carefully, "I will give them your message."

"How many are there—two? . . . three . . . ?"

"Yes."

"Three. And they're armed. How—machine guns: three? . . . two . . . ?"

"Yes."

"Two machine guns. Then the third must have a rifle . . . revolver . . ."

"Yes."

"Revolver. Right. Can you open any windows?"

Suddenly Yusuf snatched the telephone from Joe's hand and slammed it down. "Okay, enough!"

"They were trying to explain that there will be a little delay before an answer, you must give them more time—"

Hamid, the third guerrilla, pushed Joe toward the door. "See about barricading the staircase," he told Yusuf.

The hostages were ordered to bring chairs and small tables out of the room. Then Yusuf flung them down the stairs, the chairs splitting and splintering with the impact. After a few minutes there was an effective barrier across the stairs. No one could rush them now.

By day two everyone looked bad. People washed their hands and faces, and those women with makeup in their bags shared it, but the crowd had grown edgy, with a drawn look about even the plumpest faces as they realized that the gunmen's power over them was total.

Quietly, and at first somewhat self-consciously, Jonathan began to pray aloud, saying the morning prayer, the Hebrew sounding not unlike the Arabic the Palestinians spoke together. As Jonathan's voice steadied, others joined in, murmuring the familiar words, wondering perhaps whether they would be there to say them tomorrow.

This time when coffee came it was allowed, and for a while its comforting effects were evident. One group played cards. A couple had drawn a chessboard on a white tablecloth and were playing a game of chess using pieces improvised from paper and cardboard. Nearby a man was doing exercises, deep breathing and bending and stretching.

The day passed slowly and that night was bad. Galina was feeling discomfort and Joe rubbed her back and neck, soothing her and trying to relax her tense muscles. "Such elaborate preparations," she said, laughing, "room booked at hospital, everything. Maybe I'll have baby right here!"

He smiled back, trying to conceal his fear.

The next morning again, coffee was sent up, but nothing else except a sheet of paper. Hamid showed it to Mahmoud while the coffee was being drunk. "No discussion. And no surrender. We will give them one day more." Mahmoud raised his voice. "One day more, only."

Yusuf had been methodically unloading and reloading his machine gun. He looked up now. "We shoot one, then two, then four, then eight . . . pretty soon they will agree."

That day all food was sent back, the gunmen themselves taking none—simply returning everything untouched. No one complained of being hungry, but several began to suffer in other ways—with rashes, or stomach cramps or headaches.

Manny had been worried about Leah at the beginning, but she seemed to have achieved a state of guarded alertness that made her appear years younger. There were no deep sighs or histrionic recitals.

She said to Simeon, "You could negotiate, suggest compromises, it's what you're good at. If we could get them to agree to some compromise—"

He looked across at the Palestinians, at their gaunt faces and strained eyes. "There is no compromise possible for them." He did not draw Leah's attention to Yusuf, who sat, quivering slightly, slumped in a chair near the windows, his gun across his knees, his eyes wandering over the room with a sort of frustrated hostility. The man's nervousness had grown worse as time went on, and Simeon feared that at any moment he might snap and start shooting people out of hand.

As Simeon watched, Yusuf took out from a small tin in his pocket a shiny razor blade. He held it between his finger and thumb and thoughtfully drew the blade across the back of his left hand, pressing just hard enough to slice fractionally into his skin. A thin worm of bright blood followed the razor as it plowed across his hand, and he smiled as it suddenly spilled out over his skin. Around him the crowd had fallen silent, their eyes fixed on him. Simeon recognized the signs, and his anxiety for them all increased.

Late that night, Joe was walking back from the bathroom when Mahmoud beckoned him outside. The Palestinian looked exhausted. He was a handsome man with round, glowing eyes and curly black hair, but his mouth was drawn down in a bitter line.

Joe waited.

"You are not unique, you know. Your people are not the only ones who have suffered. But they *have* suffered, and they should have learned understanding. There are more than three million Palestinians today. Half of us are in exile. The other half are under Israeli occupation."

Joe's shoulders moved in the slightest of shrugs. "Your situation is the same as the Jews'—do you realize that? You want to return to your homeland. The Jews wanted to return to their homeland. You want the identity of a Palestinian state. They want the identity of a Jewish state. Why *not* a Jewish state? There are Islamic states. You have thought about returning for more than twenty years. The Jews dreamed of returning for two thousand. But there is one big difference: your people have all the vastness of friendly Arab lands where you could go. The Jews have nowhere they can call their own, just this small patch. It's all they have, all they want. That's why they have to fight—to save themselves from being pushed into the sea. You must know your friends have used you for political purposes. You've been encouraged to remain refugees. If the Arab states had wanted to do it, by now you could all have been found new homes—"

"We don't want new homes. Yes, we have remained refugees. The refugee camps forge the Palestinian identity. Refugees can return. And we want to return, to move freely across our land, work our fields, see our oranges growing—"

"Not all the oranges are yours, you know," Joe said gently. "Do you really know what that land was like when the Jews took over? Who drained the swamps? The Jews. Who planted the trees? Irrigated? The Jews. Who got rid of the malaria? The Jews. Your grandfathers neglected that land. The Jews picked the stones out of the dust with their fingers, they brought life back to dead earth. You were a child in nine-teen forty-eight. The others are younger; they can't even have *seen* Palestine—"

"But they're ready to die for it! We've been robbed of our best land, the land laws make sure of that. Even those of us who stayed, many of us are nonpersons, 'absent-present' the authorities call them. They're there in the flesh but officially they don't exist. I went to college in Beirut. I read Kafka. Have you read Kafka? That's Israel for an Arab today. We're the Jews of the Arab world! You find that funny? Palestinians also need their dignity."

They leaned against the wall, the lights of London visible far below them through long, narrow slit windows. It was as though they themselves were floating in space, far above the petty problems of a small planet. Their isolation from it all prompted an Olympian de-tachment.

"Your people have suffered from so-called laws in the past," Mahmoud said vehemently, "in Poland, in Russia, in Germany. Your people should know about laws. Your people say the laws are for the protection of the land, but they will reap a harvest they did not look for. How can you condemn us? Our problem is the same."

"Not quite the same," Joe said. "You have never been labeled. Do you know what it means to be condemned on the strength of a label? When people's perception of you is dictated wholly by a label? Why am I here, Mahmoud? Because of something I have *done*? Or because of that label?"

Mahmoud shook his head and seemed about to speak. At last he, too, shrugged. "I'm sorry," he said. But they both knew it was use-less.

There was much more Joe wanted to say, to try to enlarge this limited area of understanding. The greatest tragedy in a conflict, he appreciated, occurs when there is right and injustice on both sides. He was prevented from speaking by the thought that now filled his head: with a feeling of desolation, he realized that what he should be doing was to try to work out the problem, to try to take even one tiny step toward resolution. To hold out a hand. But what he was going to have to do was fight, in order to survive.

Inside, everyone was beginning to settle down for the night, winding up chess or card games; some women offered their moistur-izing cream to others whose skins were beginning to dry up visibly.

Joe checked that Galina was resting easily, spoke to Manny, and walked on, pausing here and there for a word, to where Mordecai sat propped against the wall.

They had never been close, and Joe squatted down next to him with an initial feeling of reluctance. He disliked the rigid ideological basis of Mordecai's thinking, and he found him too ready to criticize —cold. But he knew that Mordecai could provide the key to their problem.

Joe said, "I think they'll start shooting tomorrow. Their nerves are very bad."

"I'd say that was about right," Mordecai agreed.

"Then we have to do something."

"What did you have in mind? Prayer? Mass-suicide, Masada-style?"

"We jump them," Joe said conversationally.

Mordecai laughed, genuinely amused. "Who is going to jump them—you?"

"Yes. And Isaac and Scott."

"Scott? Your nephew? He's a schoolboy. And my grandson Isaac is a *nebech*. He couldn't jump a fence, never mind a gunman." Mordecai glanced at Joe, frowning, "Don't waste my time."

"In Peszno, as a boy," Joe murmured, "you did jujitsu. I've heard all about it. You don't need to be strong—isn't that the whole point? Now: I've been told there's a judo hold . . . a man, if he's quick and is willing to risk it, can disarm somebody pointing a machine gun at him."

"The theory is," Mordecai said, "you seize the barrel of the gun and give it a wrench and at the same time—" He stopped. "But it's absurd."

"We'd have to synchronize it perfectly, so that we jump them at precisely the same moment. Otherwise we'll just get ourselves killed," Joe acknowledged.

"Oh, you'll probably get yourselves killed anyway. Have you spoken to Isaac and the boy?"

"Yes." Isaac, to Joe's secret amazement, had agreed at once. Joe could not have known that since boyhood Isaac had longed to try his skill at martial arts. With a rabbi for a father and an all-enveloping mother, he had never found the opportunity. As for Scott, who had improved considerably since his chocolate-gobbling days, he simply said, "We do it at school. No problem. But don't let Mum know."

396

Mordecai closed his eyes and leaned his head back against the wall. He seemed to have gone to sleep. With his white hair and pouched face he suddenly looked incredibly old. *Perhaps he's too old,* Joe thought. *Perhaps I should not have asked him.*

Then Mordecai roused himself, flexed his shoulder muscles, and said, "We'd better have a game of cards. Get Isaac and the boy." He got up and went into the bathroom, first pausing beside Yusuf for permission.

When he returned to the room, Mordecai dealt the cards. As he collected his, Joe felt an extra slip of paper in his palm. On it Mordecai had drawn a diagram showing the judo movement, with a few lines of instructions. The other two studied theirs.

They talked quietly, passing the cards meaninglessly. "As you jump, you yell as loudly as possible—it rattles your man. That's all-important. That, and to make sure the three moves are at exactly the same time. What we need is some kind of coordinating signal."

Isaac said, "Leah used to sing a song, a Polish song, I remember from when I was a kid. How would it be if she sang the song and then on the last word she clapped? That could be our signal."

"A song's good," Mordecai said. "It'll throw them off their guard a little. Yes. Talk to your grandmother, Joe."

He got up and wandered over to Leah. She was crouched next to Manny, small and silent, her black silk dress creased like crumpled tissue paper. He sat down and waited until she looked at him. Then he said carefully, "Gran, we need your help. We want to try to do something to stop this. But we can't do it without someone's help. Will you help us?"

She seemed not to have understood. She gazed at Joe out of the long, gleaming eyes. Then she looked at Manny. Just as Joe was about to repeat the question she said, "Mordecai's in it, I suppose."

"Yes."

"Well, you just look after yourself. Revolutionaries don't care what happens to people. His wife died, you know that. Revolutionary, trade unionist, it's all the same. They don't care, these—humanitarians. What do you want me to do?"

She listened closely, then she got up, asked permission to go to the bathroom, and a few minutes later came back to where they were waiting. She sat down, settled her dress about her, frowning down at her stockings, which were wrinkled and sagging at her ankles. Then she began to sing.

At first the song was barely audible. Leah's voice was cracked and weak, her breathing erratic, and she sang uncertainly. From nearby, a few of the older ones who recalled the song from their youth began to join in softly.

The song curled around the room like a wisp of smoke, drawing everyone in, lulling them. Gradually Leah's voice grew stronger, more confident as the rhythm drove harder, the pace quickened.

The Palestinians listened too. They held their guns, but they listened, their hands slackening a little, and very slowly, casually, Isaac and Scott and Joe moved closer, circling them on the left and right.

Leah's voice was ringing through the room now, and all the song's power and passion swept through the listeners, holding them in a taut web of sound. Then, without warning, in the middle of a phrase, Leah stopped. Her eyes flickered over the gunmen. "Why don't you finish now? Just put down your guns and go away. Don't try to make history."

Mahmoud said, "We have to."

"No," she said, "You choose to. Everyone chooses. Listen to me, I'm an old woman. I've seen it all before."

Yusuf's head gave a violent, involuntary twitch. The other two stared, angrily, resentfully at the small, wrinkled woman talking to them as though they were children stealing apples. Leah sighed and took a deep breath. The song went on.

The last ringing note was reached, and, as she ended, Leah gave a crisp clap of her hands. Nothing went as planned: the interruption to the song had thrown them off balance. They forgot to shout, and there was a moment of total confusion as the three banged into, rather than leaped on, their targets.

Luckily the gunmen, too, were off balance. Joe hurled himself into the throw, grabbing Yusuf's machine gun, simultaneously lunging with his knee as Mordecai had instructed. The gun went off, deafening him; his hands felt shattered by the explosion. Near him, two more guns were discharged. People screamed and threw themselves flat on the ground as bullets splattered the ceiling, bringing down a shower of plaster and bits of concrete. Joe clubbed Yusuf with his own gun, then stared around, blinded by the clouds of swirling plaster.

Isaac and Scott stood over their men, Scott now trying to shake off his mother, who had rushed across the room and was overpowering him, as the gunmen had failed to do. Isaac's sleeve was dark and wet and he was wincing with a combination of pain and pride. People were scrambling forward now, binding the prone men's wrists with neckties, pulling off nylon stockings to secure their ankles. Deborah was still trying to pull Scott away from the danger that was already past.

Joe went out to the wall telephone and picked up the receiver.

"Hullo?" a voice answered at once.

"You can come up," Joe said.

Inside the room, the plaster still swirled like a snowstorm, disturbed by the movements of the crowd. In the noise and euphoria, a few moments passed before anyone noticed that Simeon had not risen to his feet. The revolver had wounded Isaac. One burst of gunfire had hit the ceiling, the other had struck Simeon.

Joe knelt beside him. Outside the police were breaking their way through the barricade; the elevator was bringing up stretchers and ambulance men. People milled about excitedly, shouting, laughing. Mordecai hugged his grandson, a hero of the hour, and then, almost apologetically, threw an arm around Jonathan's shoulder, the rabbi's black suit thickly coated with white dust, and casually embraced his son.

Leah came hobbling and waddling across the room and got down painfully on her knees. "Simeon . . ."

He was having difficulty breathing and his words came unevenly, almost inaudible. "Sorry . . ." He tried to catch his breath. "About this . . ." Another pause. "Sorry I let you down . . . always meant to . . ." his voice was rasping, the mellowness gone.

"I wanted . . ." he mumbled a phrase, the words lost. ". . . take you away from it all." He coughed. "Sorry about the cliché."

She wiped the blood away from his mouth with her sleeve and his grip tightened on her hand. "That day, when I came back to see you, after Chaim died . . . Mordecai was there, I thought he would stay, I thought there was nothing I could do. To help, you know . . ." He smiled ruefully. "Let you down."

She leaned over him, crooningly soothingly, her tears dripping unnoticed onto his hair. "You never let me down. You were a baby brother to me. You made the days brighter."

The big, heavy body gave a slight shudder, and the smile died. Suddenly, with the strength of his personality no longer animating it, all that remained was a lumpish, misshapen body, like a collapsed balloon from which the air had gone out.

The ambulance men lifted Simeon and took him away covered with a red blanket, and Leah climbed slowly to her feet. In her crushed, bloodstained silk dress, her silver hair sticking out like a mop, she looked like an old, paint-daubed rag doll. She saw Joe and detached herself from Manny's protective arm. "Well, Joseph," she began.

"Yes, Gran," he said.

For once she spelled out nothing. She saw that she did not need to, and she allowed herself to be led away by Manny.

The police were inclined to be severe with Joe and Isaac: "We were making our arrangements. You should leave these things to the experts." They untied the Palestinians, and, looking dazed, the three stood by the door, waiting. Hamid bled from a cut on the head. Someone took a photograph, the flash winking briefly.

Galina gave a surprised exclamation and sat down abruptly in one of the chairs. "I think excitement has disturbed emerging generation," she said. "I think maybe I need go to hospital now."

Joe dashed across to the police. "My wife is starting labor."

"Leave it to us, lad." They directed stretcher bearers to Galina, and the little convoy made for the elevator, Joe holding her hand.

By the door they paused, and Joe looked into Mahmoud's slack, resigned face. Yusuf stood next to him, hugging his arms as though frozen.

"What will become of us?" Yusuf asked.

"A public hanging, I should think," Mordecai said with grim satisfaction. "Disembowelment and your bodies left for the crows to pick clean."

The man's eyes widened, and Mordecai's mouth turned down in a sour smile. "That's what you'd get if *your* friends were running things. Don't worry. Going on past history, you'll be back where you came from in a week or two. Your kind gets away with murder."

"Were you in Palestine in nineteen forty-six?" Mahmoud asked.

"Yes."

"What did you get away with?"

"I was lucky. I got away with a broken arm. Others weren't so lucky."

The police were moving them on, toward the elevator. Mahmoud looked at Joe and at Galina on the stretcher. He nodded. "Go again to Palestine and see my oranges growing. And think about what I said."

"Who planted the first oranges? Can anyone be sure whose they are?" Joe asked.

No handshake was possible. There were too many people between them.

The hospital seemed only a minute away. Then Galina was whisked out of sight. Someone brought Joe a cup of tea, and, as he reached for it, he found he was shaking so violently that he had to hold the cup in both hands. He placed it on a window ledge, steadied himself, and scooped the cup up quickly, gulping the hot liquid.

An hour passed, endless, echoing with fears, spinning faster and faster as though toward the end of a long voyage. Joe refused to go to bed, but agreed to rest in an armchair, forcing his taut limbs to go slack. He dwelled on an image that had always delighted him: Galina playing her violin, eyes closed, face pursed into severity, swooping, attacking, then relaxing, breathing with the music. He thought of her practicing four hours a day as a child. He could hear the husky voice: ". . . always with father watching, listening, correcting. I discovered I loved music only after my father died." Her father would have been made happy had he known she loved music, but his very presence had prevented him from finding out. *The ironies of parenthood.*

As he sat on, the room appeared to waver and change its shape. Manny and Becky came by, hazily, mouthing reassurances at him, and accompanied, improbably enough, by Sarah. They said things, but their voices were oddly muffled and he nodded at them without comprehension. He must have slept.

Then a nurse called his name. "You can see your wife now."

Expecting to feel exhausted, Joe felt instead a great surge of energy. To confront death and survive gave an extraordinary sweetness to the passing moment. To be within nodding distance of the grand perhaps did after all wonderfully concentrate the mind. How belatedly he had taken up the torch and how briefly needed to carry it. But his existence in a particular place at a particular moment, arrived at by how many million moments of history, had proved necessary. Almost, it now seemed, ineluctably, he had needed to fulfill a small, unique,

401

Darwinian role in some vast pattern. As he had already begun to suspect, he had been making decisions all along. Not one, but many, continually, like a man unwittingly entering a maze, who turns this way and that, slowly making his way nearer the center. Neither rejecting nor cleaving to the past, he had been accepting its demands within himself.

Galina looked drowsy, lying in the geometrically neat hospital bed.

"You look so flat," Joe whispered, bending over her, his hand stroking her dark curls, frizzy and moist with perspiration.

"I *feel* flat," the deep voice was slurred. "You had better go look at him."

"She needs to sleep," the nurse said briskly, and opened the door. She led him along the corridor to a large window set in the wall. On the other side of the window, in a cot, lay a baby: minute, furious-looking, with a faint fuzz of dark hair and long eyes, closed tight.

Joe could see the transparent shell of the tiny fingernails; the skull so fragile that it moved in and out with each pulse beat. To this tiny creature he would give his protection and his love—or was even that much certain? Between them lay an uncharted future: would he betray or be betrayed? A hopeless role, fatherhood. For a moment intimations, not of mortality—which he had learned to accept—but of failure, nudged him.

Acknowledging them, he remembered that he himself was still a son, and he reached out again toward hope. There was no nourishment in despair, and hostages to fortune, too, must fight for survival.

He pressed his palms against the window, resting his forehead on its coolness. The glass wall lay between them. He could see his son but not touch him. Already, he realized with a shock of wry amusement, they were divided.

Lee Langley was born in India and traveled extensively during her childhood before her parents returned to Britain. She has written novels, poetry, screenplays, and a stage play which was performed in London's West End in 1976. As a free-lance journalist, she has also written on travel and the arts. She is married and lives in Richmond-upon-Thames, England.

The text of this book was set on the Linotype in Baskerville, based on a typeface designed by an English calligrapher, John Baskerville (1706–75). The punches for the revised Linotype Baskerville were cut under the supervision of the English printer George W. Jones. Baskerville's identifying characteristic is the crisp definition of the strokes: the thin strokes are hair thin, while the thick ones are positive and black, making it a very versatile face.

This book was composed by Pyramid Composition Co., Inc., New York, and printed and bound by The Book Press, Brattleboro, Vermont.

Typography and binding design by The Etheredges.